VERNON SUBUTEX 2

Also by Virginie Despentes in English translation

Vernon Subutex 1 (2017)

Virginie Despentes

VERNON SUBUTEX 2

Translated from the French by
Frank Wynne

MACLEHOSE PRESS
QUERCUS · LONDON

First published in the French language as *Vernon Subutex 2* by
Editions Grasset and Fasquelle, Paris, in 2015
First published in Great Britain in 2018 by MacLehose Press

MacLehose Press
An imprint of Quercus Publishing Ltd
Carmelite House
50 Victoria Embankment
London EC4Y 0DZ

An Hachette UK company

This book is supported by the Institut français (Royaume-Uni) as part of the Burgess programme

A CIP catalogue record for this book is available from the British Library.

ISBN (TPB) 978 0 85705 770 9
ISBN (Ebook) 978 0 85705 699 3

10 9 8 7 6 5 4 3 2 1

Designed and typeset in Scala by Libanus Press, Marlborough
Printed and bound in Denmark by Nørhaven

"Ring the bells that still can ring
Forget your perfect offering
There is a crack in everything
That's how the light gets in"
Leonard Cohen, "Anthem"

for Fabienne Mandron
Aurélie Poulain
Roland and Schulz Parabellum

Index of the Characters who Appeared in Volume One

Vernon Subutex: The Hero. Former record dealer. Evicted from his apartment, he couch-surfed with various acquaintances before finding himself living on the streets at the end of Volume One.

Alexandre Bleach: Successful French indie-rock singer. Died of an overdose in a hotel room. A childhood friend of Vernon, he had been helping him out financially, and left tapes of an interview he did with himself one night when he was stoned and Vernon was asleep. A number of people are hunting for this "treasure". . .

Émilie: Former bassist. Friend of Vernon. She was the first to take him in, but refuses to put him up for more than one night.

Xavier Fardin: Frustrated screenwriter. An old friend of Vernon. At the end of Volume One, he finds Vernon sleeping on the streets and gets beaten up by a group of neo-Nazis.

Marie-Ange Fardin: Xavier's wife.

Céleste: Met Vernon in a bar, he thought she was coming on to him, but she simply recognised him because her father used to take her to his record shop when she was young. A tattooist, she also works in a bar called Rosa Bonheur near the Buttes-Chaumont.

Laurent Dopalet: Film producer. Warning: public menace . . .

The Hyena: A former private detective turned specialist in cyber-lynching. She is hired by Laurent Dopalet to get her hands on the Alex Bleach interview.

Anaïs: Assistant to Laurent Dopalet.

Sylvie: One of Alex Bleach's exes, she takes in Vernon and they have a brief affair. When he leaves, he "borrows" various books and a watch. She hunts for him all over social media, determined to destroy him.

Lydia Bazooka: Rock critic, fan of Bleach, she wants to write his "biography". This is how she comes to meet Vernon and give him a bed for a few nights.

Daniel: Ex-porn star, now a trans man, changed his name, manager of an e-cigarette shop, a close friend of Pamela Kant.

Pamela Kant: Ex-porn star. Online Tetris champion.

Kiko: Coke-addled stock market trader. Let Vernon stay a few nights, then threw him out.

Gaëlle: Friend of Kiko, Marcia, Vernon and the Hyena. It was as a favour to the Hyena that she gave Vernon a place to stay for a few days (in Kiko's apartment, where she lives).

Marcia (formerly known as Leo): A stunning Brazilian trans woman, hairdresser to the stars. Lives at Kiko's place.

Vodka Satana (formerly known as Faïza): Ex-porn star. Mother of Aïcha. Ex-mistress of Alex Bleach. Ex-colleague of Daniel and Pamela.

Sélim: Vodka Satana's former husband. Progressive, secular university lecturer. Bringing up his daughter single-handed since Vodka Satana died of an overdose.

Aïcha: Daughter of Vodka Satana and Sélim. Devout young Muslim. Sélim, who is a friend of the Hyena, asked her to sound out his daughter, whose personality he does not understand.

Patrice: Old friend of Vernon, former partner of Cécile. A violent, abusive husband. Cut off all ties to the music industry. He was the last person to take in Vernon before he ended up living on the streets.

Noël: A sales assistant at a major clothing chain. Friend of Loïc.

Loïc: Courier, friend of Noël. At the end of Volume One, it is Loïc who delivers the kick in the head that puts Xavier Fardin in hospital in a coma.

Laurent: Homeless. He gives Vernon some advice and some contacts for his new life living on the streets. He hangs around the parc des Buttes-Chaumont.

Olga: Homeless. Tall, fierce, red-haired woman. She insults the neo-Nazis who distribute blankets to the homeless. The streets are her kingdom.

VERNON WAITS UNTIL IT IS DARK AND THE LIGHTS IN ALL THE windows have been turned out before climbing over the railings and venturing into the communal gardens. The thumb on his left hand is throbbing, he doesn't remember how he got this little scratch, but rather than scarring, it is swelling, and he is astonished that such a trivial scratch can be causing him so much pain. He crosses the steep ground, past the vines, following a narrow path. He is careful not to disturb anything. He does not want to make any noise, or for there to be any sign of his presence tomorrow morning. He reaches the tap and drinks thriftily. Then he bends down and runs water over the back of his neck. He rubs his face vigorously and soothes his thumb, holding it under the freezing jet for a long time. Yesterday, he took advantage of the warm weather to have a more thorough wash-down, but his clothes reek so strongly that as soon as he put them on again he felt dirtier than he had before he washed.

He stands up and stretches. His body is heavy. He thinks about a real bed. About lying in a hot bath. But nothing works. He cannot bring himself to care. He is filled with a feeling of utter emptiness, he should find this terrifying, he knows this, this is no time to feel good, but all he feels is a dull, silent calm. He has been very ill. His temperature has come down and in the past two days he has recovered enough strength to be able to stand up. His mind is weak. It will come back, the fear, it will come back soon, he thinks.

At the moment, nothing touches him. He feels suspended, like this strange neighbourhood where he has landed up. The butte Bergeyre is a raised plateau of a handful of streets accessed by flights of stairs, he rarely sees a car here, there are no traffic lights, no shops. Nothing but cats, in abundance. Vernon stares across to the Sacré-Coeur, which seems to be floating over Paris. The full moon bathes the city in a ghostly light.

He is off his head. He has episodes where he zones out. It is not unpleasant. From time to time, he tries to reason with himself: he cannot stay here indefinitely, it has been a cold summer, he will catch another bout of flu, he needs to take care of himself, he needs to go back down into the city, find some clean clothes, do something . . . But when he tries to set his mind again to practical problems, it starts up: he goes into a tailspin. There is a sound from the clouds, the air against his skin is softer than silk, the darkness has a scent, the city murmurs to him and he can decipher the whisperings that rise and enfold him, he curls up inside it and he floats. Each time, he is unaware how long he spends swept up in this gentle madness. He does not resist. His mind, shaken by the events of recent weeks, seems to have decided to imitate the heady rush of the drugs he used to take in a former life. After each episode, there is a subtle click, a slow awakening: the normal course of his thoughts resumes.

Leaning over the tap, he drinks some more, long gulps that sting his windpipe. His throat aches since his illness. He thought he was going to die there on the bench. The few things he can still feel with any intensity are entirely physical: a terrible burning in his back, the throbbing of his injured hand, the festering sores on his ankles, the difficulty swallowing . . . He picks an apple from the far end of the garden, it is sour, but he is ravenous for sugar.

Painfully, he climbs over the railings separating the communal garden from the property where he has taken to sleeping. He grips the branches and hoists his body up, almost falling flat on his face on the other side. He ends up kneeling on the ground. He wishes he could feel sorry for himself, or disgust. Anything. But no, nothing. Nothing but this absurd calm.

He crosses the yard of the derelict house where he has set up camp. On the ground floor, what was intended to be a patio with panoramic views of the capital is still no more than an expanse of concrete at one end of which he is sheltered from the wind and the rain, the space is marked out by rusting iron girders. Work on the site had been abandoned several years ago, Vernon had recently been told by a guy working on a building site opposite. The original foundations had been threatening to collapse, there were cracks in the supporting walls so the owner had decided to entirely remodel the house. But he had died in a car accident. His heirs could not reach an agreement. They bickered and fought through their respective lawyers. The house was boarded up and left derelict. Vernon has been sleeping here for some time now, whether ten days or a month he could not say – his sense of time, like everything else, is murky. He likes his hideaway. At dawn, he opens one eye and lies motionless, struck by the sweeping cityscape. Paris is revealed and, seen from this height, it seems welcoming. When the cold gets to be too biting, he curls up and tucks his knees against his body. He does not have a blanket. He has only his own body heat. A fat, one-eyed tabby cat sometimes comes and nestles next to him.

On his first few nights in the butte Bergeyre, Vernon slept on the bench where he collapsed when he first got there. It rained non-stop for days. No-one bothered him. Delirious and running a high fever, he had embarked on a fantastical journey, feverishly raving. Gradually, he had come back to himself, reluctantly re-emerging from the cosy cotton wool of his hallucinations. An old wino found him on the bench at daybreak and started hurling abuse at him, but seeing Vernon was too weak to respond, he started to worry about his condition, and developed an affection for him. He brought him some oranges and a box of Doliprane. Charles is a loudmouth and pretty crazy. He likes to kvetch, to ramble on about his native Northern France and his father who was a railwayman. He laughs like a drain at his own jokes, slapping his thighs, until the laugh turns into a phlegmy cough that all but chokes him. Vernon has taken up residence on "his" bench. After a cursory evaluation whose criteria are unknown even to him, the old man decides to be his friend. He takes care of him. He comes by to check that all is well. He warned Vernon: "You can't go on sleeping here now that the weather's cleared up," and pointed to a house a few metres away. "Get yourself in there and hide out in the back. Make sure you disappear for a couple of hours a day, otherwise the council workers won't waste any time shifting your arse for you. Do it now, because you need to get some rest, get yourself fit, lad . . ."

Vernon did not heed the warning, but on the second sunny day, he discovered that it had been sound advice. The street cleaners were hosing down the pavements. He didn't hear them coming. One of them trained the hose right on his face. Vernon scrabbled to his feet and the cleaner flushed away the cardboard boxes he was using to shelter from the cold. The young black guy with delicate features gave him a hateful stare. "Get the fuck out of here. People don't want to have to look at your shiftless mug when they open their windows. Go on, fuck off." And, from the guy's tone,

Vernon realised he would be wise to obey, and fast: otherwise he was in for a kicking. His legs numb from spending so long lying down, he had staggered away and aimlessly roamed the neighbouring streets. He listened for the sound of the street sweeper's engine and tried to get as far away as possible. The injustice of the situation left him completely unmoved. This was the day that he began to understand that there was something seriously wrong with him. He wondered where he had washed up. It took him some time to work out why the area looked so unfamiliar: he could see no cars, could hear no sounds. All he could see were old-style, low-rise houses with little gardens. Were it not for the fact that the bench he had just left had a view of Sacré-Coeur, he would have thought that in his bout of fever, he had hopped on a train and wound up in the arse end of nowhere. Or in the 1980s . . .

Too weak to carry on his perambulations, he went back to the bench as soon as the street sweeper drove away. Rubbing his cheeks with his palms, he was surprised to discover how much his beard had grown. His whole body ached from the cold, he was thirsty and he stank of piss. He had a clear memory of the events of the previous days. He had abandoned his friend at a hospital after a street brawl that had left Xavier in a coma, without so much as asking whether he would pull through. He had wandered in the rain and found himself here, sick as a dog and happy as a fool. But though he has been expecting it, he has yet to feel the vicious sting of fear. Fear might have prompted him to react. But he senses only his aching body, his own smell which, truth be told, provided pleasant company. He no longer experienced ordinary emotions. He spent his time staring at the sky, it occupied his days. Just before nightfall, Charles had come back to sit next to him on the bench.

"Good to see you emerging from your lethargy. About time too!"

Charles had explained that he was in northern Paris, not far from the Buttes-Chaumont. Charles had offered him a beer and half a soggy, squashed baguette that had obviously been lying around in his rucksack for some time, and Vernon wolfed it down. "Fuck sake, go easy there or you'll make yourself sick. You gonna be here tomorrow? I'll bring you some ham, you need something to buck you up a bit." The old man was not a tramp, his hands were not calloused, his shoes were new. But he was not exactly fresh as a daisy either. He seemed to spend his time boozing with guys who smelled of piss. He and Vernon sat together for a while, not saying much.

Since then, Vernon has felt weightless. An invisible hand has fiddled with all the buttons on his mixing desk: the equalisation is different. He somehow cannot leave this bench. For as long as he is not forcibly ejected, the butte Bergeyre hangs suspended, a tiny, hovering island. He feels good here.

He takes short walks to stretch his legs, and so that he does not spend all day on the bench. Sometimes he will sit on the steps that border his territory, or linger in a street, but he always returns to his point of departure. His bench, opposite the communal gardens, with its stunning view of the rooftops of Paris. He begins to establish a routine.

At first, the builders working on the rue Remy-de-Gourmont ignored him. Then the site foreman came over on one of his breaks and smoked a cigarette while making a telephone call. He had walked straight over to the bench and Vernon had given up his seat, moving away, eager to be invisible, when the guy called to him: "Hey, I've been watching you for a couple of days now . . . Didn't you use to have a record shop?" Vernon had hesitated – it was on the tip of his tongue to say "No" and go on his way. He was no longer interested in his previous identity. It had slipped from his back like an old coat, heavy and unwieldy. The person he had been for decades had nothing to do with him now. But the foreman did not give him a chance – "You don't remember me, do you? I used to work next door, I was an apprentice in the bakery . . . I used to pop in all the time." The face did not ring a bell. Vernon had spread his hands – "I haven't really got all my marbles anymore" – and the guy had laughed – "Yeah, I get it, life's fucked you over . . ." Since then, he comes by every day to chat for a couple of minutes. When you live on the streets, anything that has happened three days in a row is a venerable tradition. Stéphane wears Bermuda shorts and huge trainers, he has curly hair and smokes roll-ups. He likes to reminisce about the music festivals he went to, talk about his kids and bitch about his problems with the guys on the building site. He avoids any reference to the fact that Vernon is living rough. Hard to say whether this is extraordinary tact on his part or sheer thoughtlessness. He lets Vernon help himself from his pouch of tobacco, sometimes leaves him a bag of crisps or the dregs of a bottle of Coke . . . And he allows him to use the site toilets during the day. This changes everything for Vernon, who has had to dig two trenches in the garden of the house where he sleeps, but even in warm weather it's difficult digging deep holes with your bare hands and filling them in so they don't stink . . . even short term, it would have put paid to his squat. Sooner or later, the local residents would have started complaining about the smell.

For the past three days, Jeanine has been secretly coming to visit him. She also feeds stray cats. She brings Vernon food in Tupperware boxes. She does it furtively because the locals have already had harsh words with her about encouraging the homeless to hang around. Vernon is not the first. She told him as much: at first, everyone thought it was a kindness, they wanted to help their fellow man, but there were too many problems: traces of vomit, a radio left on full-blast all night, a garrulous oddball with no sense of boundaries who wanted to go into people's houses and chat, some guy on psychotropic drugs who talked to himself and scared the local kids . . . The neighbours had no choice: they had to curb their compassion. Jeanine persists in sharing her dinner with him. She is a tiny little old lady, stooped, well-turned out, the eyebrows drawn on with pencil are asymmetrical, but her lipstick is always neatly applied, and perfect curls of white hair frame her powdered face. "When I'm at home, I wear curlers all morning, and I'm not going to stop until they put me in the ground." She dresses in bright colours and complains about the terrible summer weather, because of the pretty dresses she has not been able to wear, "and I don't know whether I'll still be here next summer to get the use out of them." She tells Vernon he is a "little poppet, you can tell these things when you get to my age, I've got the eye, you're a little poppet, and you have such lovely eyes." She says the same thing to the stray cats she feeds. She fills bottles of water for Vernon, brings him rice in which she has melted generous quantities of butter. She passes no comment, but Vernon suspects that she assumes that whatever is good for keeping a cat's coat glossy is good for people. Last night, she brought a few squares of chocolate wrapped in foil. He was shocked by the pleasure he felt as he ate them. For a brief moment, his taste buds almost hurt. He had already forgotten what it was like to put something in his mouth and enjoy the taste.

AS HE DOES EVERY DAY AT ABOUT SIX O'CLOCK, CHARLES LEAVES the betting office on the rue des Pyrénées and walks up the avenue Simon-Bolivar to the grocer's near the gates of the park. The boy behind the counter isn't one for smiling. He barely tears his eyes from the television on which he is watching the cricket as he gives him his change.

The old man slowly trudges into the parc des Buttes-Chaumont. He is in no hurry. Outside the little Punch and Judy theatre, parents are waiting in silence. Inside, their brats are screaming: "He's behind you!" Charles' bench of choice is on the left, not far from the public toilets. With the flat of his hand, he wipes down the green wooden slats, invariably daubed with mud where some arsehole propped his trainers on the bench to do elevated push-ups. He pops the cap on his first beer using a cigarette lighter. Opposite, two cats are circling, sizing each other up, unsure whether to launch into a scrap.

Charles has always liked this park. Having spent the afternoon sheltering from the pale afternoon light in the dark recesses of a bar, he always comes here for his aperitif. The only problem with the Buttes-Chaumont is the gradient; one of these days, he'll drop dead climbing the hill.

Laurent comes to join him. He knows his schedule. He always has a beer for him. He endlessly trots out the same five or six stories, punctuated by a booming laugh. The tenth time they heard him bragging about the same punch-up, anyone would feel like telling him to change the record, but Charles does not ask much of his drinking buddies. You can't be a boozer and be choosy about the company you keep. Laurent is part of his day. Obviously, he would rather it was fat Olga who joined him for his aperitif. He's always had a soft spot for crazy women. He would happily put up with a whole heap of shit if on a summer's evening Olga would whisper sweet nothings in his ear. The first time he saw her, she was wearing apple-green clogs, he had mercilessly taken the piss, calling her Bozo the Clown, and she had given him a slap around the face. Charles had to give as good as he got. Olga would have liked to return blow for blow, but she can't help it, she's soft-hearted. When she punches, it is like a kiss. The old man was touched, seeing her hold her own with such conviction, he feels nothing but affection for her. She still bears a grudge because of that first encounter. He likes his women mad and ugly. He's always pretended the contrary. He nods and agrees when friends talk about women who are no trouble as though they are gems to be treasured, he has often pretended that he dreams of a pretty little thing who wouldn't bust his balls or throw things but that's just part of the bullshit men like him tell each other: back when he could have landed himself a nice woman, he stayed with Véro, and every time he's cheated on her it's been with women who are no oil paintings. It takes all sorts to make a world. Nice women bore him rigid.

The paths in the park are quagmires. It rained for hours. It's all anyone seems to talk about in the bar these days, the terrible spring they've had. It'll be a while before people come back for a Sunday stroll. The only people around are the joggers, who seem to have been hiding out in the bushes ready to jump out, panting like they're being tortured. Some of them, it's so obvious that what they're putting themselves through is dangerous to the health. Laurent stares down at his shoes in disgust:

"I don't suppose you take a size 40?"

"I wear a 44. Why are you asking me that?"

"You always have nice shoes. I'm looking for a pair at the moment . . . I don't like these."

"Those are work boots you've got on. They're really uncomfortable."

"I dragged myself all the way down to the *Secours populaire* to get shoes . . . they didn't have anything. The economy is fucked, people are hanging on to their stuff."

"Tough shit."

"I'll head up to rue Ramponeau tomorrow, maybe they'll have something in my size, these are chafing my heels, I'll end up with blisters."

On the next bench, a heavyset black man in a silver tracksuit is hectoring some puny little white guy in shorts. In a booming voice, the trainer roars: "Don't stop, don't stop, pick it up, come on, pick up the pace!" and the scrawny wimp is bobbing up and down, staring into space, dog tired and looking like he might have a heart attack. Laurent wastes little time on them, he is fascinated by a big lump of a girl staggering up the path in blue overalls like a drunken cosmonaut. Charles passes Laurent another beer and says:

"If it was down to me, I wouldn't allow any sports freaks in the park. They ruin the atmosphere."

"You'd deprive us of all the pretty little things running round half naked? I mean, take the girl coming towards us right now – it would be a terrible shame if she didn't get to show off her wares . . ."

The problem with guys like Laurent – and they are legion – is that you can always predict their reactions. The slim, blonde-haired student jogging down the path is of no possible interest. The sort of girl who smells of soap even when she's running. Not that Charles has a moral scale he applies to the libidos of others. But guys these days are all the same, it's like they take night classes to be as much like each other as possible. If you split Laurent's brain in two to look at the inner workings, you'd find exactly the same bullshit dreams as you would in the wheezing middle-manager doing abdominal crunches at the next bench: fat-free, zero-sugar girls, a bit of bling by Rolex and a big house by the sea. Dumb fuck dreams.

There is an order of magnitude between his generation and Laurent's. His generation didn't idolise the bourgeoisie. Whatever they claim, the working classes today all wish they'd been born on the right side of the tracks. In Lessines, the town where he grew up, the day was governed by the rhythm of the sirens at the local quarries. They despised the middle-class people from the other side of town. You didn't drink with your boss. It was a law. In the bars, people talked of nothing but politics, class hatred nurtured a veritable proletarian aristocracy. People knew how to despise their boss. That's all gone now, and with it the satisfaction of a job well done. There is no working-class consciousness any more. The only thing that matters to them today is being just like their boss. Give a guy like Laurent power, and he wouldn't want to force the rich to redistribute their wealth, he'd want to join their clubs. There has been a standardisation of desire: they're all free-market reactionaries. They'd make good cannon fodder.

Further down the path, standing next to a bank of flowers, four park keepers are smoking with a man in a grey suit. A smiling, broad-shouldered Asian guy, a regular in the park who always wears a Stetson, is walking backwards up a steep lawn. He always does this when he comes here, he never talks to anyone. A short-legged, long-haired grey dog runs around him in circles. Charles turns to his drinking buddy:

"Any idea why the Chinese do that?"

"Run up hills backwards? Not a clue. Different cultures, isn't it?"

"That's true, it's not something we'd normally do."

Since spring, Laurent has been living on the abandoned railway track that runs through the park at the bottom of the hill. Not many of them sleep there, and the park keepers turn a blind eye as long as no-one walks on the grass at night.

A woman hesitates near the bench where they are sitting as though she has lost her way. She is wearing a long red coat buttoned up the front, the sort of coat a little girl might wear; it accentuates her wizened face. She must be a schoolteacher. If she had more contact with adults, she wouldn't be wearing a coat like that. Laurent raises a hand and waves when he spots her. She seems surprised at first, then recognises him and comes over:

"Hello. How are things?"

"Cool. Fancy a swig?" he says, proffering his cheap plonk.

Instinctively, she takes a step back, as though he might force the bottle into her mouth.

"No, no, no thanks. I'm looking for a bar called Rosa Bonheur, do you know which way it is?"

"Always looking for something or other, you . . ."

Laurent is playing the ladykiller. Charles is embarrassed for him. Fucksake, what are you thinking, expecting a clean, well-dressed woman to drink out of your bottle and listen to your shtick?

"If you're looking for Rosa Bonheur, it's simple, take that street there, go straight on, about five hundred metres. Did you ever find that guy, Subutex?"

"No. You never saw him again?"

"Nope . . . but I can take your details and if I hear anything, I'll let you know . . ."

Laurent reels off his patter in the tone of a receptionist. He puffs out his chest, opens the zipper of his thick khaki gabardine, takes out a battered orange notepad and, flashing a toothless grin, asks the lady to lend him a pen. He's a pitiful sight when he tries to seem urbane. The lady in the red coat gives a slightly irritated pout and mechanically tugs at a hair between her eyes. Laurent carries on blethering as usual – when he finds himself a new audience, he doesn't give up easily.

"Vernon got into a right mess because he was hanging out with the wrong tart . . . You see it a lot in newbies: too easy-going. If I'd seen him with Olga, I would have warned him to watch out. Everyone gets fooled. She seems nice enough at first, but if you hang out with her you end up face down in the shit . . . It's no life for women, living on the streets. And anyway, it's easier for them to avoid it. If Olga had squeezed out two or three brats when she still could, she'd be entitled to loads of benefits, and let me tell you something, if you're a single mother, they'll find you fucking social housing, let me tell you. Guys like us, single men with no kids, we can drop dead . . . oh, but families, they're sacred! Not her though, oh no, too much effort to crank out a kid . . . a useless bitch, that's Olga. She has to do everything like a man . . . except when it comes to brawls, oh, she's more than happy to throw the first punch, but the one who takes the punches is the guy who's with her . . ."

"If you do see Vernon, tell him we're looking for him, yeah? Tell him Emilie, Xavier, Patrice, Pamela, Lydia . . . we're all looking for him. Tell him we're worried . . . and that we have stuff to tell him, important stuff . . ."

"So, you gonna give me your number? And what did you say your name was?"

The woman in the red coat does not know how to say no. Her name is Emilie, reluctantly she mumbles her mobile phone number, then rushes off. She is a little wide in the hips, she moves unsteadily. "Where the fuck d'you know her from?" Charles says.

"There's a whole bunch of them," Laurent crows. "All looking for Vernon Subutex, but I've no idea where the bastard's got to . . ."

"Who is this guy?"

"A waster. New guy. The sort you know can't hack it. Too weak. Too delicate. I dunno where he's gone, but it was obvious that the guy would never cut it, living on the street. At least ex-junkies have some experience of sleeping rough, not him though . . . too la-di-da. He got in one brawl after another until some mate of his got beaten senseless and left for dead on the street. And then, the guy ups and disappears. His friends have been trying to track him down ever since . . ."

"She didn't seem angry."

"Oh, no, I don't think they're looking to give him a beating . . . they're just a bunch of headbangers who've been hanging round the park looking for Subutex the last three days."

"So what does he look like, this guy?"

"French, skinny, nice eyes, long hair, comes on like some faggotty rock star . . . He's not much to look at, actually, but he's a straight-up guy."

The description sounds a lot like the guy up on the butte Bergeyre. Charles is wary. The guy was so sick, the old man thought he would croak right there on the bench. If he's in hiding, he's probably got good reason. We all have our secrets, and we all have our own way of dealing with them.

"So you've no idea why she's looking for him, this woman?"

"Why are you so interested?"

"It's not exactly common, a lady like that looking for a homeless guy . . ."

"Never trust women. They're always hiding something . . . it's probably something to do with death."

"Death?"

"Women are always banging on about how all they care about is kids . . . having kids, looking after kids, all that shit . . . and we'd like to believe them. But think about it. The only thing women are obsessed with is dead people. That's their thing. They never forget. They want to avenge them, want to bury them, want to make sure they rest in peace, want people to honour their memory . . . women don't believe in death. They just can't bring themselves to. That's the real difference between us and them."

"I don't know where you came up with that bullshit theory, but I suppose at least it's original."

"Think about it when you're sleeping off the booze tonight. You'll see. It makes sense."

"That still doesn't explain why she's looking for this guy."

"No. But I'm happy to shoot the breeze with a lady. I'm an obliging sort of guy. And I like women like her, timid, strait-laced, makes me want to give it to her, wham bam, thank you ma'am . . ."

Charles leaves him to his lecherous ramblings. He is still surprised that the woman in the red coat deigned to talk to them. Charles looks like a tramp. People are reluctant to talk to him. But when he feels like talking to someone, he knows how to go about it. It's like pigeons and crows, you have to regularly feed them little crumbs of attention. His approach is the same as the little old lady he used to run into around the neighbourhood until last summer. She lived on the rue Belleville, and when she came out of her house at six o'clock, the pigeons recognised her. They would flock to her in huge numbers, in the air and on the ground and follow her. She would scatter fistfuls of seeds and breadcrumbs around the bases of the trees along the avenue. Feeding pigeons is banned. To anyone who didn't know what she was up to, the flights of birds synchronously swooping along the avenue Simon-Bolivar were very unsettling. One day, her kids put her in a home. Charles heard the news in the bar opposite the park gates. The old woman owned her apartment. The kids probably sensed the wind changing, the housing crisis coming, they wanted to sell up before the market crashed. Off to the knacker's yard. She was a frisky old dame, had never touched a drink, the one pleasure of her dotage was feeding the pigeons when she went out for a walk . . . she wasn't doing anyone any harm. It makes Charles laugh, people who have kids thinking it's an insurance policy for their old age. He's long enough in the tooth to recognise that they're just feeding greedy baby vultures. No-one likes old people, not even their own children.

There's someone just like her who comes to the park. An old guy who walks with a stoop, he shows up every day, listening to something on his headphones. He has long hair and wears a threadbare black jacket. With him, it's crows. As soon as he shows up, they spot him and gather in a circle around him. Crows seem to be much more organised than pigeons. They're as big as chickens, their feathers are a beautiful glossy black, and they're unnervingly intelligent to people who assume that animals are dumb. The crows in the park know who they're dealing with. They don't need this old guy to feed them – they rip open rubbish bags with their beaks and help themselves. But, seemingly, they like to socialise. They don't just appear when he shows up with the bird-seed, they wait for him. And if the guy has to change location because the park keepers are watching, they're not flustered at all: they follow him and tell each other in crow that the meeting point has changed. The old man stopped coming in early spring, Charles never found out why. He was probably hospitalised. He's far too young to have been put in a home; however desperate they are to get their hands on the cash, it's difficult to get rid of a parent who's fighting fit, especially if he's still got all his marbles – you just have to grin and bear it. Charles asked Véro to do a search on the internet to find out what birds eat. And he showed up, every day, at the same spot, and fed the fucking things. He figured someone had to take over. And he realised why some people do it – the crows are as much company as his drinking buddies. They have beady little eyes and they're funny. Every morning, Charles goes to the pet food section of Bricorama. It stinks to high heaven, and there are flies swarming over the split sachets of dog food – he has to wade through all this, with his back giving him gyp and his gammy knees, he's none too steady on his feet, he's circling the drain, that's old age for you, it's normal. But he clings on. It was only with age he developed this mania for being kind.

Charles won the lottery. No shit. This dried-up old boil. What a joke. He often puts money on the horses, rarely on the Loto. But like all the suckers down the betting shop, he sometimes filled in a slip, tempted by some rollover jackpot. What was most surprising was not that he won, but that he was in front of a television on the night of the draw, was too lazy to get up and change the channel, and there were no batteries in the remote. It was only as a result of the sequence of coincidences that he bothered to watch the draw – he never imagined he would be among the winners. Then again, that's the whole point of the lottery: it could be anyone. Even him. He always plays the same numbers, his mother's birthdate. Easy to remember. The balls started to roll down the tubes – he has never understood people who play regularly, there is nothing more boring than a Loto draw. And, one after another, his numbers started to come up with the terrifying precision of fate seeking you out, you and no-one else. It woke him from his doze. His chest tightened as his heart hammered faster. It is not a pleasant feeling, intense joy. In an instant he was stone cold sober. Véro was lying next to him on the sofa, sleeping like a stone, mouth gaping, lips stained with wine. If she had woken up at that moment, he would have given her a wallop – anything rather than admit that he had thought he'd won. Because, obviously, at first, being unaccustomed to life serving up pleasant surprises, he assumed that he was off his rocker, that any minute now he would spot the catch.

Staggering between drawer and jacket pocket, he managed to find the play slip. This was nothing short of a miracle, since he had carelessly crumpled it into a ball. Ten minutes earlier, he would have been incapable of walking as far as the toilet without collapsing, now, suddenly, he was nimble as a goat. His synapses were firing at random. In the moment, he was too shaken even to feel happy. He tried to reason with himself – you old shitbag, stop tying your brain in knots with your drunken bollocks, you made a mistake, you'll see things more clearly tomorrow, O.K., so maybe you've got a couple of winning numbers – but the jackpot? Come off it! You haven't got the brains you were born with. He had not slept a wink that night. He lay on the bed, fully clothed, then got up and dragged himself to the armchair, tried to wake Véro, cracked open a beer, drained it standing by the window, then went back to bed. But it was no use.

In the morning, he was down at the bar by 8.00. He had carefully copied out his numbers, checking twice to make sure there were no mistakes, examined the play slip this way and that, but could see nothing suspicious. He had sat himself at the bar, right at the back, settled in the shadows – it hardly mattered, at this time of the morning there was no-one there that he knew and the Chinese couple who had taken over the place when Ahmed, the previous owner, had kicked the bucket – a burst aneurysm while he was sitting watching T.V. one night – were not likely to engage him in conversation: they had chucked him out more than once when he was in his cups, he was not in their good books. But this was his local, and he still came here every morning.

Charles had opened the newspaper and checked the numbers again. In the morning light, on an empty stomach, it seemed even more monstrous than it had the night before. This brutal disruption in his rhythm inspired more fear than joy. He almost bitched that life never left him in peace. It just went to show we don't know we're born: he could have sworn that he hated his life and would have given anything to change every single aspect of it. But now that it had happened, he was clinging to old habits as though someone were threatening to evict him from his home with a kick up the arse. Two million. What do you say to that, you fat fuck? Overnight, it seemed, Charles had lost his happy-go-lucky indifference. For more than sixty years, he had trudged through the day from alcohol-induced coma to early evening aperitif, bellowing at everyone in the bar about how he didn't give a flying fuck about anything, and not to bother him. The easy life was over.

And yet, he'd already lived several lives. He had watched his mother rake the ground with her teeth to be able to feed them, he had seen his father disappear overnight and never attempt to see his wife or his kids; he had been an apprentice when strikes broke out in Belgium in the '60s, he had been a champion pétanque player and a truck driver, a penpusher and a ruthless card sharp, a bill poster and a cuckold, a brawler and a plasterer. His greatest passion in life had been the bottle, the bars and the twenty-four-hour corner shops. He was a lucky drunk. The bottle had never disappointed, never let him down. He has offered flowers to silly cows and mooned like a love-struck idiot over pretty girls, he has had dozens of lovers, each more moronic than the last. The sluttiest was a posh bitch with a handle to her name, her family still had a tumbledown château but she liked to slum it in seedy bars. She'd had his kid. He'd told her: I don't want to be a father, this was back in the '80s, she said she was having it anyway and if you don't like it, tough, you should have had a vasectomy, arsehole. She wasn't wrong. He had never acknowledged the kid. Never tried to see him. Véro got pregnant too. But when he said I don't want to be a father, she had got rid of it. She had sulked for a bit, held it against him, but she got rid of it. And she did it on her own, didn't ask him to go with her, didn't ask him for a single franc. She's ballsy. She took it like a prole. Nothing binds people like adversity, working-class people learn to stick together. Véro is the old fashioned model, the sort that come when a teacher marries a farmer, they never betray their man. He could tell it hurt her, not being able to have the kid. And it did something to him too. But you have to be realistic, a couple of pissheads like them, the poor brat could have spent the whole night bawling, it wouldn't have woken them. And with the face on the two of them, what would the little fucker turn out like? Anyway, she got rid. Unlike the bitch with the posh name. If news of Charles' good fortune reached the ears of the phoney baroness, she'd be banging on his door with a paternity test in seconds. And men don't get any say in the matter, they're fathers whether they like it or not. She'd demand a wad of cash and drag him through hell and back to get it. Véro would end up climbing the walls and screaming at him, and she'd have every right.

In fact, he didn't plan on telling Véro either. At least not yet. He'd do some thinking before opening that particular Pandora's box. He had trudged up the rue des Pyrénées and gone into a post office to consult a telephone directory. He wanted to track down the number of Française des Jeux, but the woman at the counter, a sly, fat, black woman, had laughed in his face. There were no telephones and no directories in post offices any more. He saddled a high horse, "You're telling me I can't make a phone call at the P.T.T.? Now I've heard everything!" and she smiled and took him down a peg or two, "Come off it, you're a bit young to still be calling it the P.T.T." Not as dumb as she looked, it turned out. Mollified, he had sighed and walked out without making a scene. He had headed up to the place Gambetta, but the brasserie that he remembered having a phone booth in the basement had been completely refurbished. They can't help themselves. You have something that works just fine, it's solid, sensibly designed, everyone's happy, but then someone has to come along and knock it down and replace it with some new-fangled gizmo no-one understands. The latest thing, apparently, is bars where drunkards feel unwelcome. Your key target group, and you chuck them out. And then they complain that places are closing all over the place. But a bar can't survive on three tourists chomping on a croque-monsieur. You need regulars propping up the bar if you're going to make it, guys who would sell their house for a drink. If you're selling booze, you need alcoholics, not lightweights sipping strawberry kir.

So Charles had bought a telephone card. Shit, if this turned out to be all in his head, if he hadn't won anything, he'd have blown ten euros on a phone card he would never use again. Charles is wary of telephones. His hearing is not good these days, he doesn't understand what people are saying. It's a pain, he ends up yelling random stuff into the receiver. He had set off in search of a public phone box, a quiet spot where no-one was likely to recognise him, push open the door and yell: What the devil are you doing? Come on, let's go and sink a few quick ones.

He did not know how to phrase the question he wanted to ask. "I have a winning slip in my possession," or "I'm calling to get a little information about the jackpot." Like all working-class men, he found it difficult to have to deal with organisations. He didn't want to sound like he was a moron, and the more effort he made to speak properly, the more blatant it would be.

The girl on the other end of the line had heard it all before. She put him at ease. He obviously was not the only pleb to contact Française des Jeux. And probably not the worst. She quickly understood what he was getting at – a winning ticket was something she often dealt with, please hold the line, he had listened to Ravel's "Boléro", then some other henchperson had listened to him reel off his confused story, asked him to repeat the numbers on his ticket, and said, why don't you come here now and we'll check it out together, and Charles had panicked, it was a reflex he had when dealing with organisations – No, I can't come right now, I've got a lot of things on, and the guy on the other end said patiently,

Monday, come on Monday, here's the address, don't worry, you can remain anonymous, completely anonymous, no, don't worry, there's no-one hanging around outside the building waiting for jackpot winners, all sorts of people come and go in this place, it would be impossible to tell you from a winner coming to make a complaint, or an employee – obviously, within the organisation a number of people will know your identity, but we have very strict confidentiality clauses, as you can imagine, you're not the only person to be in this situation, no, even if you're too old to be an employee, there won't be photographers trying to take your picture at the door, if I can offer a little advice, don't try to disguise yourself, sometimes with the best intentions we end up making things worse, so no glasses, no wigs . . . Clearly, he was not the first person to win the jackpot.

Back at home, he had regretted postponing the meeting until Monday. He was scared even to go and take a shit in case a window might blow open, knock over a radio that might open the drawer of the nightstand, a gust of wind and *pff* – no ticket. If you thought this was a flippant joke, you could think again . . . He had even gone easy on the sauce, in case he did something stupid. That's how bad it was . . . And it was not just this fear that fate would play him a nasty trick, a reaction typical of his class, the glitch that screws everything up, fate devising some improbable ruse to ensure that proles stayed in the shit where they belonged . . . There was a deeper fear. What was he going to do with all this cash? Jesus fucking Christ, in three days and three nights without a wink of sleep, he had had enough time to consider the problem from every possible angle: a house? What the fuck did he want with a house? And where would it be, this house? In some godforsaken hole where no-one knew him? In the South, with all the fuckwits and the fascists? With bars full of hunters who can talk about nothing except slaughtering coypu. In the nineteenth arrondissement, where the bars are about as friendly as an open prison? Normandy? What the hell would he do with himself anywhere but here? A house – that was all he needed. Had he ever wanted to buy a house? The idea of being a homeowner bored him rigid. And the thought of having to visit a solicitor and all the bloody paperwork . . . No, no, no. This was not how he intended to spend his old age.

He had gone, as arranged, to Française des Jeux. They expected him to be thinking in terms of investments, shares, long-term funds . . . As he listened, stoically, to the gobbledygook of the junior manager, he felt as though he were slowly turning into Jean Gabin in a gangster movie, as though at any moment he might declare, "listen, sonny, are you planning to bust my balls for much longer?" But he said nothing, he waited patiently until they allowed him to leave with his cheque. Having spent a lifetime sneering at those who made money without lifting a finger, he was not about to start speculating on the stock market now.

At home in his kitchen, he felt more deflated than anything else. So what you going to do with all this loot, old man? Buy a new suit? Couldn't give a monkey's. Travel? I'd rather die. He didn't like suitcases, sunshine, sandy beaches and certainly not "getting away from it all". What then? Talk about a problem . . . he would treat himself to a couple of young things. He was not remotely bothered by the idea of some hot babe rimming his arse just because she was after his money . . . but how would he find them? The bars where he hung out were not exactly teeming with sexy young things . . . Jesus, he hadn't even got his hands on the money yet and already all he could see was hassle, trips to the bank, mountains of paperwork, new friends, hypocrisy, complications of all kinds . . .

For a long time, he sat in a daze, staring at the fridge. Véro had woken up by now and kicked up a hell of a racket because apparently he had forgotten to buy olive oil and it was his turn. She swallowed a dessert spoon of oil every day at four o'clock before her first aperitif, supposedly it lined the stomach and made it easier for her to hold her liquor. Charles had let her rant, he had slipped on his coat without a word and thought, I'm going to find myself a whore. This is what he would spend the money on. But when he got to the massage parlour on the rue de Belleville – the one he'd heard so much about from his drinking buddies – he had popped his head round the door: plastic chairs and reflexology posters. And turned on his heel.

He had had his fair share of prostitutes, back when they used to hang out behind the gare Saint-Lazare. Sometimes, he would hang around for half an hour before plucking up the courage to ask a girl "how much?" He was shy around women, except when he was drunk. For all that, women tended to like him. He had known the great ladies of the night, the sort you didn't mess around. They were no prettier than the working girls today, but they were witty, they could reduce a man to silence, you had to behave yourself. Later, when you had to go cruising for them on the boulevards, it was less practical. He didn't own a car. He had to walk everywhere. They never had a room. When they moved out to the suburbs beyond the *périphérique*, he gave up. He wasn't about to take a train just to get his cock sucked . . . When the Chinese invaded Belleville, he had got his leg over once, down a dark alley, with a woman in an anorak who was energetic and good-natured, but she didn't speak a word of French and he didn't find it as exciting if you couldn't even pass the time of day. He had thought: There you go, even whores were better in the old days, and he had never bothered to find out about the girls working the boulevard de la Villette. He hadn't been interested, just as he wasn't today. He wasn't about to force himself just because he'd come into some money. He had paid for a round of brandies at Le Zorba, then met up with Véro, as always, at the betting office on the rue des Pyrénées. If anyone had told him that one day he'd hit the jackpot only to find himself, as usual, him and Véro, at each other's throats . . .

Véro is like an old shoe, he slips it on and he feels comfortable. There is no such thing as chance, twenty years with the same woman, however ugly and annoying, must mean you like something about her. He had still not said anything to her. He had decided to keep it to himself. He was afraid that news of his good luck would spread like wildfire and hordes of women would spring out of nowhere, claiming he was the father of their children, demanding D.N.A. tests and grasping for his money.

Gradually, he had become accustomed to his circumstances and had decided what he was going to do with the money: nothing. It came as a surprise even to him, but having thought about it, his life seemed to him the best that he could lead. He would carry on, but better. He visited the barber more often, he had always cared about his appearance. Now he could afford peanut butter, brand-name beers and razors with five blades . . . The days of hunching over chill cabinets in Dia, checking the price of camembert, were over: he picked whatever he liked. Véro was suspicious. She came up with the idea that he had secretly inherited money – a dead uncle whose house had been sold off. As though he came from the sort of family where uncles were likely to own anything other than their own arsehole . . . but when she noticed that, on the whole, they were eating better, drinking more, she distinctly smelled a rat. And it intrigued the old cow. From time to time, Charles thought he should probably marry her – the problem was, it would not be easy to pop the question without arousing suspicion: why would he suddenly want to marry this fat lump? From this point, whenever he heard about someone or other unexpectedly kicking the bucket – a heart attack, or run over by a moped – a nagging worry would ruin his whole day. Shit, Véro would be seriously pissed off if he popped his clogs without making sure she inherited . . . This whole thing with the jackpot was a nightmare. It was a constant fucking hassle.

His first real pleasure as an old man with money had been a pair of trainers from Go Sport. It just sort of happened: his old shoes were uncomfortable and he'd decided, fine, I'll buy a new pair. In his head, he was imagining an elegant pair of brogues, but he had no idea where he would find such a thing and instead found himself sitting in Go Sport while a young man presented him with various types of trainers. He had tried on a pair, out of sheer curiosity. Suddenly, a whole world opened up before him: here, finally, was a field in which progress was not a meaningless word. Shoe design had reached a scientific perfection and there he was, still lumbered with a pair of old clogs. After that, he bought a new pair of trainers every month. Though he tried to hide them, Véro had sharp eyes and she launched into a tirade: "Looks like you've been frittering away your pocket money – you're losing your marbles, old man."

He had never invested the money. It had been an instinctive decision. He was not about to become a crook at his age. The young manager who looked after his Post Office account practically wet himself when he saw the new balance. He started inviting him to high-profile football matches, but Charles had no interest. Stupid fucking sport. No, he had no intention of talking about his money with anyone. This was one of the more pleasant surprises that came with being rich. Until you are in a position to say "no", it is impossible to say you are incorruptible. He would never have thought it of himself. He had assumed he would be vile, self-seeking, that he would lose his head over the zeros on a cheque. Not at all. He discovered that it cost him nothing to say "no". No. Even so, he took a real pleasure in watching the snot-nosed manager at the post office jump up like a jack-in-the-box every time he came in to post a letter. Charles gleefully tore him off a strip: What the hell were you thinking, coming to talk to me while I'm in the queue? Are you out of your mind? Do you want the whole neighbourhood trailing after me begging for money? The poor kid could only blush and stammer his apologies. Charles was the most important customer in this branch, probably in the whole arrondissement. What a carry-on.

One afternoon, after seeing a film on T.V., Véro had wedged a cigarette lighter in the crack of her arse and was walking around, careful not to let it fall – apparently it toned your buttocks. Charles teased her as she strutted about, and pointed out that, in the movie, the actress had a pert little arse, whereas she could barely get hers through a doorway – the real miracle would be if the lighter did fall.

"How can you expect to tone that flabby arse? Before you could start toning, you'd need to melt off the fat."

She launched into a rant about how, before she met him, she'd been slim and curvy, Belleville's answer to Mariah Carey, how he was the one who filled the fridge with sugary shit and the cupboards with crisps, so it was hardly surprising she was losing her figure. In the twenty years he'd known her, Véro had always been built like a brick shithouse, but she was convinced that she had once been beautiful. Whenever she cornered some sexy young thing at the bar, she would launch into endless stories about back when she was a stunner and had all the men panting after her. Urban myths. She'd always been ugly as sin. At least in her case, growing old involved no regrets.

But by now Véro was in full flow: it was his fault that she was no longer svelte, and while she was at it, she wanted to know where he had suddenly got all this money from, it made her sick to think she was sharing her life with a man who'd had kids behind her back, and had obviously come into an inheritance, a tidy packet too, but was obviously ashamed to admit it.

"You're such a miserable fucking bastard . . . do you really thing that just because some uncle left you ten thousand euros when he pegged it, everyone's going to be hanging around you like vultures. I pity you, I really do . . . Well, spit it out then, how much did you inherit?"

"What difference would it make if I did inherit money? Would you know what to do with it? You're hardly going to go out and buy clothes, you've got the classy chassis of a battered old rattle-trap. So what then? You want to go to the hairdressers? You've barely got four hairs on the cue-ball head of yours. Get your moustache waxed? If that's all, just wait there, I'll go get my razor. Come on then, what is it you want? You want to get liposuction? So do it, get yourself liposucked, you old hag, just let me drink my beer in peace."

He thought she might trot out her old lady dreams, talk about a house in the country where she could live out her days. Like all the working-class women who've had it drummed into their heads that nirvana is owning your own little house with your own little garden. One look at the state of Véro's bedroom, and you wouldn't want her to have a little house – Christ, no. The woman is feral.

Véro had simply shrugged, she was resigned to the fact that her dreams were in vain, but was content to nurture them, and without a flicker of hesitation, she said: "If I had money, darling, I'd go to see New York. New York, Los Angeles, the Grand Canyon, Chicago." Her tone was one he did not recognise, there was no bitterness, no resentment; in fact she sounded like an excited little girl; and he could have gone for the jugular, mocked her for letting down her guard so easily, but he said nothing, he allowed himself to be moved. She had this in reserve, the old bag. She had no idea that he could afford to pay for such a trip, she had just blurted it out, not trying to be shrewd, to hoodwink him. It was a dream she had set aside, one she cared about, one she nurtured. Twenty years he had been trailing after her from bar to bar, propping her up when she stumbled, listening to her throw up at home, and never once had she told him about it. And now there she was, smiling, showing her rotten teeth – she still has a full set of fangs, but given the colour and the state of them, she'd be better off without. He snubbed her, out of habit. But she had amazed him. Three months before, with his head in a vice and the never-ending pressure to pay the bills, he could not have allowed himself the indulgence of finding her poignant, in fact he would have laid into her for talking such shit. Three months earlier, he had not even been curious to know what she thought. So this was the secret of having money: having space enough to indulge in flights of fancy.

"You're not going anywhere, you old whore. You haven't even got a passport, you wouldn't have the first idea how to buy tickets, and if you got there, what the hell would you do?"

"You really are full of shit. Going to the States is no more complicated than taking the métro, except the ticket is different.

And if I needed my passport, I'd just go and get it. All my papers are in order, I'll have you know."

"You wouldn't move that fat arse of yours an inch. Drunks are all the same, they're all mouth."

"Why am I even bothering to talk to you? You've never been anywhere in your life. You're a boor. You've always been a boor."

"I don't like travelling. Besides, what could you do there that you can't do here?"

"I'd go for a walk, dipshit. I'd drink scotch, I'd take a taxi, go see a park, if there are squirrels, I'd try to catch one, I'd listen to the locals talking with no subtitles, I'd take the subway. You've never been anywhere, you don't know what it's like, abroad."

"You'd be just one more fat fucking tourist."

Véro had had a life before she devoted herself to propping up bars full time. For more than twenty years, she'd been a teacher. Had taught literature. She's the only person he knows dumb enough to get herself fired from the state education system. Four months holiday a year, twenty hours of lessons a week, and even that was too much to ask of her . . . Charles hates the idea of travelling. There is nothing he hates more than the thought of packing a suitcase, unless it is the prospect of brushing his teeth somewhere far from home. He has never taken her anywhere, the old nag. There was no way he was going to fritter away his cash on pathetic trips.

A late, blazing sun has obliterated all trace of the earlier downpour. Charles feels the heat stab at his thigh through the fabric of his trousers. A park keeper in khaki overalls is pushing an empty wheelbarrow and whistling. A couple passes, the man striding a few steps ahead of the woman, swinging his arms with a military air. Charles changes his mind. It was a bad idea to let the woman in the red coat disappear without first letting Vernon know people were looking for him.

"Can you give me the number of the woman in red? Just in case . . ."

"You know where Vernon is?"

"No."

"Oh yes, you do, I know you . . . Don't be a bastard, let me in on the secret . . . Or maybe you've got your eye on the babe in the red coat for yourself, is that it?"

"Take a good look at me. How do you rate my chances of convincing her to have a quick fumble in the bushes?"

"Depends. If she really wants to know where this guy is, maybe she'd be willing to . . ."

"There you go! That's the reason I'm not going to tell you where Vernon is. I'll open the last beer, you'll give me her number, and we'll change the subject."

"Come on, let me in on the secret. I knew this guy Vernon before you did."

"Get up. We're going for a little walk."

ON A BENCH, A GIRL IN A WHITE DRESS IS PRACTISING THE THEME from "Carmen" on an accordion. As she passes, Emilie wonders whether slip dresses are back in fashion. If she wasn't so fat, she'd love to wear clothes like that, so diaphanous, so feminine. But even if she was skinny, she's too old to pull off that look. In a way, she finds this reassuring.

The encounter with the homeless guy has left her depressed. "I suppose it was too much effort to squeeze out a couple of kids." Having to deal with the destitute is supposed to make you feel better about your life, not make you feel even shittier. But even to the homeless, women like her are considered to be pathetic losers. Emilie is looking for the Rosa Bonheur, though still unsure if she is heading in the right direction. She has always had a terrible sense of direction, and today, because she is upset, it is worse.

She has been thinking about Vernon non-stop ever since she kicked him out. Retracing his path, she realised that she was the first person he turned to when he was evicted from his apartment. Maybe she was too harsh.

But the night it happened, she had patted herself on the back. Finding herself in an empty apartment, she was proud that she had defended her territory. She'd slipped on the pair of American Apparel pants with a rip in the crotch, and the pink-and-black Hello Kitty T-shirt she only wears when she is alone. Taking off her jeans as soon as she gets home has always been a relief. She buys her jeans a size too small, telling herself she's about to lose weight. This means she spends the whole day tugging at her jumper to hide her hips. She has rolls of fat hanging over her waist, stale muffin tops. To create a cosy atmosphere she had lit a Diptyque candle that had been gathering dust for months. Who the hell could have given it to her? They cost a fortune, and apparently they're toxic. She had done a few stretches she learned at her yoga class while listening to Tibetan mantras on YouTube. She had lain on her back, palms facing the ceiling, alternating abdominal and clavicular breaths, relaxing her jaw, her stomach. The grey double-lined curtains she bought from Zara Home protected her from the outside world, from the cold, the noise, the prying eyes. Then she had put on an album of cover versions by Cat Power and told herself that she was happy being on her own. Being able to relax, to centre herself. She had heated up a Monoprix Gourmet pizza, settled herself on her bed with a tray and watched an Arte documentary about Barbie dolls on the internet. Had she not been alone, she would not have been able to do any of these little things that gave her so much pleasure. After dinner, she polished off the bottle of white wine while munching her way through a 250-gram box of Maltesers, eating them one by one, letting the chocolate melt against the roof of her mouth before crunching into the honeycomb . . . She had gone to bed early, but had been unable to sleep.

She was thinking about how cold it was outside, and though she curled into a ball under the heavy pink duvet, she could not help but wonder whether Vernon had found somewhere to stay for the night. She was haunted by the tale of the little match girl. Emilie had reasoned with herself – why should she feel responsible for a man who, when she had turned to him for help, had not even bothered to reply. A man who would be annoying her if he were here: they had nothing in common. Why would she put herself through that? Sorry, Vernon, take your shit and dump it somewhere else. She has not spent years in therapy in order to get stuck in old patterns of middle-class guilt. O.K., so her parents had bought her an apartment in Paris, O.K., so life was easier for her than if she had been born in Brazzaville. But she wasn't going to spend her whole life punishing herself for it.

She felt rather less guilty because Vernon was resourceful. Right now, while she was lying alone in her bedroom worrying herself sick, he was probably in good company, well fed and being pampered by someone else. Vernon was a liar, Vernon made no effort in life, Vernon had not worried about her when Jean-No died. But Vernon had also been a friend. She had genuinely liked him, and she had spent years bursting into the record shop mouthing off about all sorts of shit and she felt good because he had always treated her with consideration and affection. He did it with everyone; managed to make them feel that they were unique, important. And she had admired that. And now it came between them. It was ugly. She was afraid to think that what most bothered her about Vernon being in her apartment was that he was a witness to her life. For as long as there was no-one here to see how she lived, she could pretend – without really lying – that she lived a moderately rich and varied life. A life that gave her no cause to complain. This was what she most feared: being seen as a victim. But if she considers her life through the eyes of a third person, things become complicated. Her job is shit. She works all hours. Because she is terrified that otherwise it won't look good. Vernon would see that she had no friends, no relationships. No parties of any kind. He would see her online flirtations. The random hook-ups with guys encountered on Meetic, the endless hours she spent shaving, doing her make-up, styling her hair, choosing her clothes, only to see nothing but disappointment in the eyes of the man when she stepped into the room. She can no longer cut it at her age. What else would Vernon see? The kitchen on which she lavishes so much care? A wall lined with herbal teas. A rack filled with organic oils. And everywhere, funny little knickknacks in garish colours – fridge magnets, salt cellars shaped like Mickey Mouse, retro '50s biscuit tins . . . a chorus of cries for help: the more she had tried to create an atmosphere of elegance, the more she underscored her utter desperation. She doesn't even have a cat to keep her company. At night, when she comes home, she switches on the television. And pours herself a drink. In that order.

She has a map of the world pinned over her desk, with red thumbtacks indicating places she has been and yellow ones indicating places she plans to visit soon. She goes abroad every year. She saves up and treats herself to a holiday. Travel is so rewarding. But she does not want Vernon to see that. If she looks at it from someone else's point of view, she is afraid what she considers an oasis of calm and pleasure might seem like so many signs of pathos.

Emilie had slept badly that night. She had got up in the small hours, smoked a cigarette, opened another bottle of wine and stared down at the deserted street at four in the morning. Old memories had begun to take shape. Her memory is a compost heap; everything was jumbled together and beginning to rot . . . you had to study them carefully to make out the contours they had had, before they had clotted into a vast mound of bitterness. She remembered one of the first times she had seen Vernon, at the shop. She had been looking for Adam and the Ants' first album, he didn't have it, and he added without a smile, "you can do better than that" and had put on a record by The Cure. He was wearing the ring of a Red Indian chief with a headdress of blue and red feathers, it should have looked tacky, but it suited him. With hands like his, it would have been a shame not to wear rings. She remembered his movements as he handled the vinyl, index finger on the central hole, thumb gripping the edge as he turned it over, looking for the track he wanted to play. She remembered a morning when he had kissed her unexpectedly, shoved his tongue down her throat outside the all-night bakery where they bought croissants at 5.00 a.m. She had pushed him away, flattered but not as drunk as he was, saying that she couldn't do that to Jean-No. Yeah, right! She should have leapt at the chance.

But as the days passed, the guilt she felt about Vernon faded, and she would check out his Facebook page from time to time and was reassured that he seemed to be getting by. It was at this point that Sylvie made her entrance in the comments section. Screeds of vile, deranged abuse rained down on Vernon's Facebook page, accompanied by graphic photographs depicting the intentions of this woman scorned – soldiers eating their enemies' brains with a spoon, screenshots from "Cannibal Holocaust" and "Saw", decapitations, executions by firing squad, by hanging, by defenestration . . . At first, Vernon made an effort to delete the messages as they appeared, which had a perverse effect on Emilie: she found herself spending whole days refreshing the page, desperate not to miss an episode of this soap opera . . .

Not that she condoned Sylvie's unhinged behaviour. All that aggression, washing her dirty linen in public, it was grotesque and pathetic. He had stolen some book and a watch. It was hardly gentlemanly. But there was no need to turn it into a capital crime. Vernon had dumped her when she wasn't expecting it. Emilie felt like saying: it happens every day. If we trolled a guy every time we got dumped, Facebook would turn into white riot . . . She disapproved of this display of hostility, but when Sylvie sent friend requests to all of his contacts because Vernon had blocked her and she wanted to carry on making an exhibition of herself, Emilie had accepted. Without a second thought. In the same way she might read an article about Jennifer Lopez's haemorrhoids: it was disgusting to write about such things, but she was not going to miss reading it.

She was fascinated by Sylvie's madness. Emilie never loses her temper. She champs at the bit, she grits her teeth, she gets constipated, gives herself ulcers. But she has never lost control to the point where she screamed at someone. She behaves like a lady, anything else would mean making a spectacle of herself, and she knows she would die of shame. So Sylvie's hysterical rants, which broke all the boundaries Emilie imposed on herself, were somehow cathartic. The wronged woman lashed out with a fury it was impossible not to admire. She was in the wrong, she was ridiculous, yet still everyone egged her on. Everyone loves an online battle. It had to be said that her threats to castrate Vernon with her bare teeth when she found him were much more entertaining than videos of baby bats. Aware of the popularity of her posts, Sylvie created the hashtag *#wherethehellissubutex*. For the first few days, it bombed. No-one was interested in tracking down this guy. Sylvie sounded like a nutjob. One dipshit retweeted Lydia Bazooka's photo of Vernon, stoned and smiling, sitting in front of *her* computer . . . But the person who had poured oil on the flames was Pamela Kant. When she joined the comments thread – using her porn name – the hunt began. Guys would have sold their own mothers for a "like" from the hard-core porn star. Like so many others, Emilie spent all day glued to her screen, and when the discussion moved to WhatsApp, she joined the group. It was here that she had stumbled on her old acquaintances Xavier and Patrice, and got in touch. Curiously, the more invisible he was, the more important Vernon became in their lives. A bizzare group of old Revolver customers popped in and out of conversations, endlessly typing – *hey, long time no see – WTF have U been up 2?* Meanwhile, Pamela Kant, who had many thousands of followers, trailed in her wake a veritable army of slackers bent on tracking down Subutex. Some techie freak eventually spotted him in a photograph on a blog post about the old public baths in the nineteenth arrondissement. Then someone else popped up saying that they had seen him outside the gates of the Buttes-Chaumont.

Emilie kept a close watch on these conversations, but she did not take part until one day, having stopped off to buy toilet roll, milk and leeks at Dia on her way home, she found Pamela Kant standing outside the front door of her building. She recognised her from photos on the internet. In real life, she was a lot smaller than she looked in the photos. She was dressed like an American trying to pass incognito – baseball cap, tracksuit, sunglasses. As she approached, Pamela was staring at her smartphone, and Emilie noticed she was playing Tetris.

"Are you Emilie?"

"Depends who's asking."

"You know who I am."

"Not a clue."

Emilie was mortified to be carrying a 12-roll family pack of bog roll and a plastic bag with leeks poking out. At a glance, despite the baggy sportswear, she noticed the narrow waist, the perfectly flat stomach: a magazine cover body set off by huge breasts. Pamela looked like a doll from a very different factory than the one that had produced her. Emilie finds it difficult to take pleasure in other people's fortune. She admires the theory, but finds it difficult to apply in practice. Pretty girls do not inspire noble thoughts in her. With her free hand, she tugged at the waistband of her trousers, wishing the short-arsed bitch in front of her would vanish in a flash of spontaneous combustion.

"You got time for a coffee?"

"Who are you?"

"I'm a friend of Vernon Subutex."

"I've got a lot on, I can't talk for long."

"He told me he left some things at your place, asked if I could pick them up."

"And he didn't give you my laptop? That's weird. Because he left his bag and said he'd pick it up when he gave me back the computer I lent him. Then again, I'm not really surprised. I've heard that's his thing these days. Borrowing stuff and never giving it back . . . I suppose I should be grateful he didn't steal anything from me . . ."

It was a low blow. But Emilie was so furious at the idea that Vernon had the brass neck to send this bitch to do his dirty work that she had to let off steam. Pamela persisted, it was obvious she was not the kind of girl who took no for an answer. Perfect skin, glossy hair, slim nose, pale complexion, charming tilt of the head, shit, the more Emilie looked at her, the more she longed to see her mown down by a bus.

Emilie could not understand – and she had no desire to ask the question and let it be known that she was interested – what the hell did a girl like this want with Vernon? Then the penny suddenly dropped: the tapes! Vernon had told her they were unseen footage of Alex Bleach, Emilie had forgotten all about them, thinking they were of no interest. Since he had dumped his bag at her place without specifically asking her to look after them, she had assumed Vernon had filmed the singer making an omelette in his kitchen. But if Pamela wanted the bag, that meant it was not just footage of two drunks on a binge . . . And if the tapes were valuable, so too was Emilie, since she was in possession of them. Her mind made the connection: this was what that dumbfuck journalist Lydia Bazooka was looking for. Emilie had never made the connection between the rucksack under her bed and the McGuffin the whole world was trying to track down. Suddenly, she was at the very centre of this affair. This thought had pleased her. But her new-found status had not encouraged her to play nice.

"Tell Vernon I want my laptop back."

"I can pay you for the computer, that seems reasonable. Just tell me the make and model and we can come up with a price."

"I need Vernon to personally tell me that he's asked you to collect the rucksack. Sure, I'm pissed off that he didn't keep his promise to give back the laptop, but that's not the problem . . . I don't know you, I can't just hand over his stuff without his O.K. How do I know that he's agreed to this?"

Emilie knew perfectly well that Vernon could not be found. She was playing for time. Laying it on thick. It was not often that someone had the upper hand in a conversation with Pamela Kant. She was making the most of it.

"Are you sure you don't want to talk about this over a coffee?"

Emilie had noticed that the young actress was trying to avoid a strange man who seemed to be prowling around. The guy looked like a weirdo, thick glasses and a purple jumper that was far too small, there was something disturbing about the way he was acting, he had obviously recognised Pamela Kant and was making lewd gestures. Emilie had smiled, and she hoped that her smile said all there was to say:

"I really don't have the time."

The fleeting look of distress that flickered across Pamela Kant's face disconcerted her. For once she had her revenge, but it left a bad taste in her mouth. She said again, "I really am in a hurry, sorry," and, blocking the doorway with her shoulder, added:

"Tell Vernon to give me a ring, or write to me."

"He's disappeared."

"I thought you just said he'd asked you to collect his rucksack?"

"That was before. Xavier – an old mate of his – Xavier was beaten up while he was with Vernon, we went with him to the hospital, that's when Vernon disappeared."

"You know Xavier?"

"Yes, and Patrice too. I saw online that they're friends of yours."

Emilie had been so surprised by what she was hearing that she almost invited Pamela to come up to her place for this famous coffee. Patrice and Xavier were chalk and cheese. How had Pamela tracked them down? But in the end the pleasure of slamming the door in her face got the better of her, she had affected a sad pout and said:

"You have to understand, I've got nothing against you. But imagine if Vernon rocks up tomorrow asking for his rucksack? What am I supposed to say? Some girl turned up asking for it, and I gave her everything you had in the world?"

"I understand."

"Do you know where he is?"

"The last time he was seen was up at the parc des Buttes-Chaumont. I'm planning to go up and have a look round – I'm going to ask Xavier and Patrice if they'll help out . . ."

"Would you like me to give you a hand?"

That night, she was admitted to the private world of the WhatsApp group. Two days later, they all met up near the park des Buttes-Chaumont – Xavier, Patrice, Lydia Bazooka, Pamela Kant and her faggot boyfriend Daniel, who Emilie initially thought was too affected, but he was so nice to her she decided he was charming. They had spent the day talking to homeless people in the neighbourhood, and the evening discussing what they had found out in a cheap-and-cheerful pizzeria, and though she had a vicious hangover from cheap rosé the following morning, she had enjoyed seeing them again. They were genuinely concerned about Vernon, you could see it in their faces. Pamela was probably wondering what would happen if he was found dead somewhere – would she get her hands on the fucking tapes? She found it hard to hide her obsession. But all in all, she was pretty decent. She laughed too easily for anyone to be able to keep their guard up for long.

The following night, when she came home after a tanning session at the salon just up the street, Emilie had found her door standing wide open. Someone had been through her apartment. She rushed to the drawer where she kept a little cash hidden, then checked to make sure her jewellery box was intact, only then did she think to get down on all fours and look under the bed. Vernon's rucksack was gone.

She had panicked. She got in touch with the others while she waited for the police to show up to report the break-in. She was convinced it had been that bitch Pamela Kant. The two-faced little slut had probably decided to help herself, Pamela's hysterical protestations had done little to convince her otherwise. Emilie felt distinctly uneasy. The burglars had not turned the place upside down, just rummaged through a few drawers and ransacked a shelf. But still she had the unsettling feeling of being exposed; the apartment that was designed to keep her safe was open to the four winds.

They had all agreed to meet the following day at the Rosa Bonheur. And now here she was, wandering through the park, trying to find the bar. She was afraid that they would give her dirty looks; after all, if she had simply given Pamela Kant the tapes, they would all be better off.

Patrice sends a text message – he has just arrived. Emilie hasn't got the faintest idea where exactly in the park she is. All she does know is that she cannot see the bar. She walks along the banks of a man-made lake where large birds are shaking their feathers.

A friend told her that Patrice used to beat his wife. She doesn't know if this is true. Sometimes, when people split up they make up all sorts of shit. That said, she wouldn't be surprised. Patronising, assertive, rough and ready, with that arrogant, macho I'm-always-right-about-everything air . . . she can easily imagine him punching a woman in the face if she didn't immediately agree with him. He is a little Neanderthal for her taste. And the Navy tattoos on his arm don't help matters. Emilie has never understood what women see in this kind of primate. What do guys like that talk about over breakfast? Do they beat their chests and roar, sitting in the sink, waiting for someone to wring a chicken's neck so they can have their ration of blood before the first cup of coffee? It's not her thing at all. What Emilie most looks for in a man is intelligence.

Someone she can look up to. But, to tell the truth, if a guy like Patrice did try to hook up with her, she'd consider it . . . it's been so long since she slept in a man's arms. She's not so desperate that she would say yes to just anyone, but not far off . . .

Neither Patrice nor Xavier has aged well. Everything has started to droop. The shoulders, the arse, the chin. They haven't looked after their teeth. Intellectually, they've slowed down. It is strange to watch them joking around together. When they were twenty, they couldn't be in the same room without starting a punch-up. It's not that they are any more open-minded these days, their principles have probably not changed one iota, it's just that they have been spouting their drivel for so long it has become a dead language. And they no longer have the stamina to act the tough guy. They've come to resemble each other physically as they've gotten older. It's the booze taking over. Their faces are puffy, the expressions frozen. They are becoming cousins in substance. Patrice was a handsome guy once upon a time. You'd have to rack your brains to remember it when you look at him today.

Xavier has grown more bitter. It's something of a paradox, since, of the two, he's the one who's made something of himself. He wrote the screenplay for a successful movie, he has a beautiful apartment, stylish clothes, his wife hasn't dumped him, he lives with his daughter and he can afford to go on holiday. But he is more frustrated. He still has the same sense of humour, but it is not as sharp, and it is not underscored by fury but by despair. Emilie read somewhere that women survive prison better than men because, throughout history, they have been accustomed to being locked up spied on hobbled punished and deprived of their freedom. Not that it's in their blood, but it's part of their heritage. The same thing could be said about social success: women don't suffer as much when they don't succeed. They're disappointed, but they make do. For a guy like Xavier, who seemed to have everything going for him – the right breeding, the right skin colour, the right nationality – and who had a taste of success early on, failure is harder to accept. Oh well, I've fucked up my life, I made the wrong decisions, didn't take the opportunity when it presented itself, it's too late, it's done now . . . Emilie can see that the very things she can bear to think are killing Xavier. He is rotting from the inside, eaten up by the bitterness of being mediocre. You can smell it on his breath. He can't stomach it. He is spewing the same shit – Muslims freemasons Jews feminazis the Chinese the Germans the Portuguese the Romanians the Protestants the faggots and their brood – he's probably hoping that his wisecracks will make Patrice lose his rag, but Patrice just yawns, stares blankly and, from time to time, asks: "Are you keeping up with your treatment?" For some reason that escapes her, Patrice has decided not to rise to the bait. Though he's not conciliatory by nature.

Emilie doesn't find it funny. She finds Xavier's ravings disturbing, she has long since blocked him on Facebook. She didn't actually unfriend him, she simply hides his posts from her timeline. Even so, she did not manage to be as cold as her moral code dictated, after the accident, when they all got together to look for Vernon; she finds it difficult to reconcile the alt-right fuckwit whose posts on Facebook make her skin crawl and the guy she used to know so well. Xavier never was very sensitive or right-on, so she can hardly play the blushing virgin; unlike a lot of others, at least he didn't take them by surprise. And, in a way, seeing Patrice laugh at his bullshit rather than taking offence made her feel less tense. Then again, Patrice always saw himself as head of the thought police, the shepherd who welcomes strays or banishes them from the flock. In the end, it suited her to be easy-going, it had been a pleasant day, she didn't have the heart to throw a spanner into the works.

Spending the evening with Xavier, Patrice, Lydia Bazooka, Kant and her cute but queer boyfriend was a little like sleeping with a guy who's meh because it's been too long since you got laid. Obviously, she would have preferred to be spending time with people who were more interesting, more sophisticated, more on her level. But she had to admit that it felt fucking amazing to be with people who she had known long ago, to have Lydia Bazooka hanging on her every word every time she brought up some memory from her youth, or to have Patrice teasing her as though they'd seen each other just yesterday and were picking up a conversation that had been cut short. And when she had found the door of her apartment standing open, she had appreciated the fact that she could reach out to them, "You won't fucking believe it, someone broke into my place", and have them call her back within five minutes to ask what had happened and whether she needed anything. Just being in touch with them makes Emilie realise how much the sole responsibility for her life has rested on her own shoulders for years.

PATRICE HATES PARKS. HE FINDS THE NEATLY TRIMMED LAWNS where families can picnic while dimwit teenagers smoke spliffs depressing. When he picks up his kids, twice a month, he lets them play football outside his place, sometimes he takes them to the pool, despite the fact the everyone has to wear a swimming cap, but he never takes them to the park. Forty hysterical brats per square metre, and twice as many parents in helicopter mode, there's always some father sticking his oar in and his fat wife backing him up – in places like that, you're guaranteed a punch-up.

He had never set foot in Rosa Bonheur before all this shit with Vernon Subutex. They had ended up there the other night, after combing the nineteenth arrondissement talking to every homeless person they could find. The beer is expensive, but the place itself isn't too bad. What he likes most about the bar is the little waitress with the tattoos. When he arrived today, he was happy to see that she was working. But when he rolls up his sleeves to show off his ink, she doesn't react. He picks up a newspaper left on the next table. "FINANCIAL MARKETS JITTERY OVER ITALIAN ELECTION RESULTS." Anger flares at the base of his cerebral cortex like a jet of boiling pitch. How can they print this shit. They bang on about the debt, but the journalists can't even be arsed to do their jobs: to write about what's *really* happening. Make the distinction between public debt and personal debt, report the story in all its complexity – call a spade a spade: the rich have declared war on the rest of the world. Not just on the poor. On the whole planet. And with the support of the arse-licking media, they prepare public opinion for draconian reforms. It drives him insane. In the morning, the young guys in the sorting office are all talking about the *Front National.* It comes in snatches, "Marine was right about the euro, we've been well and truly screwed," as if she isn't an established figure just like the rest. They are not shocked to see the political elite enabling the *Front National,* "I mean, this is our country," they say. At the sorting office where he's on a fixed-term contract, they start work at 4.20 a.m. so they don't get paid for a night shift. That's what civil service has come to in "our country" these days: everything goes to middle-managers. They appoint more and more of them, pay them more and more, add more perks, more benefits, and everything they get is stolen from the shop floor. From the people who do the actual work. Bloody morons, why don't they realise that they're being set against each other, being wound up so they end up bashing their neighbours? The banks are being bailed out by the State on the pretext that they fucked up, their debts are nationalised, the profits are privatised, while all the pig-ignorant man in the street can think about is giving the Roms a good thrashing.

Mélenchon is better than Marine in every way. His only problem in attracting support is that he's not racist. The working class has been so brainwashed over the last decade that the only thing they care about is spewing hatred about *bougnoules.* They've been stripped of the self-respect it took centuries to win, there's not a moment of the day when they don't feel like they're being fleeced, and they've been taught that the only thing they've got to make them feel a little less shit is to bang on about how they're white so they have a right to put down darkies. In the same way that kids in the *banlieue* torch the cars outside their own tower blocks and never invade the sixteenth arrondissement, the Frenchman in dire straits takes it out on the person sitting next to him on the bus. Even in his irritation, he is passive: last night, on T.V., he was informed that there are people even worse off than he is, people who are poorer and deeper in debt: the stinking Black guy, the murderous Muslim, the thieving Rom. Meanwhile, the true culture of the French people – social heritage, the national education system, the great political theories – has been deliberately dismantled. The greatest achievement of the dictatorship of the one per cent has been its ability to manipulate minds. The alliance between banks/religions and multinationals has won the battle. They have managed to get a citizen with no heritage to give up all their rights in exchange for access to a nostalgia for empire. Well, you got screwed there too, comrade: don't think the riches of the colonies were for everyone, even in the age of empire the only privilege you were granted was the right to feel white, meaning a little better than a co-worker who wasn't white. From miners to the sheeple pushing their shopping trollies, the reign of the educated citizen didn't last long. It has to be said that the rich were at the end of their tether: they were sick and tired of having to go to Russia and Thailand in order to see proper poor people, the ones who starve to death, who don't know how to read, who go around barefoot, the ones who make you feel educated, privileged, envied. This new century has been torture for him, he is choked with anger when he hears what is going on all around him.

He recognises Emilie in the distance, walking down the central path, looking around her. She wiggles her hips, waddling as she walks. She has put on weight, she trundles like a ball, she looks devastated. Someone broke into her place and nicked Vernon's tapes. Always making a mountain out of a molehill, that's Emilie, she's capable of having a burnout just because she's lost this rucksack. Deep down, he's very fond of her, but you can tell her hormones are all over the shop, he's worried she'll burst into tears before she even sits down. "Oh, I got a bit lost in the park," she says. She is panting for breath, fanning herself with a newspaper.

She was a funny little thing, back in the day, with that look of hers like a punk from the Jura – wholesome and a little gruff. The sort of girl you ended up kissing when you were shitfaced, because she was gagging for it, because she was sweet, because she was there and you didn't have to worry about being knocked back. He'd spent a couple of enjoyable nights with her, surprised that she was so sensitive and feminine in the sack. But he'd always avoided her for a few days afterwards, feeling like an arsehole because he didn't know how to tell her that it was a one-off. Sober, he didn't fancy her at all. She had the good grace to pretend not to be hurt, even going so far as to pretend she'd forgotten it ever happened. She wasn't one to kick up a fuss in general. She has been sweating hard and her makeup is shot to shit. The smell of perspiration mingles with her perfume, which is a little pungent for the season. She looks more crumpled than she did two days ago. She probably didn't get much sleep, and spent less time tarting herself up. Her jaw a little clenched, she leans back in her chair and says:

"I can't bloody believe it . . . What the hell is the deal with this rucksack?"

"Pity you never listened to the tapes, we might have a better idea of why the whole world is batshit crazy about them . . ."

"Sure, go ahead, kick me when I'm down. That's just what I need, someone to make me feel shittier than I already do."

"Hey, chill, babe . . . I wasn't having a go. If Vernon had left three tapes of Alex Bleach at my place, I would have been in no hurry to watch them either . . ."

"Ah, you see? Thanks."

He had been surprised when Emilie popped up in the WhatsApp group. He hadn't seen her in an age, he assumed she had better things to do than take an interest in the little group of losers who were searching for Subutex. Pretty quickly he realised that she felt bad for kicking Vernon into touch when he was staying with her. She was the first person he had turned to. It must have felt weird for him, being treated like a complete stranger. If Patrice's memory serves, they had been pretty tight in the old days. He also quickly realised that she had changed: these days, she bitched about everything. It was like she spent her whole life making a list of all the people who'd been mean to her, even though she seemed to find it difficult to be kind to anyone. Patrice feels ambivalent, he wants to tell her to go fuck herself, but he feels guilty because he knows that deep down she's a nice girl who could never catch a break. Particularly when it came to guys. And he feels responsible – it's because of guys like him that girls who are basically thoughtful and kind turned into harpies.

He had had no intention of spending an hour on the R.E.R. to go looking for Vernon with Pamela Kant. The whole thing sounded a bit psycho. She hardly knows the guy, so what the hell does she want from him? But when Emilie had got involved, he had said, O.K., I'm in. He was touched that she seemed so concerned about Vernon, plus Patrice didn't feel particularly proud of chucking him out on the streets. When Subutex had left his place, he hadn't said, "I've no idea where I'll be crashing tomorrow night." He had packed his bag, he seemed chilled, he had simply said, "I think I've imposed long enough," and Patrice had let him go. Much later, he had found out that Vernon had found himself a cardboard box and was sleeping rough. It had felt weird, obviously. Vernon could have stayed two or three weeks longer and it wouldn't have bothered him. The guy's clean, keeps his mouth shut during the day, he's a good cook and a great T.V. buddy. That was the other reason he joined this motley bunch of freaks trying to track down Subutex. If he got his hands on the guy, he would have said "quit playing the fucking victim," and given him a set of keys to his apartment.

He had traipsed all the way to the park, cursing the fact that he was about to waste a whole day on this bullshit. Paradoxically, the thought of seeing Pamela Kant in the flesh softened the blow. Though he finds her obsession with tracking down a former record shop owner baffling, he has come to really like her. They chat a lot, on WhatsApp and Facebook. He fancies her. Though he has always hated porn. He finds it degrading. He doesn't like the idea of getting hard watching women reduced to behaving like slutty bitches, but he does get hard, and it fills his head with sleazy thoughts he is not used to. Not that anyone asks his opinion: he has porn thrust in his face all the time. He finds it disturbing. You can't download a game or a T.V. series without pictures flashing up of all the skanks within a 100-metre radius who are gagging for cock right now. And they're stark naked, obviously, just in case the message wasn't clear enough. So he has a look, I mean, it's inevitable. He finds it disgusting. It makes him horny and he is disgusted to be turned on by this. But who are guys supposed to complain to? They're supposed to just deal with whatever is thrown in their faces and get on with it. It's easy for women: as soon as they start complaining about how they feel sullied, they feel exploited, it's stop press! and listen to them whinge. He feels sullied by pornography. He feels exploited, but who is he supposed to complain to? Men are supposed to just put up with things and not bleat about being sensitive. Everyone proceeds from the assumption that they're obviously up for it. No-one bothers to ask whether they mind having their balls busted all the time, same as no-one gives a damn whether or not they want to be fathers, or whether they can afford to pay the mandatory child support . . . it all works on the same basis. Masculinity means "fuck 'em and fork out", there's no alternative.

So, at first, he was a little resistant to Pamela Kant. But now that he knows her, he doesn't see her as a pathetic porn star. More like a pin-up. The best thing about her is she is funny. She is sexy, he can't deny it. She doesn't pull out all the stops – her everyday clothes have no plunging necklines, nothing too sleazy. It pains him to know that she had to do that. Being a porn star is a pleb job – the boys become boxers and the girls do porn.

He had found himself wandering around the park asking every homeless person he came across whether they knew some guy called Vernon Subutex. He had chatted to a hairy young guy wearing a sleeping bag over his head like a turtle; he had knocked back a few beers with a couple of junkies, post-Mad Max freaks so filthy they looked like eco warriors, they'd played him songs on the guitar and couldn't string three chords together, and they stank, but all in all they were pretty funny; he'd met a haughty, suspicious guy from Mali and had to do the dance of the seven veils just to get him to open up and say, no, he'd never run into Subutex; he had chugged cheap red plonk with a wino of the old school who claimed he protected himself from the cold by smearing himself with seal fat, but that was probably moonshine . . .

Eventually, he and the others had got well and truly drunk at the Rosa Bonheur, swapping stories about their day with a certain unease – there were so many ways of ending up homeless none of them had ever considered. By closing time, Xavier had been belting out an old song by Les Vierges, "*Hé, les garçons, si on allait a la plage? Quoi? Plutôt crever*", with Emilie on drums, beating out the rhythm on the table, it was great seeing her so happy, remembering all the lyrics, "*On n'est pas le genre de mec à traîner sur les plages, quand on veut nous trouver faut chercher dans les caves, on n'est pas des anges on aime déconner,*" and it felt sociable rather than sordid. This was what had surprised him.

Right now, Emilie is in no mood to laugh. She is miserable, her gestures brusque, she snaps open a pack of cigarettes, takes one out the wrong way round, brings it to her lips, lights the filter end, heaves a weary sigh, tosses the cigarette away and takes out another. Patrice does not know what to do to comfort her without her thinking he's trying to chat her up – this woman's like walking on hot coals, you have to play it carefully when you try to be nice to her, otherwise she ends up imagining all sorts:

"Try to put it in perspective . . . I mean, it's not the end of . . ."

"They broke into my apartment. I feel so vulnerable now . . ."

To think that he can still remember back to when the band were on tour in Brittany and this same woman was popping tabs of acid (washed them down with coffee) first thing in the morning "because she'd just found them at the bottom of her handbag". These days, her hairstyle is like something his mother would have. Jesus fuck, but people change. He doesn't know what to say. There is an awkward silence. He feels sorry for Emilie. Sorry that men are disgusted by women of her age. This is how Patrice sees things:

forty is beyond the pale. He can't bring himself to think of fucking some woman who reminds him of his mother. Gentleness, tenderness, sure, why not. But sexual desire? No way. Emilie never had a child. That's what a woman her age needs. A kid of about ten, that's the only way for them to get the affection they need, the love that men refuse to give them. He is convinced that this is the way of things, that this is the reason that women have children: they create the last human beings who will keep them company late in life. Emilie did not deserve to miss out on life. She stubs out her cigarette and immediately takes another from the pack, realises what she is doing, replaces the cigarettes and toys with her lighter.

"When did you and Xavier get back in touch?"

"Weird, isn't it?"

"Yeah, it's strange seeing the two of you together. I didn't dare mention it the other day."

They always hated each other's guts. When he had heard Xavier had been beaten up, he had found it funny. It had been some time after he came out of the brief coma before he was back to normal. At first, when he woke up, he had insisted on being discharged immediately so he could "get back to the film shoot". He didn't want the production losing too much money . . . the poor bastard thought he was a director. His wife had to patiently explain that he was just a third-rate screenwriter, and he could take all the time in the world convalescing, there was no-one out there waiting for him. From that point of view, he could relax.

Xavier always had been an arsehole. When he was young, he had been wildly ambitious but, just because you're prepared to sell your arse on the streets, doesn't mean you'll make your fortune doing it. His only real quality was realising before everyone else that there was money to be made from the counterculture. He was prepared to do whatever it took, but incapable of doing anything much. They had always cordially despised each other, though with the grudging respect of rivals learned from years of watching gangster movies. It was here they had learned the bullshit *omertà* that served them as a moral code.

When Pamela first mentioned a serious coma in a private chat online – she had got in touch shortly after Vernon decamped from his place, and they had been chatting on and off ever since – Patrice was surprised to find himself hoping that Xavier would pull through. Out of carelessness or weakness, he had forgotten to hate him. Then he had allowed himself to be dragged into the discussions on WhatsApp, and when Xavier joined the group he didn't have the heart to tell him to fuck off. On the contrary, he had splashed out on a friendly message in a public forum. A truce of sorts. He is not a sensitive soul. Between justice and his mother, he always claimed he chose justice. But Vernon's spectacular fall had rattled his convictions. What was the point of being a die-hard, a straight edge, if you don't even give a shit that your friend is sleeping on the streets? Subutex might be dead. The possibility made him feel vulnerable.

When Xavier had rocked up to look for Vernon, scrawny and pale, Patrice had felt glad to see the dumb fuck back on his feet. When he spotted Patrice, he had smiled with that absurd pleasantness of patients who have had monster doses of legal, and had held out his hand as though the two of them were old acquaintances.

"Here I am, just out of a coma, and your ugly mug is the first thing I see?" His voice was faint and reedy. Emilie, Pamela and Lydia were poring over a map of the park, trying to divide it into zones . . . Patrice had said to Xavier:

"Don't you think it's a bit dumb to be getting in street fights at your age?"

"I didn't really have time to think of it in those terms . . . I hardly had time to open my mouth before I was K.O.'d."

Finding nothing to say to each other, they had watched the pigeons for a while, then, eyes half-closed, Xavier had said:

"'Come the revolution, we'll be on opposite sides of the barricades.' Remember how you used to say that all the time?"

"I never said any such thing."

"Sure you did. Every time you came down on us for having the wrong colour bomber jackets . . . the radical lefty . . . you always did have a thing for playing bad cop . . ."

"Well, excuse me, I didn't realise that when I criticised the Tricolour I'd hurt your feelings so badly you'd remember it twenty years later. What are you bitching about, granddad, history is heading in your direction, isn't it?"

"'Come the revolution, we'll be on opposite sides of the barricades.' You got to admit you had to be a complete dick to come out with that shit . . ."

"Are you going to bang on about this all day? Don't sweat it, it wasn't me. You're confused."

"Of course you fucking said it. Don't be a turncoat now."

"You took a serious bang on the head, that's all."

"And I used to feel like saying: 'if we're not on the same side, arsewipe, then you've got the wrong revolution.'"

"I always knew you were in love with me . . . you broke two of my teeth one day. We were putting up S.C.A.L.P. posters and you grabbed the brush and tried to plaster my face. You remember that? Right then, I could feel the love between us."

*

It was true, he had forever started his sentences "Come the revolution". It's not that he's become a turncoat. It's the shame of having been so badly wrong that means he no longer remembers things clearly. He has a feeling of utter defeat. This was a word that had defined his life, a word like a star around which he orbited. And it had never come to pass. All the conditions were there, but something else happened instead. And if someone organised the revolution today, he would not be a part of it. There would be no black flags and barricades, no *Das Kapital*, Makhno or Bakunin. It would be about something that people his age would not understand. The wretched of the earth no longer have the same and Patrice is as much a part of the past they want to make a clean break with as corrupt institutions. A crucial alliance was never made. These days, the conditions are ripe for those who have nothing to take it upon themselves to kill those who have even less, to the gleeful encouragement of the elites: go on, you poor morons, kill each other. The economy no longer means anything to a whole section of the population. They are no longer poor workers, they are unnecessary. The only institution they keep going is the prison system. Someone will have to get rid of them, and the one per cent are counting on the people to do their dirty work.

When Xavier joins them, Patrice immediately offers his hand. In fact, he is happy to see him, and smiles as he hears Xavier say:

"What's with the coat, Emilie? It looks like a cape for Wonder Woman."

"Shut up. Like you know anything about fashion."

"I don't know shit, but I know a circus costume when I see one."

"Don't give me a hard time today, I'm wound up enough as it is."

"Pamela not here yet?"

"She won't come, you'll see."

"Course she will. She posted it on Facebook – I'm just jumping in the shower, I'll be a bit late."

Emilie shoots them a black look:

"I think it's pathetic, recounting every detail of her life the way she does on Facebook. We should ban anyone who takes selfies from our friends list."

Xavier nods:

"She's not really into selfies. She just has a tendency to photograph everything she eats."

"That's worse."

Emilie scrapes her hair back. She decides to change the subject:

"Did you find the phone number for the detective you were talking about?" She turns to Patrice, "Xavier said some woman was looking for the tapes long before all this kicked off, said she came to see him . . ."

Xavier shrugs:

"'The Hyena.' She came by to say that if I came across the tapes . . ."

"What the fuck can he have possibly said that so many people are obsessed with these tapes?"

Emilie sighs loudly:

"Did you find her number?"

Patrice says: "What does she look like, this woman?"

"Hot. No spring chicken, mind. But sexy, you know, a bit of a Sharon Stone vibe. If she hadn't had plastic surgery."

"So, more like Françoise Hardy?"

"A little, yeah . . . I'd say more like Marianne Faithfull, if she was still skinny."

"In that case, you've got to find her phone number, pronto . . ."

Emilie explodes:

"For fuck's sake, nobody asked whether she was hot! So you've no idea where you put her number?"

"I do. It's just that I think it's pathetic to call her to say: 'I don't have the tapes but I was wondering whether you're still looking for them because we're searching for them and we're searching for Subutex, we're a bunch of useless cretins . . .' What the hell is she going to think?"

The tattooed waitress is clearing the next table. Her eyes meet Patrice's. She doesn't smile. He stares at her as she walks away. Emilie nudges him in the ribs.

"D'you remember what we used to think of fortysomethings with a taste for young flesh when we were her age?"

"Don't give me grief. I was just looking at her tattoo."

"You had your eyes glued to her arse like an old perv in heat."

"Was it that obvious?"

Xavier says:

"She knows Subutex. Used to hang out in Revolver when she was a kid. She heard me talking about him the other day and told me that her father used to take her to the record shop."

"Really? You talked to her? I'm really annoyed that you've talked to her and I haven't."

Emilie can feel herself tense. She is pissed off that they're desperate to fuck anything that moves – except her. Once again, Patrice commiserates. But he takes a strange pleasure in browbeating her. She plays with the zip of her handbag, making a grating jangle with the buckles. Her mobile phone vibrates and slides slowly across the table by itself, like an exhausted figure skater. She looks at the number and frowns:

"I gave my number to some homeless guy in the park who

said he knew Vernon, but I think he was bullshitting . . . I hope it's not him."

"Well, answer it."

"If it's him, I know he's going to be a pain."

"Well, you're single, aren't you?"

Emilie puts a finger in her left ear as she listens, head tilted forward, brows knitted, as though someone is talking to her in a language that is almost impossible to understand. She says O.K., thank you, hangs up and screws her nose doubtfully.

"It was the homeless guy . . . he said if we hang on here they'll bring Vernon to us."

"Did he sound serious?"

"Well, it must be worth waiting around, surely . . ."

"Especially since it's not like we were going anywhere."

GUSTS OF WIND SWEEP THROUGH THE HALL, MAKING THE DOOR rattle on its hinges. The Hyena has tried to block it by wedging a piece of folded cardboard between the door and the frame, but still, at regular intervals, the banging starts up again, like someone brutally attempting to shoulder open the door.

Sitting cross-legged in front of the coffee table, she is following the Subutex gang's WhatsApp conversation. They're in the parc des Buttes-Chaumont. Emilie has probably told them that there was a break-in at her apartment and that the rucksack has been stolen. The Hyena takes small sips of scalding ginger tea, it feels like swallowing fire. On the radio, a man with a grave voice is explaining that certain species of birds avoid hurricanes because they can sense the infrasonic vibrations that signal an approaching storm. She reaches out and turns down the volume; it is breaking her concentration.

Finding the Alex Bleach tapes had been child's play. All she had had to do was be patient and leave Pamela Kant to stir things up, rack up the retweets about how she was looking for Vernon Subutex. At first the Hyena followed her progress somewhat abstractedly, finding the coincidence a little troubling, then she began to suspect that they were after the same thing . . . The day she had posted photos of herself flanked by two police officers, shamelessly crowing: "Vernon Subutex in the house! Thx to all!" the Hyena had immediately called up a few old acquaintances to find out which police station she was at, and praise the gods, had arrived to see her leaving with Subutex . . . She had followed their taxi all the way to the hospital, but this was where she had made her mistake: seeing them go inside, she assumed she had time to park her brand new moped. It was bucketing down and it had taken her five minutes to find a sheltered parking space. By the time she got back, Subutex had vanished into the night without a word of warning. Her plans thwarted, she had kept a close eye on Pamela. It wasn't difficult, the woman seemed to spend her whole life glued to her smartphone. The Hyena had had no need to be inconspicuous, her target is determined to remain utterly oblivious to the world around her. She knows that if she looks up from the screen, it is an open invitation for some fuckwit to tell her what he thinks of her legs, her career, or her bikini wax.

The most difficult thing was staking out her building. Pamela can go three days without leaving her apartment. Thankfully, no-one has started a home delivery service for cigarettes, otherwise she wouldn't need to go out at all. On the other hand, anyone can follow her daily routine, hour by hour, just by following her on Twitter. What she's listening to, what she's watching, what time she paints her toenails, whether she burned the roast, what she thinks about Obamacare or her latest Tetris score against some deranged Korean . . . You start out thinking, how *old* are you, woman, it's like you think you're still a teenage girl. But you quickly get used to the one-woman show. Pamela Kant is endearing, especially because she is difficult to pin down. Like a lot of professionals in the sex industry, she seems to have no sexuality in her private life – not so much into fucking, more into snail farming. The Hyena spent a whole week hiding out in a hotel across from her building, scrutinising her online activities as though the security of the country depended on it. She has not quite worked out when the woman sleeps – she posts as much at night as she does during the day.

Al fin las tristeza es la muerte lenta de las simples cosas. Esas cosas simples que quedan doliendo en el corazón. Without thinking, she has been compiling a playlist. The voice of Chavela Vargas fills the space and her throat fills with a familiar sensation of gravity and grace. The Hyena's back aches from hours spent bent over the coffee table. She needs to buy a chair. But a chair would require a table, and before you know it you're living in a pigsty full of furniture . . . She likes to live in places that are almost empty. White walls, a few boxes on the floor, a low table for the laptop and a sofa in case she gets a migraine. She is an expert in vertical piles – the books, the newspapers she collects, the shoeboxes in which she keeps a few papers. A rail on which to hang her clothes next to a mattress on the floor. Minimalism reassures her. With a single trip in a minivan, she can move house, something that has frequently proved useful. She likes this apartment. Places are like people, there are some with which one has a greater affinity. She immediately felt at home here, in the dark depths of the fifteenth arrondissement, in this two-room apartment with its wood floors, high ceilings and skewed angles. There are no curtains on the windows, but there are lots of blind spots. It lacks light. This was why she could get it so cheaply. People want light. The Hyena prefers the shadows. *Que el amor es simple, y a las cosas simples las devora el tiempo.*

It is something that the Hyena has not done in a long time. Cleave to the life of someone else without their permission and not let go. Old reflexes, at once familiar and outdated, quickly resurface.

And it was Pamela Kant who had led her to Emilie's door. The Hyena had eavesdropped on their conversation, they had not noticed her peering into the window of a nearby estate agent, and, within two minutes, she had heard enough to be able to walk on and leave them to finish their conversation, observing them from the corner of the street. Pamela had left empty handed. As she walked away, even seen from behind, she seemed devastated and the Hyena felt oddly moved to see that she could be so easily discouraged. The Hyena was familiar with Emilie from the conversation on WhatsApp. She had been following them for some time now. Xavier, whom she had met early on in her investigation, had quite simply given her his password. She hadn't even asked. He had wanted to show her Vernon's Facebook page to prove that he was being honest when he said he couldn't contact him. He had told her his life story: "I always log off afterwards, you never know. I wouldn't want my wife reading some message, getting the wrong idea and being hurt for no reason. So I log off. I can't be dealing with all the passwords you have to use online these days – you're supposed to have passwords for everything, it's tedious. I always use the same one: Agnostic Front – a band no-one's ever heard of – that way I don't need to worry." She didn't need to worry either – she had only to add "66" – his birth year – to the name of the obscure band he'd mentioned, and ever since she has been able to follow every conversation thread. Never discard a piece of information freely given, even if it seems unimportant at the time, every lock has a key, you just need to be patient.

Emilie is pretty relaxed for a Parisian. She goes down to the local shop without double-locking her door. This was useful, the Hyena didn't want to creep in while she was asleep, she knows people don't like that sort of thing and she feels no personal animus towards her new target. A credit card, a little jiggling and she was in. Only the faintest rush of adrenaline. The sports bag Vernon had left with her was under the bed. It was the second place the Hyena checked. She felt obliged to open a few drawers before she left, out of respect for her victim.

Finding the tapes had been child's play. It had been afterwards that things began to go wrong. She hadn't dived for her phone to let her employer know – Hey, boss, it's all sorted, I found them. She wanted to have a quick look at the tapes. Just to get a sense of the price she could demand. It was a bit of a hassle tracking down a video camera that still took cassettes, but as she finally watched the footage, she rubbed her hands: it was exactly what Dopalet feared. He would pay whatever he was asked to be able to destroy the tapes.

Not that the stoner singer actually *said* very much. Off his face on whisky and yayo, he ranted and raved, bitching about his lot in life. There was an extraordinary beauty about him, he could read the shipping forecast and people would hang on every word. His eyes were mesmerising. It had less to do with their almond shape and long eyelashes, more their power to communicate. His gaze is magnetic: without choosing to, you connect, and he opens the floodgates of his emotions. The texture of his voice, the soft hiss of sand, accentuates the hypnotic effect. He was not saying anything interesting, but the Hyena knows Dopalet, the producer's name is mentioned, and that alone would give him a lifetime of sleepless nights. He cannot bear the idea of being hassled by the media. Actually, watching the tapes, he would be better off heaving a sigh of relief, shrugging and thinking, fuck it. If it ever did become public, he had only to say, "Just look at the state the poor bastard was in a few weeks before he croaked." The work they had done together smearing Bleach's name online would do the rest . . . But the foundations of Dopalet's egoism are too fragile to make him a shrewd tactician. The slightest contradiction is enough to have him squirming like a devil spit-roasted on a barbecue. He'd pay whatever was necessary to get the tapes, and be pathetically grateful to boot.

But she had not called to let him know. She is only half surprised. It is latent knowledge – information she has had for some time without quite being aware of it, yet sensing its shape. Once brought into the light, she does not find it startling. It is simply a beam of light trained on a corner that had been in shadow. It is there. For a long time now, she has known she would reach a fork in the road. So this is what it feels like, a crossroads. The problem is not complex. In fact, it is simple mathematics: how much should she ask. And still she doesn't phone. It's Johnson's "Cross Road Blues". Except that in the case of Robert Johnson, they say he sold his soul to the devil. Now that has a real ring to it. No-one ever talks about selling your soul to an angel. Ever. Angels don't do deals. The problem with redemption is that it's like swapping crack for chamomile tea: there's no doubt it has its advantages, but mostly it's a fuck of a lot less entertaining.

It shouldn't be complicated. She says it over and over like a mantra. She should bring the information back to her client, jack up the price and take a long holiday. That would be the best decision, the wisest decision: cynical and lucrative. And on the other hand there is an absurd temptation: get in touch with the seven or eight arseholes mentioned by Bleach, let them know she has the tapes, show them the footage. In other words, make trouble for herself, tip the world off its axis, toss a cluster bomb into a few quiet, peaceful lives, deal with the resulting shitstorm and, in the end, have everyone despising her. We might call this second option the left field solution. Why is she wavering? She's on the pitch for the cash, not the beautiful game. You don't do this job and then wallow in qualms and scruples. So what the hell is wrong with her?

She thinks back to Aïcha, when they were in Barcelona, doing her homework at the kitchen table. Her stubborn little head, narrow to the point of pettiness, without an ounce of generosity. The rounded forehead, the nose a little shiny in the late afternoon, lit by the glow of her laptop screen, the aching shoulders she absently massaged without ever taking her eyes off her work. Her single-mindedness, her intensity in everything she did. Now there was a girl who would find the tapes interesting. They'd screw up her whole life, but she'd find them interesting.

Shit – you can tell yourself you don't believe in anything, but in the end you can't help admiring the impeccably organised cluster-fuck. It's as if some pickled penpusher has been holed up in a corner plotting this whole thing for months. Because that is how it seems to her, now: the girl came to her hoping for information about her mother. At the time, it made absolutely no sense. But now, everything is different, now the Hyena can call her and say – I've got some information for you. Come to my place with the others, we'll all watch the tapes together. Just to see what happens. Out of a sheer love of poetry – of wantonness and extreme chaos.

What do you do with the truth? Pamela Kant, now there is someone else who would be interested by this. Not to mention her testosterone-fuelled friend Daniel who shows up at her place every night, it would interest him too. Everyone thinks they want to know. Truth is a blue-chip security on the open market. But what can you do with it? What can you make from it? Dopalet, the producer, wants to cancel it, repudiate it, destroy it. Well, at least someone has a coherent plan.

The Hyena fumes about not doing so, but still she does not phone to tell him the good news. A lot of people claim that they grow wiser with age. The truth is that they shrivel, they slow down. They lose their importance. They get trapped in quicksand and sink in good faith. The Hyena belongs to that rare breed of bullies – those who develop a sentimental streak late in the day, watch their armour transform into skin, and, dumbfounded, they find themselves suddenly connected to the world, and – unaccustomed as they are – suffering qualms of doubt. Many habits adopted during adolescence begin to wane with age, and she has caught a dose of conscience the way others might come down with rheumatism. She has come to the end of her pact with evil. To carry on would mean lying to herself. It is not generosity of spirit that prevents her from calling her producer. What holds her back is stubborn intuition. She will inform all those looking for Vernon that she has the tapes. And she will make sure that everyone gets to see them. It's none of her business, but she'll organise a little screening.

She has not mentioned anything to Anaïs. The producer's assistant. They don't talk about business. Though they see a lot of each other. At first, the Hyena had a classic fixation: given that her job is boring as fuck, she focussed on a scheme to ensnare the girl. She vaguely wondered what it was she found so attractive about her. Anaïs is not her type. She's too normal, sensible and easy-going. Though there are lesbians fascinated by the idea of converting someone, she has a tendency to avoid straights. You have to deal with all the bullshit insecurities of the first night, "Oh, I've no idea what to do, I've never done this before", as though they're sexual decathletes with guys, and you feel like saying, "Woman, if you don't know what to do with me in bed, I doubt you'd do much better with a prick and a pair of balls." Having fun in bed is not tantric yoga as long as there are two of you and you're both up for it. Obviously if your thing is to just lie there and let it happen, it might be little more complicated with two girls. Otherwise, just go with the flow, you'll see, you'll get the hang of it. Straight women are so fucking uptight. It's like they're always studying for a certificate of good conduct.

But she really had a thing for Anaïs and, the Hyena thought, it's not like heterosexuality is a defect – it's always possible to square your convictions and your desires – so she started hovering around, making sure there was no ambiguity about her intentions. She constantly popped by the office. And Dopalet never said, "Listen, I don't have time to see you today," quite the reverse: the Hyena was indispensable to him, like an amulet with the power to ward off fate. The mission he had entrusted to her was one that left him worried sick. She could request an audience at any time of the day and he accepted. With the producer's agreement, she passed herself off to friends and acquaintances of Alex Bleach as a documentary filmmaker who had been asked to decide whether there was sufficient material for a biopic. To justify her comings and goings to the office, she had met with a succession of Alex's personal managers, all of whom had been fired on a whim, the driver of the tour bus on his last tour, a former roadie, a P.R. girl, the trusted "friend" who had been paid to watch the star day and night, a woman who had also been canned overnight only a few weeks before Bleach's death, a photographer, a graphic designer . . . and several doctors. Bleach sought them out, and impressed them with his encyclopaedic knowledge of organs, the brain, chemical messengers and treatments. He demanded that his cardiologist come for coffee at his apartment every week, that his doctor accompany him on holiday, that his osteopath come on tour with him . . .

Not so much pushers of prescription meds as benign confidants, the doctors invariably started out feeling flattered before realising that they were being used, co-opted and exploited as part of the star's madness. Alex readily came across as polite, humble and respectful, people in his inner circle often believed they had tamed him, had forged an intimate bond to him. At some point or other, all of them believed that things would be different with them, that they knew "how to handle him". All of them had been disillusioned. The singer made no attempt to hide his vulnerability, he was funny and charming and extraordinarily affectionate. Then he fired them. Just when they least expected it, which usually coincided with the point when they needed him most. They all tried to discover the root cause of his erratic behaviour: the father who walked out before he was born, the cold, distant mother, a single mother in a village in the arse end of nowhere with a black kid to bring up, the stepfather who acknowledged the little mixed-race bastard but never forgot he was not the boy's biological father, the premature success, the enduring passion for class-A drugs . . . whichever way you looked at it, the conclusion was always the same: the guy was a self-saboteur on a grand scale. The Hyena related all this to her boss, who hung on her every word but remembered only one thing: Alex had never spoken about him to his friends. She had felt like saying, "Well, obviously, monsieur, no-one is particularly interested in you outside your offices . . ." but she kept this to herself. Nor did she mention Pamela Kant, Lydia Bazooka or Sylvia . . . Withholding crucial information is the very basis of fruitful collaboration. She also had declined to share her theory about Alex Bleach: those like him who are constantly going off the rails do it simply to piss people off. They do it because they can, and because it must be exhilarating. Fucking up three successive recording sessions and having the manager of the record label crawl back to eat out of his hand. Because he had no choice. And Alex Bleach was an equal-opportunities disappointment – from the hip tour manager to the old friend opening a neighbourhood bar and relying on him to show up, from the editor-in-chief of *Vogue* to the little quadriplegic girl to whom he had promised an interview for her blog campaigning for disability rights. His reputation as a useless arsehole preceded him, and no affinities of friendship would change his *modus operandi*: he charmed, forged a bond, created a sense of expectation and then disappeared without a word. He would say, "Sure, I'll be there," with convincing sincerity. Because, in the moment, he probably believed in his promise. Then he left them in the lurch. He claimed not to think of himself as a star all the while indulging in more whims, more cancellations, knowing that people had no choice but to forgive him. It was an aggressive stance: you need me too much to be able to treat me the way I deserve. Yet in all the confusion he choreographed, Bleach was conspicuously different from other smack-addict rock stars in that he never fucked up his records, when he bothered to record, or his concerts, when he condescended to perform. He did nothing right, except what was essential. His whole entourage regularly gave him up as a lost cause, Bleach would stage a comeback, and each time it reconfirmed his stardom. For years now, everyone had said things "couldn't carry on like this", according to the people the Hyena interviewed. His inner circle seemed more surprised that it had taken him so long to die, than by the event itself . . . but what most shocked them – all of them – was his success. With each new album, the professionals would gently shake their heads – this time, he had really lost it – but the public, in a massive sign of approbation, howled "we love you!" And his fame was not confined within the borders of France. His charm worked. As did the facile songs he wrote and deconstructed just enough to make sure they didn't sound like M.O.R., while still being catchy and easy on the ear. He had a formula that worked without fail, and he was an extraordinary live performer. Everywhere he played, audiences became devoted fans.

His ex-girlfriends were indulgent. He was the sort of guy girls fall for – he made them feel special. He never kept his promises, but it was obvious that while they were together he made them happier than they had ever been before. Having been princesses for a few scant weeks, they were intensely grateful to him and did not hate him for hurting them. Every one of them had been dumped without warning – after being idolised adored placed on a pedestal – he would vanish overnight. The only one who seemed to hold it against him was Sylvie, the online star. All his other ex-girlfriends talked about Alex Bleach wistfully, as though they believed that, if he had not died suddenly, he would have come back sooner or later and been happy with them. Alex did not have a "type" – he was magnanimous, he worshipped them all. From the young fashion model from Eastern Europe to the jaded duchess, he convinced each of them that he was happiest with her. He had a gift for grand gestures. They were more grateful that he had swept them off their feet than they were bitter that he had lied to them.

Bleach's relationship with Subutex was atypical. Though he regularly reconnected with people from his past, it was always to disappoint them at the last moment. He had never walked away from Subutex. He had even bequeathed him the videotapes. Even if the singer must have suspected – or known – that they were important.

The Hyena arranged to visit Dopalet in his office as often as possible. When she ran into Anaïs, she would come on strong, feel the girl get flustered and this would put her in a good mood. She did not think about her much during the day. This reassured her. In fact, it made it possible for her to gradually move through the stages that transform a casual fuck into a question of intimacy almost without a second thought. The Hyena thought: she doesn't obsess my every thought, so everything's fine. No, Anaïs clearly does not pose a problem. It's girls who are a pain in the arse that she obsesses over. The girls who go with the flow, who are always there when you need them, who get wet the moment you touch them, who tremble like a leaf when they come, who don't say, "When am I seeing you again?" as they put on their jacket, girls like that don't preoccupy your thoughts. They are content to shut up and do good. In her mind, Anaïs is light as a feather, a sporadic, comforting pleasure. There are tons like her. Except, Anaïs attracts her like a magnet. Pretty quickly, they settled into a routine. But this did little to calm things, on the contrary, Anaïs would wait for her in the evenings after everyone else had left the office wearing nothing under her bomber jacket except her fluorescent centrefold lingerie. She liked to fuck on her desk, standing in the stationery cupboard, lounging in the producer's office chair, bent over the photocopier in Accounts . . . It was at this point that the Hyena had to set up across the road from Pamela Kant's place, and it was when she gave the girl the address of the hotel that she realised – she doesn't preoccupy my every thought, but I can't go two days without seeing her. It is a metamorphosis. One morning, you get up, and silently, discreetly, you realise – you have become someone else. She views this new situation with deep suspicion. But there is nothing she can do about it. She has to admit it, she's crazy about Anaïs. She snuggles between her scissored legs after sex, grabbing her buttocks with both hands, so their bodies are as tightly interlocked as possible and feels a steady heartbeat thrum in her belly, stronger then the pulse in the throat, as Anaïs' pussy sends tremors all down her thighs. She cannot remember ever knowing a woman who genuinely throbs the way she does.

Where Anaïs is concerned, the Hyena refuses to send or receive text messages, she has forbidden her to call or send emails. She insists that, if anyone should look at their phones or their computers, they would find nothing overt. It is safer this way. They arrange to meet when they run into each other at the office, pretending to talk shop. She likes this. And it's mutual. Other girls always start out by saying, "Yeah, I prefer to keep my distance too, I'm really independent, I think it's best only to see each other when we decide to." Later – it takes about a week – they're asking, "When can we have dinner, what were you doing last night, why don't you sleep over." But Anaïs is a dark landscape, she is scorched earth. She asks no questions. She rarely talks about herself. She is resilient and fragile, and there is something about the tension between these things that makes her overwhelming. There is a story behind it, one that ended recently, it is obvious the moment you visit her place. An apartment that someone left too recently for there to have been time to fill all the empty spaces he left behind.

One day, Anaïs said, "I never thought I'd end up doing a job like this. I never thought I'd spend my time doing something I don't believe in. I assumed I'd end up doing social work and make a difference in my own small way. But I took the opportunities as they came. And here I am. Surrounded by people who had the power to do amazing things, but have completely given up. And I don't know how to get out." It was the first time she had talked about herself and the Hyena sensed that things had changed when she felt the urge to say, "Don't go in tomorrow, where do you want to go? Come on, let's take off together." She discovered that this was what she wanted – to take off with Anaïs. Jesus fuck . . . this was a turn up for the books. Relationships are always like this: they feed on events that seem trivial, but each one is a screw that turns and opens the way to unexpected levels of understanding.

Y siento tus cadenas arrastrar en mi noche callada. The young couple who bought the apartment next door and subjected everyone in the building to three months of noisy renovation work have finally moved in: they have a little boy a few months old, who is constantly crying. The other tenants are furious – everyone wants young people to move into the neighbourhood, but no-one wants the racket that comes with them – but it hardly seems appropriate to suggest cutting the baby's vocal cords just because he's disturbing people. She cranks up the volume until Chavela's voice drowns out the noise they are making.

The Hyena picks up her mobile and reads the messages in the WhatsApp group. They are at the parc des Buttes-Chaumont. Lydia Bazooka has just arrived with Xavier. They are waiting for Pamela Kant and Daniel. Everyone will be there. She phones Aïcha. "Hey dimwit, Satan's daughter calling, how's things with you?" Aïcha does not often laugh. You really have to make an effort. The Hyena asks whether she's free, says it's important, asks if they can meet up at the Buttes-Chaumont right now, and cancel any plans she had for tonight. Then she picks out a jacket and a perfume. She takes her time. She will let them know when she's on her way. When they know that she's bringing the tapes, they're not likely to scatter.

THE SKY IS OVERCAST WITH GREY CLOUDS LIKE A LID OVER THE CITY. Vernon studies the thin streak of blue on the horizon, as straight a line as if someone had unfurled a roll of paper above the rooftops. A last, stubborn ray of sunlight slinks from beneath the dark layer of cloud to bring a radiant shimmer to the grey tiles of Paris.

The girl showed up in mid-afternoon, she didn't give her name. She is probably younger than Vernon, but she's in a bad way. Her hair is cropped short – well, more hacked – and she's boss-eyed, it's hard to know which one you're supposed to look at when you're talking to her. She's clean, she doesn't smell, she has decent threads. She threw herself at him while he was chilling on his bench, enjoying the cigarette given to him by Stéphane, the site foreman. "'Scuse me monsieur I've got AIDS it's terrible I saw my social worker but she said she can't get me into a shelter before Friday I have to find a hotel please help monsieur please this woman was gonna to get cash from an A.T.M. she was gonna give me eighty euros but she'd left her card at home so she couldn't monsieur please for a hotel please."

He had faked a smile and shrugged, "I would have thought it's pretty obvious that I'm homeless . . . if someone gives you eighty euros for a hotel room, let me know, I wouldn't mind sleeping in a warm bed myself . . ." She had looked him up and down: "You're sleeping the streets? You don't look homeless." As though she suspected him of usurping the title. She had sat down next to him and taken off her shoes – she wasn't wearing socks. "Look, it's terrible." If the filthy nails on her hands – red and swollen from the cold and the meds – were not impressive enough, her toenails are positively spectacular: thick orange claws so long they've curled inward and meshed with the others. Vernon could not tear his eyes away. Thinking about his own swollen finger, he wondered: how long before you end up like that? How long before he was no longer like that person he had once been? Though he felt no nostalgia for his social identity, whose contours and pressures now seemed perfectly absurd, he still feared the idea of his body decaying. He still had some way to go before capitulation.

"See? I have to have it treated, it's really painful, my feet are killing me. But it costs twenty-five euros. I haven't fucking got that kind of money! I need treatment . . ." Vernon mentally calculated, eighty euros for a hotel plus twenty-five for a pedicure, you had to admit, the girl certainly set her standards high. He tried to reason with her: "If you don't want to sleep on the streets tonight, you'd be better off heading down that way . . . Back towards Belleville, there are a lot more people, it's easier to beg. You're not likely to run into anyone here. And Belleville is full of poor people, and they're much more generous than the rich fucks who live up here, they're more likely to relate . . ." Here he was giving tips on urban survival, as though he knew anything about it. All he wanted was for her to go away, because he could tell that she would bring him trouble here.

"But I can't go begging people are scared of me just look at me I've got AIDS they're completely freaked." Vernon nodded sagely. "Maybe best not to mention that straight off, you can tell them you need somewhere to stay without telling them you're sick." It was true that, when trying to start a conversation, AIDS was probably not the best icebreaker.

She was frantic, anxious and convinced that Vernon had money and that if she busted his balls a bit more, he would eventually give it up. Or take her somewhere where she could get help. But he had no idea where he could take the girl, even if only to be rid of her. She clutched his arm, fell silent for a minute or two, then launched back into the same spiel. She had probably been through some bad shit, the thought of sleeping on the streets panicked her to the point of convulsions, and it was obvious that what most terrified her was not the cold. She clung to him relentlessly and he quickly abandoned the idea of asking her questions: her name, where she was from, whether she usually bummed around this area . . . The standard small talk of the homeless that he'd picked up over the past few days did not work on her. She was too far gone. Every time he tried to ask her something, she showed him some revolting wound. He didn't know how to shake her off.

Darkness had fallen and still she was glued to the bench. Vernon knew that, if there were two of them, they would not be allowed to hang around for long. The very people who had been sympathetic to him – the labourers from the building site, Jeanine, and the two young lads who had given him a blanket – would quickly lose their patience and call the police as soon as it started to look like a gathering of pox-ridden warthogs.

In the distance, the Sacré-Coeur glimmered with a ghostly whiteness beneath the full moon. That night, he had shown her how to step over the low wire fence to reach the courtyard of the house, and the young woman set up camp, occupying a whole corner, and marking out the boundaries with pebbles she brought into the house. By the light of the moon, she had tossed out everything that former occupants had left strewn across the floor: two used condoms, a rusty cigarette lighter, an empty plastic container . . . While she settled in, she was watching him with wary hostility as if to say, lay a finger on me and I'll merk you, and he wondered whether this was why she started conversations by talking about having AIDS – to cool the passions of guys like him. Vernon watched out of the corner of his eye as she futzed about, sorting out her sleeping area, taking pathetic pains over it, her deft, precise movements at odds with her apparent mental illness. How long before you end up like that was the question that haunted him. This was probably the night that he realised he could not carry on the way he had been doing. He had to tear himself away from the butte Bergeyre.

Unable to sleep, the girl had talked in the darkness, responding to someone who occasionally made her laugh but most of the time terrorised her, someone she had to reassure – "No no I swear I'll go see her Friday morning she said she'd find a shelter for me." Vernon let her ramble on. In the middle of the night, she had let out a series of harrowing screams. There was not much chance that the neighbours would put up with that for long.

The following morning when he got up, she did likewise and he did not even make an attempt to talk to her, to tell her that if she stayed much longer she'd get them both evicted and he had a good thing going here . . . He always left the house unobtrusively, through the courtyard, checking to make sure there was no-one in the communal gardens or on the balconies opposite. But the girl just settled herself in the small back garden, everyone could see this homeless skank lounging in the shade of the oak tree and talking to herself. And Vernon had left her there, thinking – oh well, it was a good gig while it lasted . . .

*

Euphoria is a fragile thing. One wrong word and you're back to earth with a bump – he is expecting to go back to the way he was, the cramps, the panic, all that stuff. The calamity, the distress, the fear, the denial, the whole shitstorm of overpowering emotions. And then, nothing. He needs to move on, and he tells himself there's no hurry. He thinks back to Marcia. It happens to him sometimes. Her feels her beside him more often than he misses her. He has no fight left. This must be what they mean by depression. Watching things from a distance without thinking of taking part. No-one ever said that it can be quite bearable. He assumed it was accompanied by hopelessness, tenseness, a host of unpleasant feelings. Not at all. The clouds fascinate him as much as ever. He could stare at them for hours, he feels nothing but the emptiness inside him – a calmness that should be chilling but is as white as those fucking clouds.

At some point during the day, the girl comes to join him, forcing her way through the wire fence he has been carefully stepping over, kicking it down and shamelessly trampling it. She almost seems to take some twisted pleasure in tumbling over it, yelling at the top of her lungs. She's not the sort to retreat into the background. She is furious at what is happening to her. She has no intention of being forgotten. He watches her, amused. Feeling sorry for her, but thrilled by the chaos she trails in her wake, it highlights just how much effort he has made to go unnoticed. She comes and sits next to him on the bench and immediately goes back to begging him for money. He thinks about the story of Hansel and Gretel. He could walk down the hill with her, lose her in the deep dark city, and come back alone.

When old Charles appears at the far end of the street, he is happy to see him. He does not immediately recognise Laurent, who is walking beside him. Watching them as they approach, Vernon is reminded that he takes damned good care of himself given that he's homeless. The guy thinks he's God's gift, but he's got every reason. You have to be pretty single-minded and very stubborn to cultivate a look – worker's boots in good repair, jeans the right size for him, three-day stubble – but it is mostly his bearing that is remarkable. Laurent walks with his back ramrod straight, chest forward, chin up, he has not been bowed or broken by living hand to mouth. Laurent has said to himself so often that he is a dropout, an exception, that he has chosen this life and despises the working classes as much as those who exploit them, that he has ended up believing it: he bears none of the scars that attend his circumstances. They exchange a manly handshake and Vernon winces, his swollen finger sending shooting pains all the way to the small of his back. Laurent gives him a conspiratorial wink: "Well, well, you little bugger . . . Found yourself a cushy spot here . . . I don't know this area . . ." With a majestic, sweeping wave of his arm, Charles gestures to the view, like an estate agent: "Boasting a magnificent view of the Sacré-Coeur, if you please . . . a basilica erected over the mass graves of the communards, like an old whore belching in our face every day: 'Die, you fucking proles!'" But he does not have time to launch into his solo on this theme before the woman launches herself at him like a starving creature who has stumbled on a banquet: "Monsieur I've got AIDS it's terrible weeks I've been sleeping rough there's no hostel available till Friday I need a hotel I'm so cold I'm sick." The old man pats her on the shoulder, there is not a flicker of revulsion, a moment of recoil, he rummages in his pocket and takes out a five-euro note and a two-euro piece: "This is all I have, my darling, there's nothing more I can do, but on the other hand, I have some beer, would you care for a beer? We broke our backs carrying a six-pack up here, so there is more than enough to go around," and falling to her knees, without a word of thanks for the money she is stuffing into her pocket, the girl wails, "Please I can't do anything with that, go and get some money from the cash machine." Vernon spreads his arms in a helpless gesture: "She's got this thing about cash machines."

Laurent pays her no heed, he lets her snivel, does not even look at her, but sits on the bench, perching on the backrest, parking his muddy boots where Vernon usually sits. Hands in his pockets, he gazes out, "What a fucking view! You're really landed on your feet – I'm not surprised we haven't seen you around . . ." He hawks a gob of spit so thick it looks like egg white, Vernon stifles the urge to retch and listens to his commentary. "Except that, with your girlfriend here, you're in the shit . . . women like that, they're a scourge . . . they're worse than illegal immigrants, if you want my opinion. When I started living rough, people like that were taken in by the hospitals, that's where they belong, not on the streets . . . You'll see plenty like her. There's nothing you can do. Now, with the Chechens, the Malians, the Africans . . . at least you agree the boundaries, come to an arrangement about territory, you can tell them to keep away, and if you've got a knife and you know how to use it, there's a good chance that they'll understand the language . . . But people like her . . . They've got a piece missing and every month spent living rough grinds them down a little more . . . it's the pits, no-one wants to deal with them. And there's no point talking to them, there's no possible solution . . . What are we supposed to do? It not like we can burn them, is it?" Vernon nods, agreeing at least with the last statement, perhaps even relieved to know that Laurent does not envisage anything so radical.

Charles talks to the madwoman for five minutes, tries to reason with her – he has a whole list of organisations she can turn to for help – but she refuses to listen, she wants money from the cash machine for her eighty-euro hotel room, full stop. Eventually, the old man loses his patience and changes tactic: "Listen, either you shut your trap or I'll give you a good thrashing, do you hear me?" Terrified, she scrabbles over the mesh fence that she has all but demolished, cuts her hands in her panic to get away – Vernon can see blood on her palms – and hides in the garden. He is minded to go after her, her whole attitude completely changed as soon as the old man raised his voice, she was genuinely scared and she scurried away like a frightened animal. Laurent stops him with a click of his tongue. "Don't even think about trying to comfort her. There's no point. She will just start talking about the cash machine again. She does it deliberately. Crazy people are very manipulative. Have you got any money for her? No. The phone number of a decent shrink? No. Then leave her be. You don't have anything she needs. Let her look elsewhere. She'll bring you nothing but grief and you'll give her nothing she wants. It's a lose-lose situation."

Charles listens to this little right-wing peroration, not taking the trouble to respond, but from the look on his face it is clear that he is not of the same opinion. He stares at the garden, frustrated. The old man is a sensitive soul. Vernon remembers the doddering figure looming over him in the darkness as he lay on the bench delirious with fever, and the old man screaming: "Bastard, that's my place you're squatting" – then, realising that Vernon was in no fit state to answer, Charles had become annoyed: "You're burning up, you little shit, I can't even give you a kicking in peace – you're barely fit to push up daisies." He had wandered off, half yelling, half reeling, and had returned several hours later with a net of oranges he'd tossed onto Vernon's chest. "You need to eat them, and you need to get yourself indoors. You're going to peg it if you stay here . . ." And Charles had come back again a few days later. Panting for breath – "Those steps will be the death of me. I like coming up here, but God Almighty it's steep. I should check whether there's a house for sale. I could see myself living here. Piss off the whole neighbourhood." And he chuckled as he opened his bottle of red wine. "Looks like you're on the mend there, sonny. Though you're still bogarting my bench, I'll have you know . . . Usually, I stick to beer during the day, but I'm making an exception, declaring this a public holiday. So, not dead, I see? All thanks to my oranges, am I right?" And they had chatted as they drained the bottle. The old man was chilled. Ever since, he shows up every other day with the same greeting, "Brought a little bottle of red. Just to toast your health," to which Vernon quips, "I was just thinking that the sun was over the yardarm so it must be wine o'clock," and Charles responds, "So, what's new up on your perch?" and Vernon counters with a joke – common courtesy seems to demand flippancy – "Not great, they still haven't installed the central heating," or "I'm still waiting on the bedlinen to be delivered . . ." and they shoot the breeze and drink. Charles plays the grumpy old man but is sensitive as a budding daisy. From the pocket of his raincoat, he takes out a corkscrew, wedges the bottle between his ankles and screws the worm into the cork. He hands the full bottle to Laurent and, in an affectedly jaunty tone, says to Vernon:

"I suppose you know there's a tribe of nutjobs down there looking for you?"

"What do you mean?"

"There's a bunch of them. They show up every day asking about you and getting on everyone's wick."

The blood drains from Vernon's face but Laurent raises a soothing hand:

"They don't seem angry. More bewildered, I'd say . . . unless they're playing their cards close to their chest, they don't mean any harm . . ."

"It's more a case of them being worried, from what I can tell . . ."

"No. I had no idea."

"But you know who they are? They did tell me their names, but I don't remember a single one . . ."

"I've no idea why anyone would be looking for me . . . O.K., I did borrow a couple of things . . . but from that to organising a fingertip search of the Buttes-Chaumont seems a bit much . . ."

"Like I said, comrade, they don't seem to have it in for you."

"You think they're hunting me down to give me a hug?'

"Well, maybe . . . they look like a troop of teddy bears. But anyway, if I were you, I'd go down and clear things up."

Charles signals that he will be right back and totters off, his body stooped, his shoulders hunched – the old guy doesn't have problems with his back or his knees, but when he is in his cups, he likes to adopt the gait of an invalid. Vernon assumes he is going for a piss, but he carefully steps over the wire fence and, clutching his bottle, sets off in search of the psycho.

Laurent tilts his head back and belches so loudly that it sounds as though he's got an echo chamber hidden in his chest. They are the result of a lifetime's work, these spectacular eructations . . . Satisfied with the effect, he says:

"You should go down and say hello, if only for the sake of politeness. Do you mind if I ask you a question?"

"Ask away."

"What are you afraid of? Have you done something stupid?"

"You know how it is . . . little things. At the time, you think you'll pay them back, make amends . . . for example, I cadged a laptop from someone and promised to give it back, but in the end I had to ditch it . . . I certainly don't want run into the woman it belonged to . . . and another time, I borrowed a couple of books and a watch . . . from the wrong person."

"It's important to choose your victims carefully, some are less forgiving than others."

"Exactly. In my case she was very vindictive. Very."

"She's entitled, I suppose."

"She's absolutely entitled. And I'm entitled to make sure I don't bump into her."

"I can't imagine eight people ganged up to track you down because you hocked a couple of books and a watch . . . Not that I agree with what you did – all I'm saying is that they don't look like a pack of angry villagers pretending to be nice just so they can lynch you for some minor offence."

"What the hell is Charles up to? Has he gone to talk to the psycho? Just when she'd finally shut up . . ."

"Don't worry about that, he's not the type to . . ."

"I wasn't thinking about *that*."

"If you're going to be hanging around with hobos, I'd advise you to think about that . . . there are some who'll take advantage and try anything on the pretext that they're drunk . . ."

Laurent spreads his arms and yawns, then says:

"But Charles is not the type to go for a girl who can't defend herself, he likes them surly. Right, shift your arse and we'll head down. Don't pretend you're thinking it over, it'll still be here, your bench. No-one's going to rip it out overnight . . . You know that you can sleep on the railway lines? Coco and Pako left their duvets and a couple of places to crash . . . if you fancy a change of scenery . . ."

"You sleep on the train tracks?"

"There haven't been any trains for years now, so you don't need to worry about the noise . . . It's four-star accommodation, a hobo's palace . . . Quiet, bucolic, spacious . . . Obviously, I don't have a view like yours, but there are lots of wild flowers and you're not so overlooked."

"Are there a lot of you down there?"

"I'm offering you a golden opportunity, so don't go turning your nose up at it . . . There used to be three of us, but the other two left. They were fed up with the cold winters, they decided to head down to Toulouse. By bus. They managed to save the money for the tickets, but I said to them, boys, I can't see anyone letting you on a bus in that state, but I assume they caught the bus: they never came back. I've got the place to myself at the moment, like a king. I defend my territory. They're highly coveted, the train tracks. You're sheltered from the wind."

Charles comes back to join them, throwing up his hands in a helpless gesture:

"She's completely off her rocker, that girl . . . Vernon, I'm sorry to have to inform you that you've lost your peace and quiet: she's made herself at home here. She's not going to be leaving in a hurry."

Laurent gets to his feet, zips up his jacket.

"Shall we go? Do you want to fetch your stuff, Vernon?"

"I don't have any."

Laurent gives an appreciative whistle:

"Wow, you're really hardcore . . . You haven't got a duvet? Even a toothbrush?"

"Nothing."

"I bet you stink like a fucking baboon . . . For their sake, I hope the friends looking for you don't plan on kissing you . . . Anyway, shall we?"

Slowly, they descend the steps that lead to the rue Manin. Half-way there, Charles has to stop. He steadies himself against the wall, gasping for breath, brings a hand up to his chest, then sits down on the steps.

"God almighty, we're high up, my heart is going like the clappers. This must be how it feels to be in Bogota."

The old man tugs on the thin navy-blue socks that clash horribly with his brand-new Nike trainers. They are the socks of an office drudge and Vernon wonders from what period of his life they hail. He tries to imagine a clean-cut Charles, hair neatly coiffed, racing for fear of being late for work, briefcase under one arm, but it is difficult to picture him as having once been a model employee. The old man mops his forehead and shakes his head.

"The pair of you have got sturdy sets of pins, you carry on without me," he says, like a soldier asking to be left to die on the battlefield. Laurent and Vernon say they'll wait, there's no hurry, and an exasperated Charles shoos them away as he might a dog:

"Leeches, the pair of you . . . Go on, leave me to relax in peace."

Laurent is about to protest, then changes his mind, grips Vernon by the elbow and firmly steers him down the steps, whispering into his ear, "I've just worked out he wants to go back and talk to the mad girl without us around . . . he's like that, is Charles, sometimes he gets a bee in his bonnet." Vernon nods. He knows Charles. Right now, he is probably buying a bag of oranges for the lunatic. Hopefully she won't throw them at his face.

*

As they cross the rue Manin and go through the park gates, a steady drizzle seeps into their shoulders. Vernon thinks to himself, there'll be no-one there, whoever they are these people will have gone home, they won't be waiting around for us. The thought is comforting rather than disappointing since he is unsure of the welcome that awaits him. Laurent strides ahead, Vernon follows behind. They walk along a steep lawn – the whole park is laid out in terraces, a confusion of greens and slightly different leaves, the sounds of the city have all but faded. Vernon is surprised by the quiet. His nostrils fill with the smell of damp earth, above his head trees he cannot name stretch out their branches, a reassuring arboreal guard of honour. They pass an artificial waterfall. On a level patch of ground, Chinese people, indifferent to the drizzle, are performing a strange slow-motion choreography – they look as though they are pushing away huge invisible clouds. Without a moment's hesitation, Laurent steps into a bar, and Vernon warily trails after him. The noise in the enclosed space catches him unawares, as does the heat – a sensation he has completely forgotten. He recognises some of the faces around the table as they turn to him, surprised, but not at all angry. It is at this point that it happens. Immediate and subtle. A sudden shift. The closest comparison from his previous life might be a blunt of pure weed smoked on a deserted beach at 10 a.m. on an autumn day, after his first cup of coffee – the moment you decide to stand up, legs turn to cotton wool, there is a pleasant dizziness. You are physically present. You walk. Every now and then, your vision fades to black, the sense that reality has been replaced by a film set is palpable, but hangs by a slender thread. You are a helium-filled balloon. It catches him at the worst possible moment, but he has no choice. He barely has time to think – this is why if that mad bitch hadn't chased me away and these guys hadn't come looking, I'd never have come down from the Butte. Up there, these feverish delusions felt like exhilarating swoops in a hang-glider – they had no repercussions. He would tune out, happy to take the trip, in private communion with the Sacré Coeur. Here, things are different, his blankness causes concern: they'll think that he has lost his mind. He can feel their worried glances. He has probably changed physically. Deteriorated in some way he has not yet noticed. All he can do is smile ingenuously as he shakes their hands, allows Emilie to put her arms around him. He clearly remembers all of these people. But he is elsewhere. He watches the scene, plays his part, yet cannot invest it with his actual presence. He hopes that it will pass, he wants to talk to them, he can see they are disappointed, that they are studying him, assuming that this is how he is now, permanently absent. Patrice has the sleeves of his red and black checked shirt rolled up to reveal his tattooed forearms, from his guileless expression, it is clear he is happy to see Vernon. He takes him by the shoulder and gestures to the seat next to him. Pamela Kant is wearing a long black coat, she obviously arrived only moments before they did because it is still soaking wet, her eyes are elegantly outlined with kohl and Vernon wonders what she is doing here. He knows there is something strange about the fact that she seems to know everyone, but he feels himself hurtle backwards, like a tape being rewound, he wants to ask questions, but he lacks the coherence. He is incapable of uttering a single word. He lets himself drift away. Lydia Bazooka is watching him out of the corner of her eye, she raises a glass to him, and says a little too loudly: "Jesus, Vernon, it's good to fucking see you!!!" He would like to talk to her, too, but all he can do is smile, creating an awkward atmosphere around the table. His mouth is full of clouds – he cannot make a sound. Xavier is calm: he places his hand on Vernon's. He has changed. He has lost a lot of weight and seems overwhelmed by sadness. Vernon can see a greyish veil around him, as though a spider has spun a pale web over his skin. A flicker runs around the table, they look at each other, talk amongst themselves, leaning together and Vernon realises that the faint unease his drifting off has caused is not too serious – it weighs less than their joy at being together.

A tall woman in a black raincoat, belted at the waist, steps forward, hands in her pockets, she stares at him, amused:

"So, you're Subutex?"

She proffers her hand.

"People call me the Hyena. You don't look your best."

Instinctively, Vernon shakes her hand and her palm is warm and reassuring – he would like to keep it pressed against his own for a long time, and from the look she gives him, he has the illusion that she understands and regrets the fact that she has to greet the others. Her entrance cast a pall over the assembled company. All eyes are on her.

"It really is me . . ."

Then Patrice grins and, clearly smitten, says: "But you don't look anything like Françoise Hardy."

Emilie is annoyed and, determined that everyone should know it, says in a loud, somewhat affected tone:

"You broke into my apartment, now, I am not going to report you to the police because . . ."

"I'm sorry. But I was hired to track down the tapes first."

"That's not the issue, I really must insist that you . . ."

"You insist, you insist, you insist . . . If you don't mind me giving you a piece of advice, quit while you're ahead. The real miracle is not that someone went into your apartment – anyone could just walk right in – it's that I'm here to suggest that you watch the tapes. So, you say 'thanks, mum' and dial it down a notch, darling . . ."

Vernon has no idea what is going on. A waitress comes over and taps him on the shoulder – hey, remember me? He knows he has seen her before. But the memory eludes him. He smiles at her like a loon. She gives him a wink. She seems so gentle that Vernon suddenly feels the urge to burst into tears. The waitress goes back to her work. Then the memory comes back, a blinding flash: he was dog-sitting for Xavier and ran into her in the park, she was the daughter of one of his regulars at Revolver. No sooner has he thought this than his mind disengages again: the sounds and colours all around become a blurred confusion. On his bench up on the hill, when he felt himself losing the plot, he didn't give a shit whether it lasted two minutes or two hours, it made no difference . . . This time, he would like to take control and focus on the present situation, which seems quite pleasant. The conversations carry on, a distant murmuring, figures lean closer, stand up, pull up a chair, throw their heads back and laugh, these faces have names, but they call to mind nothing in particular. He feels a stab of fear. They belong to a world he has left behind. He longs to get to his feet, walk in the park on his own. He is terrified that someone will ask a question, that he will say the wrong thing, that things will turn nasty. People are talking to him, he feels his lips tighten in a feeble smile that will not go away. You sure you don't want to eat something, it's amazing having you here today, you know you can crash at my place, how are you feeling, we've been searching for you all over the shop. It's amazing you showing up like this, it's like a sign, huh? You sure you're O.K., you look pale, fancy another beer? He hears these distant comments, but his mind is elsewhere, he cannot bring himself to focus. It is Laurent who comes over and helps him to his feet when the group decide to move on somewhere, he leans close to Vernon, "When we get there, at least try to eat something, you've had too much to drink, you're in no fit state. It's a shame, you're lucky, they're being nice to you. Make an effort or they're going to think that you've totally lost it."

As they walk, Pamela Kant slips her arm through Vernon's and tries again to recap the story of the video tapes. Her words are evanescent, joining the dots of her story requires an effort he cannot sustain. It is dark now. They make a strange procession, their shadows flickering on the glistening street. Vernon does not recognise the sullen teenager in the group who has not said a word to anyone. Feeling his eyes on her, she growls: "I don't know what I'm doing here, I don't know any of these people, the Hyena called and told me to come." "I've no idea what I'm doing here either," Vernon says. She has no desire to talk to him. This is the first sentence he has managed to articulate, but the teenage girl in the hijab is not interested. They walk silently side by side. From around them, here and there, come clusters of words. They continue to stream past, a waltz in monotone. "Oh for fuck's sake get over it already" "Your little prank cost me a new lock I'll have you know" "I bet they're going to be boring as fuck" "Yeah, like anything you've spent too long anticipating" "I hope they're not going to be too depressing" "I'm really excited that I'm going to get to see Alex again" "Would you ever quit sulking, I'll pay for the bloody lock".

They take the métro, Vernon finds it hard to deal with the deafening racket, he is no longer accustomed to cramped spaces, they emerge on the banks of the Seine and, when they reach the Hyena's apartment, he is relieved to be able to collapse onto a sofa. He still cannot get used to the noise. Too many voices, too many walls, too much ceiling, not enough open windows . . . Patrice immediately puts a fistful of almonds into his cupped hands and waits, watching until he has eaten them, before saying: "Do you want to take a shower? It'll perk you up, you're looking a bit off-colour." The Hyena comes over, looks Vernon up and down with a mixture of concern and exasperation, before finally guiding him to the bathroom: "Clean towels are on your left as you go in, help yourself." Vernon balks. He is taken aback. How can he have forgotten how to negotiate walls and doors so quickly? When he sees himself in the mirror, he is dumbstruck: who is this stranger? What is most surprising is that he finds him handsome. He caught his reflection in the mirror before he recognised himself and had time to think – he's got the most amazing eyes, the poor fuck. The Hyena pushes the door closed with her foot. She talks to him calmly: "Do you feel alright? You're whiter than the sink there. Don't you want to take a shower? Frankly, you smell like a rotting corpse. The others are too polite to say it, but it's disgusting. Would it really hurt you to have a wash? Or maybe you think I'm being a clean freak." Vernon feels dawning panic: not only can he not bring himself to answer, but nothing comes, he can hear her, but not a single word passes his lips, he is drained, unable to make the slightest gesture, even if only to reassure her so that she will leave him in peace. This time, it is categorical: he is completely insane, like the walking dead, he can stand, he seems to function, but he cannot speak, and his thoughts are unhinged. She locks the door behind them. "O.K. Just let me do it." She undresses him. Her movements are those of a nurse. "Don't panic, everything is going to be alright. I'm sure you'll come round. I don't have a degree in batshit crazy, but I think yours is just temporary. You're going to take a shower. I'll lend you a T-shirt and pair of tracksuit bottoms. I think we're about the same size. You're not particularly heavyset and neither am I. We'll put your things in the wash, dry them, so if you really want to, you'll be able to leave tonight wearing your own clothes, O.K.? I should even have a pair of boxers somewhere." It is the soothing monotone of someone who is reliable, reassuring, who will take care of everything, he allows himself to be manhandled, relieved that she is behaving as though there is nothing terrible or grotesque about the situation. She removes his shoes, peels off his socks. "Jesus, you haven't change your clothes in fucking ages, have you . . . it's not just that they stink, have you seen the state of your feet?" She chuckles as she snaps the buttons of his jeans. "I can't say I'm an old hand at this. And you're not likely to make me regret it. The state of your trousers, what a nightmare."

Then seeing that he has still not moved, she takes him by the shoulders, spins him around and guides him into the shower cubicle. Stoically, she gets undressed, keeping on her white underwear and, to Vernon, she looks like a nurse. Checking the temperature of the water on the inside of her wrist, she adjusts the thermostat, talking without wondering whether he is listening, "I knew I was getting myself into deep shit when I phoned a bunch of people instead of just doing the job I was paid for, but I have to say, I didn't think it would come to this . . . Don't worry, just relax . . . You cracked up . . . happens to a lot of us . . . You'll get used to it. I know you know what I'm saying. You'll be back. You won't be like you were before, but you'll come out of this blank daze . . . At least, I hope so . . ." The feel of water against his skin brings him pleasantly back to the present, to the shower cubicle, hands soap his back, his shoulders, massage the knots, there is a searing pain followed immediately by profuse relief, and Vernon feels himself relax. She kneads his head, takes her time rinsing the soap away. She massages his ankles and he feels exhaustion draining from him, she runs the water over his feet, as though she can tell what he is feeling – she relieves his burden. Suddenly, without warning, and before he realises it, he's got a raging hard-on. He feels a rush of energy. When she notices, she is unfazed, she smiles and apologises, "Don't take this the wrong way, it's for your own good," and with a brusque movement, she turns the thermostat and, like a slap, the freezing jet of water jolts him back to reality. He protests and she lets out a loud laugh, "You see, it worked, you're feeling better already." She slips on a dressing gown and leaves him in the shower, "take your time, dry yourself properly, I'll come back with clean clothes. Are we good?"

He is himself again. He feels exhausted. He longs to sleep. He has no desire to go next door and be forced to make conversation; he knows more or less what has happened, the scraps of information gleaned here and there while he was delirious begin to connect. But he would rather not face up to all that. He is troubled by his reflection in the misted mirror. He has lost a lot of weight. The beard suits him, it changes his appearance. His cheeks are so sunken that it looks as though he is pursing his lips into a pout.

When he emerges from the bathroom, he realises that everyone is concerned, but has no idea how to behave in this situation. They treat him like an invalid, bring him bread and honey, smile benignly, make no sudden gestures. He takes a sip of coffee, he has not drunk coffee in a long time. He had forgotten that it tastes revolting. Everyone settles down, the lights are turned off, gradually a silence falls and the living room is filled with the sound of Alex's voice. On the laptop screen, Vernon recognises his old apartment. He waits for the sudden wave of emotion it should provoke, now that his thoughts are once again linear. But he feels only a pang of bitterness. He was so miserable there, though he never admitted it to himself. He does not regret what has happened. Then Alex's face swims into frame and Vernon feels an invisible hand lift him up – he remembers back when Alex was still here, a rush of images of things they used to do together ebb and flow. What was he thinking, back then, that stopped him talking to his last friend when there was still time to grab his arm, shake him hard and say, let's make the most of it, mate, let's make the most of it while we're still alive.

WE ENTERED INTO ROCK MUSIC THE WAY YOU ENTER A CATHEDRAL, remember, Vernon, and our story was a spaceship. There were so many saints everywhere we didn't know who to worship. We knew that as soon as they pulled out the jack plugs, musicians were human beings just like everyone else, people who went for a shit and blew their noses when they caught a cold. We didn't give a fuck about heroes, all we cared about was that sound. It transfixed us, floored us, blew our minds. It existed, we all felt the same way in the beginning, Jesus fuck this thing exists? It was too big to be contained within our bodies. Tearing through our youth, we didn't have a fucking clue how lucky we were . . . I remember the guy who first showed me the three chords of "Louie Louie" on the fret board and that night I realised that with those three chords you could play almost all the classics. The first time you had callouses on your fingertips was like getting a diploma. The first song I learned to play all the way through was "She's Calling You". Took me all summer. We were fighting a war. A war against half-heartedness. We dreamed up the lives we wanted to live and there was no fucking killjoy there to tell us that, in the end, we'd give up. When I was sixteen, no-one could have convinced me that I wasn't right where I was supposed to be. Sitting on the spare wheel in the back of a pick-up truck, freezing my balls off with six mates, not knowing if we'd remember to put enough petrol in the tank to get home, but not one of us had the slightest doubt. This was "the last adventure of the civilised world". As for the rest – you remember how it was – nothing was taboo, we weren't pissed off with anyone or anything: the rest of the world simply didn't exist. We lived our youth in armour-plated steel bubbles. There were alchemies of enthusiasm, things we didn't yet know had a down side, we gave ourselves nicknames, everything was fascinating, even the dumbest fucking shit. "We gigging tomorrow?" that was the only question I ever asked myself. We were living in the feedback of open mics, the hiss of a jack plugged into an amp, the heat of the spotlights, playing support to les Thugs and believing that comp drinks vouchers were the most important part of our adventure, and it was fulfilling. Between the ages of sixteen and twenty-three, I haven't got a single memory of a T.V. programme, we didn't have time, we were out on the tiles, we were listening to music, I have no memory of going to a mainstream movie, or watching a video by Madonna or Michael Jackson, lamestream culture just wasn't part of our scene. No-one even talked about it. I didn't know that it wouldn't last. We called it the network, anyone with an answerphone was a total pro, those who had a fax machine were at the bleeding edge of communications. None of us ever thought about buying meat, or going on holiday, only surf rats gave a shit about going to the beach, we hung out in the city, where there were gigs. There was no sacrifice involved – we didn't give a fuck about anything else.

The scene was the only thing that mattered. And we were right. Weekdays were spent week putting up posters, weekends we were gigging somewhere, there were always just enough punters so it didn't feel like a rehearsal, we pressed records, we made no major declarations, there were no interruptions, there was no world outside our own. We set up non-profit-making associations, we were treasurers, presidents, we were community workers. We toured from Italy to Germany, to Switzerland and Hungary and Spain, to England and Sweden in clapped-out vans, we were kings of the world. Later we had a rock star appointed minister of culture, suddenly there was talk of music grants, we watched venues like lavish youth clubs opening up, the scene was flooded with suits who could put together a grant application, they had mastered establishment-speak, they were more articulate, more astute. We started filling out application forms. C.D.s replaced vinyl. The single disappeared. We hardly noticed. We knew it was happening and we didn't know. Taken individually, each change was trivial. We didn't see the bigger picture. And before we knew it the dream we held sacred had been turned into a piss factory. It was a Cinderella story – our fairy fuzz pedal turned our pumpkins into carriages, and now the chimes had struck midnight. We were back in rags and tatters. Nothing belonged to us anymore. We all had clients now. Rock music was a useful adjunct to the official language of capitalism, the language of marketing: slogans, pleasure, individualism, sounds that could manipulate you without your consent. We hadn't realised that the magic beans in our hands were pure diamonds. A treasure in the hands of a bunch of misfits. Not one of us had a career path. We didn't even know such a thing existed. That was what saved us. We may have lost everything. But we'll never talk to those who never succeeded in living their dream as equals. These days, I come across kids who, by the age of twenty, have learned everything about competitiveness at school, or about marketing in business, who try to convince me they had the same youth that I did. I don't say anything. Forget it, dude, just forget it. My aristocracy is my biography: I've been stripped of everything I had, but I experienced a world that we tailor made to our own specifications, a world where I didn't get up in the morning thinking, let's go conform.

The 1990s. The time had come to sing the praises of pragmatism. Ethical considerations were no longer allowed to get in the way of profit. That was old school. Anyone who didn't run with the pack was a retard. Everything we loved was ransacked. Destroying things is easy, anyone can do it. Faster, faster, another full-page ad., another grant, a couple of sponsorships, and maybe throw in a little partnership agreement, could you make it as restrictive as possible so I feel the tug on the leash when I try to run? It was glorious, this brave new world, you had to be an arsehole not to believe. And the politicians we counted among our number were no more responsive. They carried on spouting hoary old clichés as though they were sacred texts. The prospect of thinking in real time didn't interest them – the more time passed, the more they loved the Commune. That massacre became our descent from the cross. We weren't going to get very far.

You asleep, Vernon? You're not even listening, are you? You asleep? C'mon bro, wake up, how can you fucking sleep, you've put three grams up your nose! You'll always be a mystery to me – you never do what people expect, but in the end, we always think thank god he did what he did. It's something I've noticed about you – you tend to throw a little chaos into the best laid plans. You can't fucking imagine what Revolver meant to me, man. How happy I was when I stepped into your shop. Often, you'd put something on the turntable that I didn't immediately find particularly interesting. A fluke. Something that would really take me forward later. I'd never have been able to make so many different records if you hadn't opened so many doors for me. You were a mentor. People really like you. You had no idea. The shop was always heaving. You did everything you could to keep the place afloat. I always respected you for that. When people stopped buying records, I still came to see you. It was weird, seeing you perched on your stool. You'd start banging on about your accounts. Something you'd never done. I realised you were going to have to shut up shop. No-one was interested any more. I remember the last two weeks, when you sold off the stock. Everyone came back for the sale. You greeted them like royalty. But you were the king. I watched you, at the time, there wasn't a flicker of bitterness in your joy at seeing all these people who had left you high and dry.

I've got a hole in my chest. An emptiness that's eating me up. And I hate everyone. You know, Vernon, Jesus only ever gets angry once in the gospels. Just once. When he drives the moneylenders from the temple. Everything else – everything else doesn't matter. I know, I've been talking a lot about Jesus these days. Why should I leave him in the hands of impostors?

Tell me something, Vernon, when was the last time you listened to a record that did what music is supposed to do? Quit the fucking snoring and answer me . . . I'll just have a little line to toast your health. It's not the music that's changed, you know. It's us. We're petrified with fear.

You know why I respect you? You knew everything there was to know. You had shelves of vinyl behind you, L.P.s lined up in their white inner sleeves. You only ever put empty albums in plastic sleeves in the display racks out front. And you have every single one of those records filed away in your head. Someone would mention a track and you'd turn around and, without thinking, pick out the disk you were thinking of, play the track, set down the stylus in the groove that interested you. You knew fucking everything, Vernon. You were the keeper of the flame and I was just some kid. And never, not once in your life, did it occur to you to play me ska, or reggae, or jazz, or funk. The only time you ever mentioned that

I was black was when you got the limited edition white vinyl Bad Brains album. You can't imagine how often people have talked to me about Coltrane or Bob Marley since. You'd never have put on Max Romeo and told me that I'd dig it because of the colour of my skin. There weren't many like you. I think it must be sheer stupidity that saved you. First off, you spend your whole time sleeping. It's as good a way as any to make sure you don't get taken for a ride.

I never wanted to be number one. That's something you're not supposed to say. Get with the programme, fucker. Success is great. If you don't want it, fuck off and don't piss on our parade. I never wanted to be number one. There is an intoxication to the depths, you know you should go back to the surface, but you linger, enthralled, on the bottom. I sold my fair share. Fuck knows, I sold a shedload . . . I learned to count. But what god do you pray to with numbers?

By the late '90s, it was over: we were past it, past everything. Past the phase where you worry about dumb questions. Questions of principle, of emotions, questions of mutual aid, the questions about playing not to satisfy the basest instincts but to serve your sense of what is beautiful. We were past the time of questions. We laughed at utopias. We were biddable, but we were no fools, we controlled everything. We weren't worried about getting our hands dirty any more. We should have been. People say it's no big deal, selling your soul is no big deal, you'll get it back, intact, at the end of the show.

I had my share of success. And I discovered I was black. I don't see how I could have been expected to work it out before, being raised by a blonde mother in a village in Creuse. Yeah, sure, people sometimes called me Snow White and laughed, yeah, I was the only black kid in the class. But I was good at football. Like a black guy – not that anyone said that at the time. I never really had any grief in the playground: everyone wanted me on their team. I concentrated on whatever worked. What else are you supposed to do when, in your mother's eyes, you are the embodiment of sin, of the fall? I grew up to be a white guy like everyone else. These days, people call me a Bounty Bar – even pasty-faced white freaks think they're entitled. And, yeah, maybe I am white on the inside: how could I possibly feel otherwise? Bounty Bar. So what? I'm descended from the Gauls, so fuck that. They make me laugh. "Bounty Bar". What did they expect? Did they think African culture was going to spring from my blood in the deep dark arse-end-of-nowhere in Creuse? I loved Motörhead and the Stooges. First time I ever heard them. It was a cousin – one of my step-father's nephews – who used to listen to them. This kid showed up one weekend with a mixtape. I didn't realise music like that even *existed*. It was a revelation. I remember watching Aznavour on T.V. and I thought, they can't share the same name, these things. They can't both be called 'music'. Don't ask me why, but that was my first thought. Somewhere inside me, the wolves had been unleashed. A minute earlier, there was nothing but desert, and suddenly I was a pack of howling wolves. It swelled in me. And it's not like I thought, I'm a black guy who listens to white music. Though God knows, that's what everyone has been telling me ever since . . .

You remember the lyrics – "He's white, I'm black, the difference is only visible in the eyes of racist fucks"? NTM – remember the first time we saw them on T.V.? Some show on F.R.3 I think. We didn't know shit about hip-hop. The lyric just made sense to us "the difference is only visible in the eyes of racist fucks". But times changed. I was put back in my box. Every which way I turned. The people who were angriest with me were other black guys.

I'm a traitor. Alex "Bounty Bar" Bleach. Not that that's something I can complain about – all I had to do was stay pure. What the fuck did I care about purity? I don't listen to Iggy Pop to feel pure . . . Blacks look down on me. I don't care. I can ignore them, I don't have to work with them. But there's no way to avoid white people. They're music journos, producers, booking agents, record producers, designers, photographers, they're the people who decide radio playlists. You can't ignore the boss man. You can't diss the white man.

By the time we got to the late '90s, I thought that if I talked about other stuff, people would stop obsessing about the colour of my skin, but it just got worse. I adapted. I met Victoire, she was pretty intense about anything to do with post-colonialism, she was pretty intense about everything, I suppose. The relationship didn't last long, but she was the one who made me read Frantz Fanon – she was shocked when I told her I hadn't really heard of him. I started reading *The Wretched of the Earth* because she gave me no choice, but after a couple of pages, I felt a chasm open up inside me. Not only was I a fucking Negro, but I'd never been given the opportunity to be anything else. And the worst thing was that I'd pretended it didn't matter. That intolerable violence. In my innermost being. I'd just looked the other way.

The *tombeau des Caraïbes,* the Negro parks, the quality of the cargo, the suppression of the Haiti riots . . . I read other books. No-one has forgotten, but that's the past, we've moved on. So, you do your job – you talk to the white guys at the record labels, who work with the white guys in the P.R. companies and the distributors who are financed by white guys and you deal with the white record producers, the white managers, the white photographers, the white journalists and the white T.V. presenters. Everything is white when you reach the top. People are always asking what difference it makes. And the truth, at least for me, is "not much" – I'm in the inner circle and I'm thinking about all the people who are excluded and have to accept that that is their place. It's not just about black people. The most important thing is to stop saying: this thing that's going on inside me, this constant bombardment imposed on me, I will no longer look away. I will no longer turn a blind eye.

You know people often suggested that I record an album of Zouk. Every time I met a new label manager – Jesus, there were a lot of those bastards, it was like they grew between the cracks in the pavement – he felt he had to come up with a suggestion for my next record. Hip Hop. Reggae. Funk. Even fucking Zouk. They'd listen to my records. They'd hear me play rock. I sold a shitload. And all they could think was "world music".

I'm glad you're asleep, you little shit, 'cos otherwise I couldn't bitch like this. I know what you think when I start bellyaching. You think: I'd give my right arm to have problems like that. Because your life is shit. And mine isn't. It's not fair, I know, do you know how much this jacket cost? Twice your monthly rent, man, twice! And I'm not even going to tell you how much I paid for these shoes. That's the last thing you need, me pulling a guilt trip.

There's a monster inside me that's been growing ever since other people started to think I was important. You know, that moment when you walk out onto the stage and the whole place howls. It can be amazing or it can be horrendous. I've felt both. But by the time it gets to be truly enormous, the monster has taken control, and it's hell. Stepping out under the spotlights is like stepping into a blazing oven. That precise moment – and the hours that come before it – I feel like a kid who's been beaten black and blue and locked in a cupboard under the sink. It's like there's an inner eye watching, and when it sees me playing the big I am, it gets angry, it corners me and beats me senseless, "you little shit," the voice says, "how dare you?" and I get the punishment I deserve. For the pleasure I was about to receive. I don't know where it comes from. I don't remember ever being locked in a cupboard under the sink. I had my share of beatings. These days, if I saw a kid being disciplined the way I used to be, I'd be fucking furious. But back then, it seemed normal.

I complain a lot. Too much. I know I do, but that doesn't change anything. Does it make me happy, having a *carte bleu* that can make money spurt from any hole in the wall without me ever having to wonder how much I'm withdrawing? Oh, yes. If money didn't give me a buzz, things would be very different. But money is much better than drugs. It's the same basic principal, but overwhelming. And people say there are no side effects.

You mind if I close the shutters? Hey, you're crashed out, why would you mind? I'm a vampire, I swear. I can't stand to see the sun rise.

The main side effect of money is fear. This shit is so pure that the fear of going into withdrawal is unbearable. You'd die if you couldn't just walk into a branch of Benz tomorrow on a whim and treat yourself. Money whispers in your ear *you're nothing without me* and the fear is so bad that you end up wanting more and the more you have, the more distance you put between who you are now and who you'll be if you don't keep going: a bum.

I remember the first time I was on T.V., Canal+, that was the first time I felt loneliness. After the gig, the record company threw a party – I wasn't a local hero any more, I'd become someone everyone wanted to meet, but no-one gave a shit about. I was an open door – I was supposed to grant everyone access. I didn't get off on the idea. I didn't much like that fact that anyone could come and tell me what they thought – about my latest single my T.V. appearance my haircut my latest remix my record sleeve my answers in some interview the lyrics of my songs. While they waited around for the next big thing – someone younger, more exotic – I was the latest gadget, the stuffed toy you use to jerk off. It wasn't the highpoint of my existence. Every fucktard felt they had a right to expect something from me. I'd be out somewhere and some loser would come up and say, "Oh, I'm not disappointed at all, you're just how I imagined." Meaning I made a lot of mistakes in French, and the guy found that exotic. Or you'd get someone making that little pout of disappointment when you think something's fake: "I expected you to be a bit more ethnic."

Jesus, Vernon, do you never get bored of snoring? If you were really a friend, you'd wake up and say, "Don't talk shit, I love you the same as always, nothing's changed." Because you haven't changed. When you were hanging out in your record shop, you never looked down your nose just to prove you weren't impressed.

Then we come to the 2000s, record companies start cancelling contracts with artists who weren't generating enough profit. They were summoned, one by one, to the office of the guy whose whole job was downsizing. The artistic directors responsible for the genocide got terminated as soon as they'd completed their mission, no-one wanted to run into a contract killer in the hall. Everyone knew, when they were asked to prepare a purge, that they would be next. The music business turned into a concentration camp. Imperious orders, arbitrary decisions, dimestore management consultants, suicides, tumbrils, threats . . . and the terrified submissiveness that goes with it. Not that this stopped us making rock, hip hop, anti-establishment music. After all, we were told there was no contradiction, only retards worried about *issues* any more.

I never got a thank-you from my record company. No way. Back then, people like me were filling stadiums. The sacred cows who, when the gig was over, trudged back to the barn, heads down, good, honest milch cows. There's no strategy. No-one offers you a drug so you'll enjoy spending the whole day in a stall, unable to move, being milked dry. But the drug is there, it's fun, that's the whole point. Every night, they let you out of your stall and put you on stage: you're one of the lucky ones. And you get off your face, because even an hour of sanity would be more than enough for you to realise what you're becoming.

I found my rhythm – getting wasted. First spliff before my morning coffee, booze with lunch, first line of yeyo as soon as lunch was over – and in the evening, whatever, take it as it comes. But never sober. I didn't write songs anymore. That wasn't a problem – my old hits were being used for T.V. commercials and ringtones. You can earn a pretty good living that way.

Personalities are like stones on a riverbank: it takes time for the elements to mark their passage. In the early days, you're vigilant, attentive, you keep yourself in check. But over time, you let your guard down, you go to seed. You learn to adapt as though learning your place. There is nothing reprehensible about adaptation in itself. It all depends on the demands of the system you're adapting to. Because compliance quickly becomes the ability to look the other way when you walk past the slaughterhouse . . . did you even think about that, Vernon? With all the improvements that have been made to abattoirs, how many human units could we exterminate per day. And don't try telling me that the day they start testing high-tech human slaughter on homeless people and undocumented immigrants, people will rise up and say: Stop, this is unconscionable. We've been the victims of government brutality for years. We behave like the battered wives you see on documentaries: we are so gripped by terror, we have forgotten the basic rules of survival. And as soon as high-tech human butchery is a booming business, we'll watch our nearest and dearest head off to the slaughterhouse with only a single shudder before the unacceptable. Our neighbours will put on their headphones and their dark glasses, pop a pill and go shopping. Pills will be our best friends. When night draws in, very few people want to be in a fit state to think about what they've done during the day.

You still dozing? I need to talk, and you're zonked out. I like that about you – you're never in time, but never really off-beat. You're a syncopated guy. I don't care, I'll talk to you anyway – you're asleep but at least you're here. One day, you'll listen to me. You're the one I have to leave all this with.

There was no turning point. No red-letter day. Just a protracted exposition leading to an extremely restricted middle: the circles of power. I was a first-class pain in the arse. That was the only opposition I could muster. I swallowed all the lies, I drank the Kool-Aid. Oh, I kicked and screamed a bit, but I did it. I felt like it was worse because they put me out there, in the public eye, everyone could see. But in the end, I endured the mandatory treatment: in a totalitarian system, submitting to humiliation is a mark of good conduct.

I could no longer be unselfconscious. I couldn't wash my own prick without wondering whether this was how Alex Bleach would do it and what the haters and the trolls would think. I couldn't make a single spontaneous gesture. That's another reason why you end up getting wasted all the time – you're no longer capable of keeping yourself in check. If you chug enough booze, other people's voices fade. After that – how could I have known what was happening to me? I'd lost sight of myself – in a raging sea, I was trying to stay afloat.

Satana died. That's when I realised. You remember Satana? I'm surprised you didn't wake up when I mentioned her name. I had a lot of girls in my life, Vernon, but the only one that made my friends jealous was Vodka Satana. When she died, I didn't say anything. That was when I knew. What it felt like. To live, to behave like a living being. When there's nothing inside. It's not the fact that I didn't say anything that really shocks me. It's that for months, I thought it was no big deal. Sad and unfair. But, well, logical . . .

Then, the morning after a gig in Marseille I was down by the beach, watching the skaters, hoping one of them would fall on his arse, I was sitting in a bar and suddenly the speakers started blaring out Burgalat's "Cyclades Electroniques". In that split-second, I was sitting next to Satana in Greece that time we went on holiday together. I had the album on my iPad, and we were listening on separate sets of headphones connected with a Y-jack. She went into a trance – later, it would be her favourite piece of music, but that first time, she laced her fingers through mine and there was a strange intensity to the moment – some moments are like that, they seem to have hidden depths – like when you're swimming underwater and a gulf opens up beneath you. Listening to "Cyclades Electroniques" I found Satana again, and I realised. I'd assumed she had been murdered and I found that sad but unsurprising. I had disappeared, Vernon. Swallowed up, body and soul.

I had first met her outside l'Olympia. I was with a mate, Gabriel, we were going to see Bowie. She was already in the queue, but it was taking people ages to get inside so Gabriel, who knew her, said come with us, and we walked straight in. Because a guy like me can't be expected to hang around waiting with other people. Everyone wants a photo with the V.I.P. They want him to listen to their demo, give them some random singer's number, they want him to come and play their bar, hear what they think of the production values on his album, take them on his next tour as lead guitarist. Satana was wearing a short kilt and a Ramones T-shirt slashed at with scissors to show off her cleavage. Her breasts made no attempt to appear natural. I had no idea who she was. But when we went into the concert hall, I noticed all eyes on her. I asked if she was a T.V. presenter. Gabriel burst out laughing and Satana said: "I'm a porn star". I was shocked by the pride with which she said it. She was as famous as Zidane back in the day. I had probably seen her in something, I watched porn in every hotel room where I stayed. But I was never interested in finding out more about the girls in the films.

Not all porn stars are alike – I met quite a few while Satana and I were together. You get all sorts of women doing porn, romantic airheads and mercenary sluts – a smatter of everything . . . and then there are the superstars like Satana. I wanted her from the way she sat next to me at the gig. It was clear that she was interested, but she was clever enough to know that she shouldn't make it too obvious. I remember her that night – she was like a little kid wielding a gladiator's sword. She went into battle weighed down by her artillery, but she rode to the front with a self-assurance I found touching. I was used to girls wanting to sleep with me. That's one area where I can't complain about racial prejudice. If there are any preconceptions, they work in my favour. But I found Satana's approach attractive. I like women who know how to shine. I've rarely met anyone who eclipsed me like she did.

The very next morning, on some dumb pretext, Satana sent me

a text message via Gabriel. We met up immediately and threw ourselves at each other. She had that weird little body that I loved from the moment I saw it. She looked like Betty Boop. She loved to clown around. She'd run around the house bare-arsed shouting bullshit, having her there was like having a wild bird in the house. Her smell was incredible, I was so happy with her. Obviously, she noticed that I never invited her to public engagements. I was thinking about my mother who was embarrassed enough when I went home to the village to visit and people recognised me – she didn't want to be mother to a rock star, she found it embarrassing. And she took a dim view of all the money I made. So I could just imagine her at the hairdresser, flicking through pages of *Voici* and seeing me with a porn star on my arm . . . But in the end, I cared more about making Satana happy than my family. I genuinely loved the girl.

We didn't last long as a couple. I'm too much in demand, Vernon, simple as that. It's not like I meet a pretty girl and by the time I get home that night, I've moved on. It's like women who would take your breath away are determined to get me into bed, whatever it takes. You knock them back once, maybe twice, and the third time, you wake up – you'd have to be stupid to resist that kind of temptation. I adored Satana. I wish I'd been the one who treated her right, spoiled her, made her laugh. But I was the one who made her suffer with my senseless one-night stands. The one who always had a stash of coke hidden in her fridge. She got a taste for it. I could tell. Four nights she went without sleep, ranting incoherently. I watched her pull away. And I thought, shit, I can't throw her out on the street while she's in that state, I have to help her kick the habit. But I couldn't imagine passing up all the girls either. So she stayed at my place, and I never went home, and she got more and more wasted, and I was waiting for the right minute to help her get clean. What I should have said was, "O.K., babe, I've cancelled everything, we're going to get on a plane and go into rehab together, and when we're clean we can decide what we're going to do." Instead I said, "You've gotta get a grip, babe. Ease up a little . . ." while I was packing a suitcase and leaving with another girl. She had fits of jealous rage, and all I could think about was getting the fuck out, and fast. But I would come back. And she would be there. And I was still happy to see her. So it carried on. I never went away without making sure that she had a stash of coke and Stilnox that would last her until I got back. I'd put a straw up her nose the minute she stepped out of the shower and say, "You've gotta get a grip, babe." I loved drugs more than I loved my girlfriend. And that was my way of taking care of her. "You've gotta get a grip, babe." Satana was an amazing dancer. Her body was tuned to rhythm – even when she was at her worst. You could tell how good a piece of music was from the way she moved. If she sat a song out, it meant the song was shit. She was the one who got me into writing music again. I felt good when I was with her. She made me feel safe. And just at the point when no-one thought I had it in me anymore, I released a record. "*Loin du Cœur*" was a massive hit – remember? No-one expected it to be so fucking huge.

Meanwhile, she was foundering. She wasn't doing any more films. I wanted to help, but everyone just wanted to meet the porn star, and they had nothing to suggest beyond "do you fancy playing with yourself in front of me?" She used to say: "Do I regret doing porn? Every single day. You end up being blacklisted. People wave you in, give you the red-carpet treatment, but as soon as you're inside, they can't find your name on the guest list, and you watch as everyone else heads off to get their slice of cake while you're stuck in the cloakroom. Forever. Yeah, I regret it. Why didn't I just become an escort? It's much less hassle. I wanted people to look at me. If I hadn't done porn, I wouldn't be with you. I would never have dared talk to you. It's complicated. Everything good in my life, I owe to doing porn. But I could have done without the incredible amount of shit that comes with it. I can't even see my little girl. Can you imagine me picking her up from nursery school? Better to just let her father get on with it. He's a decent guy. You can't fuck up everything in life. I send them money every month. And I'm okay with that. I'm not really the maternal type. When she is with me, I don't know what to do with her. But, still . . ."

She would get nosebleeds, she'd trail blood all over the apartment before she noticed, then she'd walk around holding a pack of Kleenex to her nose. We fought a lot. We always made up – it was worth it. She was hurting herself. Her jaw twitched uncontrollably, she'd tear at her eyebrows while she was talking to you. She wanted to beat the shit out of the caretaker in our building, she wanted to sue people she'd worked with. I was on tour with "*Loin du Cœur*" so I was never home. I didn't even try to get back as often as I could. By now, her mood swings were out of control. She fell in love with a cop. Swear down. She packed her bags and walked out to be with a fucking *cop*. I was furious. Being unfaithful never stopped me being jealous, but for her to leave me for a cop – it took months before I forgave her.

We were more chilled together as exes than we had ever been as lovers. Satana is one of the few women I dated with whom I stayed friends. I loved meeting up with her. I called her all the time, I answered all her messages. She started saying people were watching her. I didn't believe her. She told me a story: "This guy came up to me and asked if I wanted to be in a movie. I said, 'Sure, why not?' At the last minute, his assistant called to tell me that they wanted to push back the meeting with the producer to early evening if that was convenient. And because I'm dumb, I said, 'Sure, I'm free.' I called the guy who had set up the audition to check and he screamed down the phone – this guy's not just anybody, he's a major producer. The guy fucked me on the office sofa I swear I barely had time say hi. He asked, like, two questions and fucked me up the arse, he was so rough, so crude, that I thought about kicking the shit out of him, but he'd already shot his load and I felt so stupid, I hardly moved, hardly said a word." And me, I played it down – the guy must have thought she was up for it, you know what it's like, guys are arseholes, we see a girl who's done porn and we assume she does the dishes in high heels and a thong. Then I found out that she'd seen the guy again, and she didn't want to talk about it anymore. Her drug consumption skyrocketed. From time to time, she'd tell me these sleazy stories: "We went from the whole libertine orgy thing to this. What really turns this guy on is seeing me fucked up. I get fucked by old guys, let guys piss on me, get tied up in dungeons. He can't get enough. He pays me in coke. During the day, I think: I'm never seeing that fucking pig again, but that night I'm round his place. If I struggle, they hold me down. If I start crying, they just carry on. That's his thing. And I keep going back. He's got blow, he's got money. I'm just shit."

And I said, "That's terrible, babe, you need to chill. I'm here. You can stay at mine, you'll have everything you need and we can get you checked into a good clinic if you want." And she gave me a look of disgust. "I'm better off in that sleazy grind-fest. I suffered more at your place than I have in my whole life." I didn't take it well. I didn't call her back for a while.

She came back in a terrible state. She mentioned lots of names.

Famous people. It was impossible to know what was real and what was deranged fantasy. She wasn't particularly lucid. Her body was covered in bruises. Satana said she'd slept with a bunch of politicians, that she'd kept a list of names and that she was going to tell all. She was raving. She didn't want me to help, she burst out laughing, "It's way too dangerous you don't want to know but it's gone too far, I'm planning to dish the dirt. I've told him if you want me to keep my mouth shut, you're going to have to pay, and pay dear. He said he's going to kill me and he'll do it."

Don't worry, babe, nothing's going to happen to you. If you like I can pay for you to spend a couple of weeks in Los Angeles? You've always loved L.A. . . . No, I can't go with you, I've got too much on.

Satana stayed holed up in my apartment for four days. I pampered her. I looked after her and gave myself a clear conscience. To be honest, I deserve some credit: she yammered on all the time, jumping from one subject to another, I had no idea what she was on about. She was terrified of dying. That much at least was clear.

Then one night she said, "I really need to go out," and I knew what that meant: since I'd been rationing her drugs, she was going to go score herself a gram somewhere as a treat. She was in no fit state to manage on her own. She was bound to do something stupid. But I couldn't stand having her around anymore. Too much pain. So I thought, fuck it, I've been pretty cool to her, like I was pinning a medal on my chest. What a stand up guy.

She died a few days later. A cocktail of jellies coke and booze – her heart couldn't take it. Everyone immediately started saying suicide, because she was a porn star, because people think "girls like that" are – or should be – constantly suicidal.

She'd told me a hundred times: "He said he was going to kill me and I don't know where to go where to hide he said he's going to kill me."

Do you know what I did, Vernon? Do you think I called up any of the journalists I have on speed dial and said: maybe it's worth looking into this more closely . . . No, Vernon, no. I didn't talk to anyone, I put on my best suit and went to her funeral and I cried behind my Ray-Bans. And deep down, I thought it was normal. Sad and pathetic. But she was a lost cause, wasn't she? It was terrible, because I adored her. And I'd done everything I could for her, right up to the end, hadn't I? At the cremation, I could shake hands and look devastated. I'd been a good friend.

The worst thing is, that if it had been some minimum-wage fuckwit who had done this to her, I'd probably have made more of an effort. But Dopalet is a bigshot, and somewhere in the back of my mind I never forgot that he wasn't the kind of guy you want to antagonise. Too powerful. Way out of my league . . .

But sometimes, when I was ripped, I'd call him up. Big fucking cojones, yeah? I call him up and I say I know every sleazy thing he's done, the scumbag. He doesn't like that. He tells me I should be careful. Be very careful.

Fuck, Vernon, you could sleep for the Olympics. I've never told anyone that story. I'm too scared. Too ashamed. And I'm lucid: no-one gives a fuck. You know that Jewish expression: "They will never forgive us for the wrong they have done to us"? The Jews are fucking optimists. They can't stop themselves trusting other people. The truth is that they'll never forgive us for being alive. They will never sleep soundly as long as they know that we get some small pleasure from life.

EVER SINCE SHE BECAME DEVOUT, AÏCHA GOES AROUND TELLING anyone who will listen that her role is to deal with the housework and that she's perfectly fine with the division of labour between men and women. But this is purely theoretical. She hangs out the washing, clears the table, empties the dishwasher. When it comes to anything else, no matter how nicely Sélim asks for her help, she has an essay overdue she needs to finish right now. Bent over the laundry basket, Sélim is sorting dirty clothes to put on a dark wash. He is used to doing this. He takes a certain pride in the way he pilots the domestic ship. Aïcha grew up in an apartment that was always perfectly turned out. Just as he did before her. Sélim's mother was an exceptional homemaker. As a little boy, he loved the fact that when he came home everything was in its place, that when he washed his hands the taps were gleaming, that at dinner, the tablecloth was immaculate and the corners perfectly straight. Aïcha is like him. Meticulous – untidiness upsets her. He has always made time to keep their home ship-shape. Just as he has always made time to be there when she is doing her homework and has never missed a parent-teacher meeting. While she was in primary school, and in her first year at high school, no-one had ever mentioned his origins. But France made a U-turn – in her second year in high-school, people expressed approval that a Muslim father should take such an interest in his daughter's education. On one occasion, another father asked in a confidential tone, why he had not given his daughter a French name. "It's a pity, if you had you might pass for Spanish." The remark caught Sélim unawares. It was only some hours later that he felt a rage surge through him. What possible response was there to the insanity gripping the whole country?

He is proud that he has done his best to be a good father. He has boasted about things that others belittle. He would find it difficult to think of anyone among his friends and colleagues who puts any value on a man's desire to be a good parent. No-one cares about the fundamentals. They have a different scale of values. They think he would have been better off marrying a young girl from the *bled*, let her take care of the housekeeping and devote himself to his academic work. When he found out that the mother of his child had become Vodka Satana, professional degenerate and one of the lumpenproletariat of the entertainment industry, it took an almost superhuman effort on his part not to go insane, on the one hand, and not to rip her eyes out and call her every name under the sun. He had drawn on his reserves of strength to accept the situation and behave like a man: accept his responsibilities and take care of his daughter. Everyone had thought he was weak and not very manly. If he had stormed out, dragged his wife home by the hair, beat her black and blue, ripped her heart out with his bare hands and howled, "I wish the slut were still alive so I could kill her again" as the police dragged him away, in the world we live in, people would be making T-shirts with his face printed on them and demanding he be granted a full pardon. These days, it's the national mantra: glory to the crazy man, honour to the brute. And women are the first to agree. They don't like sensitive men. They want a slap, a clout, a guy who wears a wife-beater and demands to know what's for dinner as he belches in front of the

T.V. Even his own daughter thinks like this. He would give his life for her. He is not even sure she loves him anymore. She is disgusted by everything he stands for, otherwise she'd never have done what she did. It is her way of defying him, the prayers, the hijab, the Suras she intones all the time.

He forced himself to be the father he wished he'd had. His father is dead, he died when Sélim was very young – it was at night, his mother screamed, the telephone rang, but he has no memory of any of that, all he remembers is the howl of his big sister, Louisa, who though barely tall enough, threw her arms around her mother's waist and sobbed. A fall from a roof earlier in that day. They had waited until dark to inform the family. Perhaps if they had called earlier, there would have been time to say goodbye. Sélim never knew exactly. As it turned out, it had taken the foreman too long to confirm his identity. How many Algerians who came to work in France died on the building sites of a country that cherished its luxury apartments and its ability to build on the cheap?

When his father died, he was so young he did not know how to tie his own shoelaces. On the day of the funeral, he remembers his sister bending over him, tongue sticking out of the corner of her mouth, helping him to tie them. Until that day, their mother had never taken a bus by herself. The kitchen, the corner supermarket, a little cleaning in the next street over. She had never needed to go any farther. She spoke rudimentary French. Enough to understand what her children were talking about, or what the postman was saying when he came to the door. But she did not talk to the other women from Oran who lived in the neighbourhood. She was probably afraid that she would not be able to learn a new language. His father's death changed all that. She learned to write, only their names and addresses at first, then how to ask someone for directions, how to tell the time, she learned the names of the things she bought. In her own way, she emancipated herself. His mother was very funny. There was no-one like her for spotting someone's weak point and ridiculing it. They laughed a lot at home. She could come through the door in a black rage and snap out of it in a second because something distracted and amused her. She could burst out laughing while holding a slipper and just about to give one of her children a spanking – she could not keep a straight face. After she was widowed, she never went back to the old country. She never explained why – she wasn't the sort to give press conferences about her feelings. Whether because of the unrest in the 1990s, or perhaps for personal reasons . . . she never went back to Oran, but she was disappointed that Sélim refused to do military service there. He emphasised the importance of his studies, how he could not afford to lose two years. He did not dare admit that he didn't care about military service, regardless of the country where it would be served, and he certainly couldn't see why he should do it in the *bled* . . . his brother Abdel had come back half-crazed from his two years there – if the French did not see them as ordinary citizens, the Algerians didn't much care for them either. The boys who served their two years in Algeria rarely came back with a smile on their faces. They had a rough time of it, they were ashamed to talk about it, and they came home even more unsettled: citizens of nowhere, reviled on both sides of the border. But his mother did not like her sons to make a fuss. Having a son like Sélim made things difficult among her friends in the neighbourhood and with her family back in the *bled* – the women would nod irritably when she told them he had decided to teach in France, she would say that the most important thing was keeping him out of prison, but they implied: you poor thing, your son has no respect for his family, he is a nonentity, I pity you, you're lucky you have two other children. Louisa and Abdel were easier to manage. His mother was constantly telling Sélim to stop deluding himself: "You think people here are waiting for you? Do you think we're here just for the fun of it?" She had never been proud of him. She had been relieved when he introduced Satana. At least she was not French. And she was not like him, either. A pretty unsophisticated little thing. As for what she became later . . . as far as Sélim knew, no-one had ever told his mother, who cursed her for deserting her husband and her child, but that was all.

Aïcha never had a mother. She had to make do with this protective, methodical little man. A man who rarely told a joke. Sélim did not inherit his mother's good nature. The more Aïcha grew, the more Sélim forgot to laugh with her. Many things happened that he only understood when it was too late.

With the washing machine set to thirty degrees, Sélim sits down at his desk. He feels helpless, he has so much work overdue. He spends much of his time drawing up schedules, he tries to be methodical, to classify tasks according to their urgency. Email has become a nightmare. What did people do in the '90s with all that time not spent replying to emails? Baptiste cannot make the dates for the seminar, he has to go down to Avignon for his daughter's birthday. He had forgotten what month it was when he originally agreed the dates. The guy is infuriating when it comes to his kids. He has two, by two different mothers, his new girlfriend is not even thirty so he's probably already working on a third. Baptiste gives the impression that he is the only member of staff at the university who needs to plan things around his commitments as a parent. No woman would ever take the liberties he does. Maurice has cancelled a whole week of classes, he has huge problems as director of staff training and facilities, it turns out there has been a misappropriation of funds and his signature has been forged. It looks as though he may face charges, he has other things to worry about. Laurence has managed to get everybody's back up, the students are complaining that she is authoritarian. She claims it is sexism. She is an exceptional teacher, but right now things are not going well. She has missed all the appointments they have made for her, she has stopped replying to emails, except this morning, when she has decided to send a particularly long and abusive email about a student who had complained about her failure to attend tutorials. If things carry on like this, the whole programme will implode. François, who is coordinator for the seminar on techniques with the body politic, is having a nervous breakdown. Every time someone asks him a question, he shrugs and mutters, "Doesn't matter what I think, nobody gives a shit." No-one knows what to do with him. He didn't get the promotion he was expecting and that undermined his morale. And now, Sélim has been lumbered with organising one of the ceremonial meetings that universities so love. As if that were not enough, he has to deal with his assistant, Mireille. A dragon. Her approach is very effective: the minute someone asks her something, she screams. Needless to say, people think twice before bothering her.

When Sélim was appointed director of the in-house training programme, he bought a case of champagne and threw a party at his place. That was two years ago, he felt he had been rewarded, that he had finally been acknowledged. He imagined he'd be able to put a number of pet theories into practice, to delegate more. He had been warned that the post came with a lot of administrative responsibilities. He had not been told that he would effectively become a supervisor for a bunch of deranged fifty-somethings.

Two years ago, Aïcha had just started her final year in school. She was his pride and joy. For Sélim, who had raised her single-handed, her success was his crowning achievement. They had dodged the raindrops of misfortune, he had proved to be a good captain for his little princess. They had just spent the summer together in Brittany. Though he did not know it yet, it was the last year they would be so close. He hopes that it might come back. Because autumn had not gone according to his expectations. His department had been the first affected by budget cuts – what can you destroy without anyone noticing? Research and training. He also came to understand why no-one had ever held the job for more than two years: the workload was insane. It did not matter how many hours you put in, you were doomed to fail. As a father, he had been less available, less attentive. His daughter was not a problem. He had not been vigilant.

She had found her faith. To him, it was a condemnation of everything he was. It meant: your love of French cinema: fuck that. Drinking wine without your friends: fuck that. Your tickets to the opera: fuck that. Reading Guyotat and Deleuze: fuck that. Your lectures about Godard and Pasolini: fuck that. Everything you represent, everything you hold dear, everything you are: trash it. Your efforts your commitments your hobbies your friends: trash it all.

Islam seemed to him no more stupid than any other religion. But knowing it better than any other, Sélim knew that it demanded a complete abnegation of critical faculties. He would have been beside himself at the thought of his daughter embracing any religion. An intellect like hers should not be checked. Her memory, her ability to see connections, her curiosity – the very thought of his little girl subjugating her mind to any theological system sickened him. A mind like hers should not be denied books, nor prevented from embracing complexity on the pretext of following some obscurantist mumbo jumbo . . . Nonetheless, it had been particularly heartrending to see her turning to a religion that he knew, one that he had spent his life freeing himself from. He saw her taking advice from imbeciles. He heard her talking about Islamic scientists, halfwits capable of claiming that the earth is flat. His daughter was prepared to idolise any idiot if his beard was long enough and he refused to shake her hand.

He could not take a step back, put things into perspective, as his friends advised. He trotted out asinine arguments about the importance of post-colonial identity – he would like to hear someone explain how, by going to mosque, his daughter is freeing herself of the colonial yoke, at this stage he is prepared to listen to anything. Others take the opportunity to get on high horses that are mettlesome to say the least – suggesting in no uncertain terms that the Left was wrong not to take a more radical approach to the immigration problem. He has not the faintest idea what they mean – more prisons, more assessments, perhaps more executions? The sort of solutions that turn out to be problems more serious than those they claimed to solve.

He doesn't give a damn about immigration, he is talking about a girl who was brought up here. His daughter should not have to worry about where her grandparents came from. If she had been fascinated by the language, the literature, the history of the country, or the music of the Gnawa, he would have seen things very differently. But he finds it painful to hear certain colleagues hold forth about the right of girls to wear hijab or to reconnect with their roots. They're the same ones who cry when they hear that Chavez is dead. If the French president stood up tomorrow and called on Jesus to cure his cancer, they would be incensed, but in a tin-pot country, a brain-dead megalomaniac is a charismatic leader. Someone like Chavez is good enough for Arabs, the same way that Putin is good enough for the Russians. If their own daughter married a royalist, they'd take to their beds for a fortnight, but when *his* daughter starts wearing the veil, they remind him that it is an ancient tradition and start banging on about couscous and the Algerian War. This is what it has become, the Left Wing that so inspired him as a young man. On the one hand, there are those who still nurture a contempt rationalised by exoticism: let the darkies take comfort in their prayer mats and their Suras, it's all their brains are capable of. And on the other hand, there are those who misappropriate secularism to demand that the sons of immigrants be zealous renegades, ever ready to dissociate themselves from their own kind in order to win the medal for exemplary integration. Submissiveness – that is what both sides expect of Arabs – he can submit to the barbarism of his own kind or the violence of the French state, it doesn't matter, as long as he surrenders his dignity. And when they talk about Arabs, it is the poor they are really talking about: deep down, what his left-wing colleagues are demanding is that the destitute learn to suffer in silence. Through his daughter, Sélim has recovered his status as the child of immigrants: he is faced by an irreconcilable double bind. He is torn apart. He refuses to accept Aïcha's choice just as he refuses to condemn it and side with those who have not experienced what she is experiencing.

He loved this country madly. His school, the spotless streets, the railway network, the preposterous spelling, the vineyards, the philosophers, the literature, the institutions. But all around, the French no longer live in the France that he so loved. They are suffering. It is difficult to say what is tormenting Europe's pampered children. Living here, he thinks, it is true there is a part of the collective memory that he does not share: the double humiliation of the Second World War which made France a country twice defeated, forcibly occupied and forcibly liberated.

When it all began, when he first heard the French start to attack immigrants to the thunderous blast of "Beaujolais and *saucisson*", he did as many others did: he pretended not to understand. And yet, it said all that needed to be said: this was what the French thought of the country of human rights. Wine and pork products. This was their great cultural programme. Even from the right-wing, he expected better.

A girl like Aïcha could have become a scientist – she had the unbelievable good fortune to be gifted at maths, when she was in high school, the finest career paths were open to her. But her encounter with the Qur'an means that she is forbidden from studying science. She also avoids literature, which would expose her to too much moral filth, film, obviously, since in movies everyone is constantly fornicating, which leaves languages (studying grammar poses no ethical problems) business studies and law. Being more pragmatic than she would care to admit, she chose tax law, keenly aware that, to the great displeasure of the country in which she was born, the bulk of capital these days comes from governments who would take no offence at her wearing the veil. Quite the opposite.

He misses the closeness that he and Aïcha had shared. Things were easy between them. Their shared life was effortless, they did not weigh each other down. He did not worry. When holiday came around, they enjoyed going away together. There was no awkwardness. They were not joined at the hip, Sélim never felt suffocating or suffocated. They had never felt isolated, like some single-parent families he knew. Aïcha had always had friends and hobbies and Sélim had a busy social life that he found fulfilling. He never brought his girlfriends home, but he never felt as though his own daughter was judging him. They had an understanding – movie evenings, spring cleaning, Sundays at the swimming pool, eating pancakes all week during Candlemas, a series of rituals that, as Aïcha grew up, evolved but never disappeared. He knew that this made him happy, but he did not know it would not last. His daughter trusted him, asked his opinion on subjects he found complex, he enjoyed formulating his answers. He loved being her papa. She had been, and would probably always be, the woman who had brought the most joy to his life. Things fell apart. He had been anticipating her teenage years, the surreptitious spliffs, the boyfriends who were a bit too forward. Things did not go as he had expected. He had been unable to take a step back, what was happening hit close to home, it challenged him directly. He had not been able to stay calm. People talk about adolescence as a period of raging hormones and confused identity from which children emerge as adults. In fact, Sélim now understands, though the knowledge is useless, it is an unconscious dialogue: Aïcha comes to him and, as best she can, says this is the shit you've bequeathed to me, papa, by pretending you were in control of the situation, this is all your shit, and this is my contempt. Adolescence is played out between two parties: the parents struggle not to hear what the alien is trying to tell them. There is nothing more painful than having to give up his role as a beloved papa.

In the space of a few short months, they found themselves

separated by a yawning chasm. He began to fear dinner time, the protracted awkwardness that was an uninvited guest at table. They would turn on the T.V. so as not to have to look at each other. She only had to open her mouth and he felt like screaming. All this mumbo jumbo, so impenetrable yet so familiar. Not her. Not his little treasure. He had felt a certain fondness for the faith of his mother and his aunts, the way one passionately cherishes something that is fated to disappear, beliefs for which they could not be held responsible. He could never have imagined that they would manifest themselves again in his daughter.

The worst thing is the feeling of being judged. Aïcha would never say: "I despise everything you are." But her choices speak for themselves. Her terrifying fervour, her piousness, are a daily declaration: I think you're pathetic. Sélim often thinks about Satana. There was someone else who had not really been susceptible to what he considered his intellectual qualities. She would rather have been with any moron, as long as he had a well-defined six-pack. His daughter is doing the same thing, except that she is trading washboard abs for a goatee beard. History stumbles.

Sélim is hulling strawberries for dessert. When Aïcha comes home, he feels a knot in his stomach. This is what their relationship has come to: they are tense whenever they see each other. He is late. She is usually punctual. She seems worried. He does not immediately ask: "Where were you? Is something wrong?" He fumbles for words that will not seem intrusive. He is afraid of blundering, they can argue for hours over nothing. He would like to be able to be frank, to say – things are not easy for me at work right now – he would like to be able to grumble to her and for her to help him to see things clearly. She would say: "Papa, I've got problems at uni," and he would put his arm around her shoulders, what's the matter, baby, are you stressed? He does not touch her anymore. He does not kiss her. He can tell it makes her uncomfortable.

When they are in the street he has noticed she lowers her eyes when a man walks past. It is not a sign of submission. She avoids their gaze to show that she is pure. He could weep.

Usually, when she comes home, she rushes up to her room. Throws herself into her work to avoid him. But tonight, she leans against the counter, arms folded, a stubborn expression on her face. She stares at the floor, her jaw tensed, unable to decide whether to say something. He sprinkles sugar on the strawberries and puts them in the fridge. He will add the cream when he serves them. He tries to appear relaxed, he knows whatever he says will ring false.

"Is something wrong?"

"I know . . . about maman."

He has been preparing to have this conversation with her ever since she was a tiny creature. But, as with every carefully rehearsed scenario one has never found the opportunity to broach, he finds himself disconcerted by the circumstances. He has imagined this scene a hundred times, but it never happened "just like that". He wishes he could press "pause" and engineer more appropriate circumstances. For a moment, he is speechless. Aïcha reassures him:

"Don't worry. I've known for ages. I've talked to my Islamic tutor about it, he's helped a lot. I'm not responsible for my mother's actions. Any more than you are. I didn't want to embarrass you by bringing it up. But a couple of days ago I found out some other things, and I need to know what you think."

"Other things? What things? Who . . ."

"The Hyena. She invited me at the last minute. She said it was important. You know the singer, Alex Bleach . . . ?"

"Of course."

"He says she didn't kill herself. He says she was murdered."

"She took an overdose, darling, I'm sorry I didn't have the courage to talk to you about this long ago . . . She overdosed, but they think it was a suicide. I know it must be hard for you to find out. We should talk about it. Don't get caught up in the sort of morbid conspiracy theories people–"

"I don't think the guy was raving. Let's say I'm not sure. And I thought it was something I shouldn't keep to myself. I thought you had a right to know. Your friend, the Hyena, still has the tapes, but I don't think she's planning to keep them for long, so if you want . . ."

"What the hell gives that idiot the right to interfere? What nonsense has she been filling your head with?"

"Listen, papa, you were the one who went looking for her? You don't like it when I listen to the Imam, you don't like it when I listen to your friends . . . If you don't want me to talk to anyone, you're going to have to lock me in my room."

Angrily, she turns on her heel and leaves the kitchen. Sélim thinks he reacted badly. He did not ask the right questions. She caught him off guard. He had promised himself he would talk to her about this when she was old enough to understand. But no-one is ever old enough to deal with something so difficult. And, if he is honest, he has to admit that he has never come to terms with Satana's profession. The simple fact that she changed her name was a problem. While she was still alive, she killed the woman he had loved.

Shortly before that, she had left the marital home. Her "I need to live life, shit, I'm too young to be locked away" had seemed to him a little facile. She felt trapped with a baby she took no joy in looking after. "You'd have to be a halfwit to feel fulfilled with a life like this, don't you think?" So be it. Sélim believed that motherhood was something that all wives took to. But his was an exception. You can't force someone to stay. It had broken his heart, but neither he nor his daughter were reason enough to keep this young mother at home. She was shrivelling with boredom, she had other dreams. It had been difficult to accept. When she'd accidentally fallen pregnant early in their relationship, she had been thrilled, she said she felt fulfilled, that she dreamed of family life. At the time, he was the happiest man alive. During the first year, she too had seemed happy. Then she had started to complain about being on her own all the time. A slight depression. She wanted to find a job. She spent all her time popping round to the neighbours for coffee. By the time Aïcha could walk, her mother had no desire to spend time babysitting her. Things were breaking down. Sélim did not know what to do. Then there had been the handsome guy from the eighth floor. That was when the problems really became problems. He may have been a pathetic loser, but he was built like a Greek god. She left.

Left alone with his daughter, he refused to let himself be discouraged. In fact, the blow Satana dealt when she abandoned them was so brutal that, at first, he did not feel its full impact. Like a man stumbling from an accident who doesn't realise he has split his skull open until blinded by the blood, at first he had determinedly thrown himself into the daily routine.

At the time, he smoked a pipe. One day when he had gone into the tobacconist to buy a pouch of Drum, he had scanned the magazine rack while waiting to be served. He had not recognised her at first. The make-up utterly transformed her. But when he looked a second time, there was no doubt. From the cover of some pornographic rag, the mother of his child was smiling at him lasciviously. He had gone to the nearest video rental shop. She stared back at him from an astonishing number of video covers. Pornography was being produced at the speed of light. In a few short months, she had made dozens of films. He had prowled the streets of Paris like a madman. Heading for a role in a harrowing human-interest story, to hell with happiness with everything he held dear in the world to hell with his daughter his job his friends. He was going to strangle that slut. He was going to buy a can of petrol, burn her alive, then strangle her, or maybe not in that order, but one thing was certain, he was planning to kill her several times over. The resentment he had been choking back ever since she had left now burst forth in wild spurts, poisoned his blood and distorted his features: he would track her down and she would pay. But he did not even know where she was living.

She had reappeared some months later. Having never tried to respond to the threats and the forlorn messages he had left on her voicemail, she caught him completely off guard. "I'm so glad that you know!" She told him that she had found it very painful having to hide her "new life" from him. "If you only knew how happy I am!" What was he supposed to say to that? She was out of her mind. She loved her new friends, the first-class flights to the U.S.A., the easy money, the *Hot d'Or* awards at Cannes. She finally seemed to be living life, and the lifestyle had gone to her head. Thirteen years after her death, he still resented her.

He had promised himself that he would talk to Aïcha. But there was no hurry. Shit . . . now that her mother was dead, they had a right to forget what had happened. It had been difficult enough when it happened without going over and over it, to say nothing of tainting his little girl's life with a memory she had no use for. When the internet had come along, with its tidal wave of porn from all over the world, he had felt relieved. Video rentals shops closed down. The infamous video cassettes vanished and their sleazy contents with them. No-one thought to archive such material. Maybe Aïcha never needed to find out. He wanted to talk to her but, honestly, there was no rush.

When she had turned to Islam, it all came back to him and he had thought it might be karma. That, without realising, she was compensating. One madness atoning for another. He had to find a way to start the conversation. But he had no time, he had to find time. Not one of the Sundays they always spent arguing. The right moment never came.

That night, the hardest thing was not the fact that that she had found out, but that fact that her first response was to talk to someone other than him. Her Islamic tutor. An ignorant halfwit who wears Nikes under his *djelleba*. She had not come home and sobbed in her father's arms. She had gone to see someone else. Did this guy teach you to swim did he comb every shop in the city to find the toy you wanted did he give up his evenings to make sure you knew your reading test by heart did he teach you how to do an oral presentation did he spend nights in his bedroom racking his brains trying to understand mathematics so he could talk you through tomorrow's homework did he stand in the bitter cold watching you go round the merry-go-round ten times on the little elephant you loved did he put you on his shoulders so you didn't miss the Princess Parade even though his back was in agony did he get up in the middle of the night to bring you a glass of water when you had nightmares did he take you to see the dolphins seven times in a row because you loved them did he iron your clothes and fold them until last year did he worry how he was going to pay your registration fees when they were increased did he stand in line for two hours to make sure you'd get to see Lorie in concert? If you break him in two if you grind his bones with a millstone will you find nothing in the marrow but love for you, a longing for you to be happy, for you not to make too many mistakes? Then why is it that my words are no longer important why do I have to keep my advice to myself why can my arms no longer protect you? When did I show myself unworthy? Why has life done this to us? Why has this country gone mad?

Sélim has already been to check him out, this tutor. He hoped he would encounter a fanatic, a dangerous manipulator. He would have liked to uncover a recidivist paedophile – no-one can tell him that Catholics have a monopoly on hypocritical perverts, there is nothing more universal than vice decked out like virtue. In the end, it turns out that he is a short, chubby man with no charisma, serenely mediocre, foolishly old-fashioned. Like an upstanding country curate in the midst of the Inquisition: incapable of grasping the historical issues at stake, well-intentioned, surprised at the power invested in him. What does his daughter see in this man? How can he make sense of the idea that a young woman who is free do as she pleases should decide to defer to the judgment of the stupidest man in the neighbourhood? It must be something in their blood – after all, Satana left him for a body-builder.

What exactly has Aïcha learned? As if the bullshit from the Imam at the end of the street were not enough, now the Hyena has to get involved. The revelations of a late, great rock star . . . that's all he needs. Let's add the ravings of an arrogant junkie to the general misery . . . Sélim walks round and round the kitchen, as he angrily beats eggs. He furiously washes lettuce leaves and dries them in the salad spinner with preposterous viciousness. His daughter comes out with all this shit and then locks herself in her room, what did he ever do to deserve that? What do people take him for? A real sucker, some idiot who runs himself ragged without counting the cost so that everyone is happy except himself, the guy who puts up with everyone else's moods. And why on earth did the Hyena feel the need to fill his daughter's head with this nonsense without even warning him? Betrayed on all sides. The fool in the story. As usual. A nice guy. Women hate that.

Alex Bleach. Perfect, that's just perfect! He has been spared nothing. During the summer of Bleach's first big hit, Sélim was working in a shopping mall. Selling watches. The song was all over the radio. He had bought the album. He knew it by heart. This is something he would not wish on his worst enemy. For the woman you love to be going out with the singer you have been listening to for years . . . This was not the muscle-bound hunk upstairs he could simply sneer at. He had to believe that she had fallen in love. Sélim felt he had been made completely irrelevant.

He calls his daughter down to dinner. He is going to talk to her. With dignity. But once again they eat in silence. Sélim with his stomach knotted with rage, Aïcha staring at her plate. The omelette not overcooked, the way she prefers it, not too much dressing on the salad, the way she likes it, no garlic, because it disagrees with her. Tonight he does not turn on the T.V. After a while, he can no longer contain himself: "Do you know where I can find her, the Hyena?" and for the first time that evening, Aïcha looks at him. "Why? Are you planning to blame her?" Sélim has never hit his daughter. He is not about to start now. "I want to know what she's been telling you before I talk to you about it." The girl thinks for a moment, then shrugs:

"It's a bit late but they might still be at the parc des Buttes-Chaumont."

"What do you mean, 'they'?"

"There's a whole group of them. Old guys, about your age. They've got this friend, Vernon, who lives around there. They go and visit him every day."

"How do you know that?"

"I went to see them?"

He strides through the parc des Buttes-Chaumont, casting black looks at everything and everyone. He glowers at passers-by, rolling his eyes wildly. He knows that this melodramatic behaviour is simply a means to avoid having to talk to Aïcha, who is silently following a few steps behind. Sélim has a terrible feeling that she is not terrified at the prospect of him making a scene, but sad to see him making a spectacle of himself. He throws his arms in the air like a madman. "I'm so pissed off with you, you know? I'm really fucking pissed off. Why couldn't you have talked to me about this when you found out? You realise this goes back to Barcelona? You've been lying to me ever since you went to Barcelona. What am I? Am I the enemy now? You don't think maybe you should have talked to your father?" Aïcha does not even humour him by being insolent which would only make him angrier, instead she is gentle and apologetic, "It was so hard to talk to you about something like that, papa", she pronounces the a's in "papa" like o's, barely parting her lips. It is heart-wrenching. His little girl. Everything that is happening to her. And here he is like an idiot, forcing her to follow him through the park so he can bawl out the idiots who have been playing her the deranged ramblings of her mother's former lover. His poor little girl, dealing with all this stuff on her own. And he didn't even notice what was eating her up. So much waste. So much useless love that did not reach the beloved, that could not find words to express itself.

In the middle of the path through the park, he stops. He feels overwhelmed. He has failed to do his job as a grown up. He did not help her come to terms with what she has just found out, for the simple reason that he himself has never known what to do with the turmoil that was Satana. So he gets angry, he becomes defensive, like an idiot. He slumps onto a bench. Aïcha stands, waiting, her hands in her pockets.

Sélim cannot bear the way other people are looking at her. Some passers-by turn to stare at her. He wants to chase them away – it's just a hijab veil, for fuck's sake, you'll get over it, piss off, just piss off the lot of you. Though, as her father, he has every right to ask her why she is wearing this thing on her head, other people should realise that it is none of their business. After all, it's her hair, she's entitled to do what she likes with it. He says:

"Aïcha, I don't know who we're looking for, but they're not here. Forgive me. I wasn't expecting you to bring this up. I reacted badly. Let's go home. I'll explain everything . . ."

"No, papa. I want you to listen to what the singer has to say. I need to know what you think."

And she waits for him to get up and follow her. He wishes he knew how to say, "Darling, I don't have the strength to meet up with people who are going to talk to me about your mother. She broke my heart. I can't bring myself to think about it all again. You are the most precious thing in the world to me, I wish I could give you the gift of a different mother. Her story is sadder than you can possibly imagine. I wish you never had to know about all this, because I wish none of it had ever happened." But he walks on in silence. In a feeble voice, he asks:

"What did he say, this Alex Bleach, that's got you so worked up?"

"You'll hear for yourself. Maybe you'll say you don't believe it."

"Why did she ask you to watch these tapes and not me?"

"It would have been too embarrassing for us to watch it together."

The man Aïcha refers to as Vernon turns as he hears Sélim approach. He is wearing boots that are too big for his long, spindly legs. His skin is grey, his eyes are feverish. He has a particular way of holding the gaze of the person he is talking to with disarming equanimity. He walks over to Sélim without a word. He smells of stale tobacco, damp earth, and something indefinable that is sweet and sugary. Pleasant. He takes the father in his arms and hugs him. Sélim is surprised, but all his anxiety and hostility drain away. He came to insult this man, but he has already forgotten that. Vernon's hug envelops him and he becomes a bastion, a shield, a bandage. Sélim surrenders, aware of the absurdity of the situation, but unable to escape from this comforting embrace.

"IS IT HASH OR WEED?"

Vernon asks the question as a matter of form as Lydia passes him the joint since he is just as happy to smoke either. Then he moves a few paces away from the group and settles in his favourite spot, the hollow created by the roots of the oldest chestnut tree in the park. Tall as a four-storey house, the tree has grown lopsided, its huge branches are parallel to the ground. Its leaves, yellowed by some disease, fan out like an orange wall that contrasts sharply with the green of the park in summer.

Vernon takes long, slow tokes on the spliff, he holds the smoke in his lungs and looks at the others from afar. He likes being stoned, it allows him to experience the most improbable sensations without having to worry too much. As, for example, when he lays his hand against the bark of the tree, feeling the soft pulse of the regenerating sap, the low electromagnetic frequencies, being aware of the rhythms of plant life. He would rather think it is because he has been smoking weed, but the truth is he never really came down after the trip he had before he watched Alex Bleach's tapes.

Over the course of that strange evening, Emilie, Lydia and Patrice in turn had offered put a roof over his head. They were probably worried that he would accept, given the bizarre state he was in, but they were also motivated by sincere regret – they did not want to go home knowing that he would be sleeping on the streets. To his own surprise, and without a flicker of hesitation, Vernon declined all the offers. It was difficult to justify. He had said: "Don't worry, I don't want to be a burden, honestly, it doesn't bother me sleeping out of doors." They look at him as though he were insane. Normal. He would have done the same in their shoes. The real truth was that, physically, he could no longer tolerate walls and ceilings, he found it difficult to breathe, every object was hostile, he was plagued by a noxious vibration. The worst thing was having people around him. He could feel their misery, their pain, their fear of not being good enough, of being unmasked, being punished, wasting their lives: he felt it was like pollen, it insinuated its way into every orifice and made it impossible to breathe. Which meant that no, he really, truly had absolutely no desire to move in with any of them. These days he needed space. A solitude.

That night, he had dozed off amid the words of others, even in his sleep he could make out their conversation. Alex's declarations had been like a spotlight trained on a dark corner. Some of them believed him unreservedly. Daniel saw it as proof that women who had to bear the burden of male sexuality were second-class citizens whom one could kill with complete impunity. Pamela had started out by being more reserved, according to her, Alex was madly in love with Satana, and eaten up by guilt that he couldn't save her, he had invented this story to stop himself going insane, but she could not bring herself to believe that it was true. Patrice was not surprised, to him, this was just another example of the fact that the rich are entitled to do whatever they like, and the right to kill the poor was just one more tool in their arsenal. As for the Hyena, all this proved that there was something going on in this little group, something that she could not define, but which, when she spent time with them, was almost tangible: a pleasure at being together that was completely mysterious. They did not like each other, they had little in common, they had no interest in hanging out together, but as soon as they got together, there was a congruity – she explained this to Lydia who was having trouble understanding. To Lydia, the evidence was staring them in the face: Alex had been murdered too. They had to avenge him. Xavier declared that the whole thing was bullshit. "Alex is dead because he was into drugs, Satana is dead because she was into drugs, junkies die like dogs because they've given up caring about anything except where their next fucking hit is coming from. When they're not looking for excuses, they're looking for someone to blame. Alex was an addict. He was always denouncing people who had betrayed him or abandoned him. But the one person who betrayed him, who abandoned him, was himself." Patrice nursed his can of beer and laughed. "In that case we're all addicts. Because what you're describing is not addicts, it's the human race." Emilie was unsure. She didn't give a shit whether someone had helped Vodka Satana take an overdose, but she had found the early part of the tape unsettling. She thought about her youth, wondering whether it had really been as magic as Bleach described it. Aïcha had not stayed with them. She had been too shocked by what she had heard. She had said, "There's so much going on in my head right now it's deafening," and rushed away. Pamela and Daniel had shared a long, wordless glance, then reached for each other's hands and interlaced their fingers. They were trying to imagine what it would be like for Satana's daughter when she woke up tomorrow morning and had to bear the weight of the story she had heard. It was enough to drive anyone mad. As for Vernon, he needed to be alone.

Dawn had broken and he had sat up, taken a few gulps of beer and announced that he was heading off. Laurent, who had listened to the conversation without closing his eyes all night, immediately got to his feet. "Let's go together, brother." There was a chorus of protests: "You can't just leave like that, where are you going to go, what are you going to do" and it was Laurent who silenced them, "We're happy to take a couple of beers for the road, there are a few left in the fridge . . . Otherwise, you've all been very kind, but I'm long enough in the tooth to be able to look after myself . . . And don't worry, I'll take care of your friend here." He had kept his word: since that night he had taken care of Vernon. As he closed the door, he announced to the assembled company, "We'll be at the Buttes-Chaumont if you want to come visit," as though giving the address of his local bar. But neither he nor Vernon expected that, the very next day, so many people would turn up at the park to see how they were.

In the métro on their way back, Laurent had made no comment. He had been discreetly but visibly jubilant: at last, Subutex was one of them, a free man. Laurent had been annoyed that he had to wait for nightfall to show Vernon around his new territory: the famous railway line known as *La Petite Ceinture*. "It was originally built to transport plaster." Laurent would prattle on endlessly about the Buttes-Chaumont, it made you wonder why he didn't become a tour guide. "Up here on the Butte, they used to slaughter horses and hang criminals. There were quarries, right where you're standing, and a municipal rubbish tip. There was also the Gibbet of Montfaucon. The corpses of the *fédérés* who fought during the Paris Commune are buried under your feet. Oh, yes . . . By the time this park was built, the whole area was so pestilential that the middle classes fled, it was a park frequented by people of ill repute. They looted everything they could find, apparently – I read it on the internet. The poor are like that, we destroy everything we can."

The railways lines are twenty metres below the level of the park, which they reach via a steep embankment. At night, when they reel home drunk, it's the perfect opportunity to fall flat on their faces. Vernon set himself up a little way from Laurent, in a recess between two mounds of gravel. The walls are tagged with graffiti, to find his pitch, he looks for the purple octopus on the pillar. He is sheltered and can't be seen from the bridge that overlooks their sleeping quarters.

Laurent always carries a knife on him – there's no way "just anybody" can crash here. No-one can come down the embankment leading to the tracks without literally stepping over him. It works: there is enough space in the park for everyone to find a pitch.

On their second day, Laurent forcibly took him on an adventure, "You're lucky, I spotted a mattress while hanging out around the soup kitchen near Pyrénées, but I didn't fancy asking that fucker Samir to help me carry it, I don't like the guy, I don't want him moving in on us. You and me are going to go fetch it." They had followed the train tracks as far as the high railings that forced them back up into the city, then carried on, past Ménilmontant. Laurent had hidden the precious mattress behind a billboard, and Vernon did not have the heart to say no to him, though he didn't feel he had the strength to lug the thing back to the park. It had taken them the whole day. They had dragged the thing, pushed it, carried it, collapsed onto it and lay there for a couple of minutes, giggling like a pair of tired kids. By the time they let it slide down the slope to the railway line, the mattress was as tattered as if they'd salvaged it from the nearest rubbish tip. It was dark. They had continued on their journey, and Vernon had finally collapsed between two pillars.

It had also been Laurent who helped him erect a tent that could not be seen from the park using a length of oilcloth held down by some rusty sheets of metal stolen from a building site and abandoned here. You can find anything along the railway tracks. Vernon had turned up a crate he could use as a bedside table, a stool and a stuffed Homer Simpson for decoration. Laurent had given him a duvet and, that night, Vernon had not been surprised that he felt so comfortable in his new refuge. It has become his cocoon, a fantastical structure that protects him much better than a house.

Then Olga had reappeared, looking rested, clean and altogether much better than the last time he had seen her, the night Xavier was attacked. "They kept me in hospital for a couple of weeks, I had a pneumothorax, I was treated like a fucking queen, guys!" Laurent had told her she could not go back to her old pitch a few pillars away, "You've caused enough trouble for everyone as it is," but Vernon had intervened. "Come on, leave her alone." She had hooked up with Jackie, a little guy of about fifty, smart, funny, with a face like a crafty clown. He had just come out of squatting in an abandoned multi-storey car park that the local crackheads had nearly burned to the ground, so the place had been boarded up with everything he owned inside. But whatever he was like during the day, Jackie was a lot more difficult to manage when he was drinking – he was a loud, venomous drunk. He had not had time to get on Laurent's nerves: one night, he simply did not appear. Olga had been upset, but Laurent was matter-of-fact: "That's what it's like on the streets. You meet people, hang out with them, and one day they disappear. When you run into them again three months later, likely as not, they don't remember you. We meet a lot of people. It's completely contradictory: nothing ever happens and something's always happening. It's a particular rhythm, it takes some getting used to . . ." In her corner, Olga was sobbing. "Shit, if we can't even bring ourselves to care about what happens to each other, we're don't even qualify as human." Then she moved on. She didn't have much choice.

A few days later, she had dragged Vernon to the *Secours populaire* near Télégraphe métro station, telling him, "I've got connections there." She was grateful to him for persuading Laurent to let her have her old pitch back. The uphill trek to get to the charity felt like losing a lung . . . Then, amid the fierce chaos of an unlikely mob scrabbling for jackets, socks or towels, one of the volunteers – a kindly woman of about sixty with cropped white haired, inch-thick make-up, huge red earrings, dazzling white teeth and a big smile – had recognised Olga and signalled for them to wait. She had reappeared clutching a pair of red boots with a black eagle on the side. "I kept them for you." And Vernon realised that Olga had insisted they be put aside for her. She was thrilled to be able to make a present of them to him. He hadn't had the heart to say, "They look like something Dick Rivers would have worn in the '60s, I'll never wear them." He gingerly weighed them up – they were a fine pair of battered red Mexican boots, just what he needed. It was difficult to imagine how they had come to be here – perhaps the previous owner had dropped dead. Or his girlfriend had threatened to leave him if he didn't get rid of the boots. Now here they were in Vernon's hands. And two women were excited at the idea of seeing him put them on. He had politely complied. But even then, he remained unconvinced: they were flashy and not at all his style. But the spry old woman with the shimmering smile said, "They've been sat here waiting for you," then she had headed off to deal with a woman of about her own age and just as chubby, a breezy African woman who was clearly a regular. Vernon had put on the boots. They fitted him perfectly, they felt as comfortable as slippers. His feet had been aching for weeks, so the relief was instantaneous. The boots changed the way he walked. They demanded that he thrust his leg up higher. Wearing them, he felt his thighs stretch, his hips tip forward, he took longer strides. He was teetering. Out in the street, though worried about falling from the vertiginous heels of his cowboy boots, he had thanked Olga: yes, he really liked his new boots. He was surprised by the effect they had on him. He felt like a giant.

He gets up early. The day starts with the dawn chorus and ends with the same refrain. Over time, he has come to recognise their songs. First there is a cooing, then gradually the little sparrows, whose song is disproportionate to their size, after that it gets complicated, chords ring out from everywhere and he does not even have to glance at the fluorescent green alarm clock he found to know it is time to get up and go up to the surface: the park gates are open. He can crawl out of his lair. In the morning, he meets old people walking their dogs. From time to time, the park keepers fine them on the pretext that dogs are not allowed off the leash. Then the Chinese arrive and break up into large groups who make synchronised, mostly graceful movements in the air. From a distance, Vernon tries to mimic some of their movements, trying to make sure no-one can see him. A young man comes every day and sings next to the big chestnut tree. He flings his arms wide, closes his eyes, his deep bass vibrato sounding out the long notes. It is quite pleasant. Meanwhile, the crows peck holes in the garbage bags and share whatever victuals fall to the ground.

The gardeners and the park keepers all know that Vernon sleeps here. They never speak to him about it. It is a matter of being discreet. The three who live on the railway lines are not the only ones who hide when the park closes. Shadows dawdle, dart into the thickets, climb the railings or disappear beneath the branches of the lofty trees. Afterwards, the only rule is not to make a ruckus until the following morning.

Xavier and Emilie were the first to come and find him. They didn't hang about: the day after the evening they spent in the Hyena's apartment, they were wandering the paths, studying the bodies sprawled in the grass. It was one of those rare sunny days, the park was filled with families, shady characters, lovers, students and keep-fit enthusiasts. Time passes in a curious fashion for those who live on the streets: both oddly protracted and strangely fleeting. Vernon had all but forgotten that Xavier and Emilie existed. Their opening gambit was less than subtle: "So, what are you going to do," mumbled in a worried tone. It made him want to say: "What about you? And your misfortunes? How do you handle them?" They tried desperately to persuade him to move in with them. The offer, turned back on them, seemed quite amusing.

Vernon does not have the faintest idea what he is planning to do now. He is making the most of the spell of fine weather. All he does know is that he does not want to move in with other people. This is the sum of his future plans. What is new is that he genuinely does not give a toss. Sufficient unto the day is the evil thereof. Xavier and Emilie clearly had a lovely day playing on the grass, not knowing what to say, because they reappeared the following day, then Lydia joined them, followed by Patrice, Pamela . . . Vodka Satana's daughter showed up one afternoon, she wanted to talk about her mother but tensed up as soon anyone did, which didn't stop her showing up with her father a few days later. Sélim stormed up, furious, demanding to know why they had "done that" to his daughter, but he was like an unpinned grenade: he had come to cause damage, had watched the video on Emilie's laptop – she had ripped the file and was sending it to anyone in the group who wanted to re-watch it. Sélim stayed on his own for some time after he had finished listening to Alex Bleach. Eventually, his daughter had gone over and put an arm round his shoulder. They sat, motionless, their backs turned to Vernon, making it impossible to tell whether they were speaking. Emilie went over to collect her laptop, she was leaving. Father and daughter made the most of this to wave to the group from afar and walk off. Sélim had come back two days later. He had showed up saying, "What the . . . are you guys here every day?", surprised and bizarrely moved. He had sat down with them and talked and talked for hours. He told them his life story. How, ever since Faïza had changed her name to Satana, he had been completely unable to remember people's names. How his daughter was the dearest thing in the world to him and how he could not bear the fact that he could not protect the women he loved from themselves. Pamela had said to him: "She's lucky to have a father like you, I can't see what more you could do to protect her." And he had ended up in her arms, in tears. He had left utterly drained, but happy. Since then, he has come very day.

This was what daytime in the park had become: a mixture of group therapy session, al fresco coffee shop, beer garden and debating society. The lawn was his salon where Vernon welcomed all-comers with the geniality of a generous host touched by so much attention. His life was pleasant: there were cupcakes, bottles of rosé, pleasant company, girls waiting on him hand and foot, they listened to great music on tubular bluetooth speakers, there were the regulars and those who simply dropped by for a day. An uncomplicated social life that came to him, and no paperwork to ruin his mornings.

It reminded him of the bars in country villages, you never knew who would come, who would talk to whom, who would be the butt of the jokes, whether there would be slanging matches or unexpected libidinal collisions. When the gates closed, the park keepers made their last rounds, whistling, while the last residents scattered, and Vernon enjoyed this moment of solitude, the moment when he glided down the embankment and settled into his bivouac. He could have left the park, spent an evening elsewhere as others did and climbed over the railings on his way back – but the idea of venturing beyond his territory did not appeal to him. He had become a homebody.

These gatherings do not bother anyone: they do nothing to draw attention to themselves. Laurent and Olga enjoy nightly debriefings where they lecture Vernon in pessimistic tones: "It's a passing phase, so make the most of it . . . Though it might seem that your friends have nothing much to do, they'll eventually realise they have better things to do than watch the trees grow . . . but you're pretty lucky, Vernon, usually being penniless keeps people at bay, they think it's contagious." It is impossible to tell whether they admire him for deciding to stay with them or whether they think he is a halfwit that they protect because he has his uses.

As the summer dragged on, the gatherings grew, regardless of the rain. When it rained, they sheltered in the man-made grotto by the artificial lake where they talked in low voices because of the echoes.

Nestled amid the tree roots Vernon is bogarting the spliff. Lydia Bazooka is busy watching a Lydia Lunch interview on her phone, Patrice, on his day off, is talking to a stranger about the Camera

Silens L.P. Sitting in a circle on an orange sarong of the sort you might see at the beach, Pamela is explaining to Olga and Laurent that in the Netherlands, people sign on to a waiting list to buy property at an affordable price, which is why they are almost all homeowners by the time they are thirty. Patrice brings them coffee and Vernon listens to them from a distance. He is thinking about Alex Bleach, about the tapes, about that quote from old Hank: "Forgive me, you have my soul and I have your money." What is it that stars sell that means they are so generously remunerated?

A deflated ball rolls across the grass quickly followed by an ageing poodle who catches it and lies on his belly shaking it frantically, then scampers over to Xavier who is standing, hands in his pocket, beaming. He adopted him from an animal shelter. He's called Joyeux. A grey royal poodle. His master picks him up. Xavier spotted a photo of the dog online almost by accident. His master had died in a car crash. The animal was huddled in a cage, and it was the look in the dog's eyes that broke his heart, Xavier claims. At first he had thought, no, I can't do it, I can't get another dog so soon, and besides I wouldn't dare go outside with something like that. But all day the eyes haunted him and, without a word to anyone, Xavier rented a car and went to fetch the dog. His wife threw a tantrum when got home. Look at it from her point of view, an ageing giant poodle did not complement their interior design scheme. But Joyeux won her round, apparently, that very evening. It has to be said the dog has a handsome face. And he is obsessed with his ball. His master spends entire afternoons throwing it and watching the dog romp in the grass. He has already had to pay multiple fines, and done so with a smile. But even the most hard-bitten cops find it difficult to keep a straight face when they encounter a hulking guy with a shaved head who turns out to be the proud owner of a curly-haired poodle called "Joyeux". Olga is the only one who has never commented on the breed he chose. She simply said, "Fuck me, he's a beauty!" and threw the ball for him.

Xavier had been in a bad way after the accident. When he was released from hospital, he was in bits. His foundations had slipped. He was terrified of being out in the street. Given his height and his build, fear had never been part of his make-up. For the first time in his life, he found himself looking behind him, sizing people up, if he heard footsteps behind him, his heart leapt into his mouth. He did not quite know what to do with this new-found vulnerability. He was hardly going to start writing poetry at his age . . . The worst thing was he felt ashamed. Having woken from his coma, delirious, convinced that he was a successful director worried about finishing a film had left him disconcerted. Especially as it had been two or three days before he completely shook off the hallucinations. The doctor he had asked whether the shock had affected his neural pathways had simply shrugged: "All the tests are clear. You're fine." But then, what had caused him to be delusional for two whole days? The guy in the white coat had seemed embarrassed: "These things happen, you know, and it often comes as a surprise to the patient . . . How long has it been since you went twenty-four hours without drinking alcohol?" The idea was so hazy that at first Xavier did not understand what the man was getting at. The doctor had had to explain: "I think, or rather I believe it is very possible, that you suffered a bout of *delirium tremens* due to a sudden alcohol withdrawal . . . the blow had nothing to do with this . . ." and Xavier had almost stabbed the man with the rod holding up the I.V. drip. An alcoholic, him? Complete bullshit. Later, in private, he remembers that his first words – before asking for a cigarette or enquiring how Vernon was – had been to ask someone to go get some beers. And everything had returned to normal on the day Marie-Ange had brought him the six-pack that he hid in the bedside cabinet. An alcoholic. He had always taken it for granted that he was a good father. That was the one thing no-one could take away from him. But can a good father be an alcoholic? He had never thought about it. He had talked to his mother and she had tried to reassure him: "You're never drunk. Where's the problem? You're a wonderful father. You always put your daughter first. So, you need a little beer before lunch but then . . . you're fine . . . we all have our crutches in this life." But it did not work. This discovery, which, when all was said and done, was hardly news, left him devastated. He could play the wise guy to his daughter because she was too young to judge him. He could delude himself about his wife, knowing it had been many years since he had made her happy. And he was alone. Utterly alone. Not like a lone wolf. But like an idiot who no longer knows who he is. For the first time in his life, perhaps, he no longer had the energy to lie to himself: other than damaging his liver, he was not much good for anything.

He is a pillar of the Buttes-Chaumont group. On the first evening, when they watched Alex's tape, Xavier had not grasped the poignant nature of the reunion. It was a story he liked to tell his new friends in the park: Vernon with his "total loser" look, filthy, a look in his eyes like a demented fool, unable to string three words together. Stinking so badly that he had to be pushed into a shower, and even then some sour-faced lesbian had had to soap him up. The girls fussing over him as if they hadn't noticed what was staring them in the face: the guy had blown a fuse. Xavier had felt insulted by this idiotic jollity, these so-called old friends who had all dropped Vernon and were fussing over him now that it was too late. He had not enjoyed the evening. He had sat in the corner drinking beer and bitching to himself. When Alex began to speak, he had felt like throwing up. He peered through the darkness at little Lydia Bazooka, she was probably getting wet at the sight of Alex, that fat lump Emilie on the verge of tears, Patrice that fucking show-off, pretending to be upset. Nothing of what Alex said had moved him. Clown. Rock music. Talk about an adventure. "I believed in a way of life that was nothing more than a hipster lifestyle." The whole thing had always been just clowning around. Then came the story of that crazy slut who spread her legs in every producer's office and then started whining about it – Xavier was thinking, when do we get to the part where we're supposed to cry?

The evening had been shit. But he hadn't left. He had watched them as they put on headphones and listened to "mind-blowing" music that dumb fuck Bleach had written, thinking he was creating healing sounds. When he was passed the headphones, he had put them on, it was nothing surprising: the most mind-numbingly boring music in the world. It made you wonder what drugs would have to be invented to be able to listen to it. Otherwise, Pamela Kant had turned out to be friendly, though it irritated Xavier to see that slut trying to pretend to be a well-adjusted woman. You're nothing but a cum-bucket, bitch, and you can do what you like but you'll never manage to convince any man otherwise. Thankfully, that night, he had not realised who Daniel was. He had assumed he was dealing with a coke-addled little queer, the sort of guy who didn't frighten Pamela – it didn't surprise him that a woman like her would be intimidated by real men. He had spent the evening watching them all bustle about, wallowing in bitterness and hostility. The woman whose apartment they were in, the Hyena, looked like she was as bored as he was. She sat in a corner, smoking cigarettes, keeping an eye on Vernon who was wedged between two cushions snoring like a freight train.

Xavier had gone over to ask her: "Why did you do this? Why didn't you just turn the tapes over to the producer?" She had pushed a stray lock of hair behind her ear, it was a seductive gesture: "Most of the time, we only understand ourselves after the fact." He hadn't insisted. It was obvious that she thought he was an arsehole. Then Vernon had left and that had devastated Xavier. The guy was so fucked up that he refused to sleep in a bed. It was pitiful. And the chorus of arse-licking comments about him – as though these people couldn't see what he was: a sad bastard who'd gone completely wacko. They wanted to turn him into Rimbaud when he was just a deadbeat loser.

Xavier had slept for a few hours and, when he got up, he had made a thermos of coffee and set off for the Buttes-Chaumont to look for Vernon. He could not stand the idea of leaving him to freeze to death, and was convinced that the hypocrites who seemed so concerned the night before would have forgotten him now that it was daylight. He had wandered around for a long time before finding him, sitting on the grass, leaning back on his elbows, with the laid-back nonchalance of a guy just catching some rays.

This was when it happened, Xavier tells anyone who is willing to listen. They had talked about this and that. Then Laurent had come looking for Vernon because he was going to eat at the *Restaurants du cœur* on the rue du Soleil, and Subutex had done something strange. He had hugged Xavier to him before he left. Xavier could not say how long they had stood, silently pressed against each other. But he would swear that, as he walked home, he felt different. As though a weight had been lifted.

The following day, he had seen the photo of Joyeux on the

internet, and, after a fashion, life had begun again. For a start, Marie-Ange, who had thrown a hissy fit when she had found the mutt in the house, had become besotted with the dog in less than an hour – and for the first time in months, he had made his wife laugh – a laugh that was not forced, not self-conscious, but a lovely, tender laugh filled with respect. "You know that if it wasn't for you, they'd have put him down?" and she scratched the dog behind the ears. "It's a horrible thought . . . a magnificent animal like this." And he had remembered that he loved Marie-Ange more than one ever hopes to love in a lifetime – it was more than passion or commitment, it was everything within him that loved this woman – and how much he had missed the closeness.

Ever since, he regularly gestures to the group and says to Vernon, "You're a radiator, you know that? That's why we're all here." He argues with pretty much everyone else in the group – regardless of the topic, he always manages to say something that provokes outrage, and in a way, that has become his role: he stirs things up. He still gets on best with Olga, and not just because of the dog. But the most surprising thing is the friendship between Olga and Sylvie. At this stage, you could almost call it love. They are off on their own, sitting on a bench, chatting. They do it all the time.

Sylvie had freaked everyone out when she showed up after a few days. They all assumed that the period of blissful harmony was at an end, that she would fly into a screaming frenzy, burn down every tree and plough up the earth until the park once more resembled the gypsum quarry it had been. This was especially true of Vernon – who had snapped out of his torpor the moment he recognised her. But having publicly threatened him with the most agonising tortures, she had simply given him a little kiss, relaxed and friendly, as though nothing untoward had happened. He realised that she had skilfully grilled Emilie to find out what they were up to – and had invited herself to the park. She had reacted to her exclusion from the group with good humour, and had assumed that they would all be pleased to see her – because she had changed her mind: what Vernon had done, she now decided, was not so serious after all. In its own way, life had paid him back by making him homeless. At first, she had firmly planned to take him back to her apartment and get him back on his feet but, faced with his refusal, she had adopted a different strategy: she preferred to sow discord in the group by her mere presence. The only person who opens up to her is old Charles, who comes to join them every evening at the same time. In her own way, Sylvie has become very fond of the group, and regularly brings home-made cakes. She can be a royal pain in the arse, but she is also a fucking good baker. Which means that when she shows up, people are happy to see her show up, and just a little worried: she likes to bawl out her neighbour while offering him cupcakes.

Lydia, Patrice and Daniel are discussing whether Daniel Craig has revolutionised James Bond. Charles appears next to them carrying a plastic bag full of beers in his hand, greets them but does not linger – he gives a smile when he sees that Olga and Sylvie, his two favourite girls, are lying on the grass. Vernon cannot get used to the idea that they get along so well, he feels it is almost dangerous. Olga allows herself to be meekly guided so as not to annoy her girlfriend, while offering just enough defiance and brutishness so that things remain tense, the way Sylvie likes them. From a distance, he hears Sylvie say: "Personally, I believe in intestines. You'll see, one of these days people will realise they don't give a shit about psychology, it's the intestines that control everything," and Olga reply, "So you're saying you believe in intestines more than you do in destiny?" which makes both of them howl with laughter.

A dozen girls are sitting by the stream at the bottom of the slope. Vernon recognises Aïcha, who is talking to one of them without that stubborn, suspicious air she usually adopts with groups of people. Pamela joins them, they look as though they are having a whispered conversation. Then he recognises the slim figure of the Hyena, there is something surreal, something otherworldy about her. Ever since she undressed and showered him, he has felt a particular gratitude towards her. From a distance, she gives him a conspiratorial wink about some subject that escapes him. It is her mannish way of letting him know that she is fond of him. Their relationship goes no farther than that – they rarely speak to each other. As though their intimacy prevents them from engaging in small talk. She has still not turned the tapes over to the producer, she is letting him sweat. Her decision is as impenetrable as Vernon's to carry on living in the park – and he suspects that she herself does not really know what is guiding her actions at the moment. The women on the banks of the stream have an anti-globalisation look, but more punk. Daniel chats with them, then comes over to Vernon, sits on one of the roots of the chestnut tree, plucking blades of grass. Vernon says:

"They look amazing, your girlfriends. They look as though they've been listening to Manu Chao and Pantera and are trying to find a happy medium."

"They're Bolivian. Indigenous, lesbian feminist punk shamans."

"Fuck . . . must be good to be young . . . So what do you talk about?"

Daniel flashes him a half-smile.

"Life, death, madness. They're super woke."

Like Pamela, he has been more affected than the others by Alex's confessions. They often say, "They can snuff us out, just like that," with a click of their fingers, "and no-one will bother to wonder what happened because in people's minds, we're zombies, in fact we belong to a category of human beings less protected than others," and Laurent, who never misses an opportunity to try to get closer to Pamela, always gets fired up: "They treat you like they treat the homeless. We're pariahs – we're not even considered an adjustment constant. Do you know how many of us die every year? Do you know how easy it would be for them to house us all during the cold weather? No-one gives a damn about the names of those who die on the streets." He perches on a low branch, feet dangling just above the ground. "We live like dogs, we die like dogs," is Daniel's usual response and Olga shakes her head. "No. Dogs have masters who mourn them."

Vernon can no longer tear his eyes away from the group of girls down the slope – they're plotting something. He asks Daniel again: "What were they talking to you about just now?" He looks at Pamela, standing, motionless, hands on her hips, face turned to the sun, eyes closed, a faint smile he has never seen before lighting up her face. He turns to look at Daniel perched on his branch, he too has a strange look on his face. He is still happy, smiling, but his features are more relaxed. Something about him has changed. Realising that Vernon is staring at him, Daniel points to a panther he has just had tattooed on his arm.

"It's healing really quickly, it's insane. I hardly had to put any cream on it at all."

"Did Céleste do it?"

"Yeah, she's so talented."

"You really like her, don't you?"

Daniel has already been twice to have himself tattooed by Céleste.

"Yeah, I do."

"You think she feels the same way?"

"I think so, yeah . . . But I need to talk to her first. I haven't found the right moment."

"Talk to her about what?"

"Let her know that if we fuck, I'm not going to get out a big swinging dick. I'd rather let her know in advance."

"I slept with a girl who hadn't had the op. Just to let you know that I didn't find it strange – at least not in a bad way. I was crazy about her."

"You? I'd have thought you were more of a macho bastard . . ."

Pamela, flanked by two women, interrupts their conversation:

"We're going to make a move, Daniel, you coming?"

And, seeing Daniel immediately jump down and go to join them, Vernon thinks – they're up to something that they don't want to tell him about.

The tallest of the women is staring at him. She is as tall as Olga and at least as beefy. She tramps through the damp grass as though her red shoes with vertiginously high wedge heels were rubber boots, she is wearing a long black dress, a studded leather jacket that is several decades old, a pink boa of moth-eaten feathers around her throat, her hair is shaved at the temples and the extraordinary collection of rings on her fingers give the impression that she has steel fists. She looks like nothing on earth. She eyes Vernon with such astonishing boldness that he should feel uncomfortable, but the girl has a strange charm. He recognises in her the self-confidence of beauty. And that self-confidence trumps her appearance: she is attractive. Vernon is the first to be disconcerted by this thought: his libido has long since been running on empty.

Pamela musters her troops. It takes some time for the group to get moving. The girl is still staring at him. As Daniel wanders off, she comes over to him: "*Tu, te quiero besarte.*" Vernon smiles and pretends he does not know what the words mean – he does not know how to politely decline the invitation. She leans against the trunk of the chestnut tree, she waits. Someone from the group calls to her in Spanish and she waves for them to piss off. The women exchange a few words and, clearly unsurprised, do just that.

She turns to Vernon, takes his hand and says: "*Ven conmigo.*" No-one is looking at them. She gestures for him to follow her, leading him gently by the hand and he follows without offering any further resistance. They walk up the grassy slope to a densely wooded area; she seems to know the place and guides him towards the shade of a towering fir tree. Intrigued and strangely bewitched, he allows her to slip her tongue between his lips – it is the kiss of the century. Later, he will wonder what drug she could possibly have passed from her mouth to his that could have worked so quickly and so spectacularly – an electric shock shudders through his body. He just has time to think – your lips are amazingly soft – before lift-off. He is a tree whose roots delve so deeply into the earth that they touch the fiery core, through the soles of his feet he feels the empty space of tunnels, electrical cables, grains of sand and the woman is a huge serpent coiled around him, the warmth of her reptilian belly comforts every pore of his skin-bark. The kiss lasts only a few seconds – Vernon experiences an eternity. She takes a step back, "*Quieres más?*" and he does not move. She removes the ring he wears, a Mexican death's head someone gave him more than twenty years ago, kisses it, licks it, then slips it back onto Vernon's finger, "*Ahora estas mío*" and he takes off again. He is a bird, he can clearly feel wings emerging from his shoulder blades, their weight as he unfurls them, the muscles involved in moving them. The woman is on her knees now, she kisses his ankles, his knees – for a moment he comes back to himself and remembers the Hyena soaping him under the shower – but quickly loses consciousness again, he is gliding above the park, above the city, he is high above the fields, there is an extraordinary pleasure in feeling the wings bearing him up and the air beneath his belly supporting him, his pelvis is spread wide and thrust forward, it is a powerful, languid wrench. He does not know how long it lasts, this brutal ecstasy – when he comes back to himself, the woman places her hand on the nape of his neck and says, this time in his own tongue, "You are the shaman of Europe." A sudden urge to weep shudders through his chest. She walks away. He has been a tree, he has been a bird, he has felt his beak, his wings, his broadened field of vision. He has completely lost his mind and, for the first time in weeks, that knowledge terrifies him. He stands for a long moment, racked by sobs, sitting alone beneath this tree. Then, amid this paroxysm of despair, he feels something else encroach, a feeling of boundless joy that triumphs over his tears.

CÉLESTE CUTS THE STENCIL WITH SCISSORS AND POSITIONS THE waves around the carp. She worked on them while studying a Hokusai drawing on the internet. They are listening to Sia. The guinea pig is squealing in his cage, he wants some cucumber and he wants it now. The giant internet T.V. is streaming a live feed from a Canadian zoo of jellyfish rising and falling. The customer is rolling a spliff, she rips out the innards of a cigarette filter with her teeth and replaces them with a cardboard roach. Then she takes the flint barrel from a Clipper lighter and tamps the joint. The hash, the weed, the cigarette papers and a few crumbs of tobacco are arranged on a small pink plastic tray decorated with tiny flowers that probably came from China. She is chatting with her friend who is sitting on the sofa, resting on an electric massage mat bought from Nature & Découvertes. Wondering whether she should set it to rolling massage or shiatsu. Céleste pulls on her black gloves, the customer changes the music: "You into electro-pop? I've got a shit-hot playlist . . . perfect for tattooing. It's perfect for everything."

She says that she can hold out for two and a half hours. After that, she starts to feel the pain. Céleste is sitting on a pouffe. She doesn't have a stool. Over time, she has crippled her back. She really should go to the swimming pool so she can relax and build up her muscles, but she can never find the time. Between the job at Rosa Bonheur and the hours she spends tattooing, she would have to set an alarm for 6 a.m. if she wanted to go swimming, but she gets to bed too late to do that.

Arms folded, the friend sitting on the sofa relaxes into the massage, takes a toke on the spliff and stares up at the giant T.V. screen. "It's insane to think that these are, like, real jellyfish . . . It's amazing to think that things like that exist and we waste our time on random shit instead of looking at nature and animals, yeah?" Céleste is detached from the conversation, focussed on what she is doing – dotwork shadows on the crests of the waves. She needs people to commission her to do big pieces so she can get a rotary tattoo machine to do the dotwork, like Mike Amanita, the Russian guy who did the mandala on her shoulder. They cost two hundred euros. It's not like it costs a bomb. But most people ask for small designs, butterflies and short quotes. She can never manage to save the money. The two friends babble incessantly, both stoned out of their gourds. The customer fidgets a little, Céleste lays a hand on her shoulder to calm her. It can be hard sometimes to concentrate with all the chatter of a hair salon. But she enjoys it – some tattoo artists insist on silence, she prefers to be surrounded by life and to have to detach herself. It's electropop with jangling guitars, she drifts away. The needles she bought in Bastille are super-fine, tattooing with them is a pleasure. The customer is happy, "It's cool, Céleste, its really beautiful" and the friend nods. She is still poring over the remote control of her massage mat, she's been twiddling it for almost an hour.

The customer's son reappears. He is about twelve. She bawls him out for not phoning like he was supposed to. Céleste thinks it must be hell living with a kid that tall, he could give you a slap and there's fuck all you could do about it, you have to be really strict if you're going to keep him in line. He takes a carrot from the fridge and gives it to the guinea pig.

The girl lives near métro Stalingrad, about twenty minutes' walk from the bar. Céleste checks the time on the computer screen. It's a stunning apartment, all tones of grey and burgundy. You need fifteen separate codes to get inside, but once you're there, it's quiet and comfortable.

She has no desire to go to work, she would rather take her time, finish up here, then go home and relax. It kills her that she has to do a shift behind the bar after this.

But Rosa Bonheur is a good gig. There are lots of them there who need to swap shifts and it's flexible hours. Fanny plays futsal, Elsa does her burlesque shows, Mona has her drag king workshops – they all have outside activities, so they work things out so everyone gets to do what they want. Even so, she'll be happy when she can make a living from tattooing and can give up the day job.

She finishes, stretches before she puts plastic warp over the tattoo, gives aftercare advice: "Don't put anything on it for twenty-four hours but wash it four times a day, then apply lots of moisturiser and after the first three days expose it to the air whenever you can and it'll heal in no time." She pockets the two fifty-euro notes, slips her jacket on, no, she doesn't have time for a coffee, she'd love to, but she has to run if she's going to make it on time.

The weather this year is Alcatraz. The sky is sullied by a driving rain whipped horizontal by the wind. Late June and people are still wearing down jackets, morale is overcast. It's not a bloody summer, it's a penitentiary. The branches of the trees are still bare, with not even the hint of a leaf budding. If Céleste were a man, she wouldn't be able to walk for the hard-on. It happened when she woke up, it felt like a rush from last night's M.D.M.A., she felt horny as a cat in heat. If she doesn't mate in the next twenty-four hours she's going to spiral into depression. Maybe she should take a couple of ibuprofen, see whether that takes the edge off. She has always had a high sex drive. When she was in school, all the boys called her a slut. They would call her at night on the landline at home and yell it down the phone. Her father was driven to distraction. He moved her to another school. She learned her lesson: she only sleeps with guys she'll never see again. Not that she gives a shit about her reputation, but she doesn't want to upset her father.

She runs into Lorenzo, the cute gardener. While he is chatting to her about the effect of the cold weather on the trees, her mind is a torrent of A-grade sleaze. Thankfully, she has something of Madame de Merteuil about her, a red-hot snatch in an icy glove. Lorenzo is always polite to her. Man, here you are talking to me about shrubs while I'm thinking of you running your tongue through my bush – if he could see what's on her hard-drive, he'd change tack.

Céleste has no desire to go to work. At first, she enjoyed being at the bar, the atmosphere is dope, the nightlife the drunks the jerks the lesbians with their tits out dancing on the tables and the old guys who think they're still young strutting their stuff and swaying their hips. It's funny to watch them. She hopes that she won't be like that when she's thirty, making a show of herself and refusing to go home. She's been working here for almost a year now. The time flies. These days, the customers bore her. Eighty per cent of them are jerks. They think she's there to serve them, that that's what they're paying for, so they act like arseholes. She thought it would happen quickly, being able to make a living from her tattooing. That some veteran artist would notice her and suggest she gave classes in his tattoo parlour. You have to be patient. She's sick of being on her feet for eight hours straight, of cleaning up broken glasses, dodging the puddles of vomit, the hands on her arse, the fake banknotes, and earning just enough to pay the rent at the end of the month – the tips are lousy at Rosa Bonheur, the place is always rammed, people spend three hours waiting to get a beer, they're brutal, not a cent for the barmaid . . .

After the baccalauréat, she studied at the Beaux-Arts. But before long she'd had a bellyful of the atmosphere. Too much bullshitting. She is interested in *doing* things, not learning how to pontificate about pissweak art installations. After that, she dabbled in this and that – some theatre, a little video editing – and each time her father would tell her about an exam for some civil service job and sulk when she said, "That's all over, papa, no-one gets a job for life these days, just let me do my thing." Not that there was much else she could say. When she turned twenty, her friends clubbed together and bought her a tattoo machine – a Lauro Paolini Prestige . . . And that was what triggered it. She practised on bits of pigskin, she didn't enjoy doing it and they rotted quickly and filled the whole house with a disgusting stench. Luckily, there was Chris, the guy was tattooed from head to foot and he had a thing for her. Chris had said: "I'm giving you my body, practise all you want." That's when it had really taken off. She loves Russian tattoos, black and white. But customers have crap taste, they want multicolour lotuses or corny fucking swallows. It won't last forever. You have to be patient. In the meantime, every time anyone at the bar finds out she's a tattoo artist, they spend hours telling her about the tattoo they've always wanted to get. She feels like saying: "I don't need to hear your life story, make a fucking appointment and be done."

By the time she arrives, Rosa Bonheur is open. This is not

always the case, sometimes she ends up hanging around outside for half an hour before the guy who has the keys shows up with his head up his arse . . . In the main bar, it's colder than a witch's tits. Everyone is wearing scarves and hoodies. They're listening to Bjork with the volume jacked up, it doesn't make you want to put down roots. Straight off, Mimi, the manager, tells her to get down two crates of food for the disciples of Subutex. Like this is the most important task of the day. Mimi met up with some girl she used to know who hangs with them, says she used to be a bassist and she worships her. Looking at the old hag these days, you'd have a hard time imagining her swaggering on stage. At first, the manager used to send them food left over from the night before that they couldn't sell, but now she makes tortilla for them, sends down bottles of beer and chocolate . . . She's been indoctrinated by the sect. She says that one day she spent the evening with Subutex and the next night she had the most amazing dream, with dead people visiting her and telling her important stuff, like life-changing shit. Yeah, right, at her age, with all the drugs she necks, it's hardly surprising she has Technicolor dreams. Ever since, she's stopped smoking weed at night because she wants to be able to remember her dreams. And it's true, she does look a lot better . . . but this whole Subutex thing is wack. They all hang on his every word like he's a prophet. The big dork with his red cowboy boots. Oh well, we all have our own heroes . . . It can't be much fun being old. There are about twenty of them who rock up every day, a horde of old fogeys – not that all of them are old, but the average age is prehistoric. But they must be happy hanging out there, because otherwise, with the cold weather, they'd call it a day. They spend their time running off at the mouth. It's hard to know what to think: on the one hand the whole thing is too cute, on the other it makes your flesh crawl.

Céleste takes the two crates of food down to them, they wave when they see her coming – it's not surprising they're happy to see her: good food, gratis. Vernon is peacocking around under the big tree in his brand-new Canada Goose parka, a gift from a humble admirer – a woman who can drop a grand to make sure some homeless guy is tucked up warm at night, gotta say, he must be giving them some kind of motivation. The guy is a lot more chill than he used to be, Céleste can go right up to him without him staring at her breasts like a perv. There are rumours that at night, girls go down to the train tracks and hang around in the cold waiting to slip into his tent . . . Probably an urban myth. But with these guys, anything is possible. And Jesus can they talk! It's, like, their favourite hobby. They eat and they chat shit. Story of their lives. They're getting more and more batshit paranoid, "Not a word about what's happening down here is to go on social media." Just as well they warned her. Otherwise, how could she resist Instagramming thousands of photos of #washedup #hasbeens picnicking and yakking about rock at the Buttes-Chaumont? And the guy with the name like an orthopaedic mattress, Subutex . . . She could flood the socials with photos of their afternoon gatherings, there was zero chance it would go viral. They've even got a hairless poodle, ffs, that should tell you how zoned they are.

Aïcha's father is sitting astride a crate talking about *"la République, la République, la République"*, he sounds like a crow on a branch . . . But that's what he's like, he knocks off work and rushes down here to rant about stuff no-one gives a shit about. The national debt, public services, corruption . . . he's always got something to say about problems he'll never do anything to fix. If what people actually *want* made the slightest change in politics, we'd have heard by now. She is a bit of a gerontophobe. It winds her up seeing these people believing in stuff that doesn't exist. It's hard not to feel a bit sorry for old people. They act like they're still young. Except they're shrivelled and mouldy. They can iron out the wrinkle all they like, it doesn't change anything. They're still living in the steam age when everyone else has moved to touch-screen. They are still harking back to May '68, every right-wing reactionary like her father.

Daniel gives her a smile, she ignores him. Though he's a good customer. Someone who comes to her to get beautiful tattoos, who lets her get on with it and doesn't come out with bullshit comments when he sees what she's drawn . . . Every time he asks her to change something, he's right . . . The guy has good taste when it comes to ink. Not a single duff tat. It's almost an honour to have him as a showcase . . . He flirts with her. He disconcerts her. She's used to dealing with older guys who come to get inked and get turned on when she slips on the black gloves. It comes with the job. But Daniel is sexy. And cute. He's macho but sweet. If he was really what he claims to be, she'd do him, just to see what he's like. Despite the age difference. But she knows. She picked up something in conversation one night when he dropped in for a beer. He's trans. Céleste has no problem with that. But she doesn't want to investigate. There's girls, there's guys, it's been that way for, like, twelve million years – can you imagine telling your dad and saying: "I've got a boyfriend and when he was young he used to get his period"? So she avoids him. She doesn't bother to ask how the panther has been healing. She feels a bit bad about it, but it's better this way.

She goes back to Rosa Bonheur, Mimi has already left, the speakers are blaring out Pissed Jeans. The manageress claims that the afternoon customers with their baby buggies aren't fans of hardcore. But at least it gives you a boost before your shift. Vernon was the one who turned them on to Pissed Jeans. Because sometimes he does a D.J. set here. She's heard him spin a set, not exactly **Mind = Blown**, but O.K., does the job.

Aïcha is sitting on the terrace, all smiles. This, this kills Céleste. The girl disappears for a week, not a word, not a text, *nada*. Now Miss Kebab is back, fresh as a rose, expecting her BFF to rush over with a big hug, no questions asked. Aïcha is completely bogus. She's always fifty-fifty. Half the time she's chill, half the time she's *#zerofucksgiven*. That's not how friendship works. You don't show up at the bar looking for me one day and blow me off the next. Aïcha has manic phases, she laughs, she's gassed, she talks about her life, takes an interest in your life, gets you to trust her and then suddenly, without warning, she flips, she's depressed, she disappears. Nothing. You had a friend and now you've got nothing. Céleste isn't having it. She's not a punchbag, something for Aïcha to take her rage out on. The trouble with Aïcha is that she thinks she's responsible for everything, including other people's lives. Which means Monday they're inseparable but Tuesday her conscience is nagging and, bang, she's throwing shade, Céleste is a bad influence, and she's gone as if she's going to be tainted by just sitting next to her. Céleste is who she is, take her or leave her, but no part-timers. Either Aïcha thinks she's a heathen slut who might contaminate her in which case she doesn't have to talk to her, or they're friends and they can count on each other. She's had enough of the mood swings. If Aïcha is freaked that demons in human form are trying to "turn her from the truth", as she puts it, she shouldn't be hanging out in bars.

They only met a little while ago, but there have been so many ups and downs since then that Céleste feels like she's been riding a rollercoaster for ten years. The first time they talked, she was just showing up for her shift and she spotted Aïcha lying stiffly on the grass, arms by her side, gazing up at the sky. Some guy who looked really sus was crouching a couple of metres away, staring at her with a mixture of hatred and fascination. Céleste had seen the guy before, he buttonholed girls on their own and offered to give them "an Egyptian massage" and when they refused to talk to him, he'd get aggressive. It was obvious that right now he was on some sleazy trip – it was probably the hijab that did it for him. When pervs aren't dissing you for wearing shorts, they're insulting you for covering your hair. So Céleste sat down nearby. When the guy went over to Aïcha, Céleste kept a close eye on him, ready to intervene. She wasn't scared of him. Aïcha must have sensed something was up, she turned her head, and seeing the guy standing over her, she jumped to her feet, he made as if to spit in her face and Céleste screamed at him, "Fuck off, arsehole, just fuck right off now or I'm calling the park keepers." He'd had trouble with the keepers before and scarpered. Aïcha had looked at Céleste in silence, and it had taken a moment's thought before she said, "Thanks." It's as though it pains her to be friendly. They didn't say much else, they walked towards Rosa Bonheur together. When they reached the bar, Céleste was about to say, "Well, this is my stop," but at that moment, Aïcha broke down. Her body was racked with sobs, she looked at Céleste, her eyes wide – she was like someone who is bleeding and cannot believe it. Céleste could hardly just leave her standing there like that, even though they didn't know each other. She had taken her upstairs to the staff room and given her a Coke. Coke heals all wounds. She had not gone down to start her shift straight away, there were no customers that day. It had been raining since earlier, no-one came back to the park and the bar was deserted. Aïcha was in a state of shock. They had started chatting

– her mother with her vajayjay on display all over the net, this girl who'd thought she was the daughter of a self-effacing, depressive woman when in fact she was the daughter of a notorious, shameless hussy. The story was mixed in with details of Satana's death and her father's grief. Céleste had talked about her own life, about the mother who'd woken up one day and decided she'd never wanted a child, that she wasn't cut out for maternity, and had herself transferred to Shanghai and now only saw her daughter for a month every year, and even that seemed to be a burden. Her father had been inconsolable too. This was how they had become friends – by telling each other the things that mattered. As daughters of absentee mothers, they found they had a lot in common.

She had liked Aïcha from that first day. She had wanted them to be friends. Though Céleste doesn't have much truck with people who think they're superior and spend too much time studying the behaviour of others. But she likes this girl who talks like a man. She is driven by a secret fury mingled with timidity. There is a howling truth inside her. A repressed violence. When she speaks, she barely enunciates, as though she does not dare open her mouth. It distorts her features. Aïcha keeps her chin up, but her eyes lowered, her arms folded defensively across her chest, and there is a constant pain in her eyes that makes everything she says more interesting. She is fiercely intelligent. She needs to be tamed, but once you have earned her trust, you realise you haven't gone to all that effort for nothing. You want to know what she is thinking, she is capricious, and categorical. Before now, Céleste has never been a fan of smart-arses. She had to deal with a bunch of them at school. They were not the most cruel to her, but nonetheless she had been happy to leave them behind after the baccalauréat. What she likes about Aïcha is her body language. She has an intensity, a style.

Except now, Céleste is sick and tired of her friend's mood swings. She decides not to acknowledge her. In theory, she should be serving at that table, but she ignores her. The first thing you learn as a waitress is how to make annoying customers invisible. Your eyes drift over them, past them, anywhere as long as they never meet the eyes of the customer who is about to ask something that will screw everything up. But Miss Thing is in one of her manic phases, so tries to catch her attention by waving her arm over her head until Céleste, exasperated, goes over to her.

"What the hell are you doing here?"

"What's wrong? Are you angry with me about something?"

"When it suits you, we're best friends, then from one day to the next you're giving me the brush-off . . . For God's sake, find someone like you to be friends with and leave me the hell alone."

"I didn't realise we were joined at the hip. I was away for a few days, I wasn't being sulky, what's got you so paranoid? Sit with me. There are no customers, so stop trying to pretend you're slaving away . . ."

"I don't have time for you right now."

"What time does your shift finish? I want you to come somewhere with me."

"I don't like the way you use me."

"Don't be horrible, Céleste, I just want you to come with me somewhere . . . we haven't seen each other in ages and I just thought . . . hey, I'll ask Céleste if she wants to hang out for a bit . . . I've been really busy, that's all."

One of the problems with Aïcha is her smile. Not that she uses it often, but when she does it's a powerful weapon. Her eyes light up and you just want to start over. Two minutes after telling herself she's not going to let herself be taken in again, Céleste is back with a *café au lait* for herself and an espresso for Aïcha, who has a delicate stomach and can't handle the combination of coffee and milk.

"So, what do you want from me?"

"Can you keep a secret?"

"Who exactly do you think I'd blab about you to?"

"Swear on the most precious thing in your life that you'll keep what I'm going to say to yourself. It's really important, so think hard before you say anything."

"Bloody hell, you're a ball-buster, I'm shocked."

They watch as a handsome jogger runs past, heads turning in unison as they follow him with their eyes. They play a game where they guess what sport the joggers play. Céleste announces:

"Boxer."

"Cyclist. Look at his calves."

"Did you see his back? There's no way you get back muscles like that from cycling."

"Pedalling uphill works every muscle."

This is how they manage to talk about boys without it seeming sexual. Céleste finishes her coffee, tucks her cigarette papers and her filters into the tobacco pouch, announces that she has to work, gets up and makes to leave. Aïcha is not about to give up.

"Do you get off early?"

"Yeah."

"We need to be at the Palais de Tokyo by eight-thirty."

"Give it up, Aïcha, I'm not going to take a métro across Paris to go to an art gallery. Are you raving?"

"Don't worry, I'll be waiting for you there. I don't need anything."

*

Two hours later, they are in the métro. Céleste is irritated, she keeps saying that she is tired, but curiosity gets the better of her. She asks:

"So, what are we going to see?"

"It's a lecture. 'What is a performative exhibition?' The guy is the son of a producer who did horrible things to my mother. I want to make his life hell."

"You're planning on defending your mother, all of a sudden? A lot of shit has obviously happened in my absence . . . You're off your head, this is insane . . . And why are you dragging me into your pathetic plans?"

"You're part of the plan."

"In what sense?"

"In the sense that you're coming with me to put pressure on him."

"I can only see problems in this plan of yours: for a start, how are you going to put pressure on him?"

"We cough."

"We cough?"

"Yeah. All the time. It'll screw up his lecture."

"Girl, are you telling me we're making a forty-minute métro journey to cough?"

"Yep. This is first contact."

"O.K., you really are deranged. Question number two: why have a go at the son when it's the father you're angry with? My father's a policeman, but that doesn't mean I get to carry a gun . . ."

"Well, I didn't do anything either. I'm my mother's daughter whether I like it or not. Same goes for this jerk. You think the day he gets his inheritance he's going to say, no way, I want nothing to do with it? When it comes to ready money and real estate, you bet your life he'll be his father's son. So we're going."

"I don't know who's been messing with your head, but you're completely brain dead: you don't have two firing neurons to rub together. And what exactly did his father do that was so terrible?"

"I know you, when you find out, you'll say, what's with the coughing, we should be buying Kalashnikovs."

The more she talks, the quieter her voice gets. Céleste practically has to press her ear to Aïcha's lips to catch what she is whispering. Not that it matters – no-one in the carriage has even clocked them. In a voice so low it is barely audible, Aïcha says:

"His father is responsible for my mother's death."

"Don't tell me, someone from that gang that hangs with Subutex told you . . . if it's something that came from Alex Bleach, I swear, I'm taking you to hospital . . . we've talked about this already. The guy was fit to be locked up. And that Vernon is a clown. You should stop hanging around with them . . ."

"It's true. Of course it's true . . . What do you think? It's so normal for rich people to get away with things, they've got no limits."

"Look, we need to stop and talk about this. There's nothing normal about what you're telling me. For a start, when did you become your mother's avenger? And for another thing: do you listen to all the bullshit those old codgers spout? But most importantly: you're told someone killed your mother and you want to go and cough during a lecture? Get a grip, Aïcha, for fuck sake . . ."

"We've done it a bunch of times . . . we go round to their place at night and graffiti the front of their house. It was the Bolivian girls who came up with the idea. They do it in Bolivia when rapists get off. We borrowed the concept. We've got a list, Pamela and the Hyena came up with it. Everyone who abused my mother and knew that she was murdered. We've got their addresses."

"You're giving me a migraine. I don't see you for a week and everything goes pear-shaped . . . You've been spending your nights tagging a few houses? You've got a list? Wow, you're a real threat . . . what the fuck do they care?"

"We're showing them up."

"No surprise that this idea came from Bolivia. It doesn't travel well."

"Trust me. When this guy gets up in the morning and sees RAPIST and MURDERER sprayed on the front of his house in letters three metres high, he knows what it means and he freaks out."

Céleste decides to say nothing, she watches the métro stations flash past. A cute young black guy gets on with his guitar and starts singing, howling "*La vie est belle, la vie est belle, belle, belle . . .*" He has a powerful voice and he is pushing it to the limit. His mother probably said: "Go and play that thing outside or I'm going to kill you." He's making everyone's ears bleed. They all remain astonishingly calm. It is even more difficult to make out what Aïcha is saying.

"I didn't see the point of it either, at first, spraying graffiti on doors and walls, I thought it was kid's stuff . . . But they're right: these guys can't stand it. It drives them insane. For once, all their money is no use to them – except to clean it off every day . . . And they don't dare call the police or alert the media, because, deep down, they know what we're talking about . . . when you've spent your whole life with your trousers round your ankles fucking girls who are too desperate for money or work to keep their dignity . . . the day someone rubs your nose in your own shit, you've got too many things on your conscience to go complaining to the police . . .

"How do you know all this?"

"For a start, the producer that Bleach accused tells the Hyena everything, and every night she passes it on to us . . . it's fun to think we're driving him mad. I'm tired of being the only one who lies awake at night thinking about this stuff. I never did anything wrong. We can hardly call it justice, yet . . . But I know he has a shitty day, and that's a start."

Céleste does not say what she is thinking. She feels sorry for them. Aïcha has gone off the rails. But you can't blame her. She told Céleste what Alex Bleach said. Whether or not it was true, it was bound to traumatise the girl when she heard it. She finds it difficult to imagine Aïcha chatting with the oldsters at the park. She's got absolutely nothing in common with them.

'So your father knows about this?"

"No. He'd be dead against it. My father's old school, he still believes in the justice system of his country."

"Does Subutex go with you?"

"He doesn't know either. The girls say he's too unstable. It's impossible to predict how he'll react."

"So all this time you've been missing you were hanging out with those crazy old people in the park? I knew it's like Angel Grove down there, but I didn't realise that at night everyone transformed into Power Rangers."

Céleste is upset that Aïcha got involved in this whole scheme without telling her first. She might have been able to dissuade her. Or gone with her. Either way she should have been involved.

At the end of his song, the goofball singer does not stop to pass the hat. He segues straight into another song. The same excruciating melody but with different lyrics. His voice is ear-splitting. Céleste is quietly hoping someone will give him a kicking. The only positive is that they can talk about whatever they like, no-one is likely to overhear.

"I find it difficult to imagine that these guys are really pissed about you spray-painting dumb words on their doors . . ."

But as she says the words, Céleste remembers what it was like when she was in school, the sound of the telephone echoing through the apartment, and when she picked up the receiver she would hear some nutter say, "Fucking slut you're gonna blow us all at school tomorrow and then we'll fuck you up the arse, got it?" And that was the best possible scenario, managing to get to the phone before her father did. And she didn't have anything to feel guilty about. Even now, ten years later, she still wonders why that gang of boys focussed their aggression on her. She knows what it's like to be threatened at home, to go to bed praying that the telephone won't ring. She does not want to talk to Aïcha about it. She says:

"What's all this got to do with the Palais de Tokyo?"

"Like I said, the producer's son is giving the lecture . . . we just want him to know we're there. We want people to know that they can't just get away with this shit anymore. When it's over I want him to call his father and cry down the phone and for his father to realise that this is going to extend to his whole family."

"Pretty dark."

"You feel different when you take action rather than standing around doing nothing. Being passive drives you insane."

The cringe-making guitarist finally stops. People are so relieved that some of them even give him money. Céleste thinks to herself for a moment, then says:

"Couldn't you get money out of them? Some sort of blackmail?"

"We've thought about that."

"If you think Bleach was telling the truth, you could pump

this guy for tons of cash . . . and you're just vandalising buildings?"

"I don't want to sell myself to the highest bidder. None of us do."

"The day they find out who you are, you'll be standing in the dock like idiots, charged with harassment without the money to even pay for a lawyer . . ."

"We're very careful . . ."

They are fast approaching Iéna métro station when Céleste finally blurts out the question she has been dying to ask since they set off:

"Have you forgiven your mother?"

"No. But Pamela and Daniel have talked to me about her a lot."

"Don't tell me you're listening to a whore and a fucking tranny . . . They've completely fucked your head up, it's sick . . ."

"I listen to the people who knew her. Even if they are degenerates. They really care about her. My mother was lost. She was someone a bit like you, but she'd fallen in with a bad crowd. It means a lot to me that she also had a sense of humour, that she was an amazing dancer, that she had friends . . . That she was a normal person too, not just a freak. I can't say that I've forgiven her. Let's just say I've got some perspective."

"I suppose it's not like you've got a choice."

The Palais de Tokyo is heaving. A vast concrete space with canapés at the front, a bookshop in the middle, and families everywhere with kids running amok. Céleste has not set foot in a gallery since she dropped out of the Beaux-Arts. She always found them dull as shit. Little did she know that, in the intervening years, they've come to resemble an Aquaboulevard waterpark, minus the flumes.

They spend a long time wandering lost, before finally finding the basement room, a low-ceiling affair with no windows, where lectures are held. About thirty people perched on uncomfortable chairs are listening to a young man who seems terrified at having to talk into a microphone. Just stepping into the room you can tell that the guy is no orator. "That's him," Aïcha whispers as she spots two empty seats in the front row and decides to make her presence conspicuous. Not that she needs to do much to attract attention, the hijab is enough. The audience turn to stare at her, some wonder whether she is a cleaner who has arrived early for her shift, others nod approvingly at the idea of minorities trying to further their education, some hide their handbags, still others are wondering whether she has a bomb in the back pocket of her jeans, while the most radical are whispering amongst themselves, "Can't we ask her to leave? Is she even allowed in here? Are you sure?" Aïcha is living proof that, when it comes to style, accessorising is everything.

The speaker is a guy of about thirty. He has shoulder-length hair, and though he doesn't have the standard-issue hipster beard, he has the look. He probably gets around by bicycle and spends a lot of time in Berlin. He grips the microphone in both hands as though clinging to it for support. From time to time, his left hand detaches itself and flaps about in counterpoint to what he is saying. He is reading a prepared text: he would be incapable of ad-libbing three words. He is too scared to look at the girls. Aïcha coughs and Céleste does likewise, but with little conviction. The lecture is so disastrous that a couple of coughs are not likely to ruin the atmosphere. Céleste checks her watch. Time is crawling by even more slowly than it does at work. The guy's fingers are stubby and graceless. She finds that there is something touching about his struggle to speak in public. She has seen so many people spout reams of bullshit with considerable aplomb. He has caught some sun, or has been to a salon, his skin is slightly tanned. It comes to her completely out of the blue. She wants to fuck him. Precisely because he is second rate. She whispers to Aïcha:

"Your plan isn't working. If you like, I'll go back to his place, slip him some tranqs, wait till he's asleep and redecorate his bedroom."

"Where are you going to find tranquillisers?"

"In the bottom of my bag. I work in a bar, we all take speed to get through the night shift, so I've always got some downers to take the edge off when I get home."

That's it. She has finally worked out how Subutex's gang manage to mess with people's minds: they propose innovative activities. "I'm planning a direct action. You want to come with?" and at the time you say, no way, it's a dumb fucking idea. But five minutes later, there you are on the starting blocks. Between powerlessness and the great unknown, you choose the latter. At least it means action. It means making something happen. Go home with this guy who's never done her any harm and get payback for all the arseholes who made her childhood a living hell. And she gets to help her friend into the bargain. Prove that she can be counted on. That they form a whole. She wants to be a part of Aïcha's adventure.

"And how will you get into his apartment?"

"Guess."

"That's disgusting."

"I'm hardcore. Can you go up to the lobby bookshop and buy me a couple of thick marker pens?"

"CURSE THE RANCID PUSSY OF THE SUCCUBUS WHO GAVE YOU birth" "Bourgeois shitwank!" "Filthy money-grubbing bastard!" "Die, fucker!"

He is pleasantly surprised by her spelling and syntax. It is much better than he would have imagined from the way she spoke. The comma between "Die" and "fucker" is full-on grammar Nazi. Antoine wanders through the apartment. She has redecorated every wall, every kitchen cupboard, not to mention the bathroom. She used the fat red marker favoured by taggers, the thick strokes dribble down the wall, though she has no real flair for calligraphy. He's definitely not dealing with a seasoned graffiti artist.

He picks a golden coffee capsule from a bowl, then sends a polite text message telling Olympe, the cleaner, not to bother coming this week – the poor thing doesn't need to see this. Now Antoine understands why he woke up with such a hellish hangover having barely drunk last night – the girl slipped a roofie in his drink. It's noon, he slept like a dormouse, slept right through the alarm and missed his early morning meeting. He will have to call his assistant and get her to push back his return flight by a day. Besides, he needs to arrange to have the apartment cleaned before he leaves.

"You suck power like the bitch slut you are." To be truly humiliating, an insult must address the victim in the feminine. He is not even surprised that a girl would do so. They have so internalised their own oppression. The only redemption lies in motherhood, and this puts them in a delicate position: in order to marry, they have to be sexually attractive, and this places them in the role of the whore. And in order to get pregnant, they have to spread their legs, which simply makes matters worse. In less than ten years, these chaste virgins will all procreate via artificial insemination, it is the only way for them to be spared what they see as the taint of sex. Which will be a relief for guys of his generation: when they want to fuck, they will have professionals, and when it comes to family, they will finally have respectable virgin mothers.

Last night, she had gatecrashed the dinner. Physical force had been required to evict her. The problem with young women who know they're beautiful – in her case, it's a rank overstatement – is that it never occurs to them that their persistence is simply harassment. He had no desire for her company. He had made himself clear. She had imposed. Not that he was surprised: he had assumed she was an actress. It frequently happens. It is impossible to make them understand that sleeping with a producer's son is not going to open any doors. The younger the actress, the more stubborn she is. They know that, without contacts, they will never get anywhere and they are prepared to do anything to fill their address book. To them, sleeping with him is a matter of professional survival.

She had come on strong, done such an extravagant number that he had felt embarrassed for her. In the end, it had seemed less trouble to take her home than to shake her off. What he finds most surprising is not that she scrawled insults a metre high all over his living room, but that he does not encounter such problems more often. He is weak, shy and awkward, he is rich as Croesus and likes to slum it. He is a perfect target for someone who wants to redecorate his apartment. It will take him all afternoon to deal with the problem. He has so many other things to do. It puts him out of commission.

She had thrown herself at him like a third-world country at a sack of rice. He does not know her first name. In bed, she proved a pleasant surprise: she was passionate as an ex-con who has done a ten-year stretch but never adapted to girl-on-girl action. He had enjoyed the way she clung to him, tender and slutty, a debauched romantic who knows exactly what she wants, not the kind of submissive little wallflower he usually attracts, the ones who pant and pretend. It had been better than he expected, but he had quickly become bored, his mind was distracted. For a woman to truly excite him in bed, his image of her fully clothed plays a crucial role. She had thrown herself at him with too much ardour to leave room for fantasy, he had no opportunity to sublimate anything, clothes, gestures, words. In the end, he had to fantasise about the girl she had been with in order to get off. The other girl, the one in the hijab, was not as pretty, but she was more arousing, more unavailable. Who wouldn't want to romance a princess from a harem? He had noticed her the moment she arrived. She was surly, proud, exactly the sort of girl he would like to impress. But she had not even waited for him to finish his talk before gathering her belongings and leaving. He had been terrible. As always. He has never been comfortable with public speaking, he reads from his notes and feels unable to ad-lib. Then, afterwards, he had let himself be picked up by the other girl. Serves him right. He needs to buy himself a little personality.

At least the bitch had a good reason to hook up with him. One point to her. A desire to wreak havoc. She did a good job. He warms his hands against the coffee cup as he contemplates the devastation. He counts twelve slogans. He pictures himself sleeping like a baby while she was wrecking the apartment. She could have killed him. Cut his throat. He would have died snoring. Then again, the coincidence is troubling: someone vandalised his father's apartment a few days earlier.

He wishes she had stayed. Right now, he would give a lot to know more about her. Standing motionless in the middle of the ravaged room, Antoine finds himself unable to move. It works, this thing they're doing. It is brutal. He sets his mobile phone to charge. Before the clean-up, he wants to take some photographs. It's a piece of performative art, he could exhibit it as is. He does not know whether he would have the balls to suggest it. Poor vandal, if she thinks he is going to call his father to share the overwhelming feeling of shame . . . She would have done better to interrogate him last night, before offering up her body as a sacrifice. When his father discovered the door to his apartment daubed with obscene graffiti, he had told his children he was the victim of an ugly conspiracy, probably the work of jealous colleagues, then he had told them to say nothing to anyone, and the subject was closed.

Antoine is staggered by the extent of the damage. He does not wait until his phone is fully charged before starting to take photographs. He knows artistic activism when he sees it. When his father told him about the hurtful graffiti on his door, Antoine immediately knew the apposite term. Less than a year ago, he attended a lecture by an Argentinian curator on the subject of *escrache*, about how the mothers of those "disappeared" during the dictatorship attacked the torturers who had gone unpunished, publicly shaming them by daubing slogans on their homes.

What he should do is not bother to repaint. Leave it as it is. It would be interesting. Take the insult on board. He is bitterly aware of the irony of the situation: he had found the lecture on *escrache* fascinating, he had written page after page in his notebook about the alternative political strategies emerging in countries where justice was not dispensed through the judiciary. He does not know what his father did to bring these problems on himself. But it comes as no surprise that he too is paying the price. He is not the son of a choirboy.

Antoine would like to track down the girl who did this. He would like to warn her. They will be caught. They have no idea of the means his father has at his disposal. He will find them. They have no idea of the lengths he will go to if someone confronts him. They will pay dearly.

The little vandal could not possibly hate his father as much as Antoine has learned to do. She does not know him well enough. Maybe he raped her in his office after a drinking binge one night . . . but she did not have to endure his presence through her childhood. He hopes she has no illusions that a man like his father might feel remorse. Whatever his father has done, he is convinced he was within his rights – his desires trump all else.

Antoine grew up the son that all great families find themselves lumbered with – the embarrassing idiot. He collected endless diagnoses in the course of countless therapies: dyslexia, A.D.H.D., learning difficulties, memory deficiency, deafness, Asperger Syndrome, intellectual giftedness and oversensitivity. Eventually he was sent to school in Switzerland. Whether the teachers arranged desks in a circle, left him to run around the playground or brutally punished him . . . the results were the same: he had no idea what they were talking about. When explained in a pedagogic context, the simplest notions eluded him, they became abstract, impossible to grasp. In order for him to pass the baccalauréat, his family has shelled out the cost of a duplex apartment in the sixth arrondissement.

Antoine never came to terms with his environment. Feeling second-rate among his peers, from early adolescence he sought out misfits – the shady characters of the neighbourhood. Perhaps he hoped that contact with the less fortunate would rid him of his own complexes. He knows that this is how it generally works: guys like him tend to gravitate towards people they feel are innately inferior because they prefer to dazzle the destitute rather than deal with their sense of inferiority among their peers. He does not think that he is like that. But you never know. He felt genuinely drawn to the intelligence of people from the sink estates in the *banlieue,* the swiftness of their reactions, the sureness of their instincts, their first-hand knowledge of life, and above all the inflammatory humour they used to mock their hardship and transform it into a badge of honour. He loved their use of language, their way of crowbarring their way into every aspect of life, of misappropriating all the things that were denied them. It was a different era, back then. Being able to rock the mic earned you respect. The culture of the *banlieue* was everywhere in the late '90s, and the guys he hung with weren't likely to be impressed because he had been taught a solid command of Latin. Antoine had had to fight hard, to push through several panic attacks to get himself accepted by the guys he wanted to hang with.

Before that, in the schools he had gone to, he had always had the impression that the other pupils from his social class were privy to some secret that he had not been told. They seemed naturally confident. They were good at sports, effortlessly learned languages, they knew what clothes to wear . . . He had been twenty years old when Booba released "*Temps Mort*". All the kids were listening to Snoop Dogg, Dre, Tupac and The Notorious B.I.G. He had found a home in this music, like a surrogate womb. Hip hop was suddenly mainstream and he set himself up as an agent for tag artists.

A lot of tag artists were happy to work in fashion, galleries and institutions. At the time, he didn't think of it as anything other than a strategy for making friends. A few of the artists had talent, charisma, he was in awe of them. Antoine had a surname that opened doors and a predisposition to split personality: he already spoke the language of art galleries, and he learned the language of the streets. Like certain bilingual children, he was never completely comfortable in either. He was convinced – though the history of street art proved otherwise – that he had only to open the doors and the two worlds would be able to communicate. He chose his protégés with care. They made him a little money, but mostly they made him an international reputation. He quickly became a go-to curator. His artists pocketed some serious skrilla. But very few of them really took off. Most of the artists he worked with ended up back at square one, bitterly disappointed. Once you've had a taste of a world where you can breathe freely, had access to those privileged spheres where money flows continuously, it's difficult to deal with the suffocation of going back to the block. Some guy would get a contract, pocket a couple of grand, get to know what it felt like to breathe, then a younger guy would come along, Contemporary Art was obsessed with innovation, and yesterday's star would go back to collecting welfare. This was the rule, Antoine and his artists discovered it at the same time, the difference was that he was here for the long haul.

Antoine can brag about exhibiting some of the biggest names

in street art in New York galleries and at glittering private views on the West Coast only to have to drop them one after another. Rich kids are enthusiastic and have the means to subsidise their gullibility: the invoice life presents them for their mistakes is not excessive. Antoine worked on the – specious – principle that, if given the opportunity, the destitute would eagerly conform to the diktats of the system. But fucking things up remains their preferred option. They are sensitive souls: at the mention of the first compromise, they get bent out of shape and threaten to merk people. They lack something that only an education at a prestigious private school can provide: an imperviousness to criticism and an unshakeable conviction that you are important.

In his early years as a curator, he had seen his apartment burgled, his papers stolen, his galleries torched, his lawyer fleeced, his sister harassed, witnessed a diplomat's nose being broken and the Institut français in London being tagged . . . But his career was made. Though it was not a conscious decision, he gradually gravitated towards more conventional artists. Now that his reputation was established, he could associate with people like himself without feeling inferior. The current trend – the investor profile – is for emerging artists from the Middle East and Eastern Europe, so Antoine slakes his thirst for radicalism by working with other rich kids whose culture seemed exotic yesterday but today has become the new Universal. He rarely listens to hip hop anymore; he worships Leonard Cohen.

He can't leave the apartment in this state. He is leaving Paris tomorrow and Francesca might come back while he is away. She wouldn't appreciate the new décor, even if he sells it to her as art. It would be difficult to explain that he brought some girl he didn't know back to spend the night. Four coffees. He makes the same mistake every morning. He dry heaves and his stomach is in knots. It is his way of getting himself in gear. Since he is stranded in Paris, he makes a list of things he might do. He needs to add a ream of stuff to his Twitter feed – there is never a clause in his contract, but it is taken for granted that he has a certain presence on social media. People see him criss-crossing the world, spending half his life in departure lounges, a rolling suitcase permanently attached to one hand. The jet lag nation are a people apart, they immediately recognise their own and have a faint contempt for airport amateurs. This mania for organising meetings in far-flung countries for things that could be dealt with over Skype. Nothing turns the brain to mush quite like prolonged sojourns in first class lounges. From one hotel room to the next, with his travelling case and his perfectly folded shirts, he racks up air miles and gradually loses any ability to think.

He leaves a message on his father's voicemail: "I'm in Paris till tomorrow, if you've got a minute I could swing by the office for a coffee – and pick up a couple of D.V.D.s." Usually, he avoids seeing his father. It took him many years to formulate a simple thought: the man's an arsehole. For a long time, Antoine saw him through his mother's eyes: a loving, upstanding man with a formidable intellect. A good father disappointed by wayward children. Then he had an epiphany: his father did not love him. He had spent so long hearing about how his father was devoted to him, that he had never thought to wonder: precisely when and in what manner was this devotion expressed? His father was neither loving nor upstanding. He was narcissistic, mendacious, quick-tempered, obsessed with money and incapable of controlling his libido . . . To him,

Antoine was a burden who cost him an arm and a leg. The father took an interest in his son only to lavish him with his contempt.

Antoine would like to be able to say that, professionally, he is utterly unlike his father, that he has convictions, that he is a man of the left. But he is too perceptive not to have noticed that, objectively, he has had fewer opportunities than his father did to be corrupt. If he is honest and upstanding, it is for want of temptation.

He had sworn to himself that, when his turn came, he would not be a distant, demanding father, a ball-breaking bastard who only comes home to complain that his kids are badly brought up. But heredity is a patient spider. It spins in the shadows, unbeknownst to its host. Now his turn has come, he can barely conceal the contempt he feels for his own son. While Pablo was still a child, everything was perfectly fine. But he does not like the boy he has grown into. Family has nothing to do with it. He is a part of his generation. He had not even turned ten when he became obsessed with reality T.V. Emotional saccharine. His child would sit blissfully watching "*Les Anges de la téléréalité*". A pile of steaming horseshit nothing could tear him from. And Antoine had watched, devastated, as his child's intelligence melted away like snow on a sunny day. If forced to do something else, Pablo did not actively resist. He would passively wait until he could go back and stare at the screen. The rest of the time, the little brat whines about wanting a new jacket, a new phone, a pair of thousand-euro headphones, expensive holidays. Antoine is aware that he looks at his son the way his father used to look at him. Francesca does the best she can to try and ensure that her son has skills beyond being able to name every contestant from every season of "The Bachelor". She and Antoine had stayed married, but, by tacit agreement, they do their best to avoid being in the same country at the same time. Their relationship reminds him a little of his parents'. Except for the fact that she does not admire him, and does not suffer his infidelities in silence: she quickly lost interest in him, and it is she who stubbornly avoids him. He can see her point. He gets it.

Being the daughter of a high-ranking Cuban family and armed with a Venezuelan passport, Francesca was working on the South American contemporary art circuit when they met, through mutual friends, in San Francisco. Their initial harmony slowly crumbled. He does not know how to make her happy. She cannot stand the fact that he works, she cannot stand the fact that he has no ambition. She can't stand having him around all the time, she can't stand it when he travels. If they go away for the weekend, she starts crying as soon as the plane takes off, if they stay in a hotel, she can't stand the noise from the neighbours in the next room, if they stay at home, she complains that she doesn't get along with any of his friends. There is no way of predicting what she will complain about, she is mercurial. All he can know for certain is that she is never happy when she is with him.

When she is not around, Antoine cherishes the idea he has of her, her frankness, her irreverent intelligence, her radicalism, her exuberance. But whenever she is near, he is terrified of her outbursts, the constant criticism – she makes him feel small. It is one more thing that recalls the nightmare of his father: Francesca reminds him of his stepmother.

Antoine had been seventeen when Marilyn first came into their lives. Until then, theirs had been a family in the classic tradition: the husband, the wife, the children, the regular mistress, the occasional prostitute or discreet orgy. But the wife had now turned forty and the husband decided to perpetuate a different tradition: he left her for a younger model. Marilyn wore large hats and was passionate about interior design and alternative medicine. Twenty years on, the smell of lavender oil still makes Antoine physically sick. His stepmother was impossible. She imposed a reign of terror at home. His father was often absent. Unable to deal with the separation, and reduced to living in a studio apartment in Porte Dorée, his mother had tried to end her life in the months after the divorce and, in the years that followed, his visits to her were in one hospital room or another. Then Marilyn got pregnant. And the horror truly began. She got it into her head that her son would get a raw deal when it came time to inherit, that the children of the first marriage would get more. Antoine learned to hide under the bed when she flew into a rage. She had a diabolical intelligence: she could always find the weakest point, the most humiliating punishment, the most hurtful word. She crushed brother and sister with the zeal of a torturer. Their father could see what was happening. He made no attempt to protect them from the situation he had imposed on them. Marilyn was the military wing of their relationship.

The production offices have moved to a new address. The lobby is so vast it could be used as a skating rink. There is something pathetic about the sheer excess, it says much about a man who no longer knows how to assert his existence, whom nothing seems to reassure. His father's god is Capital. She is a capricious and demanding idol capable of hurling thunderbolts at harvest time, raping virgins, drowning innocents and ordering her subjects to cut the throats of their own children because she has a sudden thirst for fresh blood. You do not argue with such a deity: you sacrifice everything, without question.

Everything about the company has changed – the name, the

address, the scale – but the girl at reception has not changed in ten years. Antoine can never remember her name. She has lost a lot of weight and is wearing a lot more make-up than the last time he saw her. It makes her look old. He has come at a bad time, she cautions him, it is a particularly trying day. He is used to it. For as long as he has known his father, every day has been difficult and demanding. Antoine has time to leaf through several issues of "*Ecran Total*" before being allowed to take the private lift that leads directly to the lair of "*le grand patron*".

"Antoine? I didn't realise you were in Paris . . . Come in . . . Would you like to have dinner with me this evening? Just the two of us, my little *chouchou* is away on business."

"I'm leaving this afternoon, papa."

This curious habit he has of calling that bitch of a girlfriend "my little *chouchou*". He is clearly on edge. He looks terrible. Antoine is dying to simply say: "What did you do, papa, why is everyone out to get us?"

In the presence of his father, he feels a nostalgia well in his chest, a longing for a closeness that never existed. And yet he has the feeling that something has been lost – a mixture of respect, admiration and tenderness, an easiness between them. But he does not say what is bothering him, he says: "No, no I still don't take sugar, no, no milk, just short and black. New York? Good, everything's good, better than here, the market is bouncing back . . . I hear all the gallery owners are leaving the capital because of the taxes . . . that most of the art business these days takes place outside Paris . . . I don't believe it, people have been saying that for years and nothing ever changes . . . At the moment I'm working mostly with the Germans and the Dutch. It's insufferable, the way they look down on us since the crash."

His father is seated, arms folded, buttocks perched on the edge of his Eames chair, listening distractedly, his smile is insincere, the only thing that is genuine is the tension. He scratches the back of his neck, glances out the window, then brusquely gets to his feet and apologises:

"I've got a little problem with one of my colleagues, I need to have a quick chat with her. Just give me five minutes."

And, as is his habit, he does not close the door separating his office from that of his colleague, the moment he steps through the door, his tone changes, the anger he has briefly been forced to suppress becomes a murderous rage:

"How dare you! I will not tolerate your uncalled-for remarks about my friends. I have politely brought this to your attention on several occasions, so you can't say you haven't been warned. Where do you think you are? What do you take me for? Do you think we're friends? That you can laugh and joke with me? It's my fault, I suppose. I should have realised the first day you showed up, you lack maturity, you have no idea what is required of you, and to make matters worse, you're insolent . . . Who do you think you are? I've given this serious consideration and I've made my decision: clear your desk, as soon as you have packed up your belongings I want you out of here, and I don't want to set eyes on you again."

He concludes the conversation with a door slam that sets the paintings on the wall juddering and roars over his shoulder:

"Oh, and *thanks* for forcing me to dismiss you with immediate effect! I mean, obviously it's *so* convenient to be lumbered with your projects as well as my own. So, thank you. You have spent every minute here making my life more difficult, so bravo! Bravo!"

He is spluttering and turning purple. He has always been a coward by nature: all sweetness and light until something snaps.

When that happens, whoever he is addressing is made to pay for all the times he did not dare to be honest. But this time, he is absolutely beside himself. Antoine thinks about his little graffiti artist, he would like to be able to tell her: it works! He is convinced that she has good reason to hate his family. Suave and considerate, he says:

"Problems?"

"A dumb bitch. I have to stop giving opportunities to people who are simply not equal to the task. You try to be generous and you end up kicking yourself. All the years I've been in this business, and I've never become hard-hearted . . ."

"What happened?"

"She doesn't have a clue. It's not enough that she always shows up late – with her, the métro is always breaking down – she comes in here and makes jokes about Sarave – a brilliant man who has given his whole life to French cinema – and, yes, it's true, he walked out on us, but that doesn't mean . . . she parks her fat arse on that chair and calmly insults him, *she* thinks that he shouldn't have argued over the new contract . . . Does she really think we pay her to have an opinion, that bitch?"

The bitch in question opens the door without knocking and interrupts his diatribe. Pretty, dark haired, she addresses the producer bluntly and without ceremony.

"I never said that. I wanted to raise the matter with you because . . ."

"Get out!"

He is foaming at the mouth. He repeats the words over and over: "Get out!", but only after she has closed the door.

"I am going to destroy her, to obliterate her, that little bitch will never work anywhere again."

A strange intuition: she knows something embarrassing about him. And the father is aware that he has made a mistake in firing her. She is more likely to talk about whatever is bothering him if she leaves than if she is still in his employ. Antoine feels a searing flash jolt through him, something confirmed by his father's unwarranted hysteria. He fires people all the time. He regularly takes his anger out on those weaker than he is. But this time, his fury is entirely disproportionate to the situation. There is no joy in his threat to have her blacklisted, no pleasure in humiliating someone. Only exhaustion. And perhaps a certain panic. No-one would worry about firing such a woman. Antoine trusts his instinct. He glances at his phone, gets to his feet, claims to have a meeting, clumsily hugs his father, "See you very soon." "Come for dinner, give me a call and come to the house." They both know that Antoine will not come. He quickly leaves the premises. Standing on the pavement, he waits for the woman to clear her desk. His instinct is urging him to follow her.

ANAÏS HAD BEEN EXPECTING IT FOR WEEKS AND, IN A SENSE, IT felt as though she had been forced to wear something grubby and could now get rid of it. Dopalet had always been polite to her, respectful to the point of magnanimity, and for a time he had made her his confidante. Just now, when he had started to scream, it had been like a nightmare. And no-one on her floor had intervened to protest – they helped her pack her boxes and promised to promptly send them on; already, they could not bring themselves to look her in the eyes, she was a plague victim. She knew that she was not the first to suffer this fate. Which made it all the more humiliating.

No-one had ever dismissed her like that. No-one had ever addressed her in that tone. She had been thanked for her services – her contract was not renewed, she would be called into an office and told that they needed to make economies, there would be some mention of the financial crash, or the possibility that a young woman her age might get pregnant, or the curse of the 35-hour week . . . She had always been let go with a modicum of tact and courtesy. Not that this ever stopped her from being plunged into sheer panic, dreading the idea that she might end up unemployed for six months straight. She has a phobia of any unexplained gaps in her C.V. that might make an employer suspicious, it comes from having been a model pupil, or perhaps from having parents who worked hard and inculcated in her the idea that merit demands constant effort. Her parents own the largest pharmacy in Tours. They had started out with nothing and this was their legacy: she never rests on her laurels, she knows that nothing can be taken for granted, that you cannot always assume that there is still plenty of time to prove yourself. But what, in her early years working, had seemed like a series of enriching experiences – she has been assistant to a food photographer, an intern in an advertising production department, a runner for a fashion house, a props manager in a theatre – is beginning to make her résumé look like that of a flighty young woman.

She had hit rock bottom when she met Dopalet. She was writing news copy for a cable T.V. channel, the newsreader cordially loathed her and, if she made the slightest mistake, he informed his bosses. She could not take it any longer, having to get up at 5.00 a.m. in order to cobble together stories from the A.F.P. news ticker. The producer had come to meet with someone at the T.V. channel, had flirted with her over the coffee machine. She had pretended not to know what he was hinting at when he had invited her to lunch to "talk about young, experimental cinema", a subject about which she knew a great deal. He had taken a fancy to her. He had offered her a job, paying a little more than minimum wage. She had created her own role: internet talent scout. It was new to her. Previously, all her posts had been as an intern. On her first few days in the office, she was dazzled by Dopalet. His charisma, his decisiveness, his intuition, his spirit . . . He valued her. He showered her with compliments about her aptitude for the job, the perspicacity of her thinking, the breadth of her culture . . . She knew that he was attracted to her, but he never made her feel that he had hired her to be a pretty piece of ass. He had never come on strong. And yet, all too quickly, she had become disillusioned: the guy made most of his decisions based on the *I Ching* or the Tarot. If he drew a "Darkening of the Light", he would cancel a meeting. If he turned over "The Tower", he fired someone in accounts. "The Chariot" and he would hire a new intern. This was probably how he had made the decision to hire her – mid-way between pervy fantasies and the luck of the cards. He has no real interest in anything. Disturbingly superficial, he shoehorns the world "culture" into every sentence so he can complain about the movies he is reduced to making and imply that he is working far below his potential. But he would never go to see anything other than box-office blockbusters, never opens a book, never visits an exhibition, has no interest in music and the sum total of his knowledge of the internet is checking profiles on IMDb. The topics of conversation that most interest him are those that directly concern him. She has never heard him offer an interesting opinion about cinema. He insists on innovative ideas but only respects formulas that have already proved themselves. He finds it difficult to focus on anything for more than two minutes without texting someone, opening a door or changing the subject – any meeting with him feels like running a marathon. Dopalet needs to make his interlocutor ill at ease. He waxes lyrical about a project he will have forgotten within the hour, makes promises to anyone and everyone then reneges on them. His only virtue is that he has surrounded himself with talent. But the hierarchy changes from one day to the next – this is the only thing he has in common with Fassbinder: every morning, he likes to make it known who is in and who is out of favour.

Anaïs was supposed to unearth talent from "outside the box". She quickly realised what this entailed: finding "the best" YouTube channels (translation: "channels with a million plus subscribers") and persuading them to "pitch a project" (translation: "write for free") that he found "high concept" (translation: "demonstrably commercial but shot by unpaid amateurs"). She thought she had understood the brief and had acted accordingly, but on the rare occasions she had managed to drag kids into the office, they had never sufficiently impressed the producer. Dopalet constantly parroted the line, "I don't want people I run into at the César awards every year," yet he could not bear to be dragged from the "old boys' network" he claimed to disdain. In his own world, he was a major player. He expected anyone working on the internet to fall over themselves with gratitude at the prospect of being "discovered". But the adolescent stars of YouTube have an inflated sense of themselves and don't give a flying fuck about the silver screen – the clash of egos did not go well.

For some time now, Anaïs has been feeling that she is in the hot seat. He is no longer dazzled by her. He is no longer counting on her to bring him an online Stanley Kubrick who can shoot a twenty-first century "A Clockwork Orange" for three euros fifty.

She walks down toward Tuileries métro station. There was a brief sunny spell, but already the sky is clouding over and it looks likely to rain any minute now. It feels like autumn in Paris. Anaïs takes the steps down into the métro station, surrounded by tourists speaking languages she does not recognise. In the corridor, a violinist is playing a piece by Kreisler. She slows. She studied the piece as a girl. She never managed to play it without murdering it. Her parents insisted that she study music, and her sister played piano. But Anaïs had chosen the violin and had no talent for the instrument.

She has no desire to let her parents know what had just happened. It would only upset them. They were thrilled when she got this job. They had been disappointed when she and Kevin split. They had spent seven years together. Everyone around them was waiting for the patter of tiny feet. They had assumed they had lots of time.

On the platform, she has a searing memory of what it felt like being with him. When she walked next to him. She felt complete. They were a single, solitary unity. When she comes back to reality, she feels off-balance. Since he left she bumps into things, breaks things. It is all down to this feeling. The glacial emptiness beside her. She cannot call him to tell him what has happened. This is an idea she must get used to. For some time, he has been sending her text messages, like: "Search for the light deep in your heart, I wish you every happiness in the world." And silly stuff. But mostly the kind of messages you get from a guy who has moved on. When you send things like that to the girl who was the love of your life, it means: I don't really care what happens to you. He contacts her to salve his conscience, so he can tell himself he is a good guy. She replies: "Fuck off, Noddy, you're bothering me," and it takes her a week to get over it. Now when he sends her text messages, he adds a ☺. Something he learned from his new girlfriend. Anaïs would never do such a thing. Emojis. Jesus fuck.

He left her for someone else. He never cheated on her. He told her the moment he met her. He had seemed preoccupied, he was busy framing a photograph, struggling with the clips of the Habitat frame, she had said, "Are you worried about something?" he had said, "There's something going on between me and Karine." At first Anaïs had thought it was a joke.

They had not watched "Game of Thrones" that night. They had sat, sobbing, on the sofa. She had woken up the next morning convinced that she had been mistaken. This could not be happening to them. He packed his bags that week. The new girl works in politics. With the U.M.P. It's impossible. Everything about the situation is impossible, and still it keeps happening. They are not together any more.

Anaïs opens the playlist on her phone, scrolls down to Neil Young and listens to "Big Time". She knows it makes her cry. She wants to cry. How can she forget how they were together, the promises they made each other. For years they had been twin planets in the same orbit and, overnight, gravity had shifted – they had gone their separate ways. Anaïs knew that even if he were to come back tomorrow, he would not be the man she had trustingly loved for so many years. That love is dead. She is like an exile who dreams of her home country, yet, when she can finally return, finds it unrecognisable: nothing is as she remembered it.

They had believed that their relationship was special. All lovers do. Their relationship was different. The one that could withstand anything. She had kept the apartment. The red and white checked oilcloth he had laid to protect the kitchen countertops is so worn that it is now white. She does not touch it. The freezer is still full of frozen vegetables he bought in bulk – he watched his waistline. She knows everything about him. She misses everything about him. She cannot believe that he does not miss their life together as much as she does. When life was fun – having dinner in the pizzeria opposite, going to the cinema on Sundays, going to bed early and sitting up reading, bickering over whose turn it was to get up and make a hot drink. They were happy, for fuck's sake. Why could Kevin not have honoured that?

She has seen pictures of his new girlfriend online, in her huge apartment in the eight arrondissement. A Haussmann building, high ceilings, impeccably furnished. Throw rugs over the sofa, everything exquisitely tasteful. Anaïs surveys her own place. The Ikea shelves, the stained, rickety white table they never had the money to replace. They didn't give a damn about bourgeois comforts. And yet. You're nouveau riche now, Kevin. Had he always dreamed of a double living room, crown mouldings, French doors and chic restaurants? Had he simply pretended to despise these things because they were beyond his means, or has he changed? She wondered whether he still drank Ricoré with warm milk for breakfast, or whether he drinks coffee like his new girlfriend.

Is it possible for someone to change so completely? He has become a stranger – she thinks of Kafka's *Metamorphosis* – one day, her prince charming had begun to mutate into a louse. She had thought this was something that only happened in fiction. When they had moved to Paris together, they had both assumed that Kevin would become a great painter. Anaïs wanted to work in documentaries. They loved the films of Wang Bing, Chris Marker, or Watkins and Oppenheimer . . . They did not care if they struggled financially. Their parents helped them out a little. They had had to go without most things. They abhorred consumerism. When Kevin had started writing freelance pieces about contemporary art for *Libération* it had just been a little pin money now and then. *Libé* was the sort of left-wing newspaper Serge Daney accused of being bogged down in "private conversations". Journalists treated their readers as embarrassing appendages rather than readers, writing articles that were exclusively directed at advertisers, lobbyists, friends, colleagues, editors-in-chief . . . But Kevin played the game. He was offered a job as a columnist on the film pages. She had watched as his wardrobe and his behaviour changed. He was sometimes embarrassed when she heard him introduce himself, "I work at *Libé*." He had become someone else.

He would have dinner with the bigwigs from the newspaper and would come home jubilant. The articles he was writing sounded less and less like him. And he had left her for a girl he had met at the fiftieth birthday party of a photographer he knew from the paper. Anaïs had been at the party with him. It had never even occurred to her to be wary of Karine. But ten days later, she should have suspected something when she heard Kevin say: "It's old hat, the whole left-wing/right-wing thing. The only thing that matters these days is where you stand on globalisation." How could anyone say something so bloody stupid? It is the kind of remark guys make when they are leaning towards the right. Two months later, he left. He had changed so quickly . . .

The solitude in itself is not unpleasant. It has been a long time since she has spent time on her own. She reads more. But she smiles less. There are lots of things you can do alone. Laughing is not one of them. With Kevin, she laughed all the time. Is she funny, his new girlfriend? She doesn't look like she's a laugh. Anaïs is the only girl she knows to have been dumped for an older woman. Karine is nearly forty. She's bound to have a baby straightaway.

Anaïs is also sleeping with an older woman. That's it, she's done it. She has jumped the fence. She waited out the twelve months' mourning, celebrated the anniversaries of all the things they had done together the previous year. And then it had happened. Someone else had undressed her, and she had been dying for it to happen. Her lover is stunningly beautiful. The Hyena snaps her in two with a rapturous brutality. It is magical. So magical she finds it shocking. At least she is not sleeping with another guy, so the comparison is less direct.

The Hyena is brazen. She flaunts her desire with disturbing audacity, and the effect on Anaïs is the same as if it were a man.

Anaïs feels herself being looked at with a passion that is almost predatory, and it gets all her worked up. She has come to a realisation: it is not a cock that makes a man but the impetuousness of his desire. What she finds most surprising is not that she is attracted to a woman, but that she allowed herself to emerge from her grief so soon. Later, they fucked. And since then, problem solved, all she wants is to do it again.

What is fabulous about this thing that is happening is that each wonderful moment is another step away from Kevin. A gradual amputation. Sometimes, she will make a gesture she used to make with him, or use some word she thinks of as "theirs". She feels something ripped from her. It is as though she is putting a bullet in the head of what was their love. "You were the love of my life." That past tense, like a dagger driven into her chest. She did not think it was possible to get through the days that followed. But there had been no way out. She is not the person she was before that wound. Now, she knows: every "I love you" is a dagger in the making.

This thing with the Hyena allowed her to pick herself up. She has gradually come back to life. How are they going to see each other now that she has been fired? She can't believe he just booted her out like that. It's all tied up with the graffiti incident at his place. Ever since, Dopalet has been off-kilter. With good reason. At the time, she had still been part of his inner circle. He had taken her into his confidence. One morning, he had locked himself in his office the moment he arrived. Everyone had noticed he was in a foul mood. Then he had summoned her. It was 10.00 a.m. and he was lying on the sofa holding a glass of whisky so full it might as well have been orange juice. His breathing was ragged, he was having a panic attack. Sounding like a man on his deathbed, he had said:

"Anaïs, what I'm about to say has to stay between the two of us. I can trust you, can't I? I'm being persecuted by a bunch of degenerates, I don't know what the hell started it. They came to my apartment last night and spray-painted the whole front of the building. It's grotesque . . . Grotesque! You can't begin to imagine . . ."

He wanted to avoid any scandal – Anaïs had been immediately dispatched to the scene of the crime. Dopalet had called a taxi. He needed to be sure that the painter he had hired would respect the instructions he had given about discretion. Neither he nor his wife could stay there, they were too devastated. Everything needed to be painted over by evening, but there could be no question of letting *two* painters in on the secret. Anaïs had gone, a little irritated at being treated as a general dogsbody. She had expected to find a couple of tags sprayed on the wall, nothing that warranted such an outburst.

A painter was already at work. He had covered the slogans with sheets of paper thick enough to hide them – which had meant the whole front of this magnificent building of which Dopalet occupied only one floor. Each sheet of paper she lifted revealed new accusations: "pervert" "murderer" "everyone will know" "rapist" "FUCK YOU DOPALET". She had been shaken. She had not been expecting something so outrageous. It was like a war zone. Even Anaïs, who was not personally concerned, had felt distraught. The painter, a taciturn redhead, was there to repaint the whole façade in white before a team sent by the insurers took over and finished the job. She had tried to engage him in conversation.

"Someone would really have to be twisted to do a thing like this . . . luckily, with the C.C.T.V. cameras, it shouldn't be too difficult . . ."

"Yeah, if someone was prepared to press charges."

He was not forthcoming. Anaïs asked:

"How long do you think it's going to take you?"

"I can get it done today, if I don't stop to chat."

"I'll leave you to it."

She could not simply stand there, watching him paint. She had crossed the road and gone into a bar on the corner. It was impossible to get through to Dopalet, who was in a meeting with Canal+. She did not know what she should do. Help the painter? She was hardly dressed for the task. She tried to imagine what the producer had felt when he had seen the building in this state. It had probably been someone who knew him. A madman, or some vindictive junkie bitch. He did have a habit of having affairs with girls who were into drugs . . . She had seen her fair share pass through the office. Maybe one of them had wanted revenge because he wouldn't leave his wife. It was so humiliating – whatever Dopalet had done, he did not deserve this.

The Hyena pulled up in front of the bar on her motorbike. The wave of joy Anaïs had felt when she recognised the helmet left no room for doubt: when you're this exhilarated, it's not just about the sex. For the first time, Anaïs had thought, I'm in love with her. Beaming, she had rushed to the door and thrown it open, making no attempt to hide her excitement, and got shot down in flames. The Hyena had stopped her in her tracks, her reaction had been strange: "Dopalet called me, he wants me to make sure that they've left no trace . . . Just act like we're in the office, we hardly know each other." She seemed worried that someone was watching and might find out their secret. She had come into the bar, but did not order anything, she didn't have time. She had said to

Anaïs: "You're right, there's nothing for you to do here. Go back to the office, tell Dopalet I said I'd stay here with the painter." She had sent her packing. Anaïs had felt hurt. Here it comes, the little disappointments, those moments when you take someone's hand and they shrug it off. All the things she had never experienced with Kevin, but which she well remembered from her teenage years. She didn't want a relationship flecked with little pieces of shit. But the next day, she was back at the hotel, she could not keep her distance.

Their first kiss had been in the lift at work, they were both going down, they had been circling each other for some time. The Hyena had not moved except to place her hands on her hips. The chain glittering around her wrist had held Anaïs spellbound, hypnotized by the bony protrusion at the base of her hand, her square palm, those long fingers that radiated an authority that made her feel faint. Anaïs ached to fuck so intensely it hurt. It had been so intense and so unexpected that she had felt the ground give way beneath her. They had stood, motionless, until the lift doors opened, then the Hyena had pressed the button for the top floor, the doors closed and they moved towards each other.

Ever since, they have been on the down low. In the office, the Hyena will surreptitiously slip a folded piece of paper into her handbag noting the time and place of their next tryst, and Anaïs is allowed to call only if there is a hitch, using the precise code: "I couldn't find the documents you asked me for." Secrecy probably adds to the excitement. They meet up in hotel rooms.

Her hand, when they are standing and her fingers are fucking her, her smile every time she finds Anaïs already wet, her hips shuddering convulsively, a delicious terror and that feeling when the other person comes, the profile of a delicate face resting on a pillow, in utter surrender, that enigmatic expression.

Today, the Hyena has a meeting in the Marais. She mentioned it on the phone in front of Anaïs the last time they met. Anaïs steps into a métro carriage. There is a stink of piss and sweat. A boy in a beige pullover with long curly hair is sitting on his own – everyone has moved as far away as possible. The stench is at odds with how he looks, he is quite handsome, with just a slightly hippy look about him. The other passengers look at each other but say nothing, some disgusted, others smiling, two girls are giggling hysterically, a guy wearing Converse trainers is thinking about opening a window, another holds a handkerchief to his nose and changes carriages as soon as possible. Anaïs resolves to stay. The smell is so strong she feels she might throw up.

Her iPhone is set to Shuffle, she is listening to Mary J. Blige, "No More Drama", and she pictures Dopalet's secretary, Audrey, with tears in her eyes – she wasn't faking it, she was genuinely devastated. She was the only one in the whole team to show even a glimmer of empathy. All the others disappeared as soon as they heard she had been asked to clear her desk. As Audrey unlocked the storage cupboard and stowed Anaïs' boxes, promising to send them by courier tomorrow, she whispered not to worry about compensation. "He's like that. But he makes up for it with the severance package. He's generous. He doesn't want to be dragged in front of an industrial tribunal. And he knows he's a monster."

Dopalet would sometimes call her at 11.00 p.m. and demand that she join him for a drink with him because he needed to talk. He knew that she lived alone. She would get dressed again, put on her make-up, jump in the cab he had sent, and go to meet him. She would listen to him for hours. He never asked how she was.

She was grateful that he never insisted when she declined his offer to "come for one last drink in a club". They both knew what sort of club he had in mind, she would shake her head and smile and he would let her go. He had other girls for that in his little black book. She did not have to worry about him on that score. She would get to bed at two in the morning, shattered, and always remembered to set her alarm for 6.00 a.m. so she had time to prepare before heading in to the office.

She gets off the métro at Saint-Paul. She will walk past HellBabe. She could send a text message to say she is on her way. But the Hyena does not like people using her mobile number for anything outside work.

AS SHE ARRIVES AT THE RUE VIEILLE-DU-TEMPLE, GAËLLE FEELS like a lightbulb on its last legs, when it starts to sputter to warn that it is about to fail. She has spent the whole morning online trying to order a new mobile phone. Just to access her invoices, she would have needed to remember her code, or at least the email address she used when she first signed up. She feels as though she spends her whole life creating online profiles – she can never remember her passwords. Then, when she wanted to pay, they sent a code to her mobile – when the whole reason she needed a new phone was because the battery in the old one was dead. And there seemed to be no number she could call to extricate herself from this catch-22 situation. From that point, everything became preposterously complicated. By the time she managed to access the code, the transaction had been cancelled. She had had to start all over again. To make matters worse, the prices listed on the website came with so many different tariffs and criteria that it was impossible to know how much the new phone was going to cost. In despair, she started an online chat with an advisor. It turned out to be a chatbot, every answer she got was well wide of the mark, it seemed she was incapable of asking the right questions. In the end, she had cancelled her contract, something that penalised no-one but her. It was at this point that a demented dyslexic took over from the chatbot – the guy, or girl, refused to spell any word of more than two letters according to correct usage. Deciphering the abstruse messages demanded a level of concentration that was beyond her. The dyslexic demanded that she schedule a telephone conversation in a specific three-hour window the following day. On a landline. She doesn't have a landline. She gave up. Besides, she knows the routine, they would have insisted on sending the new telephone to her home: no-one wants to have to deal with the postal system, which effectively means lunatic courier services who claim you weren't home when in fact they never rang the doorbell, who leave your package at the other end of Paris in some shop that, when you finally trek all the way there to collect it, turns out to be closed. Everything has become so complicated. She'll do without a mobile phone.

The Hyena has arranged to meet her in the Marais. The old cow wants to talk. Gaëlle is a little early, so she stops for a burger. She wants red meat. Not because she likes it, but because she is convinced that she needs to eat it, for the iron content, just after she's had her period. They last for seven days and she loses so much blood it is like she is bleeding to death. She has a 21-day cycle. It's a nightmare. She avoids sitting down in other people's houses, she has already ruined several sofas. The third millennium, and she is still using the same sanitary towels her mother used at her age. They stick to her, it feels like walking around with a badly-fitting nappy between her legs, but given the efficacy of tampons, she has no choice: she has to use both. Besides, by the time she works out how to insert tampons correctly, she will have hit menopause. And her aim always seems to be off when she applies sanitary towels – they always leak blood on one side. If guys had periods, the industry would have long since come up with a high-tech solution to protection, some stylish, minimalist and elegant gadget you insert on your first day and excrete on your last. And Big Pharma would have devised a decent drug for dealing with premenstrual cramps. Men wouldn't be expected to slosh around like this, obviously. They are capable of littering outer space with recon satellites, but when it comes to P.M.T. symptoms, they come up with fuck all.

She lifts the bun from her burger and slathers it with ketchup and mayonnaise to disguise the taste. Otherwise it tastes like dead bodies. She doesn't want to know about the abattoirs where the meat is produced. Online, whenever she sees a photo of caged chickens or pigs being bred for food, she closes the window. The burger joint is cosy, like a retro American diner, but the food is revolting. The frozen fries have been dusted with some kind of herb that tastes so strange it must also have been frozen. She drinks her Coke and pushes away the plate. She leaves a generous tip, because she has often worked as a waitress, and knows they are not to blame because some con artist makes disgusting food.

The Hyena is already sitting on the café terrace when Gaëlle arrives. They have known each other for more than twenty years. Gaëlle talks about protest marches. It's either that or the shitty weather, this year.

"Did you go on any of the demos for gay marriage?"

"Not my thing."

"My bae didn't give me the choice, I went on the first march with her. It was a beautiful day. We sent off from Bastille. I made it as far as Hôtel-de-Ville, then sat on a café terrace and watched people march past."

"You need to watch your girlfriend. It starts out with one demo and you end up chained to a railing of some embassy on hunger strike."

"She's young. She's hot-headed. I couldn't bring myself to say that I didn't give a fuck about going on a demo. I mean, I get that she cares . . . You can't imagine the number of people who've felt the need to tells us that they're against gay marriage. And not just right-wing Catholics, either. Socialists these days are completely shameless . . ."

"I've never met anyone who's opposed."

"Because they wouldn't dare talk to you about it."

"I'd rather they said nothing. Personally, I'm opposed to gay marriage, but if I hear a hetero say that, I'd lynch the fucker."

"You're against it?"

"Marriage? Of course I am."

"I get you. Our generation, we're dykes, real dykes, we've suffered for it and we don't want to be like fucking straights."

"It's not like that . . . adoption, test-tube babies, marriage – I'm opposed to everything for everyone. I'm in favour of sterilising the entire population at puberty. Seven billion of us. You don't think maybe that's enough? We need to slow things down and sharpish. I see people with strollers, I look at their faces, and I think: but why? What do you think you're doing by reproducing? Stop being so fucking arrogant, the world doesn't need your third-rate genes. Take up painting if you need a hobby, but don't annoy us with your offspring. If I had my way, I'd have them all rounded up in a stadium: vasectomy, hysterectomy and you can all head home . . . Seven billion, and still they're infesting the planet . . . The day they have a demonstration for the sterilisation of humankind, I'll be there, and I won't be sitting on a café terrace, I can tell you . . ."

"Fuck it, you're right. My girlfriend's too reformist. I've allowed her to influence me. It's really good to see you, it's like having a booster shot."

*

Despite the fine drizzle wetting the toes of their boots, they stay out on the terrace smoking cigarettes. They both order glasses of muscatel from Alsace. Gaëlle likes the Marais. The sunlight gilding the ancient stones, the ersatz atmosphere – the shops are so chic, the whole neighbourhood looks like a film set. She loves the rich streets, the girls walking hand in hand – although in the past decade the area has becomes overrun by families and tourists, it's still the place to see the prettiest dykes in Paris. She likes to see the happy boys – nowhere has she ever seen guys look so happy. And it's not just because they're young, rich and handsome, otherwise they would be just as happy in the sixteenth arrondissement, it's because they're queers, and you only have to look at them to know that queers are more fulfilled than other guys.

But she loves all of Paris, from the Porte de la Chapelle all the way to Montmartre. She likes the succession of contradictory layers, the intersections and the brusque shifts. Sometimes, you only have to cross two streets to be in a completely different neighbourhood, at other times, you have to cross the no-man's-land of zones that have no identity. She loves the melting pot of tourists, riffraff, Chinese, hicks, culture vultures, fashionistas, bankers and checkout girls – they feel at home while at the same time living in a city that is not quite the same yet not quite different. Someday, people will think of the cosmopolitan city of Paris at the dawn of the third millennium as a crazy Babylon, and find it difficult to imagine that so many different people managed to live together in peace. Beardy geeks and right-wing queers, Jewish drug dealers, Sorbonne supermodels, bohemian Americans and reactionary junkies . . . All forms of expression are possible, and she is a part of this mosaic. Even if she never stops complaining that everything is changing and always for the worse, she still feels at home in this convoluted city.

Being with the Hyena changes Gaëlle's mood. As it does whenever they meet up. Not long ago, she had been furious with the Hyena for asking her to track down Vernon before disappearing into thin air as soon as he'd been found. Gaëlle got into serious shit with Kiko at the time, and was pissed off at getting herself into a sticky situation for nothing. But this is not the first time that the Hyena has got her into hot water, nor the last time she will forgive her. Besides, things have changed since. Kiko tracked down Subutex and, instead of smashing his face in, he's been sucked in just like he was before.

There was a time when the Hyena got mixed up in seriously shady stuff, when she was a real player. She is going downhill. She doesn't seem to give a shit. Gaëlle has rarely met anyone with such contempt for what other people think. She has always been that way, so arrogant that you can't help but respect her.

She cuts her own hair, and it shows, and it's a domestic dye-job too. The teeth are healthy, the eyes disdainful. In fact, she has lost everything except her haughtiness. The Hyena is staring at her glass of wine. She is thinking. Gaëlle leaves her to it. She knows exactly what she wants to talk about, what everyone is talking about this season: Vernon. Has she seen him at Rosa Bonheur recently, has she heard anything, that kind of thing . . . What Gaëlle doesn't get is why the Hyena has risen to the bait too. What is Subutex doing to these people to hold them in thrall? He's a nice enough guy, but he's in a sorry fucking state . . . Gaëlle has always hated dog-on-a-string punks. She doesn't like poor personal hygiene, people who let themselves go and she refuses on principle to talk to anyone with a beard. But the Hyena kicks the ball into touch:

"So this girlfriend of yours, when she's not on demos, what's she like?"

"Very pretty, a serious babe. She's twenty-five years younger than me. Broadly speaking, she is looking forward and I'm looking back."

"And it doesn't bother her, being with a babushka?"

"I'm a seriously good fuck. That makes up for it."

The Hyena smiles. This is their kind of humour. They have been coming out with the same jokes for decades now. Gaëlle drains her glass, looks around for the waitress and says:

"So you wanted to see me to ask about my love life?"

"I wanted to do a general debrief. We haven't seen each other in an age. I hear you're spending a lot of time at Rosa Bonheur these days?"

"Yeah, I'm helping out Zoudou when she organises parties. And there are a lot of them. But I've heard you've been spending a lot of time in the park too? You should pop in more often . . ."

"Do you hear much gossip about Vernon at Rosa's?"

So this is what she wants to know. Gaëlle was right. She doesn't understand this whole thing about Vernon. For a start, how did he manage to wind up living on the streets? And so quickly. O.K., granted, he got kicked out of his apartment. There's an economic crisis, the guy's not as young as he was, he's not in touch with his family. But for fuck's sake, twenty years running a record shop leaves you with enough contacts to ensure you don't have to sleep on the streets for three months at least . . . and how does a guy who's likeable enough but a bit short of change when it comes to charisma turn himself into the messiah of the Buttes-Chaumont? The guy is homeless, stinks of sweat and wears trailer trash boots, but everyone treats him like he's baby Jesus if he'd skipped the bit with the cross, he's surrounded by dozens of Magi who bring him gifts every day. Vernon chooses a tree, sits under it, and people come to see him. Of course she hears about him at Rosa Bonheur. He's pretty much all anybody talks about. She went and had a look at his merry band. Shallow straight guys out for a good time. Even Kiko has been bitten by the bug. When he found out that Subutex was hanging around in the park, Gaëlle watched him march off with that grim I'm-going-to-rearrange-your-fucking-face-maybe-that'll-teach-you-to-walk-off-with-my-stash-of-blow look . . . and he had come back the following day and spent the next three weeks listening to Jethro Tull. No parties, no booty calls, nothing but headphones, music and drugs. He had not gone to work. Something that was utterly unheard of. He had started seriously raving with a vengeance – about how he believed that God would soon exist, he would be the sum of all logarithms, that he was the only one who could save the planet and humankind – and how it was important to come up with software, the kind that would teach people how to live in a functional community. As far as Gaëlle is concerned, when urban hipsters start dabbling in spirituality, you know shit's going to get real. Kiko emerged from his three-week retreat with a grand project: travelling around Latin America. Reading between the lines, it sounded like the guy wanted to get his cocaine from the source. And why not, it was possible to imagine that this was his one true passion. But the idea of getting photos from Guatemala of Kiko sitting on a llama wearing a Peruvian *chullo* just depressed Gaëlle. She has decided that if Kiko is found washing his clothes in the rivers of Chiapas, she's going to rock up at the Buttes Chaumont and torch the whole place. She's been living rent-free with this guy for years, he's always been a rabid neoliberal, it pisses her off to see someone fuck up his whole worldview. Meanwhile, Kiko got a grip, went back to work and now only talks about Subutex late at night. He says he is planning for his trip. She knows from experience that the more hard-bitten people think they are, the more likely they are to fall for happy-clappy new age shit – a cynic is just a frustrated romantic – but even so, this was a shock. She hopes he'll forget this shit and go back to how he used to be. In the meantime, he has come to Rosa Bonheur twice to listen to Vernon spin a set. And it really is something. Even Gaëlle is prepared to admit it. It was Mimi who first had the idea. Basically, it was a way of giving him some cash-in-hand work without it looking like charity. But it had been a huge success. He has already done two. Someone needs to get him to shower beforehand, but aside from that, he's pretty dope. Spinning discs has always been his thing.

When Vernon gets behind the decks at Rosa Bonheur, they close the bar. They say it's a private party, that it's a choir rehearsal, just so they can allow the initiates to commune in private. Even Gaëlle, who is immune to all forms of sentimentality, and especially to mysticism, has to admit that *something happens.* Vernon has a gift for creating a dynamic set. At the start of the evening, she will be sitting in a corner, listening to him spin, bitching that he's not exactly on fleek, but by the fifth track, she's not so high and mighty. She's out on the floor, she's pumping. It's collective, it's a madness, it would be stupid to deny it. And she's not dancing to prove that she can still twerk it at her age, her hips are pumping like she's on an M.D.M.A. come-up, except she hasn't taken anything, she starts to feel the music thrill through her fingers, relax her neck, and all around are bodies in the same state – she's dancing and she's checked her brain at the door, it makes her sick to admit it, so next morning, she thinks about something else, but she dances to feel vertical, the soles of her feet connected to the ground and she is completely out of it, shooting stars tumble through her belly as though they've always been there, she dances and thinks about the dead, she dances with them, she dances thinking about everything that has vanished and yet still exists, unscathed, as easy to access as though she had opened a book and images, sounds, smells and every pore of skin poured out, she dances among the others and she acknowledges their presence, there is a bond that connects them all, just being together they are happy with that irrational joy of someone who has only just fallen in love, except that there are thirty of them and, without even paying attention, she is somehow connected to each and every one, they are a single undulating body and are happy simply to be there. It is impossible to say what triggers it. She refuses to go into raptures and claim that Vernon is touched by some kind of genius – she is resistant to such confusion. But she has to accept that she has never danced like this.

The Hyena finally comes to the point:

"So what's the word down at the bar, I mean, you're there all the time . . . about this whole thing with Subutex and the people around him?"

"What do you want to know?"

"I'm just keeping informed."

"And why should I help you?"

"Because you love me."

"Sorry, I've got nothing for you. He's done two private parties as D.J., all his friends came. And they were good. I don't understand what people see in him, but when it comes to spinning a set, he's the man. He's the enigma of the decade, that guy. Look, it's not like it's the first phenomenon where you're thinking, how does this work. If you want me to be more specific, I might be able to give you some information . . . Why are you still so interested in the guy?"

The Hyena flashes her pirate smile. The one that means she knows things that she cannot talk about. It is a beautiful smile. She would obviously like to ask more questions, but a pretty brunette with a strong chin is heading towards their table sporting a phony look of surprise. She's a fine specimen, though there is something Plain Jane about her. When she reaches them, she feigns astonishment when it's obvious she spotted them a hundred metres back. Everything about her exudes that famous joy of femininity, an accretion of details that scream: "It's such fun playing the airhead!" The fluorescent slimline watch that says she's *quirky*, the sausage colour nail polish because she read in a magazine that it's *trendy*, the overpowering perfume, the threaded eyebrows, this season's gloss on her pouty lips . . . "Hey, what are you doing here . . . ?" It goes without saying that as soon as she opens her mouth, she has a shrill, grating, little girl's voice. The Hyena looks at her and smiles, but doesn't invite her to sit down. "Anaïs, this is Gaëlle . . ."

It takes Gaëlle only a second to realise that they are sleeping together. Otherwise, the Hyena would not be coming on all George Clooney.

"I've been fired."

"By Dopalet?"

"Just now. Like a piece of shit. It's never happened to me before. It's terrible."

"Because?"

"I didn't really understand. He fired me the same way he hired me, I suppose: on a whim. So I'm free for coffee. Mind if I join you?"

"I'm so sorry for you, Anaïs, we'll talk about it later. I was just about to leave."

Anaïs swallows hard. She takes it like a slap in the face, but feels obliged to put on a good show. She surreptitiously glances at Gaëlle, wondering whether she is the reason for this chilly welcome. The Hyena insists:

"I'm already running late for a meeting. But if you're free tonight, I'll give you a call and you can tell me all about it."

"You'll deign to use your phone for me, now?"

The pretty brunette is suddenly brittle. She could not hold it in. It suits her better than being nice, Gaëlle thinks, and suddenly finds her more interesting. It has to be said that the Hyena went too far – though she knows nothing about their relationship, you don't sleep with a girl and then tell her you're late for a meeting when she says she's just been fired . . . Gaëlle feels the whole situation is unfair, she gives Anaïs a wink and gestures to the empty chair next to her:

"Take a seat anyway. I'm not in any rush."

The Hyena looks daggers at her. They have already stolen or borrowed each other's girlfriends once or twice. Hardly surprising, given how long they've known each other . . . Gaëlle gives her sunniest, sluttiest smile – get over it, girlfriend, it's one of the unwritten rules everyone agrees on – if you treat your lover like dirt, I've got every right to look out for her . . . Besides, there was no mention of leaving before the girl showed up. And she has every intention of ordering a second glass.

Exasperated, the Hyena grabs her cigarette lighter and her notes from the table, her fingers are long and slender, her gestures efficient, she fumbles in the pocket of her jacket for money – she is bothered by the idea of leaving the two of them alone.

"I'm heading towards République if you want to walk with me?"

"Not if you're really in a hurry. I haven't finished my drink and mademoiselle hasn't had a chance to order yet."

The Hyena is incandescent. Before she walks away, she says: "Anaïs, can I come round and see you this evening?" and Gaëlle cannot help thinking – I think she'll be in my bed, darling. Just for the fun. Nor does she feel that this would generate too much tension. When you really care about a girl, you don't treat her like that. Gaëlle has never been monogamous. That sort of thing is reserved for ugly people.

Anaïs sits down. She is shattered. She has abandoned any attempt to feign good humour. Gaëlle offers a little compassion, she has always been a sucker for victims:

"She's always been uncouth. It's part of her persona. Don't take it personally."

"Who are you talking about?"

"The Hyena, who did you think I meant? You're white as a sheet. Do you want me to order a whiskey for you?"

"We hardly know each other . . . I just ran into her here by accident. If I'm pale it's probably low blood sugar . . . actually, yes, thank you, I would like a drink."

"Honey, I've got eyes in my eyes, she's your lover and she behaved atrociously. Don't hold it against her, she's a bit touched. What do you do for a living?"

"I was a talent scout for a production company."

"Did you enjoy it?"

"Not really, no."

"Maybe it's not such a bad day after all, then."

Anaïs is on the verge of tears, she smiles as best she can.

"I'm sorry. I was fine until just now, I think it's talking about it, I've only just realised . . . I'm sorry, but . . ."

Gaëlle orders; she has always been attracted to a woman in tears. She can't help it, it's her nature. She is a Scorpio. You can't argue with astrology. Anaïs downs the whisky with a certain panache, then heaves a deep sigh.

"Better now?" Gaëlle says.

"Getting there. So do you know the Hyena well?"

"We served in Vietnam together . . . in a manner of speaking. But I can't see what a girl like you sees in her."

"A girl like me?"

"You know what I mean. Is she your first girlfriend, or have you been bi for a while?"

No point using kid gloves, otherwise her chances of reeling the girl in by tonight are slim. She needs to steer the conversation round to Anaïs and forget all about the Hyena. But Anaïs is more determined than she seems at first glance. She is not easily flustered. "I don't know what you're talking about," she says again and begins to talk about the job from which she has just been fired. Gaëlle has little patience for conversations about work. It occurs to her to bring Anaïs along to Rosa Bonheur. That way, if she doesn't get anywhere with her, there will still be time to have cocktails with her girlfriends.

They cross the roadworks at the place de la République, heading for métro line 11. Anaïs keeps prattling all the way to Pyrénées. Gaëlle listens inattentively. She is no longer sure she wants to bed the girl, she needs another drink to review the question. There are roadworks on the corner of the avenue Simon Bolivar. If it's not a new bank branch opening, it's bound to be a shop selling sunglasses or an estate agent. It's been a long time since anyone opened anything else. Along the avenue, trees grow, protected by metal girdles, the areas between the trunks are littered with cigarette butts and dried dogshit. The pavement is strewn with gravel, they pass an upturned bathtub someone has attacked with a hammer to rip out the pipes, flecks of ash and white porcelain are scattered all around.

The roadworks stretch all the way into the park, some of them blocked by hulking yellow diggers that look as though they are shipwrecked in the mud. The rain starts up again just as they reach Rosa Bonheur. Little Céleste is behind the bar, chattering away to her friend Aïcha. Gaëlle waits for her to finish, thinking she will talk to her about a tattoo – she wants an Erzulie Dantor *vévé* on her forearm. It's something she saw online – a quadrille heart pierced by a dagger. The website said that Erzulie Dantor is the goddess of lesbians and whores, and the idea appealed to her, but it's a voodoo symbol and, although Gaëlle doesn't believe in anything, she wonders whether it is a good idea. Céleste is a good inker. And she's pretty, too. Gaëlle likes the idea of being locked in her tattoo parlour with her.

Anaïs comes back from the toilets. Either she's a lightweight who gets drunk on a single whisky, or this is her way of dealing with the anxiety of her encounter with the Hyena: she does not stop talking. She manages a five-minute free-form solo about the joys of the Dyson hand dryer which she "adores" because it really gets your hands dry, and she "adores" the feeling of the hot air pushing against her palms. Gaëlle loathes this sort of conversation, it's like people thinking they are hipsters because they talk about the temperature of the milk their pour on their cereal, it's tedious.

Céleste is taking her time about serving them. Gaëlle gives her five minutes. If she has to get up to order her J.D., she is going to initiate a campaign of being very crabby. Young women these days, they have to have everything spelled out for them, especially that they are being paid to work.

But Céleste's expression suddenly changes. At first, there is a flash of terror in her eyes. Aïcha, who is sitting with her back to the door, turns around to follow her gaze and immediately stiffens and, skipping the box marked terror, heads straight for blind rage. The object of their sudden mood change is a short little man. As nondescript as a glass of lukewarm water. He is drenched, but seems stupidly happy to see them, he bounds towards them enthusiastically. Aïcha stops him in his tracks: "What the fuck are you doing here?", her tone arrogant and menacing. Anaïs immediately intervenes, as though it were her responsibility to protect him.

"Remember me? We bumped into each other at the office a couple of hours ago?"

"I followed you. I didn't dare approach you. I'm the son of Laurent Dopalet. The way he treated you made me feel sick."

"You've followed me all the way from the office?"

"I needed to talk to you. It was harrowing, what I witnessed."

Without troubling to explain further, he lays a hand on Anaïs' forearm, urging her to be patient and, turning to Céleste, says reassuringly:

"I wasn't expecting to see you here, don't worry, I won't say anything to anyone."

To which Aïcha immediately responds:

"Maybe I'll just smash your face in as a little precaution – you won't be able to say anything to anyone when I'm finished."

On the off chance, Gaëlle steps around the bar and calls the Hyena from the landline – "You walked off with my lighter. I'm at Rosa Bonheur. I need to see you right now." She has a feeling that this is precisely the sort of thing her old friend had in mind when she nonchalantly asked whether she heard "much gossip about Vernon at Rosa's".

"YOU SHOULDN'T HAVE HURT MY MOTHER. EVEN IF SHE WAS A whore."

"I guess you thought you could kill her and get away with it?"

"No, he didn't *think* he could, he *knew* he could."

Laurent Dopalet has no idea how they got the code to the private lift that leads directly to his apartment. He never gives it to anyone – usually, callers press the buzzer on the intercom and he screens them on the video monitor. He is even wary of couriers, he would rather go downstairs than allow them in. And these women didn't even check to see whether he is alone in the apartment, it is as though they knew.

Dopalet was not expecting visitors so, the first time he heard the buzzer, he decided to ignore it. But when they buzzed again, he thought, I'm going to look like a complete idiot if it's the guy next door with an urgent message. So he opened the door to find a pretty little redhead who had begged him to let her in, claiming she lived downstairs but had locked herself out and the battery on her mobile was dead, could she use his phone? His immediate reaction had been, what a pain in the arse, but he believed her and let her in. As she stepped inside, his first thought was that she had curves in all the right places; it was at this point that the Muslim mastodon with her had shoved him back into his own apartment.

The situation is so violent that he is wondering whether he has been teleported to some distant planet. His mind refuses to accept the fact that the two girls have locked the door behind them and pocketed the key. The aggressive one, the one in the hijab, is gripping the back of his neck, she is incredibly strong. The other girl is glaring at him hatefully, standing so close that he recognises her perfume – Chance, by Chanel, his daughter has been wearing it since she turned twenty. He always remembers to buy her a bottle when he is passing through the duty free section of the airport.

He is so terrified, he cannot move. He had a premonition about this some time ago, and every time he did a tarot reading about Bleach, it was the same: destruction and turmoil. He is convinced that this is where it all began. He knew he needed to get his hands on those tapes. He had a premonition the moment he first heard about this "testament". That deranged singer, that odious piece of vermin had accused him before doing away with himself . . . The girl wearing hijab pushes his chin back and begins again:

"So where is it now, your fat, fuck-off bourgeois impunity?"

It seemed clear that he could dismiss the classic robbery scenario that had flashed through his mind when they shoved him into his apartment. And the idea of offering them money to let him go seems deeply misplaced. Despite his maxim: "Everyone can be bought, you just need to know how much to offer" . . . He can see now that there is a limit to such axiomatic truths. He is petrified, but his brain is still working as though nothing terrible were happening. Some part of him is observing the situation. Pictures come flooding back to him, images that idiot Anaïs had shown him of violent girls in the *banlieue*. She had thought he might find it interesting. But all the girls were pig ugly, it didn't push his buttons. She was a stupid cow, that assistant of his. She scammed him. Now he has violent girls right here in his apartment. The potato-head Muslim is going to strangle him if she keeps this up. She is staring at him with a vicious glee that does not bode well, and however much he asks, "what the hell are you talking about?", trying to sound as respectable as possible, she does not answer, but like a dangerous psycho she simply repeats:

"I know what you did."

O.K. Fast Forward. Dopalet is concentrating on breathing, out of the corner of his eye he can see the other girl wandering around the living room, admiring the furniture. He tries to beg. He knows that pity can disarm as well as disgust. He stammers:

"But I don't have the first idea what you're talking about."

"I'm talking about my mother. Vodka Satana."

He feels like saying, "Sorry, honey, but I can't help it that your mother was a whore." He can understand how that might be difficult to live with. But as they say: he can't carry the weight of the whole world on his shoulders. In a gentle voice, he says:

"Satana was your mother?"

If she's prepared to tell him her name and has not tried to hide her face, it can only be because they plan to kill him. He imagines his obituary: "Brutally murdered in his own home by two jihadists" and the thought is so absurd that he feels a desperate energy shudder through his body. He has to save his skin. Collect his thoughts. He cannot allow himself to be overcome by fear. He says:

"I don't get it. I knew your mother well. I did everything I could to help her. We were friends. What do you want from me?"

Terror makes him sound convincing. It is not hard for him to sound sincere. He didn't kill her. It's way more complicated. That said, Satana was one hell of a thorn in his side. He had been furious with her. She had insulted him, threatened him. But things had been good, in the beginning. She had an extraordinary charm, the body of an angel, and she loved to party. Dopalet is a dom, and she appreciated having a man who knew how to treat her with a firm hand. They saw a lot of each other. For months, he would call her whenever he was at a loose end. He had even taken her to the Cannes festival one year. He was proud to be seen with her, especially in more libertine circles. He liked being the sort of man who could have such a girl as his partner. And can share her around, if he so chooses. She was always up for it. She loved sex, she had no taboos. But she had taken a wrong turn when it came to her drug consumption. From recreational, her substance abuse had increased until it was embarrassing. He had tapered off his calls. She had felt hurt. She had probably fallen in love with him. She couldn't bear the idea of him being distant. She had become impossible. By now, she wasn't right in the head. At first he would help her out, give her a gram so as not to seem rude, he would have a quick fumble before telling her to leave. But she said he had forced her to do things against her will and she was going to expose him. He was too much of a gentleman to say, "I remember watching you drain the balls of every stiff prick at Les Chandelles, you were much too enthusiastic for anyone to think you were being forced." At the time, the girl had been insatiable, anywhere you could stick it, she was happy to take it. But after Satana went around the twist, there was no way of bringing her back. She started hounding him. She got it into her head to talk to a friend in the media, give him a list of the people she'd slept with, and all the gory details. This was a decade ago, years before Strauss-Kahn, people were not so defensive, but even so . . . He had felt obliged to warn some of his more libertine friends that Satana kept saying she was going to talk. For some of them, it was the sort of scandal to bc avoided at all costs. He was furious. He had thought he could trust her, had introduced her to important people, she had done well out of it. Now here she was, turning on them, making up sleazy stories. She was completely off her head. She had no idea of the gravity of the threats she was making. Certain situations necessitate extraordinary solutions, there are brilliant careers that cannot be derailed over some vulgar sex scandal. He warned her. She persisted. She left him no room to manoeuvre: he had to let his friends know what was happening. But, honestly, when some minor bigwig had said, "alright, then, she's left us no choice," he had not understood. Perhaps he had sensed that things might go too far. He had thought they might ask some Chinese gangster to break her leg, so what, she might have a little trouble dancing. But she had to be made to see reason: she had to leave them in peace. When they had asked him to arrange to meet Vodka Satana, he did so, and when he saw the suave playboy they had sent to chat her up and persuade her to go to another party, he had felt reassured: hardly what he would call a punishment . . . She had been found dead the next morning. Accidental overdose or suicide. There was nothing to prove it was anything other than a terrible coincidence. He had met with some of the friends involved, in Normandy, some weeks later and they had not mentioned her death. Poor kid, when you think about it . . . but what happened was bound to happen. If someone did palm her off with contaminated dope, that's sickening. But she was a car crash waiting to happen, it was just a matter of time. He had not done anything.

Her daughter is Muslim. In different circumstances, he might find this deliciously ironic. But right now, her teeth are chattering only millimetres from his mouth, compulsively repeating, "I'm going to rip your tongue out" and he urgently needs to find some way of making her understand: none of this is his fault.

Jesus Christ, Satana is managing to make his life hell even from beyond the grave. He would have been better off going and getting a prescription for potassium bromide the day he first succumbed to her charms. Because after she was dead, he had had to deal with that fucker Bleach. He had kept it up for years, his little campaign of harassment. Dopalet changed his phone number, his fax, his email address, but the little shit always found a way to contact him. And it would start all over again. The same threats, the same bullshit. Over time, it started driving him insane.

Images of Vodka Satana flicker through his mind. He didn't kill her. But he was turned on by the way she used to debase herself. He's a man, is that a crime? He liked the way she pretended butter wouldn't melt in her mouth and, at the end of the evening, he would have to persuade her to flash her tits for his dinner guests. It was part of the game, urging her to do things and watching her give in. Coaxing such a beautiful woman to do these things for a guy like him made him feel powerful. There was a dark side to it. There always is with sex. In a pleading voice, he says:

"How could you think I killed her? Just give me a chance to explain . . . We were friends, why would I have done anything to hurt her? Are you the one who's been persecuting me for weeks? This is all a misunderstanding, I swear . . . I didn't do anything wrong. I loved your mother. I don't know what you want from me . . ."

Alex Bleach. That bastard. Not honourable enough to speak out, not clever enough to capitalise on what he thought he knew. If he had been smarter, he would have taken up the offer of an inordinately well paid starring role in a rom-com with the actress of his choice naked in every other scene. Everyone in Dopalet's inner circle agreed: keeping a famous singer quiet takes tact. It was tacitly agreed that they would come to an arrangement: Dopalet told him to calm down, that the cachet he could offer was worth considering. But the little shit had neither common sense nor manners – he had hurled insults, had even mocked him. The producer had laughed when Bleach started insulting him about the size of his cock – which according to Vodka Satana was considerably smaller than average. Did the dumb nigger really think he was the first person to point out Dopalet was hung like a squirrel . . . ? But, all the same, he had not appreciated the remark. After all, he had done nothing wrong, there was no reason he should allow himself to be humiliated by this arsehole. And Bleach had continued to stalk him. Unless you've experienced it, it's impossible to imagine the torture involved. Tensing up every time you answer the phone, worrying every time you open an email that it will be abusive, constantly checking before you leave home in the morning, because sometimes that fucker Bleach would be standing, arms folded, next to the car that had been sent for him. As soon as they realised that Bleach was not interested in them, and blamed Dopalet for everything, they had left him to deal with it. He had had his revenge. He had met the Hyena and, though it had cost him an arm and a leg, it was now impossible to Google the name Alex Bleach without stumbling on pages of sleazy stories. It had done Dopalet a world of good. That was all that he needed to do. Bleach shut up. The dumb bastard. He had celebrated the day he heard the guy was dead. What a relief. He had not been able to stop himself, he had spent two whole days with a pack of Kleenex, talking to anyone and everyone. Every time he said, "Such a shame", he felt fireworks in his chest. Finally rid of that vermin. Free at last. So, when he had seen his apartment building sprayed with insults a few months later, he had gone apeshit. It was starting all over again.

He can sense that these girls have a weakness. They cannot be completely sure. They know nothing of what actually happened. He is innocent. Not exactly snow white, but not guilty of what they're accusing him of. They need to realise that. The girl in the hijab grabs him under the arms, forces him to his feet and slams him against the wall. He feels weak and feeble, a baby seal in the paws of a polar bear. He is losing track of his thoughts. He suffers a brief syncope. A black veil descends. They don't give a shit.

"I bet you haven't given much thought to my mother since you killed her. But after this, you'll think about her every day."

"At least tell me what put this idea into your head? For God's sake, I'm trying to understand!"

How old would she have been when it happened? Satana never mentioned that she had a daughter. Or maybe he wasn't listening. She certainly didn't have custody, that he does know. She didn't really have a home. She was a lost soul. A complete wreck by the end. It's such a shame, beautiful girl like that . . . He goes all-in:

"You're making a mistake. She wasn't well, but it had nothing to do with me. She got involved with that singer, Alex Bleach, and he fucked her up. I tried so hard to convince her to leave the guy. He humiliated her, beat her, gave her drugs, he treated her like scum . . ."

The pressure on his arm relaxes for a split second. She is wavering. He presses his advantage:

"Bleach was a bastard. He hated me for trying to take Satana away from him. I was the only person who never gave up on her. She was completely under his control, he destroyed her. She used to phone me up, it was tragic, he threatened her with a knife, broke her ribs, but she refused to press charges. I put her up in my spare room more than once. He was the one who got her onto smack. He was the one who gave her the fatal dose. I'm sorry to have to tell you this. Read the results of the autopsy. I did. It was an overdose. When she was dying in his arms, he didn't call an ambulance. He panicked. He left her there, in the hotel where they'd been staying, it was hours before the paramedics were tipped off by an anonymous call. He never forgave himself. Could she have been saved if he had called earlier? But all he could think about was the fallout for his career . . ."

"How do you know this? No-one ever said she was taking heroin . . ."

"Because he told me. I spent hours talking to him. In the early days. But you can't reason with a lunatic. He made my life a living hell. He tormented me for years."

"Why you?"

"Because I was the one who tried to save her. The one who did what he couldn't do."

He is still in the same position, arms wrenched behind his back, face pressed against the wall. But the girls are listening to him. There are a few little white lies in the story he's telling, they would be easily exposed. But it would take them some time to check. The version they would find on the internet would not be very different. If they use Google, he's doesn't have to worry, they'll come across the stories he paid the Hyena to spread: alleged rape, harassment, a violent, dangerous, homophobe. He drives the nail home:

"He was eaten up by guilt. He took it out on me. I became his punchbag."

"I don't believe a word you're saying."

"Maybe, but it's the truth."

"I'm going to trust my instincts: he told me you were a liar."

Behind his back, he hears the other girl open her bag and take out something. He is convinced he can persuade them to leave him alone. They don't trust Bleach any more than they do him: they haven't said a word in his defence.

"So I'm the handy scapegoat? I'm convenient? And obviously, since I'm rich, I can't possibly be innocent – so you can just destroy my life without worrying? You can burst into my apartment, smash things, torture me, insult me . . . But it doesn't matter, I'm rich, I'm paying for all the other rich guys, after all we're interchangeable, is that what this is about?"

"No, no. This is about the fact that my mother is dead. I choose to believe that things could have been different for her. That I might have had a chance to know her."

She grabs him and drags him to a kitchen chair and forces him to straddle it, facing the back. The other girl is waiting, she has ropes. They tie his hands behind his back. They have a powerful grip and enough common sense to hobble his ankles, his knees, his waist and his arms. It is like being in a straitjacket. Blood trickles from the fingers of Satana's daughter, she grazed herself while tugging at the knots, and seeing the blood galvanises her, she redoubles her fury. In the prettier girl's eyes, he imagines he can see a flicker of compassion. He pleads with her, summoning all the sincerity he can muster:

"You do realise I'm innocent, don't you?"

And the girl in the hijab gives him a clip round the ear.

"How long are you planning to whine about that? Don't tell

me that at your age you still believe in justice, that the guilty pay and the innocent are pardoned . . . ? That's not how things work in this world. You're tied up and we're free to move. It's not difficult to understand: you come off worst."

The pretty one lays a hand on her friend's shoulder as though to calm her.

"Give him a chance anyway."

Turning towards him, in an almost friendly tone that makes Dopalet want to sob, she says:

"Talk to her about her mother. How you were friends, all that. Tell her. What kind of stuff did you do together?"

"She loved music. She had an astonishing knowledge of music."

"So you listened to records together?"

"Sometimes."

"That's sweet. Sometimes she'd come round to your place, she'd be here in this room and she'd spend the evening impressing you with her musical knowledge?"

"No, not my place. I never bring people here. This is for family."

"Family?"

"My wife, her children . . . I kept my private and professional lives separate."

"So, your relationship with her mother was professional?"

"No. But sometimes we'd listen to music in the car."

"In the car?"

"Yes. She'd sing at the top of her voice, she'd dance, when we stopped at traffic lights people would laugh, she loved it."

"And where were you going in this car?"

"To dinner, to the cinema, to a party . . ."

The girl in the hijab barks:

"And where did you have dinner with my mother?"

"I don't remember . . . at the Hôtel Costes, maybe . . . or somewhere . . . anywhere . . ."

"You picked her up outside her place?"

"Sometimes."

"Where did she live?"

"I can't remember."

"Or maybe she came to see you at the office and you screwed her and then she got into your car so you could pimp her out elsewhere."

"I've already told you I didn't screw anyone."

"So you were friends. O.K. What kind of music did my mother like?"

"Rap."

"Wrong. She only listened to white music. You don't even know that. Mostly rock and techno. You've got no idea. Because to do what you did together, music didn't matter much."

This is what the Inquisition must have been like. Pathetic torturers who didn't even listen to what you were saying. Behind his back, he hears the shorter one take something else out of her bag. He doesn't know what she's doing, but it is taking her a long time. He feels perspiration trickle down his chest. He realises he is sweating as if he were in a sauna. Then he feels them slice through the back of his shirt. At the feel of metal against his skin, he is plunged into abject terror. There is no point screaming. The whole apartment is soundproofed. It dates back to the time when he used to have parties here and was sick and tired of complaints about the noise. He is going to die here. Tortured by these two little shits. A short paragraph in "News in Brief". He has a fleeting image of Satana crawling towards him on all fours, panties down around her thighs, her arse spread wide, in the living room of one of his friends; there were several of them sitting in white leather armchairs. All that for this. It's absurd. It has always bothered him that he is led around by his dick. He always knew it would be the death of him. But how can he explain to these two retards that it was a consensual relationship between adults, that there is always something uncertain when it comes to sex. Satana understood that.

Out of the corner of his left eye, he catches a glimpse of the pretty girl, she is pulling on black gloves. He is about to pass out. Then they blindfold him, he hears the sound of a motor whirring behind his back and feels a glacial fear steal over him.

LOÏC IS LISTENING TO "MODERN WORLD" BY THE JAM AS HE RIDES along on his moped. The traffic is clear. The sun is shining, but Loïc has kept his gloves on. According to the forecast, it will rain around midday. The weather is all the guys talk about before their shifts this year. For a motorcycle courier, the weather is much more than just whether you're going to wear your shiny new shoes. Apparently, there hasn't been a summer this cold and rainy since 1988. He can't remember what the weather was like back then. He would have been twenty-four – the weather was the least of his worries. He was living in Montpellier. 1988. The year Mitterrand was re-elected. Loïc hadn't bothered to vote. By then, he already knew the whole thing was a farce. Back then, he would have been listening to Les Shériff's "*A coups de batte de baseball*". He always liked fucktards. The past couple of days he's been having trouble with his cervical vertebrae. The doc says there's nothing to be done except take it easy. Not something he can do in his job: being a courier is non-stop pressure. Stress is part of the job, if you're not constantly on the alert a car will sideswipe you, if you're not the fastest, you won't get your contract renewed. He's the oldest member of the team. He's not the best anymore. The kids are faster. And more reckless.

The light turns red at the bottom of the avenue Marceau. A bunch of people from Virgin are holding up traffic. Though not for long. There's maybe fifty of them. Loïc heard about the protest on the radio this morning. It's just a handful of employees. The queue outside Virgin the day it shut its doors, now *that* was a crowd. Everyone had set an alarm clock so as not to miss out on the closing-down sale. It was a full-scale riot. But the number who've turned out to defend workers' rights this morning could be a bunch of friends off on a stag party. Loïc feels bad for them. Buildings have become more important than the people who work in them. Have to say, it was a beautiful building, the Virgin Megastore. He wore the red waistcoat himself. Worked for six months on the information desk. If people had questions, they came to him. The Champs Elysées will seem weird without Virgin. Not that he could afford to go there and buy anything on what he earns, but at least it was there.

Besides, he hates Paris. He's been working here for more than fifteen years. He never liked this fucking city. He crosses the sunlit place Vendôme, deserted at this time of day, then heads along the banks of the Seine, overtaking taxis, crossing bridges, the Musée d'Orsay with tourist coaches parked out front, the waters of the Seine are high, muddy, almost yellow. Within minutes, he reaches the lines of garden centres along the quai de la Mégisserie. Pottery chimpanzees astride plastic alligators, fake palm trees and garden gnomes.

The difference between a broken love affair and a broken friendship is how long they take to heal. At the time, a break-up is more painful, there is a lot of craziness involved, that sort of shit can easily become obsessive. It's unbearable. But it passes pretty quickly and leaves no trace. A girlfriend is easily replaced. It's not hard deciding you want to sleep with a girl. Most of them have got something or other that warrants taking an interest. If you want to settle down, you've got to be realistic. The half-decent girl who knows how to cook, has no bad habits, accepts you for who you are and doesn't try to change you or get you to eat your vegetables, that's about as much as you can ask from love. It's always the same story, give or take a few details. The important thing is not to go looking for things in a relationship that you're never going to find. Loïc has long since realised that, to be happy in love, you have to make do with what's on offer.

Friendship, on the other hand, brooks no compromises. It demands complete sincerity from both parties. It's easy to find someone to sink a few beers, tell a few jokes. But finding someone you can really talk to, now that's rare. Loïc is dealing with a broken friendship. He feels betrayed. And alone. He goes through phases of anger, contempt, misery. But the worst thing is the withdrawal. Last night, he was watching T.V. at his place in Garges-lès-Gonesse – there's footage of a young black guy in London, hands covered in blood, wielding a machete, his bagging jeans slipping off his arse, in the background you can see the body of the soldier he's just murdered, and the young black guy is just standing there, chill, talking straight to the camera. Immediately, Loïc thinks about the text he wants to send to Noël. He still can't get used to the break-up. Now he's got no-one to share his thoughts with. He's lost his best mate. They laughed at the same stuff, they had a sort of secret code. They constantly quoted Maradona at each other – they would look up Spanish quotes online. They knew every insult he'd ever made against Pelé by heart. They would watch every goal by Ronaldinho. That Brazil 2011 free kick. He knows the defenders are going to jump, so he shoots it underneath. Not going for the corner of the net. Straight in. Counter intuitive. They could watch it a hundred times. The intelligence of the guy. They didn't want to like Messi, but watching his goals side by side, they had to admit he was the true heir to the master. The same command in midfield, dodging diving defenders, and that same genius for putting the ball exactly where the goalie least expects it.

I mean, obviously he's got Pénélope on the sofa next to him in the evenings. But she's a girl. Which means she takes everything hyper-seriously. If he makes one of his dumb jokes, she goes ballistic. It's like she's paid by the P.C. brigade to make sure no-one has any fucking fun.

He and Noël used to have a good laugh together. Loïc would regularly crash on Noël's sofa, it was easier than catching the last train on the R.E.R., and saved him a two-hour commute in the morning, which was a pretty useful. Friendship break-ups are more painful. Loïc knows that a good friend is something you find only once or twice in a lifetime. Friendship isn't something you can generate. Usually, it's girls who come between friends. A guy hooks up with some girl and she gets all clingy and possessive. In desperation, the guy decides it's easier to hit PAUSE with his friend. He lays down his arms. The girl has won. A friendship has died.

The irony is that it was some bourgeois fuckwit who came between with him and Noël. He'd never have imagined that Noël would fall for that bullshit. Middle-class people are always fucking things up. Julien goes round busting everybody's balls about the Jewish lobby – the guy might not be circumcised himself, but that doesn't stop him owning a fancy apartment, on the rue de Bretagne, no less. And he slums it with guys from working-class families and tells them how they should behave. Julien's always banging on about *real* French people, but he doesn't know shit about working-class people or where they live. The bourgeois fuck is always trying to get people to hand out blankets to the homeless – like *he's* ever likely to be homeless. Why the hell does the guy have to be such a monumental pain in the arse?

Loïc never could stomach the middle classes. Even when he was a kid and hung around with all sorts, the parents of the rich kids would always tell them not to invite him round. Not that he wasn't well-behaved, but the parents always took against him. He looked too much like what he was: a fucking pauper. His mother weighed, like, three hundred pounds. People would shout insults at her from their cars. There she was, holding her son's hand, he was old enough to know what was going on, but too young to run to the next set of traffic lights and smash the driver's face in. He can still hear the way his mother used to breathe on the stairs. They lived on the sixth floor. The lifts were out of order for at least one week every month. He was terrified that she would drop dead in that stairwell. She would turn to Loïc, who always walked behind her, terrified that she might collapse at any moment and furious that she had to suffer like this. For him, this is the sound of being working class. His mother stopping on the third floor, unable to catch her breath. Given her weight, she was grateful that anyone gave her a job. She was a junior hairdresser in a salon in a Carrefour shopping mall. She became allergic to the shampoo. Even if she wore gloves, it gave her eczema. She would break out in a red rash all over her torso and her neck.

Little Julien can dress up the "will of the people" any way he chooses, he'll never know what it's like to be six years old and have to watch your mother ruin her health and not even earn enough to buy you a bike. Julien doesn't know what it's like, but that doesn't stop him opening his big mouth. The left wing is full of the same sort of cretins.

Loïc's had to deal with his fair share of them in his time. He was sucked in by rock music when he was a kid. The whole industry was riddled with Trots, Maoists, anarchists, libertarians. A lot of them hated the music, but they saw it as a breeding ground for young minds they could brainwash. Loïc was really into The Redskins. And all the hardcore punk stuff: Bérurier noir's "*Concerto*", La Souris circa "*Une cause à rallier*", Sham 69's "*Kids Are United*". In the beginning, he allowed himself to be indoctrinated. He took lessons in radicalism with guys he would run into five years later living in apartments paid for by their parents. None of them ever started their sermons with: "I'm the son of landowners and I grew up in the lap of luxury." It had worked like a vaccine. If you want to talk to me, first tell me where you grew up.

The right wing has the same clowns as the left. But there's one thing that sets them apart: they're more sincere. Human beings are shit. All they want is to be told what to do. To be punished, rewarded, guided. Kill thy neighbour, that's the essence of human nature. That's how you can tell which of two civilisations is superior: who's got the biggest weapons. Put three families from different religions in a city, leave them to get on with it, wait a generation, and they'll be killing each other. An ego is like a cock: no conscience can stop a hard on. There's no point pretending human beings aren't shit. The only thing that stops people killing each other is control. They need a leader. That's what the people want. A leader is someone who says: this one we kill, this one we reward. And everyone's happy. In the end, it doesn't fucking matter whether the leader advocates this ideology or that. What the alpha male gets off on is power. He can base it on any book he likes, it's all the same.

He doesn't give a shit. What he cares about is who I hang with, who I have a blast with. After that: he's loyal. If Noël really believed that L'Œuvre française was a cure-all, they wouldn't be spending all night arguing when they could be chatting football. Go join Jeunesses nationalistes. Loïc doesn't belong to any political party, doesn't buy into any ideology. It's something that comes with age – one day Noël will realise that everyone thinks he's a fuckwit. There's no point expecting anything from politicians. Even if they were decent people to start off with, the system would turn them into arseholes. You get swept away by the discipline: once you're prepared to betray your convictions, you're ready to betray your friends. At that point, you're done for. It pisses him off that Noël has allowed himself to be suckered.

Right-wing, left-wing, he doesn't give a fuck. It's all the same shit. He's not about to have his balls cut off swearing allegiance to one side or the other. With Facebook, surveillance has been ratcheted up a notch – I noticed you liked So-and-So, why did you repost Whatshisname? He does what he likes. No-one pays his rent, so no-one gets to call the shots. It doesn't bother him, getting into arguments with fuckwits. On the contrary, he gets a kick out of it. On the Left, all anyone talks about is how things are "slipping". He is not slipping: whenever he takes a sidestep it's because he wants to shit in the flowerbeds. It's the same with the Right and their "I'm politically incorrect". Bunch of morons. All they want is approbation. The national mantra, on both sides of the fence, is "I'm not looking for a fight". Loïc is looking. He always has been.

But it has to be said that Loïc hates left-wing arseholes just a little more. They exploited people like him, clambered over their backs to get to power then pissed in their faces and expected them to say thank you. When they hire you, left-wing bosses make you sign the same contracts, accept the same conditions, but they also want you to admire them and get touchy when you talk about overtime. When they have a good job to fill, they do it like everyone else: they hire their kid, their mistress or their nephew. They pay you minimum wage and squeeze you like a lemon, and you're expected to be all smiles every morning because they call you by your first name. He doesn't give a shit whether the boss knows his name, all he cares about is his payslip. If the number under your name is ten times mine, you can keep your fucking friendly banter.

He is disgusted with the Left. All their gold medals from the revolution. Self-proclaimed champions of truth. Not that they've won anything in his lifetime. It doesn't matter: it just makes them more electable. His mother voted Communist all her life. He heard people talk about "The Worker and his Factory". Like they were a couple whose future was worth fighting for. Like "The Hairdresser and her Eczema". Still she went out to vote. She doesn't bother anymore. She's got the picture.

Noël is from another generation. He never saw the Left triumphant. He lets himself be taken in by different bullshit. But nothing's changed: it's still the same bullshit it was twenty years ago, they haven't changed the stock. The only thing that changes is who controls the feeding trough, mongrels always turn towards the smell of food. Noël will figure it out in his own time. Loïc even misses his old friend's apartment. They used to watch films about dinosaurs. Noël loved them. If they happened on a documentary about the diplodocus, it was impossible to get him to change channels. In recent times, Loïc would call round to his place with two tubs of Ben & Jerry's Peanut Butter Cup. That stuff costs a fucking fortune. They would each sit with a tub in their lap, and there wouldn't be another word out of them until you heard the spoon scraping the bottom. Before that, they went through a cappuccino phase. They'd put so much powder in the cups their teaspoons would stand up.

To be honest, Noël has been uncomfortable about his sense of humour for a while now. Loïc knew that. Ever the master manipulator, Julien was always shit-stirring between them. He convinced Noël that Loïc was jealous of their friendship. He came between them, the way a girlfriend would. It had been brewing for a couple of weeks. There had been insinuations, a lot of awkwardness. Stuff he and Noël had never experienced before.

The whole thing started with something completely stupid. Loïc should have kept his mouth shut. They were on the internet, looking at pictures of a dozen guys giving the Nazi salute on a train platform, trying to block Caroline Fourest. Julien was obsessed with that dyke. And Loïc had cracked a joke. He couldn't help himself. It was starting to piss him off, this obsession with the Third Reich. Not that he's a staunch anti-Nazi, but he was spoiling for a fight. "It makes me laugh, a bunch of French guys giving the Nazi salute. If you really love your country, what do you do? Copy the people who invaded it? What a glorious memory of France – the Germans marching down the Champs-Élysées. I'm not saying that the Americans had much respect for us, but we need to get over the idea that the Huns were our friends. I'm French. I don't like the Nazi salute. I don't like Germany. I don't go round flattering the enemy just because I lost the war."

It was banter, a joke, a bit of verbal sparring. And besides, he was tired of their bullshit. Those dumbfuck ultranationalists, most of them incapable of writing a three-line Facebook comment without making forty spelling mistakes. If you love your country so much, either learn the language or don't write comments. He should have held his tongue. But for a while now, he'd been itching to go head to head with that little prick Julien, with his sanctimonious air like a parish priest. Monsieur More. More intelligent, more enlightened, more confrontational. Loïc had wanted to show Noël that he wasn't afraid. He has always been like that. Always hated people who throw their weight around. He likes to think the opposite of what he's being told to think. Put the ball where the goalie is least expecting it. That's his thing.

What he hadn't expected was that Noël would slowly get to his feet, tight-lipped with rage, and point to the door. All he had said was "out". He hadn't been drunk, he hadn't been stoned. Five years they had been friends. Loïc had taken the shock with dignity. He had made a grand exit. In the deafening silence. He had affected a half-amused smile that said: "I really don't give a shit and you're all a bunch of tossers." But once outside, he was so shaken that he'd had to lean against the wall for support. Noël had humiliated him in front of everyone. Then Loïc had composed himself. Assumed that they would both regret the incident, and the next time there was a Paris Saint-Germain match they'd be sending each other sarcastic text messages as though nothing had happened. This is another advantage friendships have over relationships – there's no psychobabble, no post mortems. A friendship can withstand periods of distance, of silence, without crumbling.

But Noël had unfriended him on Facebook and blocked him on Instagram and Twitter, all without a word of explanation. This was how bad it was. This was serious. And there had been no way back. After a few weeks, he had thought: what the hell, I'm screwed anyway, I'll show them who's boss. He had trolled them online, on every site he could. He hadn't used fake profiles. This was open war. He knows Julien. The guy's a cardboard cut-out. He can't take confrontation. But this revenge is cold comfort compared to the crushing sadness he feels. He misses Noel's friendship constantly.

There is Xavier . . . Loïc feels fortunate to have met the guy. He's reliable. It gives him someone to talk to. When, a few days after putting him in a coma, Loïc had discovered the identity of his victim, he had been mortified. Back in the 1980s, Xavier Fardin had written the screenplay for "*Ma seule étoile*", a minor masterpiece Loïc considers one of the few French "cult films". As if that were not bad enough, he also discovered that the homeless guy the whole scuffle had been about was Vernon Subutex, the guy who used to run Revolver. Loïc hadn't recognised him. If he had, he would have told the others, come on, leave him be, let's move on. Loïc remembered the record shop. When he had first arrived in Paris in the early '90s, he used to go there all the time. It was here that he had been introduced to Rico Maldoror, Patrick Eudeline, Géant Vert, Roland and Schultz Parabellum, Alain Picon, Thäi Luc, François Molodoï and so many others . . . Subutex had been a decent guy. Open minded. Girls liked him, there was always a gaggle of them hanging around the record shop. He had even spotted Laurence Romance there once. Loïc also remembers Cécile, a little mod girl, pixie cut, khaki trench coat, who used to sell amphetamines she stole from work. She had a job making up prescriptions for pharmacies. They had once spent the night walking through Paris in fog so thick you couldn't see two metres in front of your face. She kept coming up with these wild ideas – imagine we're in London and it's 1965, and we're off to the 100 Club to see The Byrds and the Spencer Davies Group . . . You met up with all sorts of people at Revolver. But around that time, Loïc had taken a swerve from punk into hip hop, like a lot of kids who grew up in the *banlieue*. He started hanging out at the F.N.A.C. Montparnasse.

One night, Loïc had decided to face things head on. Damn the consequences. He might be a thug, a bad boy, but he wasn't a bastard and he wasn't a traitor. He had tracked Xavier down on Facebook and sent him a message. As always when he's online, he used his real name. Only torturers and traitors need to hide their identity. He had written to Xavier: "I'm the one who put you in a coma, I didn't realise who you were, and I'm really fucked off I did it." He had apologised, like a real man. He had been drunk when he wrote it. Sober, he would never have done anything so stupid – imagine the shit he'd be in if the guy turned out to be a dickhead and went straight to the police . . . But Xavier works in movies. He also asked Xavier whether he knew what had happened to Vernon Subutex. He didn't want the guy sleeping on the streets. Obviously, bringing him back to Pénélope's place in Garches might be problematic. Like most girls, she jealously guards her creature comforts. Pénélope likes everything to be neat and tidy, her beauty products, her pots and pans, her magazines. She has her little habits, she doesn't like things to get in the way, and she doesn't believe in friendship. Persuading her to allow a complete stranger to sleep on the sofa would have been a nightmare. But he couldn't bear the thought that Subutex had been abandoned by everyone. Paris is a real shithole. That sort of thing would never happen in the provinces.

It had taken Xavier two hours to reply: "Take your apology and shove it up your arse. You really think I'm going to talk to a guy who goes round with a gang beating up the homeless?" It was a good opening salvo, incisive and succinct. But an hour later he had not been able to stop himself ruining the effect by adding: "We'll run into each other again. Don't you worry." Loïc felt like replying: I knocked you out once, snowflake, I can knock you out again.

But he had not apologised only to pick a fight two minutes later.

What he liked was that both Xavier's messages had been short. On the internet, anything longer than three sentences and you're splitting hairs. That was the great thing about Twitter. He had let Xavier stew for a while, then sent another message: "Message received. Deserved. But if we do run into each other, I'm buying the beer." Xavier had waited a whole week before accepting. "O.K. I'll polish my baseball bat."

They had met up outside the Mistral on the place du Châtelet. Loïc had not known what to expect. They could have kicked off with a principled punch-up down by the river for old times' sake, but they were too old for that shit. Xavier had mumbled a couple of insults, kicked the subject into touch, and they had settled themselves at the bar. Loïc had tried a little "*la pelota no se mancha*", but Xavier did not pick up on it. He had explained things: Julien's fantasies of seizing power by attacking the country via its arsehole – the poor. How he swept people along. And how he had ended up, with his mates, getting into a scrap with a mad homeless bitch. Xavier had laughed. "Has to be said, you made a mistake picking on Olga. She's not scared of anything, let me tell you." By the third beer, the ice had been broken. Xavier was telling him how it had been impossible to write a second film. How he was sick to death of French cinema. Loïc had smiled and said, "You don't have to tell me, I only have to see a Renault in a movie and I know I'm about to be bored shitless." They understood each other on various subjects without having to explain too much. The gypsy dancers who had just performed at the Théâtre de la Ville poured in to get something to eat from the bar. They had danced the flamenco with a couple of the Arab waiters and, behind the bar, the French owner smiled for the first time that night, and the whole place went wild. Good natured, but electric. Loïc realised that he felt relieved to be with someone who could watch two *bougnoules* and three gypsies kicking their heels up in a bar without feeling the need to invoke Saint Louis of France. Xavier had nothing to prove. This was something they agreed on: if they felt like making remarks about kikes or ragheads, they did. But it was not like they felt obligated: they could talk about other things too. And that felt good. They had wound up at four o' clock in the morning, propping up one of the sphinxes in the fountain on the place du Châtelet, chugging Bavaria 8.6. They knew they were in for a hell of a hangover, but they were engaged in a passionate conversation about which they would remember almost nothing the following morning, other than a vague, persistent feeling that they had been on the same wavelength. Loïc had spilled his guts about Noël's betrayal. Xavier had talked about his coma.

"I nearly kicked the bucket. When I came round, I realised that if they told me I only had six days to live, I wouldn't have had a flying fuck what to do. O.K., I'd like to spend it with my daughter. But what would I do with her? What's important? I hadn't the faintest fucking idea. That really unsettled me. Because that's the one thing you've got to know, don't you think?"

Since then, when Loïc finishes an early shift, he goes up to the park to sink a beer with Xavier. He's always hanging out up there. He still hasn't recovered from the beating Loïc gave him. Not that he complains. But he's a bit touched in the head. He has this thing about Subutex. It's weird, seeing them all together, full-on Flower Power. They listen to Zarma music on fuck-off expensive headphones, sometimes when Loïc shows up, he thinks it's all an elaborate gag. It makes him uncomfortable. Usually he and Xavier slope off for a drink in the bar next to the town hall. When he asks what he's doing hanging out with a bunch of hippies, Xavier shrugs. "I was at rock bottom. People tell themselves 'I don't give a shit what people think about me,' but we carry their judgment inside us, the hard thing is ripping it out of your chest. And when I saw Vernon do it, I felt free. I stopped telling myself stories in which I had to be the hero. I gave up on the idea of winning. It doesn't haunt me anymore. I think I've really changed." At which point, Loïc changes the subject. They've discovered they're both fans of Vince Taylor, it's not like bonding over Maradona, but at least it's something.

Today, he finishes work, takes his schedule for the week, and heads straight round to Xavier, who suggests he swing by because his wife is away. Loïc has never met Marie-Ange, but from what he's heard, she sounds like an ice queen. He wouldn't put up with a girlfriend like that.

Pénélope is a good girl. He can't complain. But she's no beauty. You don't puff your chest out when she's on your arm. She doesn't make much effort to please him. Not that she's an embarrassment either. But she's not the kind of woman who primps herself, puts on nail polish, gets all dolled up and spends her day buying matching accessories at Zara, or doing something new with her hair to look more feminine. She's not girlie, she doesn't give a damn. She's a girl from the *banlieue*, perfectly capable of dressing like a guy and not understanding why that pisses him off. At least she's skinny, so there's that. She doesn't talk shit when she's in public, doesn't go around telling randoms her life story and she's got a decent sense of humour. She's happy for him to stay in Paris some nights. When she has the apartment to herself she invites her girlfriends round for sleepovers.

*

Standing in the kitchen with his ridiculous little dog at his heels, Xavier is trying to work the new coffee machine:

"The one I used to have was perfect. It was eight years old, but it worked flawlessly. I was the one who cleaned and descaled it, I took care of it. There was a minor short circuit with the on/off button, but I just left it switched on all the time, and it was fine. Then we had a power cut, and when I started it up again, I pressed the button too hard and it stuck. It couldn't be fixed, can you believe that? I took it round to all the local repair shops – fifty euros minimum. The thing only cost seventy when it was new. Marie-Ange's mother bought us a new one without even asking. It bothers me, chucking out things that could still work. Drives me mad. I can't do it, I can't live in a world where things are designed to become obsolete as quickly as possible."

"Just drink instant coffee. Stand your ground."

"Do you mind if we pop round to Rosa Bonheur tonight? Subutex is on the decks. Pamela Kant will be there."

"I was about to say, yes, actually, I do mind, but if Pamela Kant is going to be there, get dressed and let's get a move on."

Until now, Loïc has been unlucky – she has never been in the park when he dropped by. It sickens him that he can't send Noël a text message to say he's having a drink with Pamela Kant. She was one of their great fantasies. Because she had legs that went on forever and she was so good at pretending she really liked it. Shit, Noël would be insanely jealous if he knew . . .

"I figured that might be the deciding factor," Xavier laughs. "But like I said before: off-screen, she's anything but a slut."

"You never know. Just imagine that, in a moment of madness, she decides tonight's the night she gives everyone a blowjob."

FROM THE DISTANCE COMES THE SOUND OF CHEERS AND HONKING horns of a wedding at the town hall. The only way to get to the train tracks is via a steep embankment, clinging to the boulders strewn here and there. The grass is bare here, it is the least frequented area of the park. Someone has spray-painted their tag on a tree trunk. Reaching the bottom, the Hyena walks past the piles of timber, mattresses, railings, chairs and gutted toys. She finds Vernon sprawled on a burgundy-coloured sofa bed set into gravel. Seeing her approach, Vernon jerks his chin towards a small white rodent with the body of rat, but with a bushy squirrel's tail as white as its body.

"What do you think it is, that thing?"

"Looks to me like two animals that were never designed to meet but did the nasty together."

"It's weird. It's been there since this morning."

Vernon tries to connect a car battery to an amplifier he found by the side of the road. He smiles ingenuously. He is short circuiting as much as ever. It is as though he has epileptic fits that gently dissociate him from reality in slow motion. After a fashion he loses consciousness, but rather than suffering painful convulsions, he seems radiant. When he regains consciousness, he does not seem worried. His clothes are filthy, but he still smells nice. The three-day stubble brings out the grey of his eyes. The guy is possessed, he attracts company, like a magnet. He says:

"Did something happen last night?"

"How did you know?"

"Charles told me he saw people running. Aïcha, Céleste and some people he didn't recognise . . . And Olga saw you pass by, but you didn't come to see us . . . Is everything alright?"

"Are you DJing at Rosa's tonight?"

"Yes."

"It's probably the last time we'll see each other there. There was a bit of a ruction . . ."

"You can't stop people doing what they have to do."

"It feels like the end of the holidays . . . If people stopped coming to the park, what would you do?"

"I'll see. I have trouble planning ahead."

"I noticed. Do you want us to put you up somewhere, with someone who'll look after you?"

"The one thing I don't want is to be put up somewhere. Do you want to tell me what you've all been keeping from me these past few weeks?"

"We haven't been hiding anything. We were being discreet."

Pamela and Daniel came up with the idea. It was something they got from the Bolivian girls who had spent ten days in Paris. They rounded up five prostitutes, all of whom had known Satana, and had asked Aïcha if she wanted to be part of it. The kid had thrown a hissy fit when she found out she was surrounded by whores, but she was a little more pragmatic when she realised they were prepared to put themselves in danger to avenge her mother. She had agreed. The Hyena had become their confidential advisor. They proved exceptionally good at following orders. They memorised routes to within a metre so they could avoid the C.C.T.V. cameras, at the agreed signal they changed their clothes and pulled on balaclavas as though they had been doing it all their lives. The Hyena had suggested they get into the habit of running, so they would be able scatter quickly, and every morning since, they had come running in the park. They took training sessions with some girl they'd discovered near the place Stalingrad, who was covered in Buddhist tattoos but was skilled in martial arts and had a thing for doing push-ups. They were the perfect team. The Hyena had never thought of herself as a team leader, but felt it was worth adapting just this once: not a blunder, not a misplaced word during the day, not a dumbass question, and – rarer still – not a single overweening ego to destabilise the group. Just a gang of beautiful women hungry for action. The Hyena had taken her role seriously. She had watched as Aïcha got hooked on the adrenaline. It had not been surprising that she had felt she needed to do more. She could have predicted what happened next.

After Anaïs told her that she had been fired, the Hyena had rushed straight round to see Dopalet to make sure that he had not cottoned on. He trusted her implicitly and had been as eager to see her as always. Leaving him, she had felt reassured: he had not made the connection between her and Anaïs and clearly harboured no suspicious about her. It was at this point that she got a call from Gaëlle at Rosa Bonheur, and the Hyena realised that she had missed a step: she should never have left Anaïs alone with a shit-stirrer like Gaëlle.

From what she has been able to piece together, Antoine had made his grand entrance at Rosa's and had insisted on speaking to Aïcha alone, and Anaïs had gone out to smoke a cigarette while she waited. She had been gazing down at the lake and had seen a confrontation between two figures. Antoine was talking, waving his arms about, vehemently trying to explain, when Aïcha suddenly grabbed him by the neck. He was struggling like a madman and Anaïs had started running towards them, shouting for help to passers-by, but no-one came. By the time she reached the railway bridge, Aïcha was trying to throw Antoine onto the tracks while he clung to the metal railings. Céleste was trying to help him, but neutralising the furious girl was no mean feat. Anaïs had thrown herself into the fray, a grotesque shambles of ripped T-shirts and clumsy punches. In the end, she had sunk her teeth into Aïcha's shoulder, biting down until she heard a howl of pain. Antoine had managed to struggle free and was standing in the middle of the bridge, screaming: "You could have fucking killed me! When all I came to say was that I'm on your side . . ."

"Just fuck off! I don't want you on my side. I want you to drop dead, I don't need your support. This stupid fucker has been saying the same thing for the past hour. I'm going to kill him."

Céleste had exploded:

"Alright, so you throw him off the bridge – then what? How is that going to get you any closer to what you want?"

"It's what Dopalet deserves – to see his son's face smashed in."

"You really think it would hurt him to see his son dead? You're deluded. He'd put on a nice suit, cry for the cameras and use the opportunity to play the victim, that's all. Just think about it."

Anaïs had managed to draw Aïcha to one side. The girl was still paralysed with rage. In the middle of the bridge, Antoine was talking animatedly to Céleste, and Anaïs had to call to the tattoo artist to get her to come and take care of her friend: "You need to get her to a hospital, right now. She needs to see a doctor. You can't let her go home like that." – and the pretty dark-haired girl had promised. Anaïs had led Dopalet's son away. He seemed to have recovered from what had just happened. The little geek was tougher than he looked. He didn't want to go to the police. He wanted a beer.

The Hyena had seen them come into Rosa Bonheur. She had waited until Antoine went to the toilets and then beckoned to Anaïs. She had led her outside and asked what had happened, then she had simply said: "We won't be able to see each other for a while." Hardly had she said the words than Anaïs turned on her heel. Maybe in a few months, the Hyena had been thinking. But the situation was about to get much more complicated, and the best thing for Anaïs was to move on. The Hyena had headed off to Dopalet's apartment. He was not answering her text messages. This was not at all like him. Standing outside the building she realised she did not have the code for Dopalet's private lift, he had always opened for her. She had had to walk around for a while before she found a public telephone. She wanted to call Aïcha. She didn't for a minute believe that Céleste had taken her to a doctor to help her to calm down. That would have been completely out of character. But she did not guess that the two of them had gone straight to the producer's apartment. She had let the phone ring three times, then hung up and tried again, and then again. Aïcha answered. From the tone of her voice, the Hyena had guessed. "You're at his place?" She could hear a machine whirring in the background. Was the silly bitch shaving his hair off? "I'm right outside. I'm coming up. I don't want to use the buzzer, so could you watch for me on the videophone and let me in? And when I do come in, don't say a single word, O.K.?" At the other end of the line, Aïcha's voice was strangely calm, almost as though she were bored.

She had buzzed the Hyena in. Behind her, in the kitchen, tied to a chair, Dopalet's back was streaming blood. He was blindfolded. At first, the Hyena thought they had been whipping him. Then she had understood. The other airhead was giving him a tattoo. Silly bitches. It was all the Hyena could do not to burst out laughing. "RAPIST". Céleste was hard at work on the second tattoo: "MURDERER". She still had four letters to finish. The Hyena had dragged Aïcha into one of the bedrooms and hissed in a low voice: "I'm going to go back outside. I don't want him to know I'm here. I'll ring the buzzer, you two panic and get the hell out and I'll meet you downstairs." And Aïcha had agreed to the plan, but not the timing: "Give us half an hour, Céleste still needs to tattoo: 'YOU'LL PAY' on his lower back." They had stared at each other in silence, then Aïcha had compromised. "O.K., give us ten minutes so she can at least finish 'MURDERER'."

When the two girls had met up with her outside, they seemed so happy and relaxed the Hyena had not been sure whether to slap them or hug them.

"Antoine gave us the door codes, and we came straight here. We had to do something."

"My father's a cop. I know what we've done is really serious."

The Hyena had felt a faint, familiar pop in her chest: a discreet click, like the pull of a thread, after which everything would go to hell. She felt sorry for the girls, who were too young to realise that they had just changed the course of their lives and those of everyone around them. Or, more precisely, too inexperienced to know that they would regret this. She did not yet know how Dopalet would take it, but she was sure that he would not allow himself to be attacked like this without seeking revenge. And given all the resources he had at his disposal, criminal proceedings were the least of their worries.

"Don't look at me like this is my fault," Aïcha had said. "As it goes, I think I've been pretty restrained."

"O.K., girls, you're going to go home and pack your bags right now, we'll get you out of Paris tonight, you need to lie low for a while."

"Antoine is not going to say anything."

"So what? Do you really think that Dopalet is going to leave you alone? I'll meet you at Nation in two hours."

Then the producer had called her and asked for her help. He was about to pass out. She had helped him sterilise the needle marks. He clung to her, bewildered and disoriented. The Hyena had force-fed him a fistful of Lexomil: like any self-respecting coke addict, his medicine cabinet was full of tranquillisers. She had more than enough time to get the two girls out of the city. After that she would have a couple of days, maybe a week, before Dopalet realised that she had double-crossed him. She had not covered her tracks carefully enough, he was bound to find out. His son wouldn't say anything just yet. Anaïs was not likely to go and visit him. The Hyena ran through all the parameters in her mind as she covered the bleeding tattoos with cling film to stop them becoming infected, and lavished him with words of comfort and promises of vengeance.

The girls had left that night, as arranged. Neither of them had cried. They were hard-faced and determined. It had been more difficult for Sélim. He had stared at his daughter without saying a word. He was trying to understand how this could have happened. He was thinking that it could have been worse. This was small comfort.

*

She tells all this to Vernon as they go to join the others on the bank of the river. It is not raining, the day is bright and sunny. On the lawn, Daniel is playing football with Joyeux the poodle. A girl is shouting, "Shield your thigh, shield it, and when you kick, flex from the hip, not the knee," then she shakes her head disappointedly, "Did you never play football when you were a kid?" Olga is offering salt and vinegar crisps to Sylvie, who declines. "The Sex Pistols are a feminist group. Just listen to the lyrics of 'Bodies'." Xavier is convinced that he's right. Laurent is lying on his back on the grass listening to Alex Bleach's alpha waves on headphones. The quest for perfect sound has become an obsession with Sylvie. She shows up with a new pair of headphones every couple of days. Lighter, more powerful, better infrasonic bass definition. Charles watches her make a fuss, mocking but completely seduced. Patrice is sitting next to the cooler filled with beers. He has found himself a little folding deckchair like the ones you get at the beach. Emilie is telling him that when you smoke weed, you need to take melatonin supplements and vitamin C. He listens but does not seem overly persuaded. Sylvie interrupts the conversation: "Getting stoned is a young person's sport. It's all about recovery time. That's why kids can take whatever they like. They recover overnight and the next morning they're creative and alert. At our age, it's tough, it takes longer to recuperate." Pamela agrees, "At your age, everything is tougher." Patrice laughs, "Get ready, you're not far off yourself."

"O.K., SHE'S A DYKE, BUT WOULD IT REALLY KILL HER TO CRACK A smile? Do they get thrown out of the coven for being friendly? What happened to the cute waitress?"

"Céleste? Apparently she quit her job from one day to the next. Gaëlle is cool, you just have to get to know her. She's nervous about being a waitress at her age."

"You promise me I'm going to get to meet Pamela Kant, and here I am being snubbed by a female truck-driver. I have to say, I'm disappointed."

"Relax, she'll be here. If you hadn't insisted on running all the way, we wouldn't have been the first to arrive."

Loïc is a porn fiend. If he's honest, he prefers getting off in front of a screen than with his girlfriend. And, in this case, it is not Pénélope's fault: he's the same with all girls. They're never as exciting as the ones in the skin flicks. In fact, even when he does fuck, he's constantly thinking about the porn movies he's seen. The stimulus is too good, nothing comes close. They're randy sluts, they've got tight arses, you can see every detail, and you can't smell anything. He knows Pamela Kant's filmography so intimately that he feels like a kid at the prospect of meeting her.

The bar is beginning to fill up. Loïc recognises many of the faces. But no-one says hello. He has been pigeonholed. The fascist who beat the shit out of Xavier. He keeps his head down. Not that he cares, he doesn't like them. A bunch of worms slithering around some homeless guy and wetting themselves about his mix. He hates their guts.

Xavier is off talking to Emilie. She is avoiding Loïc. Left-wing bitch. A frustrated frump looking down her nose at him. Loïc is sorry he and Xavier didn't bring the dog along, at least he would have something to do to save face. But it was raining too hard to bring him. They had decided not to take umbrellas so as not to look like idiots. And besides, they had run the whole way here, holding their hoods over their heads. Physically, Xavier has made a full recovery. Loïc had to bust a gut just to keep up with him. Macho pride, neither of them could bear to slow down. The effort practically killed them both.

The price of beer here is outrageous, he holds off before ordering another one. Xavier doesn't give a toss, his wife is loaded. Loïc lies to Pénélope about how much he spends when he goes out. With the price of drinks in this place, he could give her the iPad she's always talking about, because all her girlfriends have one and they play online games she can't get on her ancient mobile phone. He is sorry he came. He had assumed he would be spending the evening at home with Xavier, he'd brought a six-pack of beer. Now here he is in this sleazy dump, with one eye on the door because he was told that Pamela Kant would be here, but that was just bullshit. What would she be doing with these losers?

He feels out of place here. He misses Noël. And the others. They're probably getting ready for a demo. All hell will probably break loose. He won't be there. Another group he's fallen out with. He's an idiot. As soon as he gets comfortable somewhere, he always manages to find a way to get himself rejected. He scuppers his chances. He's always been that way. He can't help it. He can imagine Noël's face if he could see him here, with his tiny glass of beer, surrounded by hipster faggots, listening to shitty techno. He has to turn a blind eye to a lot of things here to stop himself from going off the deep end. He is pathetic. He seeks out company like a stray dog looking to be petted. No matter the price. This is what he has become. And this sets him off again. He misses his best friend.

It is at this point that Pamela makes her entrance. Loïc hardly notices Subutex on her arm. It all moves as one, it is astonishing. The tits, the arse, the hips, the ankles, the hair, the eyes, even the shoulders turn him on – he doesn't know where to look, there is not a thing single detail about her that is not sexually overwhelming. Xavier is watching him, with a little half-smile. Loïc keeps his composure. He is glad that the bar is dark. His cheeks are on fire.

She is wearing a black sweater, the neckline cut low enough to reveal prominent collarbones that he finds arousing. She is probably the most beautiful woman he has ever seen close up. Some little guy comes trotting behind her, another faggot probably, handsome, though, with delicate features. Loïc has the impression he has seen him before, but he cannot remember where. Loïc doesn't like queers, he rarely notices whether men are handsome, but this guy is stunning.

Pamela Kant is wearing black jeans so tight that it's worse than if she were naked, low-heeled ankle boots. Her thighs are both delicate and powerful, they make him feel dizzy. She is wearing her hair down. In films, she always wears too much make-up, and she's not warmly dressed. But it suits her. What he wouldn't give to have a woman like that . . . Just one. Just once. In his bed. Not even to show off to his mates. Just for himself. He certainly wouldn't have to picture scenes from skin flicks he'd been watching the night before. He would be living a real porn movie.

He has never had a problem chatting up girls, but he sticks to women of his own league. Mid-level. How do you even talk to a woman like that? What do you do, when she undresses? How do you forget your own insignificance when faced with someone like that?

What the hell is she doing hanging out with Subutex? Is she sleeping with him? The guy has grey eyes, he's tall, but apart from that . . . She can't be being nice to him for the money. The fucker's homeless . . . So why does she come to listen to him spin a set?

Subutex recognises him, and stares at him intently, the way he has learned to do since he was dubbed guru of the nineteenth arrondissement. He looks a little less filthy than he does most days and he has had his hair cut. But Loïc is not in the mood to put up with his visionary pronouncements. Whenever the guy talks to you, it's like he's about to kiss you. It freaks you out. He says, "How's it going, Loïc?" and stares like he's saying I can see right into your soul and I suffer for you.

"Yeah, good, good. Just having a quiet beer. I came to hear your set. Apparently you're on the decks tonight?"

He feels like saying, if you want to make me happy, introduce me to your friend and tell her to be gentle with me. That might perk him up. But Subutex sits down next to him. A little too close for Loïc's taste. Then, the thing he dared not hope for happens: Pamela Kant strides over to their table, flashes him a big, sincere smile, like I've-no-idea-the-effect-I-have-on-men, and says, "What are you drinking?" as though they've known each other for years. She walks away, swaying her hips like a goddess and Loïc feels like taking his new friend in his arms. Finally, he can see why everyone likes Subutex. With a smile, he says:

"What about you, Vernon, how are things?"

But instead of giving a normal response, the guy grabs the back of his neck. The gesture is slow, gentle, Loïc tenses but doesn't dare pull away. Shit, just as he was starting to relax. Vernon brings their foreheads together, and closes his eyes. It does not last long enough for Loïc to kick off, but he is mortified by the whole grotesque situation. Then the feeb pulls away and gives him this look that is sad and loving. Everyone around carries on, they're used to this guy doing weird shit, no-one pays him any mind. Pamela comes back, gingerly carrying three beers, and he gets up to help her. And by way of thanks, she gives him a wink. He hears himself say:

"Hi, my name's Loïc."

The words just came by themselves. Like an idiot. He's just introduced himself like a dummy.

"I know, I've heard a lot about you."

"I'm guessing I don't have a good reputation round here."

Every time he opens his mouth he says something stupid, and to make matters worse his voice is quavering. The lights are dimmed. Pamela leans towards him, as though the darkness is forcing her to whisper, Loïc swallows hard and sits there like a lemon.

"I've kept files on everyone," she murmurs. "The day I open a dungeon, I'll send you a summons. I'll make you pay, I'll give you a spanking for all the dirty thoughts that haunt you."

She is insane to say these things to him. Even as a joke. She is chatting him up. Xavier said she only ever talked about boring things. And now here she is coming on to him. He thinks of Lino Ventura, a tough guy, imagines what he would do, and does that. He forces a smile, but his face is so tense that it must be obvious that it makes his cheeks hurt.

"I don't take spankings, I give them."

He manages to say these words to Pamela Kant, with only a flicker of hesitation, manages to sound casual. He controls his emotions, but inside, a mini-me is dancing and cheering and beating his chest. She smiles and says:

"Well, I could be wrong. Or maybe you don't really know yourself."

The slut. He is glad he does not have to stand up. She whips her hand through the air, making it clear that in a spanking, it's all in the wrist action. He does not dare say, I'll take you down a peg or two, honey, and you won't talk about spanking me again. He cannot believe that he's talking to Pamela Kant about sex. And that Noël will never know.

Subutex plays "Magic Bus" by The Who, and Loïc feels a lump burning in his throat. He loves this track. He would never have imagined Subutex would start his playlist with something like this. Fucking amazing. He's not just some pathetic loser hanging out in a bar – he's the guy who made Pamela Kant laugh in a bar where they're playing good music, at just the right volume, and around him he notices that several people are smoking. He lights a cigarette. It feels so good to be smoking in a bar. This is the first decent night he's had in ages. When Subutex segues into Eddie Cochran, he thinks, keep doing that, and I'm going to be the one kissing you. As though Vernon is choosing tracks just for him.

And then he dances. Real guys don't dance, certainly not Loïc. He hates the idea of making an exhibition of himself. When he was young, and when he was on his own, he would pogo a little when he listened to The Meteors or The Vibes. But at gigs he always stood stiff, motionless. You know, dignified. Black guys dance, alright, fine, that's normal. But not him. Between music and his body there exists an insuperable taboo. But tonight, he is dancing. Most of the lights have been turned off now. He is dancing to Bowie, wailing about being heroes. He still can't believe it. And he is dancing with Pamela Kant. It wasn't planned, he didn't have time to wonder how he would go about it. She moves slowly, as though underwater. She looks up, thrusts her pelvis forward and stares at him. And, instead of falling over backwards or throwing himself at her, he dances. Maybe she put something in his beer. Good thing if she did. The handsome little gayboy is on the dance floor. They know each other. He's convinced of it. The guy moves like a god. And it doesn't even bother Loïc that he's enjoying watching him dance. The bad-tempered dyke who was serving behind the bar earlier has climbed up on a table. He's not even annoyed. Why shouldn't she strut her stuff? It's a pleasure to watch her having a ball. James Brown. "The Payback". And there he is in the middle of the crowd. Dancing. He has never done this in his life. And fuck knows he listened to his fair share of funk back when everyone was reading *Get Busy*. Xavier is shaking his booty too. This isn't his kind of music, you can tell. But he's connected. The music jolts through their bones, moving their arms, working their hips. His body follows. For hours on end. Off in a corner, lit by a pale green light, Vernon looks out at them, his eyes half closed, an enigmatic smile playing on his lips. He has become a sphinx.

It is late when Xavier comes over and says, "I have to head back, I don't want to leave the dog on his own all night. If you're staying, just give me a call when you're outside the building?" "Let's go together." In a way, he feels relieved to be dragged away from this madness. His legs are starting to hurt. Tomorrow he will be aching all over. It's going to be a long day.

The park gates are closed, they exit through a little door and run home through the rain. Loïc loves the empty streets, the smell of wet tarmac, the orange sodium lights. He is laughing about what just happened to him, "I swear, I never fucking dance. I'm not that kind of guy," and Xavier says "Me neither," and they keep running, not bothering to say any more.

They crack open a last beer before they go to bed. Loïc noses around in Xavier's C.D. collection. It is his turn to play D.J.: Gorilla Biscuits, Agnostic Front, Sick of It All. It's been a long time since he listened to this shit. He hugs Joyeux's neck – he's drunk, normally he never touches animals, but it's late and the poodle seems *so* cute. Besides, tonight's the night for doing things he never usually does. He slips into the music. You just have to let something go. It is a strange sensation, as though he has an internal organ he never knew was there and that organ is a valve, and it has just opened. So he sinks into the music.

Dawn is breaking and Loïc realises he is crying. He has had too much to drink. He doesn't remember starting to cry, but when he comes round, he is sobbing. Xavier hauls him up and clumsily takes him in his arms. Loïc hasn't cried since he was a kid, he cannot even remember the last time it happened. He is not shocked that Xavier is hugging him. He feels no embarrassment. In general, he's not one for physical contact. One of the things he really likes about Pénélope is that she not very touchy-feely.

Loïc and Xavier stand, motionless, leaning against each other. And in his mind, Loïc is hugging Noël, because whatever had happened between them, nothing can erase the years of friendship they shared. The guy is part of his life, part of the things he has loved in his life, and nothing can change that. At the same time, if Noël could see him now, he'd be disgusted, or he'd laugh, but he certainly wouldn't be happy. Noël doesn't like the idea of letting yourself go . . .

Pamela Kant spiked his drink. But Loïc cannot bring himself to believe that it was to make fun of him. She spent too much time dancing with him for that. It was to make him feel included. If the price to pay is this slightly brutal come-down where he is blubbing like a little girl, it was still worth it. He feels ridiculous, but he needed to get it out.

It is daylight, time to go to work. Second coffee from the new machine that is still frustrating Xavier. Loïc will be late, he sends a text message – delays on the R.E.R. It could easily be true.

They walk to the métro station together. Xavier needs to take the dog for a morning walk anyway. It's so cold it feels like February. At the top of the steps, they go their separate ways, "All the best." And Xavier walks on, trailing his ridiculous poodle on a leash. As he heads toward Line 11, Loïc is thinking he is not really tired, he'll easily be able to put in a day's work. He might not be on top form, but he can hang in there.

It makes a change, being only twenty minutes from work. When he comes to Châtelet, he gets off and wanders through the labyrinthine corridors to his connecting train. He hates this métro station. He feels like a trained rat running to the lab where he works.

As he turns the corner, he recognises three figures. They immediately disappear. The tiredness and the strange mood he had been in instantly fade away. He knows he was not dreaming. He recognised Julien, Noël and Clovis. He slows down. Danger. They're waiting for him. An ambush. One more strange incident to add to his collection. He turns around, starts to walk faster, and hesitates: leave the station, or take the first train that comes?

He has a premonition, glances over his shoulder. They are behind him. He runs. Three against one, there's no point even trying to understand. He flees. At first, his body pumps all the energy he needs, he is electric, then fear fails to sweep him along, he can feel himself slowing. He spent all night dancing, he has no energy left.

The first blow hits him between the shoulders. He staggers forward, turns around. They have covered their faces. But he recognises them. He just has time to think how fucking stupid are you there are cameras everywhere you'll easily be identified he has time to think of the soldier slaughtered by the black guy who said you people will never be safe and he has time to work out which one is Noël, to turn towards him and try to catch his eye under the visor of the baseball cap he has pushed down over his ears. The second blow catches him on the temple, he has time to think that it is the kind of punch you throw when you are trying to kill.

He is lying on his back, listening to music on headphones. Link Wray, "Rumble". Heavy, sticky, it feels like a migraine. Vernon has been sleeping in Charles' place for the past three days. It is hot in the living room, but nothing can shake the feeling of cold pinned to his bones. A tenacious bout of flu wracks his body, his ears are blocked, he is trapped in a bubble of fever. Against his closed eyelids, he can see the figure of Loïc dancing with the others at Rosa Bonheur. In his delirium, Vernon cannot make out his features, only the shape of his body and the colours all around. From time to time, his skin expands and makes contact with the world, a hole the size of a fist opens up in his chest – and suddenly nothing is external to him. He has grown accustomed to this. It would feel strange to go a whole day without hallucinating. He has been sleeping on this broken sofa every night since he caught flu. The house is an unbelievable hovel. Old mother Véro refuses to throw anything out. Every available surface is piled with boxes, papers, objects she has picked up who knows where. She is a fanatical nurse. She stuffed Vernon full of pills, turning over the boxes to check the expiration date and shrugging, "They say 2004, but I can't see how a medicine could lose its powers." She took care of him. He is still pretty out of it, but he is able to get up and around.

He drags himself from his bed and knocks on the door of Charles' bedroom. He and Véro do not sleep together. She snores too much, according to Charles. The old man hardly knew Loïc, but he is insisting on coming to the funeral. He grumbles, spits, coughs, and then emerges from his room, fully dressed. Charles would not miss an opportunity to see Sylvie. It is not that she is his type, it goes beyond physical attraction, from the moment she opens her mouth, he hangs on her every word. When she gets angry, he rolls his eyes to heaven and mutters, it's preposterous, this whole thing is preposterous, enchanted to see her being vulgar.

Vernon is tired of constantly being surrounded by people. Their desires are stubborn and contradictory, and he has taken on a grotesque importance within the group. But every time he thinks of sloping off, something holds him back. He talked about it to Charles, and the old man shrugged, don't worry about it, it's not like they're going to spend their whole lives taking care of you. Just be grateful that there's something happening.

They stand outside the railings smoking their cigarette. Olga and Laurent duck through a broken stretch of fence. They do not know Loïc either, he did not come to the park very often. They want to be part of the cortège. A huge crowd is expected at Garges-lès-Gonesse cemetery. The mortal remains of Loïc, savagely murdered in the corridors of the métro, belong to everyone. Olga and Laurent think they are onto a good thing: there will be lots of free food. But Vernon knows that, deep down, they sense that this might be the last time that they will all see each other.

They walk as far as the Gare du Nord. Olga is terrified of the métro. The flame-haired giant keeps close to Vernon, her shoulder pressed against his. She is angry with him that he did not treat her like his first lady. She is the one who sleeps next to him down by the tracks, not the others. It pisses her off. He allows all the compliments people pay him to go to his head. Vernon needs to realise that when all these dickheads get tired of playing social worker, the only person he will have is her. The others are nice enough people, but they're tourists, they're just passing through. She's had her share of perks from it, obviously. She tells them what she wants the night before and Vernon's friends bring her bars of Côte d'Or dark chocolate with coconut, a jar of Nutella or sanitary towels. These days she only drinks whisky. She's built up her own little cellar which she hides in a niche far from the train tracks – not much chance of anyone stumbling on it when she's away. She's done with the rotgut red that played havoc with her oesophagus, these days madame puts whisky in her Pepsi Max. People are happy to do favours for her. But Vernon spends his time trying to make sure everyone gets something out of it. Most of the time he smiles like a halfwit and stares up into the branches of the trees, then suddenly he'll come over and decide to share her bag of roasted almonds with Zaïa, the schizophrenic who pisses herself. She's always prowling around, she knows there are easy pickings.

She refuses to take her meds, she's always completely shitfaced, why bother share anything with her. She talks to herself all day long, and sometimes you'll see her screaming "Don't worry be happy" at parking meters. Olga believes in class solidarity, but she feels hacked off to have to give a bag of roast almonds to a woman who couldn't give a fuck. Vernon has started to behave like a leader. The day before yesterday, Emilie and Lydia came by to clear out his tent, because he was going to be staying with Charles for a few days. Olga had panicked. She thought that he wouldn't be coming back. She insulted the girls. Said that she wanted his duvet. He hadn't even given orders that Olga should be allowed to divide up his possessions. After everything she's done for him. Result: the pretty little Hungarian girl who's only passing through Paris on her way to visit friends in Seville got her hands on his sleeping bag. Just because she's got a fat arse doesn't mean that Olga doesn't feel the cold as much as the rest of them. She feels angry with Vernon that he hasn't treated her better, but mostly she is terrified that he will disappear. Friendships don't last long on the streets.

The day after Loïc's death, the Feds had come to the park, rounded up the homeless and taken them in for questioning. A handful of the illegal immigrants managed to slip away unnoticed, but that still meant they were packed into the police station cells like sardines. Olga had asked in a loud voice how much it was costing the government to persecute them. Wouldn't it have been quicker and easier to find them somewhere to live? At first, Olga managed to stay calm while she was being held for questioning, but in the end, she freaked out and started screaming and insulting the police. They screamed back that she was mad as a box of frogs, but she had still been among the first to be released. Madness always pays off. The police knew perfectly well that none of them had had anything to do with the murder – the whole thing had been caught on C.C.T.V. Hauling them in was just their way of saying that they were done turning a blind eye to what went on in the Buttes-Chaumont. Some guy gets himself killed in Châtelet by a couple of ex-friends, but the homeless are the ones who have to move on. That's the rule: you don't let the homeless congregate in any one place for too long. Everyone's terrified that they'll find a loud-mouth spokesperson to lead them to the nearest supermarket – looting, pillaging, demonstrations. The day the destitute start attacking shops and businesses, the army will have to roll out the tanks. There are so many people begging on the streets now. So the police stop them from assembling.

Laurent would have preferred to take the métro to the Gare du Nord. It was fat Olga who insisted on walking. She's claustrophobic. She freaks out if she has to get a train, she spent all day yesterday banging on about it, wondering whether she would even go to the funeral, bending Laurent's ear until eventually he told her to fuck off. "Listen, Garges-lès-Gonesse is too far to walk, so either you take the train or you stay here, and either way just shut the fuck up about it." Olga never goes down into the métro stations, not even in winter, not even when it is raining. He just hopes she doesn't go nuts once they're on the R.E.R. Once she starts, she's out of control. And today is not the day. This guy, Loïc, always looked down his nose at Laurent. But even so, he was killed in action, the poor bastard. A young guy, with a girlfriend, and a job. Such a fucking waste. He just hopes that Olga doesn't go and ruin the funeral. She has been a lot calmer recently. She's in love with Vernon. She's got no chance: there's always a gaggle of pretty girls hanging around Subutex, fresh pussy just begging to satisfy his every whim. So even blind drunk on a night so pitch dark he didn't know what he was doing – there's no chance he would wind up between fat Olga's thighs. And now he's going to leave them. She's scared. And not just a little. Laurent feels sad too. Sometimes he finds Vernon irritating, the guy thinks the whole park revolves around him and puts on airs like a mad poet. But they've had a good laugh, the lot of them. Laurent has never seen the like: crowds of people showing up every day, making deliveries. No need to go begging. Large coins and small banknotes falling out of every wallet, and so many meal vouchers you'd think they were printing them at home . . . Generosity to the point of diarrhoea. So much kindness and attention that, at first, Laurent was wary, but he quickly got used to middle-class creature comforts. The only thing that stuck in his throat was the feeling of being a tourist attraction. He always believed that he could connect with ordinary people. That the only difference between him and them was that he couldn't bear to be kept on a leash. Spending so much time with those on the inside has taught him that the only thing they feel for him is pity. No-one now can tell that he's a handsome man. Even five years ago, he might have seduced some of the girls who flutter around Vernon. His teeth have rotted now. His face has changed. Even his jokes don't have the same impact. People have to strain to hear what he is saying. He is not senile. They don't seek him out, they put up with him. He is tolerated. Even Olga is more popular than he is. Sylvie remembered her birthday and made her a triple-chocolate cake. No-one has even asked when he was born. The night of her birthday, he had been horrible to Olga, so furious was he to see her so happy. "You think when winter comes your bourgeois friend will offer you a little corner by the fireside? I don't think so, you're too old and ugly, you wouldn't match the curtains." It has been a cold, raining summer. His heart is in his boots. He will head down south. It's something he has been thinking about for a long time now, but he keeps putting it off. He knows Paris like the back of his hand, and he has his little ways. He may not have a house, but this place is his home. But this time, it's decided. He needs a change of scene, a little sunshine. He will tell everyone after the funeral. These good people will surely club together to buy him a ticket. Because these days, not paying your train fare is treated as a crime more serious than breaking into a kindergarten to rape the toddlers. It's ironic, when you think about it: he and Olga are taking the R.E.R. to go to the funeral of a guy they didn't know, when so many of their friends are dead and they didn't even find out what day they were buried.

Standing on the forecourt outside the Gare du Nord, Pamela Kant lights her third cigarette of the day. She is wearing a figure-hugging trouser suit and stiletto heels. The men insulting her do not even know who she is. It is not the fact that she is a porn star that bothers them. It is her appearance, it is overly sexual. It is only 7.30 a.m. They are already irritable. Men have changed. Not long ago, men were delighted to catch a glimpse of long legs and a plunging neckline. Now they are infuriated. Pamela thought she looked elegant when she saw her reflection in the lift. But men are force-fed images of sexually attractive women. All they feel now is frustration that they are unattainable. They know they are not going to get any, so they would rather women walked round in moonboots and anoraks. But Pamela likes funerals. And she wouldn't miss this opportunity to wear her Corsican widow outfit for the world. She looks stunning in it. She did not know Loïc well, but she believes that when a woman has lewdly rubbed her pubis against the engorged penis of a man the night before his death, custom dictates that she attend his funeral and take a modicum of care in choosing her outfit. There was something about Loïc that she found attractive. Apparently he was a fascist dickhead. Worse than Xavier. Which would take some doing, because when Xavier gets going . . . you had better be in a forgiving mood. But she didn't have a conversation with Loïc. She danced. There was a certain reticence about his movements. She thinks he would be pleased to see that she has made an effort for him. But as the thirtieth knuckle-dragger says something insulting, she feels like planting a bomb in the train station and going home. This will teach her to be punctual. She was first to arrive. She thrusts her chest out and stands bolt upright, a smile playing on her lips. If you're going to infuriate, you might as well do it with style. She is the only one who knows her hands are trembling.

Daniel arrives to join her. No-one gives him shit. He hardly bothers to say hello before remarking, "I'm *so* over this." He doesn't quite understand what the hell he is doing going to Loïc's funeral. "I bet there'll be loads of neo-Nazis," he says. "There's bound to be trouble." In fact, what is bothering him is that, on the day Loïc died, the Hyena visited everyone in the group in turn to explain that Aïcha and Céleste had overplayed their hand, allowed themselves to be seen, and were leaving the city to lie low for a while, and that the rest of group should suspend any further actions and avoid the parc des Buttes-Chaumont as much as possible. Daniel had really got into this whole graffiti tactic, it was a spectacular revenge. Playing commando by night, having to be stealthy when it came to spray paint and materials, always paying cash, never buying too many cans at once, the messages summoning him to secret meetings that sometimes took place in the catacombs beneath Paris, it had been exciting, this double life. It made no sense, but it felt like being in a movie, group action, an eye for an eye. "Like an act of psychomagic," Lydia said, and she was right. The adrenalin rush when they all scattered. Meeting up the next morning and saying: "Your turn to eat shit." And wherever she was now, Vodka Satana could see them: the living have not forgotten her.

Sylvie pays the cab driver, a man she imagines must be at least seventy, he has a well-groomed grey moustache in the old style and emerald green eyes. She had not noticed his eyes until she saw them in the rear-view mirror. She had not wanted to come. Loïc was a hateful bastard. Dead or alive, her opinion has not changed. She is not about to shed a tear for him. When he beat up Xavier, he had left him for dead on the pavement. Certain kinds of individuals are beyond forgiveness. You'd have to be dumb as ten gallons of shit in a five-gallon bucket to mix with the far-right when you're working class, like he was. She is not about to feel sorry for him. Though she can understand how people like her might profit from the rise of the far-right. Many set themselves up with extremely lucrative posts that would otherwise have taken them years to reach. When the day comes that they can accuse union leaders of terrorism and shoot them, it would be easier to avoid paying taxes. But a pathetic prick like Loïc, what did he expect? A job in the militia? Why should she feel sorry? Because he's dead? She slips on her black gloves. She has come because everyone is coming. And because she feels that they are hiding something from her and she wants to find out what. Where have Céleste and Aïcha got to, for example, and why does Sélim look so devastated. She likes Sélim.

She joins Pamela and Daniel. She will never get used to the idea that Daniel wasn't always a boy. When she was young, testosterone didn't even exist. It's amazing, when you think about it, it seems so easy now. Sylvie thinks about some of her girlfriends, the Plain Janes who always had a hard time getting boyfriends. These days, *bam*, a quick dose of hormones and they could have been decent looking guys. Being ugly doesn't matter so much when you're a guy. She takes Pamela by the arm. For once, the woman is well dressed. It changes everything. She's a fine specimen, there's no denying. Pity she brought that tacky black leather purse, anyone can see it's plastic. But she's a decent woman when you get to know her. Batshit crazy, but a heart of gold. Though you can't count on her to help stop Vernon sliding into madness. If he says to her, "I think I'm connected to the trees," she just says, "Some tribes believe that stones have souls." Nothing surprises her. People her age are like that. The Illuminati, conspiracy theories, witchcraft – on the basis of "They're covering up things *they* don't want you to know" you can get them to believe anything. Vernon needs help. He's not the same man. But Pamela doesn't understand that. She thinks he's on some kind of trip. It reminds Sylvie of the lyrics from an '80s song: "Max is free, some people even say they've seen him fly." It true that it's difficult to worry about Subutex. He seems so serene . . . Sylvie sees him coming now, flanked by Charles, Olga and Laurent. The Buttes-Chaumont dream team. She gives a little wave. She is always surprised that she is so happy to see them.

THERE IS NOTHING CHEERFUL ABOUT GARGES-LÈS-GONESSE, especially arriving in the rain. Ringed by grey, forbidding tower blocks, the town centre has a provincial feel: low houses, red-tiled roofs, no aesthetic pretensions. At first glance, it is obvious it has never been a wealthy place; no-one here has ever thought I'll just build myself a little architectural gem. The trip by R.E.R. is short, it is the connecting bus that makes the journey feel interminable.

As they arrive outside the church, Gaëlle says: "There's no way I'm going in. After everything the Catholic church has done to us, I wouldn't set foot in the place. Every time we held a demonstration, people would leave piles of homophobic tracts next to the font and the priests would turn a blind eye. I'll wait for you out here." Pamela looks puzzled, she's accustomed to feeling at home in places where by rights she should not even exist. "If you think that's going to stop Christ from being with you . . ." Daniel licks a gummed cigarette paper and says: "And since when has Christ been with you?" Pamela looks in the river, arranges her veil in the wing mirror of a truck: "He died for me too, didn't he? You think I get lumbered with my sins just because I'm a blowjob goddess?"

Gaëlle is wearing skin-tight black leather trousers that make her look even thinner and more fragile. Her belt buckle is a skull and crossbones. She has bags under her eyes and she got caught in a shower. Her hair is soaking wet. Vernon is thinking that it suits her, the drowned-rat look. She spent a lot of time dancing with Loïc the other night. When she heard that he was dead, she took the blow. Her jaw is clenched as she mutters, defensively: "And anyway, just from an aesthetic point of view, I can't abide this style of architecture. Is it a church or a factory? It's impossible to tell." Ever since they passed La Courneuve, she has been wearing a mask: she has never ventured so far beyond the périphérique – the idea never seemed rewarding. Sylvie, wearing a magnificent black dress, holds her huge grey umbrella over Gaëlle's head and says: "I'll wait out here with you, I don't much like churches myself. I wasn't baptised, and I hate anything to do with religion. If you want my opinion, they'd be better off installing swimming pools. There's a terrible shortage of them in Paris." The church is gradually filling up. Laurent and Olga exchange a look and shrug, they want to go to the service, "We'll meet you here afterwards, besides we're all going on to the same place later." Daniel stands next to Xavier, who did not say a word while they were on the train. He is the only one whose eyes are red. Lydia protests, she doesn't want to attend the Mass either, so why did they arrange to meet up so early, they could have gone directly to the cemetery and had a couple more hours' sleep. Vernon takes a toke from the spliff she proffers. Charles emerges from the church to tell them that the place is already packed and they're bound to be bored senseless, it's freezing cold and the priest looks like a sinister goon; when he hears that Sylvie has decided not to attend the service, he gleefully rubs his hands, "I didn't like to say, but I'm gagging for a little beer."

Patrice comes over to say hello. He arrived earlier with the others. In a black bomber jacket, he bustles in and out of the church as though he were responsible for the order of service. He has reserved several seats, and ushers Olga and Laurent inside, then comes back out and says: "What the hell are you still doing here?

What do you mean you don't want to go in?" He pulls a face: "Have you even thought about his widow?" But, convinced by Gaëlle's arguments, he says: "You can't wait out here in the churchyard. There's a bar a little way over there." Pamela waits until he has gone before raising a quizzical eyebrow. "Am I a prude, or is there something strange going on between him and Loïc's ex-girlfriend?" Vernon nods, he too has noticed: Patrice has put a lot of effort into this funeral.

At first, no-one could understand why he felt obliged to call her to offer his condolences. It is not as though they were friends. But he has become so protective of Xavier, that he started taking responsibility for things his friend should be doing. He had asked Pénélope, the ex-girlfriend, whether she needed anything, and found himself dealing with a woman who was utterly overwhelmed. She was receiving requests for interviews, condolences from complete strangers and anonymous insulting messages. Patrice became her attentive escort.

Emilie stubs out her cigarette before heading towards the church, commenting to those still hanging around outside: "Someone should make sure to let Loïc's ex know that she's getting involved with a wife batterer." And Vernon wonders how she knows this. And why she has never said anything. All the time they spent in the park together, and she never once broached the subject. Xavier and Lydia go into the vast modern building just before the doors close. Charles says: "So where is it, this bar?", and Vernon follows him. On the opposite side of the street, they run into Sélim. He was not supposed to come. "Hurry up, you'll miss the service." "I'm not going to the Mass. I just didn't want to be alone today." Vernon slows his pace, and the two of them lag a little behind. "Any news?" "Not directly, no. But apparently she's fine.

What can I do, I have to believe it? So I wait. I think about all the things that I've never had the chance to say to her. It wasn't up to her to avenge her mother, it was up to me. But I don't believe in revenge. I believe in forgiveness." His face has changed, it is sapped by grief. As they are about to step into the bar, he grabs Vernon's sleeve. He needs to talk a little longer before he has to pretend to the others that everything is fine. "If the police come looking for her at my place, I'll tell them we had a row and she walked out. She's over eighteen, she has every right. Maybe I'll say I told her in the name of secularism: for as long as you live under my roof, I won't have you covering your hair, you pathetic weakling. What would they charge me with? Being a staunch republican? But if the police actually do come looking for her, I don't think I could say something so cynical. I'm afraid of betraying her again by lying unconvincingly." Vernon says: "The Hyena says that Dopalet is not going to press charges. The anti-terrorist brigade aren't going to come and kick your door down anytime soon . . ." and Sélim shrugs. "I need to be prepared for something, you get that?" And in silence they push open the door of the bar.

It is neither a seedy local dive nor something that has been completely renovated, the décor of the bar is reminiscent of a small town in the Eastern Bloc before the fall of the Berlin wall. Vernon finds the honest tang of bleach at once unsettling and reassuring – is it the childhood smell of cleanliness, the smell of his mother keeping house. The landlord is in his sixties. He does not look hospitable. Thick moustache, two black eyes, he has the ruddy complexion of the marathon drinker, but with none of the vitality one sometimes finds in alcoholics. He watches blackly as they invade his space, as though serving coffee and beer was not among the duties he had in mind when he opened up this morning. Sullenly, he takes their order, avoids making eye contact while he serves them, then stands, leaning over the sink, ready to kick them out should their attitude leave anything to be desired.

Sylvie is whispering, repeating what she heard on the radio this morning, news from Syria, the austerity regime in Greece, the tonnes of radioactive water spilling from Fukushima since the earthquake. Laurent and Olga join them, to whoops of joy from Charles, who is already on his second beer. In the near-empty bar, under the reproachful eye of the landlord, they push two tables together. Lydia shows up, her hair still wet: "I've been calling after you since the church, you could at least have waited! Jesus, it's brass monkeys in there . . . I couldn't stick it out. I haven't been to church since my first communion, and I can tell you now that I won't be getting married in one. Five minutes in there and you're bored witless . . ." Olga roars that she's never seen so many knuckle-draggers crammed into such a tiny space. Hanging with a bunch of fuckwits like that, *non merci* – to think she took a train out into the suburbs for this. Sylvie giggles as she pictures Olga, in the church, seething. "What about you, Laurent, why did you leave?" "I was parched." And Olga shouts: "Champagne!" Sylvia stares at her, speechless, then slaps her forehead with perfect comic timing: "You're right, that's what we need," and turns to the landlord. "Barkeep, a bottle of your finest champagne!"

He is just setting the champagne flutes on the table when Pamela and Daniel make their entrance, dragging Xavier who doesn't look at all well. "I see you're on the champagne?" but he takes the proffered glass just as Vernon raises his: "To Loïc" while Laurent, in a deep, self-assured voice that no-one knew he possessed, sings: "Don't fuck around, Manu, don't go opening a vein, one new girlfriend lost, is ten old friends regained." Xavier stares at him, dumbfounded. His first impulse is to yell shut up, what the fuck are you thinking, but then he feels somehow touched. And he sings in his turn. His voice is less confident, but the thought is there. It is around about this point that everything goes to hell in a handcart. It is difficult to say what changed. Perhaps it was when the landlord accepted a glass of champagne Lydia offered him from the third bottle, and he says in a surly voice that she can put on some music, there is a U.S.B. port. The voice of Nick Cave rings out, "Push the Sky away". Sylvie says: "Fuck, that's depressing, what is it?" while Lydia closes her eyes, "I love this song." Vernon feels the grief of the morning slip away. He gets up and begins to dance slowly, glass in hand, in front of the bar. He imagines he is a palm tree swayed by a light breeze. Olga, who has never come to the sessions at Rosa Bonheur with them because dancing isn't her thing, comes and stands next to him, shy, motionless, then she lets herself go, her huge body swaying, a strange, slow-motion choreography that is half Apache, half grunge. Those still sitting at the table hesitate for a moment: this is it, the landlord is going to blow a fuse. But, on the contrary, this prehistoric female resolutely undulating against the rhythm in front of his bar sends him into a state of unexpected euphoria. He brandishes a fourth bottle, declaring, "This one's on me" and when he has filled the glasses, as Big Mama Thornton rolls out the first notes of her version of "You ain't nothing but a hound dog", he takes up position to the left of Olga and begins to jiggle his hips, knees bizarrely bent, throws his hands in the air and – in their own fashion – they do the twist.

A RADIO IS PLAYING IN THE DISTANT COURTYARD. AN ALEX BLEACH song. "Though I'm here in your arms / it is only because / a girl who's not you / has rejected my charms". In the kitchen, Marie-Ange hums along as she washes the dishes. She is careful about her fingernails. She had a manicure only yesterday, and she does not want to chip them. The girl who applied the semi-permanent polish insisted that it is very resilient. It seems she was right. Semi-permanent polish is brilliant, no more waiting twenty minutes for it to dry. She had only to hold her hands under a mini dryer for ten seconds, and she was immediately able to leave, rummage in her handbag for her keys, and there was not a scratch on her nails. She loves the way the sun streams through the window, feeling its warmth on her shoulder. A car alarm starts to wail out in the street. Marie-Ange is used to making as little noise as possible in the morning. Xavier needs more sleep than she does. About two hours a day. Fourteen hours a week. Sixty hours a month. Two and a half days dozing while she is up and about, tidying the house. Then she gets herself ready and goes to work while he is still wearing his tracksuit. She knows that he spends his days doing nothing. But every evening, when she comes home, he invents activities.

When she first realised that she was entirely responsible for the housekeeping, she had tried to talk to him. The first time, he had made her laugh, he had pulled his clown face and categorically declared: "You can't expect me to use a vacuum cleaner. It'll make me grow breasts." It was utterly silly, but she had been charmed by the way he said it. Back then, he often caught her off-guard. He played the moron, she laughed, he disarmed her. She had decided not to bother getting into a petty argument over housework, given time he would realise that it didn't make sense – her having a full time job, paying all the bills, and him sitting around doing nothing all day. But when she saw that it never occurred to him to pick up a sponge and clean the sink, or fold the dry bedsheets, or change the bed linen from time to time, she had aired her point of view, taking care not to be hurtful – avoiding any mention of the fact that he was not earning anything. She had talked about respect, affect, not equality but mutual support, her right to lounge on the sofa at the end of a long day . . . Xavier had pretended to understand. But that was all. She had tried being pedagogical: she stuck a list of chores on the door of the fridge: the dishes, the bins, the laundry, cleaning the toilet, the bath, washing the floors, the windows, tidying their daughter's bedroom, dusting, cleaning out the fridge, the bathroom . . . It had worked: he put out the bins. Every time he did it, he felt he had to proudly announce: "I'll take the bins out for you." The phrase "for you" in that sentence could send her into a blind rage. She felt like grabbing him by the throat and shaking him, "At least get a job so we can hire a cleaner." Because living on her salary alone is tough. She no longer finds his boyish I-don't-take-any-thing-seriously patter entertaining. She feels betrayed: she is expected to take responsibility for every difficult decision. He doesn't even seem to realise. Whenever she mentions money or says that it might be difficult to take a holiday, she feels as though he is looking at her thinking that she is whining about nothing.

Xavier barely earns enough to pay for the dentist, the occasional round of drinks in a bar, and métro tickets when he miraculously has a business meeting. The subject has become off-limits to such a point that he will often refuse to engage in conversation. He flies off the handle when she suggests she might take a job in the country. He says she has no respect for the work he does. But it would be much easier to live on her salary if they left Paris. If they sold the apartment, they could buy a little house with a garden. Xavier hates Stéphane Plaza, because every time she watches his T.V. property shows, she starts talking about moving.

At first, Marie-Ange supported him – she thought it was normal for someone working in the arts to go through occasional dry spells. She listened sympathetically when he railed against the faggots who controlled the industry. He was too forthright, his ideas did not sit comfortably with the general mediocrity, the kind of filmmaking he loved got no respect in France, he didn't come from a privileged background, there were a lot of things that tipped the scales against him. She had continued to support him when she realised he had been blacklisted – though his name was still mentioned by the occasional director who had admired his early work, producers simply shooed him away. No way. Anyone but him. Too temperamental. He was screwed, though not really for the reasons he cited. His analysis of the situation was fundamentally flawed, which made it impossible for him to make changes. But she earned enough to keep the three of them, she was convinced that he had talent, that one day she would be proud to have stood by him through the tough times. But as the years passed, her patience began to wear thin. She no longer believes that his day will come. His glory days are behind him.

Marie-Ange leaves every morning at 7.30, takes the métro to the Ipsos Group offices where she is a market researcher. She spends her day juggling screenings, focus groups, and bullshit while Xavier stays at home, creating. She never complains. But she no longer finds it amusing. She is sick and tired of the struggling artist. She does not feel up to being the muse to a loser. The last time he printed and bound his most recent screenplay and gave it to her like some precious gift – she was his first reader – she realised that she no longer found him funny. He had spent more than a year on the project. Ninety pages of dialogue. Eighteen months, full time. O.K., it required him to be creative. But the fucker took his own sweet time. She had felt obliged to start reading that night, she was shattered and would have preferred to wait until Sunday, but he was like a kid stamping his feet nervously, so she had told herself that sleep could wait and read the first forty pages. She had kissed him before turning out the light, she had faked it: "I'm saving the second half for tomorrow. But it's brilliant. Bravo, my little Vévé." This is what she called him in private – my little Vévé. The screenplay was terrible. His previous projects had not been much better, she realises, now that she is prepared to be honest with herself. But up until now, at least they had been funny. She had always smiled and laughed as she read what he had written. He had a spark of imagination that he has lost along the way. And he had found little to replace it. She could no longer summon the energy to lie to herself. Her husband was a mediocre writer. He strung together clichés but thought he was reinventing the wheel, the plot was weak and slapdash, the dialogue feeble, the characters inconsistent . . . She did not need to be a professional reader to realise this – watching the occasional movie or T.V. series was enough. What had most shocked her that night, while she lay curled up at the edge of the mattress, unable to sleep, was not that she did not believe in him as a screenwriter but that she lacked the courage to deal with what would come next: he would send the script to everyone he knew and wait for replies that would never come, because people would be too embarrassed to tell him that it was mediocre and they were going to pass. And Xavier would complain, dig his heels in, and she would have to console him when she stumbled home exhausted after a hard day's work. And who was there to support her? Xavier has nothing but contempt for her job, he cannot even feign an interest. He says the opposite, but whenever she talks to him about her problems with her manager, she can sense his mind wandering.

Her father had warned her. At twenty, she hadn't listened because she thought the old dodderer could not understand the rapturous love she was only just discovering. But he had warned her. "For a woman, there is nothing worse than to marry beneath her station." She had concluded that her parents did not have a clue about the world she lived in, the world in which Xavier was an untamed beast in the concrete jungle, seductively arrogant, who was going to revolutionise the film world. They were wrong to underestimate him. Now she realises that she was the one who lacked judgment. She had bet on a lame horse. The system could have worked for her if she had only made the right choices. But in every possible sphere, with grim, meticulous care, she had made the wrong ones. She had had a diploma in her pocket when, against her parents' better judgment, she had decided to take a permanent post with Ipsos. True, she had come a long way since. And not in a sector seriously threatened by the financial crisis. But it would have been easier to spend another three years at university, learn a foreign language and allow her father to guide her.

The wrong choice . . . But she had made the best of the opportunities that presented themselves. She had not had the aptitude to attend one of the "Grandes Écoles" – as her parents tactfully put it, "Her intelligence isn't academic." Nor had she rejected a string of suitors more prestigious than the one that she had married. She had fallen in love with Xavier because he was the first guy she had found exciting, the first who had seen her as a princess. He had been self-confident back then. It had been shortly after the minor success of his first film; in trendy circles, he was spoken of as the Renoir of the slum belt. He could not have guessed that the director, a childhood friend, would decide to write his second film himself. In his own way, Xavier is a complete innocent. He imagines that everyone shares his sense of chivalry. But all around him, his colleagues have matured, become pragmatic: screenwriters are expensive. So they do without. Things were good between them in the beginning. It was the first time Marie-Ange had found what she was looking for in a guy. He was assertive, he was the man, but she had him eating out of her hand, he was madly in love with her. Until that point, she had had to make do with looking on jealously as other girls flirted with guys who, from a distance, seemed perfect. Her turn had come. This thickset brute became tender and loving as soon as she snuggled next to him. They brought out the best in each other. He came up with tailor-made compliments, noticed things in her personality that he celebrated as unique qualities. He had given her confidence. It had been a glorious time. But even then, she should have raised an eyebrow. Everything upset Xavier. Dining out, visiting a gallery, going with her to visit her parents – he criticised everything, sulked for no reason, he was so thin-skinned it made her uncomfortable. She should have noticed that he was pig-headed, even when things had been going well and he had a network of friends, when he was hanging out in what he called "his bar", a cramped, smoky corridor in the depths of the eighteenth arrondissment. It was the sort of place where people laughed riotously between hands of cards, dipping their chubby hands into bowls of peanuts, and the people he considered "colourful characters" were just alcoholics who made him feel like a god, and called him a "gentleman of the cinema". He liked to surround himself with people who were not on his level, because he had a desperate need to be reassured. But his bar friends were dragging him down at precisely the point when he needed to evolve. Marie-Ange has never had a fascination with what he calls "real people". She doesn't care how they live – she is no more interested in the daily routine of a teacher or a nurse than she is whether these "good people" read books or go to the cinema. This was her first real love. She respected Xavier. And it's true that for several years he gave her stability. He made it possible for her to finally think about something other than I'll never be married, no-one will ever want me. And when her father tried to caution her about "letting a man who was beneath her into her bed", she couldn't bring herself to tell him what she was thinking: being in bed with Xavier in the early days had been electrifying. And that meant a lot to someone like her who had experienced no thrills in that department. She and boys had never really got along. It was mysterious. She was a pretty girl, and she knew it. A honey blonde with delicate features and not an ounce of fat. Her legs were a little short, her waist a little pronounced, her breasts a little small. But she had big eyes, a delicate bone structure, a beautiful complexion. Men were not indifferent to her. But she did not kindle an erotic passion. Xavier had been the first to make her feel like a woman – to feel desired. He found everything about her arousing. It had been thrilling to discover this – when she undressed for him, she was like an epiphany.

She had been happy. For a long time. It hadn't bothered her that, after a year, she had had to start faking it in bed. She had assumed the feeling would return. When she was less tired, less preoccupied. But in fact, it had simply got worse. She had to force herself, and it became more and more tiresome. She had not talked about it with anyone. Men are from Mars, women are from Venus, men like sex and women could just as easily do without. This was the least she owed him. She had not wanted him to look elsewhere. Only after the caesarean did she finally give up. She no longer wanted to pretend.

Being pregnant had not been a mystical revelation to her. The latter months had been difficult. She had not experienced the famous hormone rush that might have made being infirm feel wonderful. Nor had she felt at ease in the months after Clara was born. She knew she was the mother of this little creature, but all this made her feel was blind panic. She had left the maternity unit shocked that no-one seemed alarmed that she had had none of the skills required to look after a baby. And it was not as though her own mother – who had jetted off to the Caribbean three days after the birth – was likely to step in and help out. Xavier had been amazing. He had had an answer for everything. He had found an online forum for first-time fathers and he knew everything there was to know, from the correct temperature for a baby's bottle to the best brand of nappies. His daughter filled him with wonder. He had cobbled together a way for the three of them to be happy. Spending leisurely morning lying in bed, kissing her tiny feet, doing Indian dances to make her laugh, spending hours in children's bookshops looking for collections of fairytales, smiling every time she did a poo, "magnificent, these faeces are magnificent." And, in a sense, Maria-Ange had only to climb aboard a family life she had always dreamed of. She had relaxed. She loved the father that Xavier had become. She no longer loved the man who still desired her.

Socially, on the other hand, motherhood has been a disappointment. All the other mothers she knows have competitive children. In the early years, Marie-Ange had been innocent, she had assumed that, once she had given birth, she would be a paid-up member of the sisterhood of first-time mothers, she too would take out her iPhone and show them pictures of her child. But it is not so straightforward. The other mothers made her depressed. "My daughter was walking at six months, we were flabbergasted when we saw her toddling across the living room." "Mine was bilingual by the time she was two." "Mine taught himself to read when he was three." "Mine was moved into the upper stream in kindergarten because of his football skills." "I opened a savings account for mine, someone asked me if I wanted her to do a fashion shoot, I wasn't keen, but she loves it, and ever since, she's been in demand everywhere." Let me just show you this video of my child turning cartwheels on a beam, rebuilding a computer blindfolded, singing an operatic aria . . . Clara is an angel, but when it comes to showing off, she is useless. She probably gets it from her mother. She has not the slightest talent that might make her stand out. When she dances to Maître Gims, she looks like Goldorak trying to keep warm. Marie-Ange adores her daughter. But a teacher has never called her back after class to share her astonishment – did you realise you have a gifted child? Never. This year, for Carnival, her father gave her the dress Elsa wears in "Frozen". A princess costume that had looked spectacular in the packaging. But when she put it on, she looked more like Shrek than anything else. Marie-Ange took lots of pictures, she does not want her daughter to feel offended. But she does not post them on Facebook. She is clear-sighted. The only time her daughter was a hit in her office was doing a zombie walk. She was wearing an orange wig and black and white striped leggings like Emily the Strange. A friend of Xavier's who works in special effects had come round to create a huge fake wound that made it look like her cheek was slashed open to reveal her teeth . . . Clara had a ball, crawling around the place de la République foaming at the mouth. It was the first time in her life strangers had stopped to take her picture. And Marie-Ange has noticed that she is not invited to other girls' birthday parties. She is not popular. When she tries to talk to Xavier about it, he growls: "You're not the one who has to pick her up from school, you've no idea, but everyone in her class is a fucking idiot."

Another child. She often thinks about it. It is sad for Clara to have to grow up on her own. And besides, couples who only have one child are weird. It says something about the relationship that Marie-Ange doesn't like. She doesn't feel happy with her life as it is, so she certainly doesn't need to start shouting from the rooftops: we've only had one kid because we're a dysfunctional couple. It's nobody's business. More and more often, she brings up the subject of trying for a second child with Xavier. He doesn't seem to be in any hurry. Though he's got nothing going on his life except raising his daughter. He's hardly likely to burn out if she has a little brother . . .

Marie-Ange gives herself a little time. The caesarean left her with painful memories. Men are so sweet when they're being condescending: "Don't tell me you're afraid of a few stretch marks?" You go and have someone cut open your abs with a pair of pliers and split your uterus – then maybe we'll have a conversation about how women are so shallow that they think twice before doing it again. And the healing process is absolute hell. This is the point when you realise that you use your abdominal muscles for almost everything. For a month, she walked around bent double. After a vaginal delivery, you can't take any serious exercise for a month. After a caesarean, it's more like six. By the time she went back to her Pilates lessons, she looked like a sack of potatoes. And she had no muscle tone – it took a year of gruelling exercises before she could stand up straight. It takes a lot of work before you can wear a swimsuit again. This was something else she didn't know – but as far as the competitive mothers' club is concerned, a caesarean is only for the feckless. Motherhood is not at all as she imagined: she assumed that it meant mothers supported each other, genuine female solidarity. But giving birth is just buying a ticket to enter the race. It doesn't guarantee you a medal.

And at the same time, she really doesn't care. Maybe she cannot show Clara off in society, but her need for affection has never been so fulfilled, and she cannot imagine any purpose to her life without her daughter. Xavier is a brilliant father. She criticises lots of things about him, but when it comes to Clara, she can't fault him. He is patient, he is firm, he plays the clown, he is attentive, he sets high standards for her, he remembers to praise her. Marie-Ange has only to fall into step and everything goes well. He is mad about his daughter, but it is a love that never excludes her mother. And you earn big points in the world of mothers. In the early days, she avoided saying, "He picks her up from nursery every day," she assumed that her friends would think she was living with an idle layabout. She was wrong. Something that she realised over time. "He's watched 'The Aristocats' with her sixty-three times, it was his favourite film when he was a kid and Clara loves it." Or: "He plays all her video games with her, he wants to make sure that there's nothing there that she can't work out on her own," it's like, "He found a miniature bass guitar and he's teaching her how to play." You score big. In fact, the other mothers are not thinking, so your guy never tidies away the Nintendo and he still has a bass guitar in a case in the wardrobe, or he's a girl, you've married a girl. No. They're thinking: creative guy, masculine but modern, and they say things like, "It's so important for a little girl, having her father take an interest. If they feel valued by their father, it changes their whole conception of men and what it means to be female." Marie-Ange knows this is rubbish: her own father was good with her. But that didn't stop him being an arsehole. But since they seem convinced that it is true, Marie-Ange is only too happy to tell them stories about how wonderful Xavier is.

One more reason for not leaving him. You know what you have to lose, you don't know what you stand to gain. She knows that if one of the guys she occasionally sleeps with made a big fuss, insisting that she leave Xavier, and if he had a good job, she wouldn't think twice. But none of her lovers have ever tried to persuade her to leave her husband. Any more than they considered breaking up their own marriage. So she stays. If leaving means living alone and never being in a relationship again, she would prefer to live with the father of her child. Some mornings, when she wakes up, she feels a bitter visceral hatred towards him. She tidies the house, going over and over all the ways in which he hinders her, suffocates her, bores her. But she never talks to him about this. And she is not sure that she would get along as well with Clara if it was just the two of them. She loves her daughter partly because she sees her through his eyes. He is so proud to be the man of the house.

You need to be wary of answered prayers. So often, when she came home in the evening, she has wished, "let him surprise me."

She was tired of coming home to find Xavier there. Happy to see her. So loving, so dependent, so affectionate . . . She had to stifle the urge to recoil. He had no idea how easy it is to suffocate a woman. Sometimes, when he took her in his arms, she wanted to push him away – inspire me to dream, scare me, make me feel alive, for fuck's sake. She prayed that he would surprise her. But this was not what she had in mind. It finally came, the surprise . . . These days, it is all about "the gang". Subutex's gang. She is no longer the centre of her husband's world. Though she would have sworn otherwise, she misses it. It all started after the coma. Doctors are morons. All their tests tell them nothing. Sometimes, she wants to beat them around the head with a baseball bat: do all the tests you like, fine, but it's obvious to anyone that the guy has lost some neurons. And no-one helped him. Vernon Subutex has become her husband's idol. The guy's a first-class loser. But attractive. She would have fucked him herself when she saw him in her living room, that weekend he spent looking after their bulldog. Some guys are like that – it's impossible to say what it is exactly. They reek of sex.

Dimitri, her current fuck-buddy is like that. Handsome as fuck. So young. He has his shoulders and chest waxed and shaves his balls before he sees her. He works as a window cleaner at the office. They ran into each other a couple of times before they hooked up. When she found out he got waxed, she felt sorry for him. Apparently all the guys his age do it. Why the hell would they put themselves through it . . . it's not as if women need it to find them attractive! She often wondered whether Xavier cheated on her. It would hardly be surprising, given all the free time he has . . . All she asks is that he doesn't tell her. When he started going to the park every day, she couldn't help but wonder. She was jealous. He said "we" when he talked about his friends, and he seemed so happy. She took a couple of days' leave to spy on him. She was convinced there had to be another woman. She stalked him. He spent his days in the park, sitting on the grass, smoking blunts. With his famous "gang". Seeing them, she thinks of stories she read about the Middle Ages, whole villages in the grip of mass hysteria. He's enjoying himself. And it's not as though he enjoys himself with her. He suggests that she come with him, he even wants to bring Clara, but Marie-Ange refuses. She has no desire to be part of this ship of fools. He is changing. He is happier. This is what most infuriates her. Compared to him, she feels worthless. Nothing has ever happened, not even something stupid, that might make her feel happier. She cannot understand what he sees in this bunch of hack and misfits. But he has come out of his shell, he has been reborn. He is drifting away. She often thinks about giving him an ultimatum: it's them or me. It would be ridiculous. But she needs him to reassure her, to tell her that he would do anything for her. She misses it, this thing she had complained about for years, this obsessive, unconditional love. And she does not know who he is anymore. She doesn't want to lose him. She doesn't love him, but she could not bear to be without him.

Joyeux, the poodle, is first to bound out of her daughter's room. That means she is awake. He comes and laps from his bowl, then nuzzles his head against her thigh, begging to be stroked. At first Marie-Angle couldn't stand the sight of the dog. He reminds her of Xavier. A big useless lump. It's unbelievable. How much she loved that man, how much she admired him. And now, the sight of an aging, foul-smelling poodle sprawled on the sofa reminds her of her husband. They loved each other, in the beginning. No-one ever tells you the truth about these things. That's all it is. Everyone gets bored after the first few years. She can see it all around her – you do your best to hide it, but everyonc in a relationship ends up bored. The most important variable is how much effort you put in, playing to the gallery. There are couples who are in love with the effect they have on other people. As long as there is an audience, they continue to pretend. But as soon as they're in the bedroom, they're bored senseless.

Clara appeared, padding barefoot across the parquet floor. Marie-Ange shouts: "Slippers!" and feels guilty for starting the day by criticising her daughter. She has a tendency to snap at her. When Xavier is around, she is more careful. The little girl reappears in her red tartan slippers, hair tousled, eyes puffy from sleep, she looks like an angel. She wraps her arms around her mother's neck. She smells so good in the morning. "Can I have my Nesquik?" "I'll make it for you now, darling. Do you want a big bowl of Cheerios or a little one?" This is a little secret they have when Xavier is not around: Marie-Ange gives her sugary cereals. They're bad for her, but Clara loves them.

"Can I watch a cartoon while I eat my breakfast, maman?" Marie-Ange sighs. When her father is around, Clara never asks if she can watch television in the morning . . . Marie-Ange is happy to plonk her in front of the T.V. sometimes so she can do the housework or check her emails. It's not good for her, every parent knows that. She should get her dressed and suggest an activity. But it is very practical. She says: "O.K., but just the one," and feels guilty, because it suits her.

Xavier has a nerve, leaving her on her own over the long weekend. The three of them could have gone away together. He might have thought of that. Or thought, why don't I look after Clara so Marie-Ange can get a little rest. This is the third time he has gone to see "them". It just gets better and better. It was bad enough when he was going to the park, but now he has to take the train. And he didn't say where he was going. He better get a grip, and soon, because she is not going to put up with this much longer. She has no idea where he is. And his phone is switched off. Well, she wanted him to surprise her, and he has. But not in the way that she wanted.

Clara puts on the D.V.D. of "Frozen". Marie-Ange cannot suppress a shudder of loathing as she hears the opening credits theme. She hates this song . . . Clara has always been like this, when she decides she likes a cartoon, you have to watch it on a constant loop until you're sick of it. Clara is snuggled between the dog's paws. Marie-Ange sits down for two minutes, strokes her daughter's ankle and watches the screen where two sisters are playing together, the elder is using her ice magic, while her little sister is playing in the drifts of white powdery snow she is magically conjuring in the ballroom . . . When she accidentally hurts her little sister, she is inconsolable and resolves never to use her powers again. Marie-Ange starts to doze, but is woken by a thought. How can she have watched this film so many times without realising that it is the story of Xavier? She couldn't work out what he saw in this fucking film, but it's blindingly obvious. Two children separated by white powder. Each crying on opposite sides of the door of their lost relationship. It is Xavier and his brother. Why does she feel so infuriated every time he mentions the emptiness he feels because he was unable to protect his brother? Everything he finds moving irritates Marie-Ange, puts her on the defensive. What happened to the tenderness between them? She sees Elsa in a different light, the young queen who builds a wall of ice between herself and the world. Is she like Elsa? Who can get close to her now, without her immediately becoming defensive? She suddenly becomes aware of the rage that has been swelling in her chest all morning. What has her husband done that is so terrible that she hates him so much? What do you do when your relationship has become a factory churning out frustrations? Xavier is changing. He took a blow to the head, and he is not the same as he was. So what? Before it happened, she was the one complaining that he never changed. She doesn't want to leave him, she doesn't want him to stay – it is a circle that cannot be squared. She is afraid. But of what?

Marie-Ange bends down and kisses her daughter's ankle, the round, bony protuberance. She will never again love the girl's father. Never feel physical passion for him. That is reserved for others. He will no longer make her dream. She no longer believes in the stories of "flames of brilliant red / bursting forth anew / from mountains long thought dead", etc. What do you do with love when there is no love left? In the film, Hans, the villain, says to the heroine, "I would never shut you out." And Marie-Ange feels the urge to cry.

AS HE DOES EVERY DAY WHEN HE WAKES UP, VERNON WONDERS what the weather in Paris is like. He misses the city. Pamela has given him a pair of Ray-Bans, gold frames, tinted glass like the ones drug dealers used to wear in the '80s. When he wears them, he looks like an idiot, but he likes the colour they give things, it looks as though summer is soaked in whisky. There is a campsite five hundred metres away, they are organising the first party of the season. On the beaches, the beach huts will soon be open. The music is carried in the breeze – Daft Punk, "Get Lucky". In the distance, a train is passing. It connects the little villages along the coast. There is a little station ten minutes' walk away. Today, the last tourist will disembark, in clusters, into this godforsaken corner of L'Île-Rousse . . . In the little house that serves as their headquarters, there is a shower outside on the terrace. The water runs along the steps made of interlocking blocks of stone. Sometimes, during the day, Vernon looks around and has trouble believing that what is happening here is his life. He knew nothing about Corsica. They have been here for a fortnight. This is the third place they have set up house. He goes with the flow. A family of wild boars passed by every night, and grass snakes slither across the terrace during siesta time. Spiders as big as his fist hide in the bushes and huge birds flap their wings above the rooftops. The beach is not far away. But he never goes there.

He doesn't like getting sand in his boots. He preferred Brittany. Here, everyone wears flip-flops. Too many toes for his liking.

Xavier is already up. He is playing with Emma, a pedigree pitbull bitch that Olga rescued. The bitch has teats that trail along the ground. Farther off, three young guys are sitting chatting under an olive tree. They are about twenty. Vernon has never seen them before. The campsite is already full. After tomorrow, it will gradually begin to empty out, like a bathtub when the plug is pulled. The three silhouettes move, one of them scratches his throat. They are joined by a girl who tries to persuade them to get up and go with her. They would rather stay sitting there, drinking beer. They slept in one of the dozens of tents that have blossomed all around the house in the past two days. With every party, more and more people come. None of this makes any sense. And it can't last. Vernon woke up with "A Day in the Life" running through his head. Already, the sun is beating down like a blind drummer. In Corsica, the summer is beginning. It is only the middle of May. Wasps buzz over his coffee. Emilie comes and sits next to him. She arrived last night. She doesn't feel as though she fits in, she is tense as always. She is wearing a blue '50s dress that really suits her. Vernon lays a hand on her shoulder and says, "So, are you ready for a little Julos Beaucarne?" It is a record he played in Brittany, Emilie had spent the whole of the next day mocking him. "I still can't believe you had the balls to play it." "Well, did it work or didn't it?" It was dawn. There were hundreds of people much younger than them on the dance floor. "Everything is about staring afresh." He knew that he could play it. On the dance floor, they were prepared. The segue had worked, perfectly. Except for Emilie, who is still giggling about it weeks later.

*

All this started after the funeral. Sylvie had remained stoic while Loïc was buried. Hands stuffed into the pockets of her black trench coat, her shoulders hunched, staring blankly as people filed past to lay a rose at the grave, then followed the gang as they discreetly headed for the cemetery gates.

In the R.E.R. on the way back, they all had a vicious hangover. They all sat at the back of the train carriage, and at first, no-one had said anything. Lydia Bazooka made her lips quiver with every breath, as though trying to relax them. Then she had said to Daniel: "I didn't realise that Loïc had so many neo-Nazi friends . . . It was really sleazy, the funeral." Daniel raised his hands above his head, stretching: "When you see the state of them, you have to think they've got a fucking nerve, claiming to be the defenders of the white race . . . If that's our genetic inheritance, we're completely fucked. If we leave them to it, France will have the ugliest population in the world." Lydia shifted her hip slightly closer to his to let him know that if he could manage to forget his little tattoo artist for a couple of minutes, she would be happy to carry on this conversation, tonight, at her place. At that point, Sylvie had burst into tears. Noisily. This was not I'll-shed-a-little-private-tear-and-hope-nobody-notices. Oh, no. She was sobbing loudly enough to shatter windows. "Can't you see, everything's fucked. Everything. It's all fucked." Everyone around her was dumbstruck. No-one really knew what she was getting at: was she talking about the grim atmosphere at the funeral, the fact that summer was almost over and they would no longer be meeting up in the park, or was it something more personal? Sélim had taken her in his arms and comforted her. Xavier had slumped, depressed, against the side of the carriage. Daniel and Lydia had exchanged a worried look as if to say, shit, we've obviously said something terrible without realising. And Pamela Kant had stepped into the middle of the group, gripping the handrail so as not to fall: "I love you all. I refuse to let us go our separate ways like this." Vernon had waited for someone to crack a joke, to break the tension, but everyone remained silent. As though thinking.

This was the day when everything had changed. Now, he was not the one who hovered over the group. He had been the astonished witness to a rare phenomenon: group hysteria. It had less to do with what was said than the atmosphere in which it was said. He had sat in his corner, thinking about Loïc, picturing him dancing. He could see him, fists raised, chest thrust out, stamping his feet and shadow boxing. A frenzy of pure joy. Pamela had slipped her arm through his, in that particular way of hers, a gesture of intimacy that was not sexual enough that it gave someone permission to slip a hand between her thighs, but tender enough for them to put an arm around her waist so that what followed took place in a twilight that was half-erotic, half-platonic – and in a serious voice, she had asked Vernon whether he would come away with her for a few days to think about "all this" and he had immediately pictured a beach, not the sand, just Pamela Kant in a swimsuit, the two of them sitting on a terrace, thinking about "all this". Obviously, he had said yes, wherever you want, whenever you want, whatever you want. He had not followed the rest of the conversation. He had drifted off into his own world, as he often did. The gang found it difficult to go their separate ways when they reached the Gare du Nord.

Four days later, deciding he was fully recovered from his bout of flu, Pamela had taken him up into the Vosges, to a deserted mountain cabin a few kilometres outside Remiremont. She had decided to leave the city. She was not planning to take two weeks' holiday. She kept saying that it was time for a life change. She had entered a phase that might have been called manic, had there been a depressive pole to counterbalance it. But no-one around her ever encouraged her to come down. Once shared with a group, madness, however raving, can become a way of life.

The Hyena had joined them. She was in hiding. She was the one who had jet-propelled the idea . . . Pamela has a taste for secret societies. The Hyena has a hyper-paranoid worldview. The two of them, together, with nothing else to do: dynamite. It was from this that the idea was born to set up a headquarters that would organise ceremonies. At first, they thought of it as just throwing a party "to get together". But from the first event, in a disused not-yet-gentrified paper mill they had clandestinely commandeered, more than fifty people had shown up.

But those who wish to attend the ceremonies are required to make some effort: the day before departure, they receive a hand-delivered message, usually to meet at a bus station. But it could be a train or a car. You never know. There are specific clauses. No-one is allowed to use their travelcard on the day they leave, only individual tickets. Absolutely no taxis and no Vélib bicycles. A series of comparable precautions making getting to the venue highly complex. But everyone diligently plays the game. Smart-phones and computers must be left at home. On arrival at their destination, guests are collected from the station. If any of them have brought their mobile phones, these are deposited in a nearby apartment. Pamela has fans even in the most remote areas of France. She knows her public: she knows the names of those who would rather rip their hearts out than break a promise to her. They provide the apartments. The whole thing is like this: highly complex and hugely improbable. It is part of the charm. And every month, there are more people. Vernon is in the D.J. booth, he spends the whole night spinning records. According to word of mouth, during these ceremonies, you dance as you have never danced before. They say he deserves the credit for that. Vernon looks around. A lot of women, not many straight people. More and more fat people. Quite a few hippies. Maybe there's a revival. A rainbow of Lesbian, Gay, Bisexual, Transgender, Queer, Intersex . . . A lot of hookers. The occasional hunky guy. Some older people, too. All of them wearing flip-flops, that's what's really irritating.

For permanent members like him who live there full time, it's about going off grid. Social security bank account digital identity rent tax insurance logbooks. Walking away from the old world. It is still vague. But Pamela and the Hyena are thinking big. And it is not as though Laurent or Olga, who joined up later, are likely to stop them. With a practicality that Vernon never suspected she had, Pamela drew up a list of places where they can set up camp for a few weeks. Between one thing and another, she has scouted enough locations for them to live as nomads for at least a decade.

Within the camp, there are potential conflicts, but none has yet burst into the open. That will come. Between those who never stop working and those who want to sleep, those who like to lead and those who can't stand being told what to do, those who only think of getting wasted and those who claim that drugs destroy groups, those who want to talk seriously and those who can only chat shit, those who want to sleep with everyone and those looking for monogamy . . . There will be problems involving money, egos, manipulation, betrayal . . . There will be every conceivable fuck up and every opportunity for disappointment. But right now, they are preparing for the third ceremony. They are not celebrating anything. They are doing it because they can. And because something happens on these nights. It is impossible to say what the people streaming here have in common. It is when they gather together that they become a supernova – they have come to dance.

"Stop deluding yourselves. This whole world is fucked. The world we knew. All this stuff you're talking about. it's already over. The retards frolicking in the meadows demanding the return of the Latin Mass, the stoning of prostitutes and the reinstatement of military service . . . it's all long gone. They're clinging to a world that has disappeared. Stop pretending that things were better yesterday and they'll be worse tomorrow. This is the intermission. Make the most of it. Everything starts again tomorrow."

He has got into the habit of listening to such conversations over breakfast. The girl speaking has a dragon tattoo that covers the back of her skull. That must really hurt, Vernon thinks. He wonders how Céleste is getting on. The Hyena says the girls are "doing great". She gives no further information about their fate. Lydia is wearing a large straw hat that hides half of her face when she leans down, and makes him want to see her eyes. She smiles as she approaches Vernon, rolling her hips as she walks, placing a filter into the cigarette paper in the palm of her left hand. "Not working on your playlist?" she asks, but does not listen to his answer. She is watching, open-mouthed, as two shirtless guys walk across the terrace. They have astonishingly broad shoulders, the curve of their backs is perfect. She tilts her head to one side. Emilie sighs: "Mansluts, the pair of them. Jesus, they're hunks. It's unbelievable. Where did they spring from?" Vernon shrugs.

Charles is settled in a deckchair under a parasol, a cooler full of beer on his left, shirt half open to reveal his paunch, a pair of green and orange New Balance sneakers on his feet. He always insists on giving them some money to be part of the events. Vernon finds it touching to think that the old guy has saved up and is dipping into his nest egg to help them organise raves in the middle of nowhere . . . When he doesn't even dance. And he hates flip-flops at least as much as Vernon. When Sylvie says, "I don't see the point of these parties," Charles invariably replies: "There is no point. That's the beauty of the thing."

Daniel sets a huge bag of fresh almonds on the table, he is trying to convince Xavier to write a zombie movie. "You know Karen Greenlee? The necrophiliac? She was completely unrepentant . . . I'm not saying it's blockbuster material, but I'm pretty sure there's a niche." He does not come often. He is terrified of spiders in the bedrooms, living in communes and chemical toilets. The hours he has spent exercising mean he is built like a tank. Sylvie takes a seat at one end of the table, she is wearing a Thee Oh Sees cut-off T-shirt. When she comes, she spends a lot of her time in the kitchen baking cakes. She says there is no point to it, this thing they're doing, but she spends half of her life with them.

Next to them, a short-haired brunette with an Italian accent is saying to Olga:

"I see what you're saying. As long as you're thinking 'defence', you're still 'prey'. If you're prey, you have to escape. You have to learn to run, to hide. To avoid contact with humans. Look at horses. They should never have allowed themselves to be domesticated. They could have run away, that's what they should have done."

And Olga disagrees:

"You're all very sweet, with your plant-based medicine and your communicating with animals, being nomads, foraging for food, a little trance, a little meditation . . . but just try to imagine

Subcomandante Marcos brewing herbs in a cauldron and chanting *Om* . . . You'd never have known he'd ever existed, guys. He'd be out there somewhere, in the jungle, communing with mosquitoes. You need balaclavas, guns and rivers of blood or you're nowhere."

"You're reasoning using obsolete arguments."

"The only way to defend yourself is to be better armed than your enemy. You need an arsenal of semi-automatic weapons. All the rest is bullshit. For as long as you run courses called 'self-defence', you might as well be teaching silk painting . . . when you decide to call them 'I'll rip your balls off with my teeth, dickwad', then maybe we can talk . . ."

Olga has changed. She drinks less. She flies off the handle less often. She learned to chop wood. In the Vosges. With a local lumberjack, a timid stutterer who loved his work. She left with his chainsaw – Vernon doesn't even want to imagine what kind of deal she and the guy struck in the privacy of the barn for him to give her his chainsaw. She dug out a bunch of outlandish dresses at the Salvation Army in Épinal – some woman of about her size had obviously just dropped off a collection of nightgowns. Chainsaw in hand, in a long print dress decorated with cornflowers and lace frills on the sleeves . . . When she lumbers around with her power-tools, she looks like a walking statue. She makes furniture. It is almost a vocation. She cuts, saws, nails and dovetails. She never stops jabbering. She is obsessed with violence. Pamela is obsessed with pacifism. They never argue: they wind each other up, each confirming the other in her convictions. Olga says: no terror, no salvation. Any movement that refuses to spill blood is doomed in advance. Pamela replies that the defining characteristic of the world as we know it is that all civilisations are built on violence. Olga ups the ante: You see, you agree with me. Pamela carries on – as long as we adopt the language of the master, we will adopt the behaviour of the master. It is never-ending. "By its very nature violence validates and reinforces the warrior system, it cannot overturn it." "Bullshit, complete bullshit . . . hugging trees and dancing naked in the forest is never going to achieve anything . . . You have to show your teeth. Then you have to kill. On a massive scale. Good people. Only then will they let you sit down at the negotiating table and listen to what you have to say . . . do you really think the guillotine was invented because someone was bored one Sunday? No. The guillotine was invented because it was the best way of getting respect."

Sélim loves these clashes. His favourite game plan is when Patrice joins in, and the four of them thrash out the subject. Yesterday, he choreographed a discussion late into the night between six of them: Sylvie and Xavier were also involved. He had a wonderful evening. He needs it.

He hears from his daughter from time to time. He gets letters that are passed from one person to another and posted from any country other than the one where she is living. He carefully archives his replies to her, since he has no way to send them. They haven't communicated as well as this in years, he says. He still has not had the police show up with a search warrant. The Hyena says that this is not necessarily good news. But Sélim is the kind of depressive who has a fanatical bedrock of optimism. He is convinced that things will sort themselves out.

The Hyena would also like to be able to send letters to the girl she is thinking about. But since she cannot go and fetch her, she says she prefers to wait. Vernon asks, "Are you planning to be out of circulation for a long time?" and she is in no hurry to go back. "These things take time." This is all he can get out of her.

After the Vosges, Laurent decided that he, too, had the soul of a carpenter. In his case, it is mostly an opportunity to strut around stripped to the waist, the guy is really well built. He would spend whole days making things and showing off his abs . . . But the furniture he made was shit . . . his approach took no account of gravity or the nature of human bodies. It was a long time before he eventually gave up. He was waiting for people to adapt to his furniture. Even with the best will in the world, a lopsided stool eventually falls apart. He left them, one morning, just before the ceremony in Brittany. He had done a lot of work preparing the abandoned train station they had taken over. He had even made hammocks. He had picked up his rucksack and headed off without a word. Charles says he is living in an anarchist commune.

Pamela brings another pot of coffee. Her hair is piled up into a chignon, fixed by a wooden hair slide, her shoulders are broad and sinewy, she always holds herself as though she spent thirty years doing classical ballet. She has been swimming a lot ever since they came to Corsica. Her body is metamorphosing, strength suits her. She sets her stubbed-out cigarette butt on the edge of the table and refills their cups. Vernon covers his with his hand to indicate that he has had enough. He gets to his feet and stretches. He needs to prepare.

When night falls, people head for the church. It is a half-hour walk. They have a few torches to light the way. After that, everything takes place in darkness. It all started in the Vosges when the generator conked out just after they arrived. They had had to spend a week in almost total darkness. That had been in winter, so the sun set early. The only light was the glow from the fire, the rest of the chalet was pitch-dark. They quickly realised that it suited them.

Their eyes had had too many things demanding their attention. They didn't speak in the same way, didn't move in the same way. Knowing no-one is looking at you and that you cannot look at them changed their behaviour. Refined it. Ever since, evenings in the camp are always the same – they never turn on lights.

The church is deserted. They have spent days preparing, the truck coming and going, installing the sound system. This time it was Sélim who brought the equipment. He borrowed it from an association in Bobigny, without telling them he was taking it down to Corsica. Moonlight streams through the side chapels, providing just enough illumination to cast shadows. In the half-light, the microphone is passed around. Patrice has the plan for the evening. He makes a good team leader. Those who wish to speak make themselves known during the afternoon, he draws up a schedule, chooses the place where they must stand until he brings them the mic and the tiny L.E.D. light so that they can read. Afterwards, they can move around, but until they have spoken, they are easily recognised because they do not move. "We will not be solid. We will unspool. We will not be pure. We will thread our way. We will be neither decent nor upstanding. We will not be heroes. We will not be conquerors. Of the warped wood of humanity, we will not try to fashion steel. We will have neither flag nor country." He recognises the voice of Pénélope, Loïc's ex-girlfriend, who arrived with Patrice. They are still not sleeping together, but they are rarely apart. The sound is pure. Some people are lying down, others are wandering aimlessly. Voices follow each other in the darkness. A boy with a surprisingly deep voice reads a poem by Lorca: "*No duerme nadie por el cielo. Nadie, nadie.*" Vernon can make out the figure of Xavier. He is sitting between his wife and his daughter. They arrived on the last train. The mother is tense, the kid thrilled to be at the beach. The father almost fainted when he saw that she had come. Vernon is not worried. They will get used to things tonight. He has never yet seen anyone stay on the edges of the dance floor. "We will forget. We will forgive. We will be the weak and the gentle." It begins to unfurl. He is no longer surprised when he feels his vessel about to take off. He still cannot control his flights, but he no longer tries to resist. On the contrary, he allows himself to be tamed by the waves of madness. And he knows that he can depend on them on nights like this. "We are the defeated – and we are thousands. We are searching for a way." Vernon does not think it matters, what is said, it is happening on a different level. He can feel it in his chest.

Then, later, a long silence. He fires up Alex's alpha waves. He takes his time. With the reverb in the church, everyone immediately gets to their feet. Still in the darkness, in the purity of sound. Bootsy Collins, "I'd Rather Be with You". Shapes peel away and form fleeting groups. The Hyena is almost motionless when she dances, except for a slight sway in her hips. A lot of people are still lying down. His eyes meet Pamela's. He makes contact with those who are absent. Mentally he feels his way along the shifting walls – the secret passages through time and the solidness of things. Whorls of moonlight open up between people. And as often in the darkness, he sees the lank silhouette of Alex, a giant among the scattered seedling stars, bending down and watching them, breathing gently on the ground, smiling. All around the living the dead and the invisible dance, shadows merge and eyes close. All around him, the movement has been triggered. It is beginning. He is making them all dance.

A New Library from MacLehose Press

This book is part of a new international library for literature in translation. MacLehose Press has become known for its wide-ranging list of best-selling European crime writers, eclectic non-fiction and winners of the Nobel and Independent Foreign Fiction prizes, and for the many awards given to our translators. In their own countries, our writers are celebrated as the very best.

Join us on our journey to **READ THE WORLD**.

1. *The President's Gardens* by Muhsin Al-Ramli
TRANSLATED FROM THE ARABIC BY LUKE LEAFGREN
2. *Belladonna* by Daša Drndić
TRANSLATED FROM THE CROATIAN BY CELIA HAWKESWORTH
3. *The Awkward Squad* by Sophie Hénaff
TRANSLATED FROM THE FRENCH BY SAM GORDON
4. *Vernon Subutex 1* by Virginie Despentes
TRANSLATED FROM THE FRENCH BY FRANK WYNNE
5. *Nevada Days* by Bernardo Atxaga
TRANSLATED FROM THE SPANISH BY MARGARET JULL COSTA
6. *After the War* by Hervé Le Corre
TRANSLATED FROM THE FRENCH BY SAM TAYLOR
7. *The House with the Stained-Glass Window* by Żanna Słoniowska
TRANSLATED FROM THE POLISH BY ANTONIA LLOYD-JONES
8. *Winds of the Night* by Joan Sales
TRANSLATED FROM THE CATALAN BY PETER BUSH
9. *The Impostor* by Javier Cercas
TRANSLATED FROM THE SPANISH BY FRANK WYNNE
10. *After the Winter* by Guadalupe Nettel
TRANSLATED FROM THE SPANISH BY ROSALIND HARVEY
11. *One Clear, Ice-Cold January Morning at the Beginning of the Twenty-First Century* by Roland Schimmelpfennig
TRANSLATED FROM THE GERMAN BY JAMIE BULLOCH
12. *The Shape of the Ruins* by Juan Gabriel Vásquez
TRANSLATED FROM THE SPANISH BY ANNE McLEAN
13. *Vernon Subutex 2* by Virginie Despentes
TRANSLATED FROM THE FRENCH BY FRANK WYNNE